CRUSADER I:
THE SERPENT CROSS

By

Karen Parker and
Carole Bullock

ISBN: 1466395125
ISBN 13: 9781466395121

Printed in USA

Acknowledgments:

The authors dedicate this book to their loving families and numerous friends who provided encouragement, critique and inspiration. The book is set in New Orleans, but the characters are fictional and any similarities to real persons are coincidental and not intended by the authors. Some of the locations of landmarks and dates, have been altered for literary effect.

VOODOO:

Voodoo Tarot is a name attributed to a traditionally West African spiritual system of faith and ritual practices designed to invoke the spirits of past ancestors and explain the forces of the universe, influence those forces, and influence humans. Adherents honor deities and venerate ancient and recent ancestors. Within the voodoo society, there are no accidents. Practitioners believe that no thing and no event has a life of its own. They believe that we are not separate; we all serve as parts of one. So, in essence, what you do unto another, you do unto you. Similar to those who believe in Karma or the popular phrase, "what goes around comes around."

In essence, we are mirrors of each others souls and there is a sacred cycle between the living and the dead.

THE SERPENT:

The Bible says, when the people of Israel complained against God while crossing the desert -- the Lord sent fiery serpents among the people of Israel as a punishment. They bit the people and many died. Moses prayed for the people. And the Lord told Moses to set a serpent upon a pole and all those who were bitten and looked upon it were healed.

CHAPTER ONE

New Orleans, La.

8:00 P.M., Sunday Night, March 5, 2000

The ribald crowd on St. Charles Avenue was growing impatient. The distinctive Mardi Gras stench — a nauseating mix of vomit, urine and Dixie beer — was emanating from the street gutters, saturating the anxious crowds with an invisible, penetrating fog. Revelers pushed hard against the iron barricades, arms, legs, or heads of those tall enough seeped through and over the railing in their efforts to gain a better view of the Bacchus parade.

Far above the smell and the noise of the crowds, the setting sun still cut through the quickly darkening streets, shining down from above and highlighting parts of buildings and groups of parade goers in a soft orange glow. But soon only the fiery flambeaux flares of the pagan dancers who pranced along side the glittering parade floats would illuminate the dark street.

Peg McGregor and her six-year-old daughter, Caitlin, had staked out a spot on the corner of St. Charles Avenue and Fourth Street. Peg's two friends, Kevin and Oswald, or "Ozzie," owned a house on the corner. The neighborhood, tucked between St. Charles and Magazine Street, had in the past been considered a seedy area. But the area had made a comeback, as many of the gays in New Orleans began purchasing the undervalued properties, restoring them to their original antebellum charm.

The "boys" as she called them, had lent them a carnival ladder so Caitlin could see the Bacchus parade above the heads of the swarming masses. On her high perch the roiling stench of the street crowds was not as strong and Caitlin enjoyed a view that must be similar to that found in the last dying rays of sunlight. Totally swept up in the anxious excitement of the crowds Caitlin's little body was in constant motion and the ladder was practically vibrating in Peg's hands. She kept glancing up to make sure Caitlin was holding on tight.

Normally, Peg hated crowds, but she took pleasure in the Bacchus parade because of the thrill it brought Caitlin every year. Bacchus was one of their favorite parades.

Bacchus was also the last of the weekend parades that signaled the grand finale of the New Orleans carnival season. On Ash Wednesday, Peg and Caitlin would be boxing up the costumes, plastic beads and comic masks of Mardi Gras to be sealed and stored away in the attic until next year. She smiled as she thought of the fun they would have, Caitlin insisting on wearing every necklace she could fit around her small neck, trying out all the different masks in her efforts to make her mother laugh or scream in mock terror.

"She's got a nice spot up high," blurted out a man standing to the left of the ladder where Caitlin was perched.

Peg turned around to face a bearded but clean-cut, khaki-clad young man and his girlfriend, who held a plastic cup of beer.

"Yes, she has been excited all week. I just hope the crowds don't get too wild."

Her words seemed prophetic as a drunken man staggered over, and fell onto the young man's girlfriend.

She screeched and stumbled toward the dirty sidewalk, just managing to break the fall with her left hand, while the plastic cup in her other hand, threw an arc of beer on those unlucky enough to be in its path.

The young man grabbed the drunk's jacket and whirled him around, pulling him in for a close range punch. The drunk tried to focus and speak, managing only what sounded like "heeeey, whaaatt cha." Seeing the booze haze and glassy eyes up close, he spun the man around, grabbed his shirt from behind, rotated ninety degrees and with a disgusted push sent him stumbling on down the sidewalk. The staggering drunk parted the surrounding crowd like a slow moving bowling ball.

"You let him off easy, but he wouldn't have felt it anyway," Peg laughed.

"Are you okay?" she asked the girl, laughter turning to concern, as she noticed her bent over brushing away dirt from the knees of her jeans.

The young woman gave Peg a cool, dismissive stare and turned to her boyfriend.

"Come on, I'm thirsty. That drunk asshole made me spill my beer."

The man pulled up his girlfriend by the arm and winked at Peg. He allowed himself to be towed away, but not until he removed a string of gold beads from around his neck and threw it up to Caitlin.

"Here you go darlin, catch."

"Be careful you two," he shouted before he was swallowed up by the rolling crowds.

Be careful he said. That is what Peg had spent the last six years doing. Having a child totally changed her life; a new city and nine-to-five weekday job. She vowed her daughter would always be the center of her life. Funny thing though, she had ended up reaping more than she sowed. Caitlin brought her so much joy and happiness that it sometimes scared her, even now, six years later.

She remembered the new mommy jitters when she worried that someone would drop the baby. Then she worried obsessively about germs. Friends laughed at her and chalked it up to first-time-mother-syndrome. But Peg knew how fragile life could be. In the blink of an eye your world can change, and not always for the good. Peg knew loss and she knew it intimately. She sometimes felt it showed on her face the way crow's feet and laugh lines show age. She felt her loss was there for all to see if they bothered to look close enough. Caitlin was her salvation. She was the only one who had ever sensed when Peg was drowning in the past. She would bring her little face close to Peg's and with an intense look say, "I love you Mommy." Then everything was right in the universe, the birds would start singing and Peg could breathe once more. Two feet firmly anchored on dry land.

Peg shook her head, physically trying to throw off the odd mood that had brought on these troubling thoughts. That life had long ago been packed away, just old memorabilia in a chest in the attic gathering dust. The last two years she had hardly ever thought of the past. She felt she might be tempting fate and did not want to awaken those old misgivings. She pulled herself back to the present and looked up at her daughter.

Caitlin carefully put the gift of beads around her neck so she wouldn't dislodge her sparkling gold tiara.

Dreaming she was the queen of the Carnival, she peered down at the ever-changing thick crowd of revelers that surrounded her.

Perched on the six-foot wooden ladder, she could see far up the avenue. She hoped to have a clear view of the gargantuan papier-mâché head of the serpent that heralded the beginning of the Bacchus parade.

Peg's favorite part of the parade was watching the tattooed dancers prance along, garbed in scarlet loincloths, holding out their rusty tin cans to catch the quarters thrown by the crowd.

Caitlin twisted her Mardi Gras necklaces round and round her neck, thinking about all the beads she would catch, when her mother's voice caught her attention.

"How many pink ones do you have, beautiful?"

Peg smiled up at Caitlin but her thoughts shifted again to the young couple. Maybe the encounter had brought on the strange mood. She realized that for just a moment, she had found herself wondering what it would be like to have a man in her life again.

But the way that young woman acted, made her remember that she never liked the game playing that always seemed to come with a close relationship. No, she was better off without those kinds of problems. Besides, Caitlin was all she needed to fill her life. She looked up at her daughter's animated face and her thoughts were verified. She was filled with a rush of happiness and love. Just looking at her daughter could drive away any cloudy day.

"Oh, I don't know Mom, but not enough," Caitlin said, with a greedy smile.

"Why, you'd have a lot more if you collected the green, gold or purple beads. Those are the colors of Mardi Gras, you know."

"But I like pink!" Caitlin thrust out her plump little bottom lip for emphasis.

"Caitlin, you always have to be different and want the unusual ones."

Peg laughed at Caitlin's pouty expression.

As the parade approached, Caitlin began jiggling her body to the beat of the glittering strutters that twirled their batons and marched along with the band. The serpent's head on the first float bobbed back and forth, large green gooney eyes rolled back and forth, taking sweeping glances at the cheering mob below.

"The parade is here Mom! Look, it's the snake."

Masked riders taunted the screaming crowds with their "throws."

The torchbearers, with their painted faces pranced alongside the decorative floats, jiving to the beat of the mambo.

Sparks from the flambeaux flares exploded into the sky sending bursts of shimmering diamonds raining down. Excitement rippled through the crowds like an electric current as the parade moved past.

Drummers in the marching band blasted out the throbbing beat of the Mardi Gras Mambo. An eruption of ecstasy roared from the crowd, as the glistening beads and handfuls of purple and gold Bacchus doubloons rained freely down on the wildly waving arms and heads of the crowded masses. The entire ground was vibrating from the blasting sounds of the screaming crowd, begging for throws.

Caitlin reached her hands high to catch the gilded doubloons and shiny strings of beads that were coming toward her.

"Throw me somethin, mister!" Caitlin screamed loudly, reaching out her open hands and slightly tipping the ladder.

"Careful baby, don't fall off." Peg shouted, struggling to be heard above the shouts of the crowds. A few strings of beads fell on the ground not far from Caitlin.

"Look, a pink one over there and a doubloon. I'll get the doubloon for you, mom." Caitlin scrambled backwards down the ladder.

"Just grab them and get yourself right back to the ladder."

Peg grabbed Caitlin's leg and helped her with the last step.

She wasn't worried, because she could see Caitlin was headed just a few steps away. She would be in her line of vision the entire time.

Don't worry Mom, I'll be right back. Don't lose my beads." She thrust her bag toward her mother.

Peg skillfully unwound the gilded rope pull string of the sequined red silk bag from her daughter's fingers. Caitlin impatiently pulled away to free her hand from her mother's. Peg gave her tiny plump fingers a quick squeeze before letting Caitlin go to retrieve the beads.

Peg clutched the bag that had been given to Caitlin just yesterday by her two favorite "uncles." She watched her daughter run to get the fallen treasure. For Peg, Caitlin was her treasure, wrapped in a tiny package of sweetness and innocence. She watched the curly blond head bounce away and disappear from view as she stooped in the midst of the crowd to grab a doubloon that had landed next to the curb. Peg kept her eyes glued to the spot, waiting for Caitlin's head to bob back into view.

Just as she saw Caitlin's blond head rise up again, the crowd swiftly shifted. Peg was picked up and moved down the sidewalk as easily and effortlessly as flood waters from a ravaging, swollen river can sweep away large trees, roots and all, downstream.

"Caitlin, stay by the ladder." She yelled loudly, in an effort to be heard over the huge crowd of inebriated people who had suddenly emerged from Washington Avenue, the adjacent street.

The crowd had become a single entity as it pushed forward up the street to St. Charles Avenue. Everyone in its path was absorbed by the mass in its effort to catch the sights of the first float that had just passed by. Peg engulfed, was forced along with the rushing crowd.

Peg pushed and pulled and yelled as she slowly navigated her way over to the wall of an old stone building. She clung to a tall, paint-chipped plantation-style shutter.

Soon the crowd slowed its pace. With great effort and strength born of a first twinge of fear, Peg squeezed her way back up the sidewalk, but she was forced back a step, for every two that she gained, as she tried to move against the flow of the slowly, moving crowd that continued to head eastward. Her eyes darted around the sidewalk, desperately searching for the sight of her daughter. She was afraid Caitlin may have stumbled and been trampled by the crowd. As she neared the ladder, an unexpected but welcome break in the crowd appeared. The mobs parted and Peg thought she spotted the pink beads still lying on the ground.

"Caitlin, Caitlin!" she yelled, frantically.

Halfway between her, and the place where she last saw her daughter, laid the pink plastic beads. She rushed to grab the pink beads, and scanned the street.

"Caitlin, Caitlin!" she screamed, louder.

Fear and distress entered her voice and made it sharp and loud, cutting easily through the noisy masses. Several people turned to stare. Her heart leapt in her chest and began beating wildly, as her mind reeled with fear. The twinge turned into a full-blown ache when she could see no glimpse of Caitlin. She can't have gone far, Peg kept telling herself, over and over. She waded through the thick masses, precious minutes ticking away as her fear mounted.

Anxiety grabbed her heart and squeezed until she could hardly draw a breath. "Calm down, calm down, I'm sure she is close by," she kept chanting to herself, all the while a terrible, sinking feeling kept spinning through her mind; flashing before her eyes all the horrible possibilities that could claim a lost child. She found herself back at the ladder, not sure how she got there. She had never felt so utterly alone, while in the midst of such a huge number of people. She climbed up to the top of the ladder, nervously scanning the street.

Her last sane memory was screaming at the top of her lungs, "Caitlin, Caitlin, Caitlin," until she was aware that a policeman was tugging at her leg and pulling her down the ladder. Then, the terrible nightmare began.

Through a panicked haze, she gave Caitlin's description to the police. Events were going by in a blur, with only brief periods when she actually allowed reality to come to the surface.

"Please God, please God?" was a constant chant invading her tortured thoughts. When the delirium began to fade, the brutal reality of the situation could no longer be suppressed, but still she couldn't believe this was happening to her. Please God, not her. She would never survive; she would die. And like others in desperate situations, she even resorted to making promises, she would be better, she would do more for others, she would give her own life if only her daughter was spared from harm and returned to her.

Between these silent prayers, she constantly replayed those last few minutes with Caitlin, her mind torturing her with all the things she should have done differently. She now knew how normal people could suddenly go insane. She knew the meaning of "insane with grief," because she was living it.

Her guilt was like lead weights. The stress of her emotions sent adrenaline racing through her veins. She wanted to question every person, stop and search every car. She wanted to run through the crowds up and down every street in New Orleans until she either found Caitlin or died from exhaustion. Instead, she was forced to do nothing but watch as others who did not even know her, or her daughter, carried out the search. She felt useless and her guilt-stricken mind was the only thing that was allowed to race away through scenario after scenario, helping her go a little more insane with each passing minute.

Peg waited at the corner where Caitlin was last seen, hoping somehow her child would find her way back. By midnight, after hours of searching, she allowed herself to be finally taken home to rest; but she would never rest again. She could never rest, not when her baby was out there somewhere, lost in the dark. By that time she had totally locked up, her mind numbed and frozen at the same time.

Peg stumbled in the door to her house and slumped in the closest chair. The female officer with her asked her if she was okay. She inquired about friends and family, someone to stay with her. She also needed pictures of Caitlin to distribute to the media.

When the officer grabbed both her arms and gently shook her, asking her again if she was okay, Peg slowly emerged from the frozen numbness and looked at the officer for perhaps the first time that evening.

What was her name? Anne, Amy, she couldn't remember. She heard herself speaking "my hand hurts." She looked down at her right hand. It was clutched into a tight fist; the knuckles white from the strain. Something pink glistening between her fingers. She couldn't imagine what she was holding, but the pain had been strong enough to cut through the haze. Slowly, her mind forced her fingers to uncurl. Pink beads trailed through her loose fingers. The beads were smudged with blood from the deep cuts her fingernails had driven into the palm of her hand. Unclenched, the cuts bled freely, dripping silently on the polished wood floor. The officer gazed for a second in disbelief and then ran into the kitchen to grab a towel.

Tears silently welled up in Peg's eyes, turning quickly into a stream as her face crumpled up in grief.

She wiped away some tears and felt soft cloth against her cheek. Pulling her hand away she noticed the string handle of the red, sequined silk bag still wrapped around her wrist. She had completely forgotten it since the nightmare began. Seeing it instantly flashed the scene in her mind, plump little fingers sliding so effortlessly out of her grasp. She could still feel their warmth and moisture as she squeezed before letting go. Oh God, why did she let go? If only she could go back, she would hang on and never let go.

Tremors began running from her fingers and up her arm and through her whole body. One cry escaped her lips before she slid from the chair and collapsed, sobbing onto the floor. "Caitlin, Caitlin, I'm so sorry baby."

CHAPTER TWO

Lieutenant Lester Hopper sipped his strong, black chicory coffee from a paper cup as he drove to the hospital. He was deep in thought about the previous night's tragedy. Today, Lundi Gras, or Shrove Monday, was to be a traditional day of celebration for the upcoming parade, Rex, King of Carnival. The frivolity of parades and fireworks had been spoiled, as the city searched for a lost six-year-old child, stolen from the streets during the Bacchus parade. Her mother, hysterical and inconsolable, was sedated and taken to Charity Hospital for the night.

"Charity," as the city natives know it, is one of New Orleans' oldest public hospitals, dating back to 1718 when it used to be located in the French Quarter. The new downtown location on Tulane Ave was erected in 1939 and like many big, inner city hospitals it had undergone renovation but remains a safety net for the poor and underprivileged, and a training ground for the University of New Orleans medical interns.

Lester Hopper and his two brothers were born in Charity, his family unable to afford a private hospital. As a cop, Lester had spent hours in the emergency department, accompanying victims – or perpetrators – of stab wounds, gunshots, beatings and other violent crimes.

Today, Lester was at Charity to see a woman with a deeper wound. She was the mother of a missing girl. The police suspected that the child had been abducted but knowing who did the abducting could change the story from a family disturbance to a much darker outcome. Lester feared the latter as he knew the mother was single, lived alone with her daughter, and by all accounts, there was not a father presently in the child's life. A massive search was ongoing. Lester came to the hospital to obtain more information about possible suspects. Did Caitlin have any other relatives or close family friends who might have taken her?

In the quick background check on Margaret McGregor he found that her father, a police officer, was killed about eight years ago in the line of duty. Her mother died of cancer many years earlier. On the surface, it seemed that Margaret McGregor and her daughter were quite alone in the world. Most surprising of all, she had also worked as a police officer before moving to New Orleans. She now was a journalist for *The Times Picayune* newspaper. He wondered what had made her switch careers. No father was listed on the child's birth certificate. Maybe the birth of her child had made her seek out a less dangerous career.

Lester came to get a better description of the child's clothes, anything that might help. Sadly, he also needed to get a toy or an item of clothing that could help the search dogs sniff for a body. But that was something he would never allow the mother to know, although with her police background, those were the thoughts that had probably sent her here, in the first place.

By habit he entered through Charity's emergency room entrance. As the well-used automatic doors laboriously rolled open, he was flooded with the familiar smells of alcohol and cleaning fluids, which didn't quite manage to mask the smell of burnt coffee, stale urine and unwashed bodies. Lester had always thought that if fear had a smell, this is what it would smell like. In his experience, emergency rooms were often places of fear for patients and those who loved them. In his job, he had the unique opportunity to be the unbiased observer, a third party in the life and death dramas that unfolded. Fear, above all else seemed to be what controlled this part of hospital. Even in the light of day it always chilled his skin with a cold sense of dread.

It was just after lunch and already the waiting room was packed. Assorted elderly people, some waiting in wheelchairs or tired mothers trying to control children, who were coughing, crying or running around trying to play, were among the miserable group of people. Barely controlled chaos echoed through the room and Lester was glad he was not required to stay, as he quickly navigated his way through the room.

Near the back exit to the main hospital, Lester recognized a cop from his own division. He was standing with a sullen, dirty teenager, who looked like he had tangled with a barbed wire fence. It would only get worse as the afternoon wore on and turned into night. Actually, 2 a.m. seemed to be the witching hour for every nut and criminal in the city to converge on the ER. Being a cop was not an easy job but every trip through this area of Charity flooded him with respect for those brave souls who chose to be ER staff and doctors.

Lester waved at the other officer and headed through the ER exit.

In the main lobby, he rapidly approached the information desk beside the elevators. Grateful there was not a line; he realized he didn't need to rush. The atmosphere of the lobby was much more sedate. The heavy, wooden door was all that kept the chaos of the ER from leaking into the marble-floored reception area.

"I'm Lieutenant Hopper, and I've come to see one of your patients who checked in last night. Her name is Margaret McGregor."

Lester retrieved his wallet from an inside jacket pocket and flipped it open to display his NOPD badge.

The receptionist, a plump woman with dirty blond hair, typed in the name. "She's in room 630. Head right down that hallway to the red elevators." Without looking, she pointed toward the elevators.

When he reached the sixth floor, he stepped from the elevator and walked up to the nurses' station to inquire about the patient's status.

"I'm Lieutenant Hopper, and I've come to see Ms. McGregor to ask her some questions." A nurse was busily writing in a chart at the desk. The young woman looked up to see the detective staring intently at her. Self-consciously, she reached up and smoothed her dark hair back behind her ears and smiled.

"Oh yes. That poor lady, losing her child; I know she must be going out of her mind. She was given a strong tranquilizer last night, so she may still be sleeping. But you can go in the room and wait if you like. It's the second door on the left."

"Thank you Miss. I think I can find my way." Lester returned her smile. She watched him walk towards the room.

"Who was that?" inquired Joan, who had just come back from answering a patient's request for more medication.

"That was a very interesting looking detective," Emilie replied, smiling broadly.

"Yeah, he may not be a movie star, but he is definitely hot. Too bad, he's too old for you and too young for me, so get back to work, girl," Joan said, laughing at Emilie's pretending pout.

"What...I like older men," glancing over her shoulder, grinning seductively as she went to make her rounds.

"I told you nurses marry doctors," Joan threw back at her, as Emilie disappeared into the first room on the left.

Lester knocked gently on the door and slowly opened it. He saw a woman, sleeping soundly. Covered up in a blue blanket, she appeared very small and fragile.

He sat in the cracked and worn leather chair that was in the corner near the window. The heavy curtains were closed against the harsh light of day. The room's meager amount of light was provided by the soft glow of a bedside lamp.

The chair's springs had given in, so Lester kept readjusting his posterior to find a comfortable position, a distraction that kept him from focusing on the sleeping woman. He was embarrassed by the thought of watching someone sleep, especially a woman. Then he took occasional glances, admiring the soft peachy skin and honey-golden hair. Something about the oval shape of the face and heart-shaped lips were so familiar. Suddenly, it occurred to him that the face he was seeing was Caitlin's, the one in the photograph that was being distributed to help in the search. The poor woman probably looked just like her daughter when she was a little girl.

He had already met Ms. McGregor late last night to get a photograph of the little girl, although he didn't remember looking at her very closely. She was wracked by grief and shock and, more than likely, did not, or would not remember meeting him when she recovered.

He rose from his chair and walked closer to the bed. He studied the planes of her face as she slept. She had high cheekbones, a petite nose, slightly freckled. Her lips were full and he noticed it was only the wide-spaced eyes that kept her face from attaining the timeless beauty that graced so many faces in today's fashion magazines. Still, there was something about her. He found himself wondering what she looked like awake. What color were her eyes? How did they change her face? People always looked different when they were asleep. As he looked at the closed lids, edged with long lashes, he was startled as they suddenly opened. Deep blue eyes were staring blankly up at the yellowed ceiling tiles above the bed.

The tranquilizers had stilled her body, but her mind was circling with vivid memories as she lay in the hospital bed. What could have happened? How could Caitlin have gotten lost or taken? She was always so careful to warn her daughter about strangers. If she had lost her way, surely she could have found a policeman or a friendly lady to help her. The uniformed cops were everywhere.

She was searching for an explanation and would not let herself imagine the worst, and yet inside, deep in her heart, she felt tormented by a recurring nightmare.

"No! No!" she screamed in her nightmare, struggling to speak.

Her eyes opened wide, but everything was blurry. Above her, stood a hulking figure. Who was it?

Suddenly, her clouded vision cleared and her eyes slowly focused on the large form, as a strong warm hand grabbed hers and called her name. She recoiled in fear.

"Ms. McGregor, I'm Lieutenant Lester Hopper, and I'm going to help find your daughter. It's going to be okay. You have to trust me," Lester's commanding voice filled the room.

She heard the words, but they meant nothing to her. The drugs had made her dizzy and weak, and she slumped back in her bed, silent. The visions returned — gold beads flying through the air, reflecting the lights from the street, clinking sounds of shiny purple doubloons, pelting the street like bullets and the glowing red and yellow sparks that flashed erratically from the flambeaux. The faces of the dancers, leering and evil and then, in the black, smoky night, from far away, Caitlin's high-pitched, excruciating scream, "Mommy, mommy, help me; mommy, mommy, help me..."

Finally, her brain shut down and her body collapsed. Darkness descended and she welcomed its release.

Lester stood over her for a few minutes, not understanding anything that was happening inside this woman. He knew there would be no talking to her today, and maybe not for many days to come. He walked out of the room, feeling distraught and powerless.

The young nurse stopped him on his way to the elevator.

"Did you get to talk to her?" she inquired, sweetly.

"I'm not sure," he answered, lowering his head in concentration, as the elevator doors slowly started to close.

"My name's Emilie, call me and I'll keep you posted."

The elevator doors slid shut, and cut off the last of her words. He certainly was a serious and intense guy; maybe he was too old for her. She turned her thoughts to daydreaming about the new intern in the ER, as she headed back to her desk.

CHAPTER THREE

Lester walked slowly back to the car. He had planned to go right back to the police station to file a report, but instead found himself headed in the opposite direction toward the Mississippi River. After driving a few miles down the river road, he pulled over to a desolate spot and parked his car. He walked up the grassy bank of the levee to the top. He stood motionless, watching a barge float slowly by. He absently massaged his forehead.

His scar was really itching today and his fingers were drawn to the small indented space above his left eyebrow. His fingers rubbed back and forth. The scar was not large or disfiguring, and would not have drawn much attention, except for Lester's habit of rubbing that part of his forehead in times when he was troubled or deep in thought. As his fingertips smoothed the edges of the permanent reminder, he was drawn back to memories of his childhood.

Lester grew up in a shotgun house on Toledano Street in the Irish Channel neighborhood, a section of New Orleans near the river, bordered by Magazine Street to the north and the Mississippi River to the south. The Catholic-Irish and German immigrants settled the area in the late 1800s, but to this day, many families still preserve their religious and culinary traditions. When Lester was growing up, the neighborhood was still a "rough and tumble" world of working class laborers struggling to make ends meet.

Lester's mother, Jean, managed to keep her family together, in spite of the meager wages they earned. She knew how to make an Irish beef stew last for days. Her jambalaya was reputed to be the best in the Irish Channel, which may explain why Lester weighed in at over 150 pounds when he was 14-years-old. Jean made the poor man's version; cutting down the smoked andouille sausage and making it up with hotdog wieners, but no one seemed to complain, least of all, Lester.

His father, a bricklayer, eventually tired of the working class environs. Having a family was just tying him down. Drinking and carousing had become his way of dealing with his dead end life and lost dreams. Late one night he jumped on a barge heading north. He was never heard from again. Although, that was not the whole truth, and in an effort to turn off the memories, Lester walked until he found an empty bench that faced the river. Another barge was coursing its way around the river bend. A lone figure walked the deck. Once again, his thoughts traveled back in time.

When he was growing up, Lester would often come to the levee to watch the barges and tug boats. He found it to be a respite from his family and during times when he needed a break from his father's cruelty.

He remembered one time when he finally confronted his father about his drinking and running around.

"When you are a man you will understand. I gave up everything for this family. What do I get back, but disrespect? What am I sayin; you'll never be a man. You would have made a better girl," his father shouted.

He had stood rigid, his eyes boring into Lester's, his large hands clinching and unclenching into fists. Lester had sensed the danger. His father's control was hung by a thread. But then, suddenly, something broke inside of him and the coils of childhood fear unwound slowly within him, their strength dissolving. He locked eyes with the man before him whom had suddenly become a stranger.

"You don't deserve respect," Lester spit out, his anger like a hot steel rod running straight through him. Lester's usually calm, easygoing nature had been transformed. His face set in anger, eyes blazing, he stared his father down. His father' eyes widened in surprise then quickly turned back to anger. Without saying another word, Lester turned his back and walked away, ending the confrontation. As he walked, he braced for the barrage of blows that were sure to follow. He forced himself to walk steadily, refusing to cringe or run. The expected blows never fell.

Lester's father treated him differently, after the confrontation. He berated Lester in front of his brothers, baiting him. Lester ignored him, making his father even angrier. Inside, Lester was seething and withdrew from his mother and brothers. He was trying desperately to deal with his anger, which threatened to explode. He became quiet and brooding. He knew his mother was worried about him, but he couldn't control the way he felt.

Lester knew his father was purposely baiting him and he was determined to not fall victim to his tirades. It was a battle of wills, but Lester felt a final blow up grew closer with every passing day.

Then it happened: It had been a legendary New Orleans steamy day and Lester had worked from 6 a.m. that morning till sundown, helping mow and trim lawns with a friend of his from school. The pay was almost nonexistent. Lester didn't care as long as it kept him away from the house. By the time he got home, he was tried and drained. He took a quick bath and fell into bed without eating supper.

A couple hours later, he had been awakened abruptly and painfully from a deep sleep. He had been grabbed by his hair and the back of his shorts. The next thing he knew, he was flying through the doorway into the wall of the hallway — his body breaking the old plaster wall as it hit and slid to the floor. Lester was dazed and not fully awake as his father lumbered drunkenly down the hallway calling for Dale and George to get their asses out there. His younger brothers appeared in the hallway, their pale faces pinched with fear.

"Get in the living room," their father boomed. Lester smelled the liquor fumes that filled the hallway. His father was in a rage.

Dale and George tore down the hallway stopping long enough to pull on Lester's hands trying to drag him down the hall away from their father. In the back of his mind, he could hear his mother yelling and his brothers crying. Although his mind was wide-awake, his body was still trying to drag itself out of a dead sleep.

"I said git!" his father yelled as they let go and fled.

Lester was still trying to get his mind and body in sync, as he was once again picked up by the hair, one hand circled the back of his neck, as he was pulled upright and propelled into the living room. His mother tried to run to him but his father backhanded her. She fell back in a heap on the sofa. Dale and George were crying louder now and his mother was screaming. It was a scene from a nightmare. He looked at his mother and brothers. They were petrified, frozen in fear. How could this be happening? Fully awake now, Lester snapped and his own anger exploded.

He sprang at his father like a crazed madman, managing to topple the bigger man. He was screaming gibberish, as he rained blows on his father's face. His triumph didn't last long, before he felt answering blows like jackhammers tear into his sides. The wind was knocked from him and he could not breathe. He heard and felt the crunch of rib bones snapping.

Then his father had him by the hair again, "Not such a big man now, is you?" he said with a drunken glare.

Lester's whole body was filled with raw agonizing pain. He stared back at his father. He saw his own death reflected in his father's hate-filled eyes, but instead of panicking he felt strangely calm. His defiant eyes locked with his father's and he spit in his face. He still remembered his own surprise as the bloody spit sprayed across his father's face, his blood. Those were the last thoughts that passed through his mind, as his father threw a crushing right that connected soundly with his head. His brothers told him later, sirens filled the air as their mother screamed, "You've killed him! You've killed him!" Their father ran out the back door, never to be seen or heard from again.

Lester was left with four broken ribs, a black eye, concussion and a permanent reminder where the Union ring on his father's hand had cut into his forehead and branded him for life. His mother called it his badge of courage.

When he woke up in Charity hospital two days later, he swore to himself that he would never let his mother or brothers down again. He would always be there for all of them. Secretly, he harbored guilt that his defiance had pushed their father to go crazy. Maybe if he had just left home, they all would have been happier. Then he would picture Dale or George being beaten in his place, and he was glad it was him who took the beating. He couldn't stand the thought of them lying helpless and bleeding, while he was somewhere far away.

To make up for the loss of their father's salary, Lester began taking on more responsibilities. He found weekend work on the wharf, which helped supplement his mother's salary from her job selling tickets at the Majestic Theater on Canal Street.

They had their ups and downs but they were more of a family than ever before. Still, Lester faced many challenges. As a teenager in a rough neighborhood, Lester was still never too far away from the seedier side of life.

The fathers of his boyhood buddies were men who worked the river, who spent their time on the wharfs, with the transients and ruffians. Lester heard their stories, their bragging, about the amount they could drink, and nightly assaults on their own wives and children. Most of his own buddies were destined to follow in the same footsteps.

Lester realized someone had to protect the ones who couldn't protect themselves. He would take a different path.

It was no surprise to his family and seemed a natural choice, when he decided to join the New Orleans police force. The biggest obstacle, of course, was his weight. Lester scored high on the entrance test. After six months of intense dieting and weight lifting, he passed the physical. He had managed not to cross the line back into obesity, but he was by no means a small man. At 6'2", 220lbs, he put fear on the face of many of the criminals who chose to cross his path. Those that knew him well called him a "big ole teddy bear," but never when he was within earshot. Lester knew New Orleans was a city that seemed proud of its criminals. You practically had to be one to be elected. Lester cut his teeth on the crimes of the French Quarter – prostitution, drug dealing and simple thievery. But there was one transgression Lester could never understand; it was the torture of a child and the anguish that it caused the families. No matter how many times he witnessed the devastation, it still managed to touch him. He knew this was one crime that he would never be able get used to, no matter how well he did his job, or how much he tried to disassociate. He thought it made him a better cop; many had no empathy left, their hearts hardened to rock by their time on the streets. He could still balance his emotions for the victim, without losing his police instincts.

He had seen many distraught victims turn out to be the criminals, such as the tortured, grieving husband who begged searchers to find his wife. She had only left to go buy doughnuts and never returned. He sat and cried on his front porch, consoled by relatives and neighbors for several weeks, after her abandoned car was found several blocks away. The poor husband put on a good show while his dead wife lay only 20 feet away. During a heated argument, he had broken her neck. Self-preservation was his only concern, as he stuffed her lifeless body into a trash bag and hid it in the living room closet. His grief was so convincing that his friends and family were afraid to leave him alone. Thus, he could never dispose of the body. The odor of the decomposing body finally led the searchers to its hiding place.

Yes, he knew objectivity was a very important skill, but that still didn't mean he had to turn into an unfeeling rock to do his job well.

Lester pulled his thoughts away from the past, and looked at his watch. It was already lunchtime. He had daydreamed the morning away and was no closer to finding anything new on the kidnapping. Disgusted, he got back in his car and headed back to the office, driving slowly along the winding river road.

CHAPTER FOUR

Troy LeBlanc was one of those lucky uptown boys. His mother and father drew large salaries from their psychiatry practice. The money paid for the luxurious lifestyle the family enjoyed, and their home, a restored antebellum mansion that was located on Soniat Avenue in the Garden District.

But like many rich and privileged kids, he easily became bored.

His one passion was his black Volkswagen beetle. He spent hours working on the engine, tuning the plugs and polishing the rims.

After school Troy took off by himself, driving for hours, humming songs on the radio. The torments of adolescence faded away, as he sped along the avenues and bridges in New Orleans, while the Moody Blues, The Eagles and Eric Clapton's songs vibrated through his car.

One of his favorite hangout spots was the levee road in old Algiers Point. He found it relaxing to sit on the grassy riverbank, puffing a Marlboro cigarette, watching the flat-bottomed barges course down the swift currents of the muddy Mississippi, towing cargo to points north. What would it be like to jump aboard?

Troy also enjoyed hanging out at the ferry crossing at Algiers Point and watching the unloading of passengers, walking along the warped wooden planks, to the cars. It was an antiquated section of the city, with shotgun houses and beer joints. Anyone could become lost in time, and even the pretty Westbank girls found the levee crossing a safe hideaway for smoking and carousing.

The teenage girls couldn't help but notice Troy, the tall, dark-haired, lanky guy in a black, shiny VW who resembled Tony in "Saturday Night Fever."

One afternoon, as Troy was leaning against his car, peering out toward the river, a pretty girl with elfin features walked up to the car and asked what he was doing there.

Troy was shocked. His hand quivered with nervousness. He was uneasy around girls. He was afraid that they would think he was a freak for hanging out there all the time.

"Why are you just standing there? Let's go for a drive." The sassy girl flipped her long red hair away from her face, drew one last drag from her cigarette, and then tossed it on the ground, smashing it out with her foot.

She opened the passenger door and plopped down on the seat. Her name was Mary and she had the face of a pixie, with a turned up nose, bright eyes and a perky smile that revealed even rows of small, perfect white teeth. She was the most beautiful thing Troy had ever seen.

"Let's go," she commanded.

After that day, the two were inseparable. Mary was different from the debutante girls who attended the Newman High School in the Uptown District. Mary's dad was a city employee and her mother, a homemaker who managed a tight budget, clipped coupons and organized the carpools.

Mary's boldness and charm delighted Troy's parents. She brought Troy out of his hermit life of cars and loud music. Mary's parents were pleased to see their girl tamed, and dating a rich and well-bred uptown boy. Everyone was happy.

After graduating from high school, they moved to Baton Rouge to attend LSU. They took classes together, both majoring in journalism. Mary wanted to be a writer, and Troy a radio broadcaster.

Their part-time jobs at the college radio station gave them a great opportunity to hone their skills. Mary was the copy-editor, Troy the broadcaster. After college they married and within months Troy secured a nighttime radio spot on station KYNO, a talk radio station. His parents had pulled a few strings to get him the job, but it was Troy's own raw talent that kept his ratings high. The show had been running for almost 15 years. It was one of the top-rated radio shows in New Orleans.

Troy developed his own style of talk radio called "Troy Talk."

His show began with a reading of the top news stories. He would then pick one news item for discussion. Callers phoned in comments or questions. His show had become a forum for discussing political hot button issues about topics, such as governmental scandals, gay rights, or fundamentalist Christians. On weekends his show focused on people profiles, and he invited local celebrity guests, like Anne Rice, or Al Hurt.

His show was lively, but never too raunchy or moribund. He became a champion of the social causes. Troy believed in New Orleans and thought the city could one day rise above its past history of corruption, racism and caste system.

But on one special Sunday, just two days before Fat Tuesday, Troy's dream of the future New Orleans was set back once again.

His program began with the news of a missing little girl, swept from the streets of St. Charles Avenue, during the Bacchus parade.

Police had contacted the radio station on Sunday night, to set off the "Angela Alert." Station managers were instructed to announce the description of the child. The Angela alert was a new program sweeping the nation that Troy had personally championed hand in hand with the New Orleans Police Department.

This was also the very first time the new alert system had been used in the city and it brought chills to his skin. He wrote down the information for the broadcast.

The alert system was started in Dallas/Fort Worth, Texas where it had been known as the "Amber Alert." Amber was a young girl taken while riding her bike in an empty lot behind her house. Dallas/Fort Worth residents held their breath for days, hoping for her to be found unharmed. Her body was recovered in a creek bed and her killer was never found. Nearby residents had seen the abduction, and wondered if some kind of a warning system to alert the public might have helped save her.

The goal was to get a photo or a description of the missing child out to the public by TV and radio as soon as possible. Studies had proven the first hours to be critical for child abduction. Texas had success with the new program, so that some children were being returned unharmed to their families. It could be a little unsettling for the abductor to hear a description of the child, himself and his vehicle on the radio within minutes. Some kidnappers became scared and ended up letting the kids go. Vigilant citizens spotted others and reported the information to the authorities.

However, in New Orleans, the name of the program was changed from the Amber Alert to the Angela Alert. Angela, the 5-year-old Morelli girl, had been abducted the year before, during a busy market day in the French Quarter. Disappeared into thin air — or so it seemed. The FBI was immediately called in and the wealthy family waited nervously, expecting a ransom demand for money from the suspected kidnappers. Two days later, Angela's battered body was found in a dry-docked, covered fishing boat by the boat-builder hired to scrape and repaint the hull. The poor man, six months later, still broke into tears when forced to talk about finding the little girl. The man was so upset he rattled on and on in Italian for over 15 minutes before the 911 operator could get another person on the line to translate.

callers suspected the worst — a child molester. One man called in and said if he spotted the girl with the kidnapper, he wouldn't call the police. Instead, he'd take his shotgun and blow the sick bastard to pieces. Troy thought to himself, "Yeah, I see your point, man."

CHAPTER FIVE

Twelve days after Caitlin McGregor was declared missing, a child's tiara was found on the banks of muddy Mississippi River. A jogger on the levee road near the corner of Tchoupitoulas and Amelia Street had spotted it, and brought it to the station. All those CSI crime shows were paying off, as the jogger had enough forethought to carefully hold and bag the item. There were several long blond strands caught in the comb of the tiara.

Lester was at home when he received the call.

"Looks like we found something belonging to the little girl and it's not good," said Detective Pierre Martens, "All we need now is to get a DNA match, and then we should get the dive team out and start dragging the river."

"I'll call the mother to get the DNA sample."

"No, I'm going to do that, Pierre," Lester said. "You stay put."

"Sure Lester," Pierre's voice was clipped, his anger barely concealed.

Lester sighed heavily, as he pushed himself out of the worn, leather Lazy Boy recliner that dominated his living room. The hardwood floors glowed and, though the room was sparsely furnished, it was tidy and filled with a wide assortment of plants that gave it warmth. The pleated drapes were hunter green and matched the two rag rugs on the floor. A handmade oak entertainment center covered the north wall, opposite to Lester's recliner and held his television and stereo. The stereo had an old fashioned record player that Lester refused to exchange for a CD player. There was something soothing and comforting about playing the obsolete records from his childhood and teen years. Just listening, brought back the good memories of his youth in the shotgun house where he grew up in. He couldn't stand that new "rap crap" or the other new avenues of sound music had taken. It was amazing how his collection had grown. His friends and family seemed to enjoy finding him records he didn't have — although some would never get played. He had two or three polka albums, one of Irish folk songs and several twangy old westerns that stayed forever in the back of the rack. A couple were given as jokes, but he was hoping one day the joke would be on the giver when the value increased with age — yeah right, even he couldn't swallow that one.

While he would never be considered handsome, Lester had a certain rugged charm. When he got lazy and let his hair grow, his sister-in-law said he looked boyishly sexy. Ever since that comment, he tried to keep it as short as possible, but sometimes it was a losing battle to find time to make it to the barber. Curly or short, his hairstyle didn't matter much when he lost weight and obtained a well-muscled body, women seemed to suddenly be waiting in line for his attention. One of his friend's wives had labeled him the strong silent type. He soon learned a close relationship with a woman took more work and time than he was able to give.

Anyone in his life would have to be happy with bits and pieces of his time. Lester had learned the hard way that even if a woman says she understands and wouldn't push, it wasn't long before she was making demands that he couldn't keep. It was just easier to keep his entanglements to a minimum and concentrate on his work and family responsibilities.

Lester put his youngest brother George through community college while Dale, who was truly the "good-looking" one of the three, caught the eye of a southern beauty whose father owned a large and successful construction company in Lake Charles. The marriage was arranged rather quickly and Lester became an uncle seven months later.

Anytime Lester needed to smile, all he had to do was think about Dale's little daughter Dominique. Dale worshipped his little family and in return they made him a very happy man. Dale soon became the son his father-in-law never had, and was being groomed to take over the family business.

George, who like Lester, also fought a weight problem, took a job in California after graduation. He fell in love with the West Coast beaches and swore he would never leave it.

Apparently the "California girls" and great outdoors was just what he needed to end his war with fat. He was a "health nut" now and seemed to live on bean sprouts and salad. The last time he came home for a visit, his mother was beside herself with worry at how gaunt he looked.

While a little on the skinny side, Lester had to admit George looked good, healthy, and seemed very happy. Lester laughed when he thought about his mother taking advantage of every opportunity to shove large bowls of seafood gumbo in front of George's face.

She couldn't understand how he could turn down his favorite childhood cuisine. Those "Californians," as his mother called them, had brainwashed her child. He really got a laugh when George confessed on the way to the airport how it had taken all his willpower to resist the gumbo.

He said the visions of crusty French bread dipped in steaming gumbo, with shrimps and crab claws floating around, and the scent of the file, would be swimming in his dreams for weeks. And then there was momma's jambalaya, spicy sausage with sweet tomatoes and puffy rice. Good God.

Not long after George left for California, Jean decided to move into a newly built retirement community near the lakefront along with several of her friends. Lester suddenly found himself alone with spare time on his hands and for the first time felt the pangs of loneliness.

He even caught himself wishing he had taken the time to start a family, though a part of him knew it never would have worked. Instead, he would be divorced and maybe a part-time, weekend father. Lately, he had found himself taking stock of his life and looking for a new direction that would fill in the holes left by his family.

His mother's retirement community was only 10 minutes away. Sometimes, he visited on the weekends, which accounted for the flourishing plants that filled the room. His mother had a green thumb and enjoyed the challenge of resurrecting a dead, neglected plant to healthy lushness. Her neighbors in the retirement community were constantly bringing Jean their sad, brown, shriveled plants. If she could revive them, they were hers.

Consequently, Lester, who had inherited his mother's skills, was given as many as he wanted. It already took him a full 30 minutes every week to maintain them all. But he had to admit he loved having growing things around him.

At his mother's urging Lester moved from his small apartment into the old family home. Another thing he had inherited when his mother moved to the retirement community was a large, fat, black and tan striped, longhaired tabby cat named "Babykitty."

Lester and "Baby" had reluctantly taken up residence together. It wasn't long before the cat had wormed her way into Lester's heart. His mother said cats weren't allowed at the center, and she also felt the old cat would never adapt to new surroundings. It was kinder to leave her where she felt comfortable and knew the lay of the land.

The ten-year-old cat was far from being a baby, but after a few weeks Lester realized how perfect the name fit. While she was rather large for the name Baby, she had retained her cute kitten face.

The cat cried and pouted when she didn't get her way. Lester called her "Bawl Bag" and "Catzilla" when he was irritated with her. Baby had an especially annoying habit of ceaselessly banging the vertical blinds that covered

Lester's bedroom window at precisely three in the morning, until Lester either got up to let her out or sailed a pillow across the room for a direct hit that sent her scampering down the hallway.

He often swore if it weren't for his mother the cat would be homeless. He ultimately installed a Babykitty sized pet door in the kitchen door and a cease fire was negotiated. Deep down, he loved the company and Baby knew it, as she always demanded some of whatever Lester was eating and was totally fearless in the face of Lester's anger.

Whenever Lester settled into the recliner, the cat took it as her cue to jump up and rub her face against his stubby chin, purring loudly, as she turned in his lap, until she found a comfortable spot to settle down for a long bath and nap.

The cat had been his secret roommate for over a year. He knew the merciless teasing he would receive if anyone at the station learned he was sharing his house with a cat, let alone one named Babykitty. Lester didn't buy his mother's story about pets not being allowed or the cat's inability to adapt to new surroundings. He had seen cats sitting in the other residents' windows and heard dogs yapping behind doors as he passed on his way to Jean's apartment. He kept quiet because he knew Jean was worried about him being alone in the house of his childhood. He had to admit it was a different loneliness than his small apartment held.

Everywhere he turned an old memory lurked to touch his heart — some good, some bad. So to keep her happy, he took the cat and before long he realized that he enjoyed the company of the demanding creature and the laughter her antics brought to his life.

Right now, Baby was curled in his lap fast asleep.

"Sorry Baby," Lester said, as he picked up the limp, sleeping cat and stood up and put her back down in the lounger. In the kitchen, he checked the cat's automatic feeder and watering container. A godsend with the kind of hours he sometimes worked.

He grabbed his jacket hanging on the ladder back chair in the small kitchen nook, and headed for the front door, his head lowered, already deep in thought.

CHAPTER SIX

The house on Meyer Street where Peg and Caitlin lived was of the small wooden frame variety. It was neatly landscaped, and freshly painted a bright white with dark green trim, unlike many of the houses in the neighborhood with their cracked and peeling paint, and ferns and banana trees running wild in the yard.

Red and pink begonias planted in alternating rows filled the front flowerbed. A painted pot overflowed with white petunias.

Light fluffy white clouds floated across a crystal blue sky. A cool breeze wafted the smell of ginger blossoms through the morning air. Lester admired the lush, carefully tended flowers. He imagined Caitlin laughing in the sunshine, as she helped her mother plant and water the flowers. For Lester, it seemed like the perfect home, the perfect day; perfect — except for one thing: Caitlin's laughter may never fill this house again. He was here to deliver some of the worst news any parent can ever receive.

As Lester climbed the steps, he noticed several wind chimes hanging from the ceiling of the porch. One was cat-shaped and with several tin bells; another was a Celtic cross with a large amber piece of cut glass that glittered in the morning sunlight. But the one that sent the softly muted tone into the morning breeze had long slender tubular bells that lightly brushed in the morning breeze to make the familiar sound. Any other time, he would have thought the sounds were beautiful, but today, their haunting cadence sent chills down his spine. He could feel the goose bumps rise on his arms. The sun-drenched porch instantly went dim as the sun vanished behind a fluffy cloud. The murkiness, like a thick layer of dust, covered everything it touched with gloom.

He took a deep breath and knocked on the door.

Sooner than he had wanted, the door opened.

"Hello, I'm Lieutenant Lester Hopper, are you Margaret McGregor?"

"Please, call me Peg. I haven't been called Margaret since I was 13."

"I may have some information about Caitlin," Lester said, his voice somber. He was dreading the news he had to deliver.

"Yes, I know, the FBI told me to expect you. Please come inside. They said you had some news." Hope washed toward him in waves, engulfing him and making him momentarily mute.

He suddenly couldn't find his voice as he looked at her face, and could tell she was hoping for some positive news.

Lester paused; He knew this wasn't going to be easy. Peg seeing the look on Lester's face pushed the screen door open to stand directly in front of him. Her face drained of color, her voice urgent.

"Where is she?" She demanded. Her mind already jumping to the worst-case scenario.

"Please don't get upset. We haven't found her. It may be nothing but we have to check it out. A jogger found a tiara on the levee. We want to see if it could be Caitlin's. We need something to match the DNA."

Jesus, he didn't mean to blurt it out like that. What was wrong with him? But he could see she had read his face without really listening to his words, and she knew, she knew. She was shaking her head back and forth.

Damn, he wanted whoever was responsible for this in front of him. He knew at that moment he could have easily squeezed all the life out of them, and to hell with courts and juries and proper justice.

"Oh God no, no, it can't be," Peg cried. "I know she is alive. I feel it. If it's hers, it must have fallen off when she was taken. Did you search the area? Have you received any leads from all the news coverage?"

"We thought we had a solid lead on the case. There was a report from a woman at a Sweet Shop on Decatur, who said she had seen a small child fitting Caitlin's description, but that's all she knew. We searched the area around her shop, going from house to house. We also got a few phone calls from individuals who said they thought they had seen Caitlin, but none of those leads were useful. We've followed every lead no matter how small. I know this is upsetting, but I have to let you know that we plan on dragging the river. We also need to know if there is a DNA match on the hairs found in the tiara," Lester finished softly, his voice trailing off as he got to the part about dragging the river, hating to cause her further pain.

Peg collapsed on the flowered sofa, holding her head in her hands, chanting, "My baby, my baby, my Caitlin. If the tiara is hers, then you think she's in the river. You think she is dead?"

The realization of what he said hitting her as she voiced the words, with the pain and shock sinking in all at once. She thought the nightmare of the last 12 days had wrung her dry of all emotion, but as she thought of her Caitlin in the river, fresh tears stung her eyes and cheeks.

Lester knew this would be bad but he was not prepared for how bad it really was. The moment he saw her face, it was obvious she had spent the last twelve days with hardly any sleep. While not a beautiful woman, Lester could tell she was very pretty if you looked past the darks circles and sadness stamped on her features. Now his heart lurched, as he watched her bend over and draw her body into a tight ball of pain, trying to hold in the wrenching sobs threatening to over take her. He knew not to get emotionally involved. There was a fine line that should not be crossed.

As Lester observed her raw pain, he could not seem to stop his hand from reaching out to caress her hair. When she raised her head and their eyes met, he felt connected to this woman he hardly knew, as he had never felt connected to another human being in his whole life. Before he was even aware of it, she was cradled in his arms on the living room sofa, clinging to him tightly, crying softly as he gently rocked her back and forth.

Lester wasn't sure how much time had passed. It could have been ten minutes — or even an hour — time had somehow stopped. He could tell she was calmer now and her sobs had lessened as she seemed to be gathering her composure. When he felt her shift in his arms, he took the opportunity to release her and rise from the couch.

He reached into his pocket and pulled out the white handkerchief he always carried, a habit that was instilled in him as a boy by his mother. To this day, Jean still gave him a set every Christmas with his initials intricately embroidered in one corner.

As he extended the handkerchief, their eyes met again and they were strangers once more. He felt relieved, but at the same time, a sharp stab of disappointment touched his heart. For the first time in his life he felt the loss of something he didn't even know he was missing.

Lester was torn between not wanting to intrude on her grief and his need to comfort Peg.

"Let me make you some hot tea." He headed toward the kitchen.

"Thanks," Peg said as she headed in the opposite direction.

Peg went to the bathroom and quickly splashed cold water on her red, swollen face. All she could think of was Caitlin and another bout of fresh tears threatened to crumble her again. She reached for the bottle of pills in the medicine cabinet and swallowed one of the xanax pills prescribed by her doctor. She had to admit the pills made the mental anguish retreat and numbed her feelings, though she hated the lethargy. On impulse she reopened the bottle and took another pill.

She stood outside Caitlin's door and slowly turned the handle. She walked over to the white dresser and picked up the little pink brush. She lovingly touched the blond hairs stuck in the bristles of the brush. She was brought back to the present by the sound of the tea kettle's whistle. She slowly left the room, softly closed the door behind her and headed towards the kitchen.

"You're very organized. I had no trouble finding anything." Lester said, trying to say something positive, but feeling stupid after he said it.

He had removed his jacket and rolled up his shirtsleeves. As he reached for the sugar, his muscles moved under the thin, white fabric of his shirt.

Peg was struck with how odd it was to see such a large man, roaming around her kitchen. Her appraisal was more out of curiosity. She had met the inner man before she had a chance to see him as a whole person. It was a little weird, kind of like pouring your heart out to a long distance pen pal before ever meeting in person. She wanted an imprint of his features to store, along with her other memories.

He had curly brown hair, though he kept it short enough so that it wasn't unruly but softened his more rugged facial features. She remembered how safe and warm she had felt, when he had held her on the couch. She wished she could have stayed there forever. Peg tried to shrug off her crazy thoughts. The pills must be working faster than usual or she had reached insanity. She instantly felt guilty for thinking of her own comfort. She just wanted to be in a place where she didn't have to think anymore.

She realized she had been staring at Lester, and was instantly embarrassed.

"It's good to see the color return in your face," Lester said, as he brought the cups to the table.

Peg blushed even more, as she quickly raised her cup to her lips. She felt like he could read her thoughts.

"Thanks for making the tea; I'm sure it is not part of your regular duties."

Peg tried to cover up her emotions. She suddenly was eager for him to leave. She wanted to be alone. She felt very tired.

"I have Caitlin's hair brush. Will this work for the test?" she asked. Her voice strained.

"Yes, that should work fine," Lester said as he pulled an evidence bag from his pocket. He carefully dropped the brush in the bag and sealed it.

"I want you to feel free to call me anytime, Ms. McGregor."

"Peg, please call me Peg," she said, forcing a smile and trying not to show how eager she was for him to leave. He had been so kind but she needed to be alone.

"Here is my card Peg, and I have written down my home number. I mean it...anytime, please call me." His green eyes shined with sincerity.

A shrill beep sounded three times from the pager attached to Lester's belt.

"Well, I guess I better check in. Are you sure you are all right? Is there anyone I can call?"

"No really, I'm fine, and thanks for the card. You have been so kind and caring. Really, you should go. I'll be fine."

Lester grabbed his jacket and took Peg's offered hand. Instead of the shake she expected, he enclosed her small hand in his and gave it a light caressing squeeze, lifted it and kissed the back of her hand.

Peg felt her hairs on her arm prickle and tingle all the way up to the back of her neck. She quickly ushered him to the door and then stood silently watching, long after his car had disappeared.

With each passing day, a small part of her continued to hope, even though her hope drained away more. But somewhere deep in her heart she could feel Caitlin was alive, but she also felt that her daughter was far away and out of reach. She didn't know if this meant Caitlin was really alive or that her spirit had moved on to a better place. It was difficult to keep despair from claiming her last bit of hope.

A part of her was sad to see Lester go, as she knew that once she turned away and shut the front door, she would slump back into her world of recurring nightmares about her traumatic losses: her mother, her father, and now Caitlin.

She thought that those memories were long gone. She hadn't had any nightmares about her father's death since she had learned she was pregnant with Caitlin. It was as if the baby had given her a new life; she could leave the painful past behind. But now that her baby had been taken away from her, the door to her past had been torn from its hinges. She was once again caught up in the painful cycle of lost dreams and should-have-beens.

Everyone in her whole life who she had ever loved, had been taken away from her, ripped from her life leaving the gaping holes that would not heal. If only she had held tighter to Caitlin.

She realized that she was still standing staring out at the darkness through the open door. How long had she been standing like a zombie in the doorway? Slowly she closed the door and walked in a trance to the couch, where she collapsed into a deep, drug-induced sleep.

As soon as Lester had pulled away from her house, he knew why he had instinctively avoided contact with her. Ever since that day in the hospital, he had found reasons why he did not personally meet with her and conduct any further questioning. She was so distraught and he felt the officers who had been involved in the search would make her more comfortable. The FBI would send strangers to talk to her also. He wanted to lessen her trauma.

That was the story he told himself as he avoided further contact. Now he realized it was because of the way he felt when he saw her in the hospital. It was like all the stories he had heard, or read about, people meeting for the first time, and being instantly drawn to each other. There was a connection between them and it was real. He was frightened by this sudden emotion. What he would do about it was something that would require a great deal of thought. He reached for his radio and called the station.

"I've got the sample DNA. I'm going to drive it over to the lab myself. The sooner we know, the sooner we can get the divers in the water."

CHAPTER SEVEN

Peg walked up the sidewalk to the Aurora Methodist Church, a modern suburban red brick building. When she had first moved to New Orleans, a little over six years ago, she rented an apartment uptown. After Caitlin was born, Peg used the money from her small inheritance to purchase a two-bedroom house on Meyer Street in Algiers, a more affordable neighborhood located on the Westbank. The church was only a few blocks away. Peg was raised a Catholic, but she had not gone to mass or confession since the day of her father's funeral.

Peg decided a change in religion might be what she needed. if she wished to raise her daughter to learn about God. When she needed it most, her own faith had failed her so she planned to give her own daughter the same exposure to religion that she had.

Since her Catholic background brought back too many painful memories of her mother and father, the Methodist Church seemed like a good choice and neutral ground for her and Caitlin to set down some roots. Caitlin had enjoyed singing in the children's choir and attending the church's vacation bible school.

But today, Peg wanted to be anywhere else. Today, she felt as far away from God and her faith as ever.

The hair on the tiara had matched Caitlin's hair from her pink Barbie brush. They had dragged the river for more than a week, but the divers found nothing. Still the general consensus was that Caitlin was gone – Dead. Even though the police had not officially closed the case, she knew they all thought it was only a matter of time before the body was found. Then, there were those who speculated that a child's body in the river may never be found when you take into consideration the teeming river life that had many days to do nature's work of dismantling fragile human flesh.

Everyone she had ever loved had been taken away from her. She felt nothing as she approached the church. Today was Caitlin's memorial prayer service. She took no comfort in the sight of the church or the preacher, who now ran out to meet her.

"Peg dear, how are you holding up?"

The pastor embraced her and suddenly her tears came rushing out in a tidal wave.

"I don't want to live," she sobbed, practically collapsing in his arms. "I don't know if I can do this. It's like saying goodbye."

"Peg, you know we discussed that this would be important for you to carry on. You have to move on. The service is meant to bring comfort to you and to Caitlin no matter where she is."

He brought her into the sanctuary.

During the service, Peg's eyes were transfixed on the gold mosaic cross behind the altar. She felt as if her blood inside was draining away onto the ground at her feet. She heard no sounds; not even the emotional verses of Amazing Graze or the hysterical weeping of friends.

Kevin and Ozzie stood on each side of her, holding her up throughout the service. She was like a body with nothing inside. Nothing left, not even tears. This is what her life had become, a crazy seesaw of emotions. One minute she felt as if she would literally burst apart into a million pieces from the intensity of the pain, and in the next instant, she felt nothing, her body desensitized.

She was also amazed and struck with gratitude at the seemingly endless bouquets of flowers, stuffed animals and cards sent by so many sympathetic New Orleans residents.

People who did not even know her or Caitlin wrote her long compassionate letters, with offers to help her through her grief. She had even had a handful of psychics tell her where to look for Caitlin's body. There was one that said Caitlin was alive and to not loose hope but it was written on old yellowed stationary in a spidery crawl of words that Peg had a hard time deciphering. It had no return address, so she dismissed it as some elderly person's attempt to ease her pain and so Peg put it in her desk with the rest of the cards and letters.

She was very touched by it all but only for Caitlin's sake. She was beyond help. She did not want to talk or see anyone.

She longed to return to her small house, where she could remember and mourn in private. The pain increasingly turned inward and was eating her alive. She felt as if she were shriveling and dying a little bit more each day. Her life's juices were draining and leaving her an empty, hollow shell that would eventually collapse and blow away like dust in the wind. The only relief was that as the essence of her life drained away, the pain went with it – at least for a while.

But, today, she would try to weather the storm of tears because it was for Caitlin. She had to follow through and see her daughter's memory honored before she could give in to total despair.

CHAPTER EIGHT

The Mississippi River Bridge was not congested, and Peg weaved easily though the lanes, making her exit to Magazine Street.

When she arrived at the parking lot, she waved her ID card to the guard, who opened the gate.

"There are no words to describe how sorry we all are about little Caitlin, it's so terrible. Peg, hon, I am glad that you have come back to work. We have missed you somethin' awful," Mr. Pete said.

"Thank you, I can't be at home by myself anymore, it's so lonely."

"That's right, but you need to take it easy, now. Don't push it, daulin." Mr. Pete lowered his head, not knowing what else to say.

Peg parked her car, and grabbed her purse and briefcase. She made her way to the entrance of *The Times Picayune* office building.

As Peg walked into the expansive newsroom, the chatter halted suddenly. Eyes darted to Peg, and the silence was broken by Bill Bodecker, her managing editor.

"Glad you decided to come back," he said in his raspy, but loud voice. "It hasn't been the same around here without you."

"Thanks Bill, I'm ready to get back to things here," Peg said, trying not to draw attention to herself.

"Maybe you should start slow. The health column would be good for you to get back into, not too much of a strain after being gone," he said, clearing his throat, and spitting out a wad of chewing tobacco in the tin trash can next to his desk.

"Bill, I'm tired of this once a week health column, I'm tired of writing about the disease du jour; it's boring. I want to go on general assignments; I need a new direction. I need to keep busy," Peg said, her conviction shining bright in her eyes.

"Whoa, whatever you say, Peg. Just don't bite off more than you can chew is all I was sayin." Bill turned around and finished scribbling edits to a story on his desk, mumbling his usual string of curse words, "What fucking asshole wrote this piece of dog shit?"

"Couldn't have been me," quipped Peg, laughing at Bill. She surprised herself with her joke and her new boldness. Now she had nothing to lose. Peg had always taken care to back off from confrontations. She was too insecure, and somewhat afraid of Bill to ask for better assignments and the raises that she deserved. She walked through life one careful step after another, taking whatever was given to her. Being a single mother meant she had to be watchful, cautious and steady. She couldn't afford to make waves.

Peg went to her desk, cleared away a few papers and turned on her computer. She removed the out-of-office reply on her e-mail and began deleting the old e-mails so her computer wouldn't crash. She took joy in deleting the masses of old e-mail and temp files, as if she were erasing all traces and remnants of the past and now focusing on the future. She felt a slow anger beginning to boil. Damn, she was mad. God what was happening to her? Suddenly she seemed so full of pent-up rage. At this rate she would have to visit the gym at noon and after work, instead of just mornings.

She had thought it would be harder to face everyone, but discovered most people wanted to skim over any emotional outpourings and welcomed her attitude of business as usual. Peg was so relieved that she was able to contain her emotions. She had been afraid she might break down in front of them. That would have been a terrible set back.

The guard's words had almost broken through her shaky reserve.

She had pushed back all the memories to their same small space, but knew the hold was tenuous at best. Only time would strengthen the door that concealed them.

The feelings of anger seemed to come out of nowhere, but she welcomed them. Anger helped her focus and drove the pain away.

Peg spent her teenage years secluded in her bedroom, watching TV, reading and filling up on junk food. She used food as a substitute for the emotional loss of her mother who died when she was just twelve.

After her mother's death, her father poured his grief into his work at the police department and seemed to forget he even had a daughter.

She always cringed when relatives would say, "You have such a pretty face." It was an empty and hurtful comment, always delivered with such sincerity, with the implied but unspoken part of the equation being "if only you would lose some weight."

But that was nothing compared to the abuse and cruelty she suffered at the hands of her classmates. She faced the trials of puberty on her own, turning to books to answer questions about the changes taking place within her body. The worst part was the recurring headaches. She was sure she had a brain tumor. It was only a matter of time before the tumor would grow large enough to kill her. Her father seemed not to notice how quickly the bottles of aspirin disappeared from the medicine shelf.

The taunts in school made her headaches worse. She started missing a lot of school from staying home sick. She was tired all the time and spent most of her days in her room. All she wanted to do was be by herself, safe in her bed, spending the day reading.

It was only after her fourteenth birthday that her father had finally recovered enough from his own pain and grief, to wake up and take a good look at his severely depressed daughter.

It all changed the day her father received the call from Principal Harris when "Maggie," as her parents and relatives always called her, was caught putting half her gym class's clothing in a pile in the shower room. She lit them with a lighter, and watched the flames. The fire alarms were triggered and the entire sprinkler system in the locker room and auditorium had sprung to life.

As she had gathered the clothing from the various lockers, all she could think about was the countless times that she found her own shirt or pants on the wet floor of the showers, or worse, floating in one of the locker room's toilets. Then the snickering would begin as she tried to wash out the item in the sink. She had told herself it didn't matter what they thought, or did, they were nothing to her. But in the end, her anger won over and she took her revenge. She wanted them all to know that she had done this. She was responsible and she wasn't afraid of the consequences.

When her father arrived, he seemed so stern as he looked at her with his stoical "policeman" face. Then, Principal Harris walked into the office. She tried to listen to the drone of their voices from inside the office, but a headache, which had started earlier in the day, reached a peak. She felt if she moved to lean closer to the wall, the nausea would take over and her meager lunch of French fries, Almond Joy and Coke would decorate the gray slate floor. Instead, she swallowed her bile down and tried to ride out the wait as her physical misery increased.

She barely noticed when the door opened and Principal Harris called her into his office. She stood and slowly moved into the open doorway.

The last thing she remembered was trying to concentrate on the middle of Dr. Harris' chin, as it moved up and down, while he was telling her she was to be suspended for two weeks. The room went black and she was thinking "who turned out the lights."

When she regained consciousness, she was at St. Joseph's Hospital. There was a rustling beside the bed as her father rose from the only chair in the small room and scooped her into his arms and said, "Maggie, I am so sorry. I know this is my fault. But things are going to be different now. I love you so much. I've been so selfish. Can you ever forgive me?"

Her arms slowly came up and circled his neck, as she began to cry.

"Oh Daddy, I love you too. I thought I had lost you both."

In that one moment of shared love, all the walls built, slowly, one painful brick at a time, melted away, and from that moment on her life with her father was forever changed.

All the tests came back negative and, while the doctors were stumped as to the cause of her headaches, they were relieved at her quick improvement. In the end, the diagnosis given was a combination of stress and hormonal changes that had caused the headaches. The doctors prescribed migraine medication.

As soon as she was released from the hospital, they packed and went on a two-week camping trip. Those days of solitude helped them rediscover each other and father and daughter found a new beginning.

She started at a new school, made new friends and a whole new life opened up before her. The next few years, she and her dad spent summers hiking, fishing, hunting, and various other vacation camping adventures taking place along the bayous and coastal canals. He took her shopping for new clothes.

Mainly, she remembered the laughter and long talks during those fishing trips. But it didn't last, nothing ever lasts for her. Even now, a hard lump grew in her throat and her eyes grew moist as the memories floated to the surface of her mind.

She would keep up her strength, with the hope that Caitlin would be found, and brought home.

She was "Peg" now; she pushed the memories of her life as "Maggie" away, before they caused too much pain and focused on the mission. She was an expert at pushing memories into a small locked part of her brain, where they stayed secluded and hidden. It was only in dreams that they usually surfaced when her conscious mind was asleep.

CHAPTER NINE

Peg wasn't expecting the voice on the end of the phone line to be a man's. It was noon, and she was waiting for a call from her friend Marsha to confirm their lunch plans. Marsha worked at an art gallery in the Warehouse district, and was trying to get Peg to try out some of the local French cuisines, cropping up in the new arts neighborhood. It was only Peg's second week back at work; the days had seemed to take on a regular ebb and flow; she was grateful for the routine, but was also tempted by her friend's invitation to try something new.

The weekends would have been open canyons threatening to swallow her whole if not also for her friends Kevin and Ozzie, who were doing their best to keep her entertained. She didn't want to think about what she would do when they left for vacation.

"Is this Ms. McGregor?"

"Yes," replied Peg, trying to recognize the voice.

"My name is Vincent Morelli. I hope I haven't caught you at a bad time," he said cheerfully.

"Morelli," why does that name sound familiar? Peg thought to herself. Then it came to her: Morelli is the last name of the little girl who was abducted last fall.

"Are you related to Angela Morelli?" Peg asked, already thinking that she liked the rich deepness of his voice.

"Yes, I am her father. And before I go on, I want to express my deepest sympathy for your loss. I, more than anyone, can understand what you have been through, which is why I am calling. I must see you right away. I think I can help you."

Peg was silent. She didn't know what to say. She was taken off guard. The man sounded sincere, but how could he – or anyone – really help her. Caitlin was gone. Nothing could change that. Why should she want to talk to this man whose life, like hers, was shattered by losing a daughter?

"Ms. McGregor, I apologize. I know I'm the last person you probably thought would be calling today. And maybe you think I'm insensitive to call you. But please, say you will meet me, just for a few minutes. We could have lunch somewhere."

"I don't know," Peg said. His voice was smooth and soothing. She liked the voice even though it was tinged with arrogance. She found herself speculating on what he looked like: tall, dark with a good build. For the first time that day Peg almost laughed out loud at herself, but instead found herself smiling into the phone. He was probably some tiny little man with a bald head and bad complexion. No one ever looked like they sounded on the phone.

Sensing her reticence, Vincent implored again in a more brazen voice. "Just say yes. We can arrange to meet somewhere. What can it hurt?"

"Oh, all right," she said, trying to sound put out, when she had already decided to meet him, if only to satisfy her curiosity, before his last convincing effort. She also felt guilty about her thoughts regarding his appearance.

"Great, where would you like to meet? We could go somewhere near your work. How about Brennan's?"

"Yes, that's fine. I can be there at noon. But how will I find you?"

"Don't worry; I'll be able to find you." Vincent's mind immediately conjured up the picture of the distraught mother, pleading for her daughter's return during the fruitless search over two months ago.

"And thank you," Vincent said, relieved that he didn't have to continue pleading. He was not the pleading type. He was used to giving orders and having them followed. He was playing it safe with Peg because he didn't want to do anything that might jeopardize the meeting he had planned.

"I think you will be interested in what I have to tell you," he said, before realizing she had already hung up.

Peg picked up the phone and dialed her friend Marsha. While she waited for Marsha to answer, she thought how disturbing it was to have this man know what she looked like and where she worked. What else did he already know about her? Marsha's voice cut through her thoughts.

"Hey Peg, so are you ready to try out something new? Where are we going for lunch? It's your call," she said in a cheerful voice.

"Listen Marsha, I'm sorry, but I just don't have much appetite right now. Can I take a rain check?" In the past Marsha would have demanded an excuse from her for breaking their lunch date when they had so much to catch up on and some great food to look forward to!

Since Peg had returned to work everyone treated her like a delicate piece of china teetering precariously on the shelf's edge. While most of the time it made her furious beyond words, at the moment, it came in handy. She couldn't explain her recent phone conversation to herself, let alone someone else.

"Well, okay, but just this once. Let's plan on doing it next week," Marsha said.

"Sounds good, and I'm sorry." Peg already felt guilty for the small lie.

"Talk at you later doll," Marsha said, hanging up the phone.

Later, Peg was nervously trying to come up with some excuse not to go through with the lunch with Morelli. But she convinced herself she had to go.

Morelli might know something about Caitlin's abduction, but how would he have any information? Again, she wondered how he got the number for her direct line, and how he knew where she worked. She was suddenly determined to find out what else he might know. She also decided to do a little searching of her own, to see if there was anything on this mysterious Mr. Vincent Morelli.

She clicked on the Internet and began searching for articles that detailed the Morelli kidnapping. "Ah, the Internet, what a great invention," she thought to herself, as she clicked on the search icon.

CHAPTER TEN

The white linen napkins at Brennan's were folded to look like pyramids. Peg remembered her mother saying that you could always tell how classy a restaurant was by how much starch was used to stiffen the tablecloth to form an elegant place setting.

As she was admiring the overflowing purple orchids, in a cut glass vase on the table, a handsome, olive-skinned and dark-haired man, who was staring at her from across the room, approached.

"Hello, you must be Ms. McGregor," he said, holding out his hand.

"And you must be Mr. Morelli."

Her eyes were drawn to his and held there. His direct and powerful gaze caused her to blush and she looked away.

"No, no, call me Vincent."

The blush spread across her checks.

What an attractive woman; He almost didn't recognize her at first. She looked different from the photograph that the private investigator had shown him. She was a young and innocent-looking beauty, without the harsh lines of stress and worry distorting her features. He immediately felt a need to protect her, from what, he did not know. She had a fragile look to her that was countered by strong and intelligent eyes, an odd combination that had caused him to stare longer than was polite.

"Well, I'm Peg, then," she said, conscious of his admiring gaze.

Good grief, what was wrong with her? She was acting like a teenager with a crush. Her embarrassment only increased the depth of her blush. She was thankful when she saw the maitre d making his way through the tables toward them.

He escorted them to the small table in the back of the restaurant.

"Good afternoon Mr. Morelli," the waiter said, as he pulled out a chair for Peg. Vincent gave a nod, smiled and then turned to Peg. He opened the napkin and placed it in Peg's lap and handed her the menu.

"Thank you for coming Peg," he said as he took his own seat. The waiter repeated the ritual; somehow, it didn't surprise her that the waiter knew Vincent.

"We don't have to order right now; let's just sit for minute. I am so glad you decided to meet me."

"You didn't leave me much choice. You seem to be full of surprises. I was curious to see how you were able to contact me on my direct phone line. You seem to know a lot about me."

Peg was wishing she had gone to lunch with Marsha, after all. She was on guard and the elaborate lunch was already proving to be far from relaxing. Right now, the two of them could be having their favorites – Bloody Mary's and po-boys.

"I hope you don't think I have been too intrusive. You'll get your answers. But first, let's enjoy some brunch."

Vincent picked up the menu and Peg followed.

"What will you have?" His smile reached all the way to his eyes as he turned on the charm. "I recommend the Eggs Hussarde; it's one of my favorites."

"You're the expert." Peg was starting to lose patience with his cavalier attitude.

Peg handed the menu to the waiter, taking the opportunity to gather her wits, regain her composure and focus on Vincent.

Instead of getting to the point he acted as if they were long lost friend and drew her into light conversation about the upcoming election, as they waited for their lunch to arrive. She was surprised how easy he was to talk to and it seemed like only a few minutes had passed when the waiter was back with their steaming plates and a basket of French bread. The small talk had put her at ease. She was surprised how much she was enjoying their conversation – and the food!

"Now you just relax and enjoy your food and listen to what I have to say. Some of this will be hard to hear, but I'm telling it to you for a purpose." His voice grew serious with tones of sadness etching each word and gesture. Earlier she had been anxious to know why he wanted to speak to her but now she found herself regretting the change in topic.

"When we found out my little Angela was gone forever, my wife truly lost her mind. She took an overdose of sleeping pills. We didn't get to her in time and she died. The pain was overwhelming for her. I went a little crazy too, but there was one thing that kept me going over the edge completely. It was the dogged determination to find the animal that took my only daughter. You see, this person – if you can call him that– didn't just take one life, he took two – the two people that mattered most to me. So I wasn't just going to sit back and do nothing. I wanted justice!"

He grew silent. Peg knew he was trying to gather his emotions before continuing.

It seemed surreal how quickly his whole demeanor had changed. Peg felt that she was being given a rare glimpse of the real man behind the charming, genteel mask he wore for others.

His voice had grown firm and fierce and his face hardened. Peg could feel her own emotions responding. She felt what he felt; she knew above anyone else what he was feeling. They were linked through a tragedy the way survivors of traumatic events are often connected. Shared trauma cuts through all barriers and puts people together at their most basic. Two people from totally different worlds can be brought together through one event, one moment that changes everything.

"I can tell from your expression that you know what I am talking about." Vincent's voice cut through her thoughts.

Peg nodded; unshed tears glittered in her eyes as she tried to blink them away.

"Now something tells me that you love your daughter, just like my Elizabeth and I loved our little Angela, but you managed to keep going. You didn't self-destruct."

"You see, when your daughter was taken, I was watching and praying for you. I was sending my own people out to look for her. When they sent out the Angela alert, you can't imagine what I was going though. I relived that whole nightmare. But it made me want to help with the searches and I hoped the new alert system might work to save your child. The thought did cross my mind that the monster who took my baby also took yours."

Peg was listening intently. She couldn't imagine where Vincent was headed with his story. But she wasn't leaving, until she found out.

"Anyway, I'm telling you this because I think you too also have a mission. You are staying alive because you want to see justice done. You want to see this bastard caught. You want retribution…and so do I."

Vincent's eyes had narrowed and hardened, expressing his growing rage. As he continued, Peg felt herself drawn in to his anger and was clinging to his every word. She couldn't believe that she was sitting across from someone who didn't just sympathize, but truly understood. As he continued, her natural caution kicked in and she tried to bury her scattered emotions. She had been caught, reeled in by his magnetism and their shared pain.

She had to back up and think more clearly, before she ended up following this man around like a Hare Krishna worshiper. Damn, if he wasn't hypnotic and very attractive, in a sensual, dangerous way.

"But in the meantime, you have to take care of yourself." He continued talking, seemingly unaware of Peg's own conflicting emotions of pain, anger and desire.

"You cannot let this destructive depression swallow you. You cannot succumb to the rage, but you must use it." His voice was hard and unyielding.

"I know. I want to do something. I have been working with the New Orleans police and doing some searches on the Internet, but I don't know what else I can do," Peg said, trying to return the conversation back to solid ground.

Vincent nodded and continued.

"When Angela died, I learned a lot about law enforcement and about kidnappers. I helped start the "Angela Alert" here, but I also experienced what it's like to be a victim, the one affected by crime, to be the 'living victim'. So I joined an alliance, a support group of sorts for parents or other survivors of children killed in violence. This alliance operates much like Alcoholics Anonymous: people meet at different locations and it's a chance to share the pain, rage and anger, with friends who understand and can help you."

Vincent stopped for a moment to try to gauge how Peg was interpreting what he was telling her.

"Please go on," she encouraged.

Seeing that he had her full attention, Vincent continued to tell her about the group.

"We don't give our names. Of course, everybody knows me and I know most of the members.

"The alliance is proactive and we have power in numbers. We push for stricter laws against child molesters. We inform neighbors when there is a child molester in their neighborhood. Some members find this to be a way to heal. We help in the search for missing children. I think you could benefit. Please, just come to one of the meetings and judge for yourself."

Peg's mind was going in several different directions. She had admiration for Vincent. He had the courage to turn the loss of a child into something helpful to society. However, Peg wasn't interested in helping a society that allows a child to die in the hands of a monster; nonetheless, like Vincent, she was driven to find out who took her child and bring him to justice.

She was not a "joiner" by nature and rebelled at the idea of attending a "group" meeting. Her father had raised her to work out her own problems and to depend only on herself. She was reluctant to get involved with Vincent's group, no matter how attractive and persuasive he was.

"Wait," he said, interrupting her thoughts.

"Before you say anything, let me tell you that you don't have to say or do anything you don't want to. We are a very sympathetic group, as you can imagine. We only want to help and to prove that, as survivors, we are more powerful than the scum that poisons this world."

"You're making me feel guilty. How did you know that I wouldn't be interested?

"So you'll come?" he said. A smile was all he offered as an answer to her question.

"Why don't we have some dessert now? How about the Bananas Foster?" Smooth as silk, again, his voice charming and soothing as he took her silence for acceptance and abruptly changed the subject.

"Oh, I couldn't eat another morsel. However, it's something I haven't had in a while and it is their specialty."

"Let's go for it!" he said with a sly smile, gazing into her blue eyes.

"By the way, what do you call your 'alliance'?" Peg asked, not yet ready to let the subject drop.

"Well, we don't really have one, per se; we are quite selective on who can join. We don't advertise. We are a pretty special group, but I think you'll understand more when you come to a meeting. If you must call us something; call us the 'Survivors,' although we are much more than survivors, as you shall see."

Peg left the restaurant feeling certain that she would see much more of Vincent. Whether that would be good or bad — only time would tell.

CHAPTER ELEVEN

The day had grown cloudy and a light rain sprinkled the sidewalk, as Peg headed back to the office. She went straight to her desk, sat down and turned on her computer to begin searching for information on the Morelli clan and Vincent's daughter. When the kidnapping had occurred, there was plenty of news coverage, but she hadn't paid much attention to it at the time. Now, Peg was obsessed with finding information. The same person might have taken Caitlin and the Morelli child.

She clicked onto the Internet and plugged in the phrase: "Morelli/kidnapping. A series of article headlines appeared. The sequence told the horrific story.

"Pops Morelli's granddaughter missing, last seen in French Market."

"FBI called in search for kidnapped Angela Morelli."

"No ransom baffles police and FBI."

"Police find Morelli child – distraught mother commits suicide."

"Pops Morelli offers reward for information on kidnapper."

"Mayor says city will begin new 'Angela Alert' system."

"Family says alert system might have saved Angela."

Peg continued scrolling down on the computer screen. She found an article written about two months after the kidnapping, titled: "Why no ransom? Angela Morelli's kidnapping remains unsolved." It had been written by her friend, Craig Miller.

"I've got to talk to Craig," she said out loud as she picked up the phone, dialing his extension.

"News desk, Craig Miller speaking," his voice sounded unusually cheerful.

"Craig, it's Peg McGregor, how are you?"

"Not bad for a Monday. My wife just called from the doctor's office; we're having twins." His happiness was infectious.

"That's wonderful. I know how much you both have wanted a baby." It was good to see life could still bring others happiness.

"I know you are going to be a great dad. I hate to switch gears on you Craig, but if you have a minute or two, there's something I want to ask you about the Morelli piece you wrote," Peg said, trying not to sound too anxious.

"Sure, what do you want to know?"

"Was there never a ransom asked for Angela?"

"Now that's a very good question. That was one of the ongoing mysteries of the case. When the girl was first taken, of course, everyone suspected that she was being held for a ransom, because the family's loaded. No one talked about it, because they figured that the police and FBI must keep those kinds of things secret. But after it was all said and done, some reporters were able to get their hands on the police files. It turned out there was not ever any ransom demanded. Nobody could figure out why Angela was taken. Was it just a random kidnapping by some sicko?"

"What do you think?" she asked, not sure what answer she feared most.

"Me? I think that maybe the kidnapper got scared, and never sent the note; maybe he was an amateur and either killed the girl himself, or let her loose and she was grabbed by some molester. We'll probably never know. If the Morelli family can't find out and they have all the connections that the police and FBI don't have, it's probably useless," Craig said with a sigh.

"I'm researching any possible connection to my daughter's disappearance and the Morelli girl. Do you know of any similarities in the cases?"

Peg was finding it very painful to discuss her daughter out loud. Maybe she could benefit from the Survivor's group on an emotional level after all. She wanted to find out why Morelli had contacted her; did he see a connection that the police hadn't seen?

"I really don't know Peg; anything's possible. I think if they are related, then the abductor never intended to ask for a ransom. Maybe they didn't realize who the Morelli child was and it was a random attack, just like Caitlin's; or, it could be that the killer botched the Morelli case; or, maybe he didn't want the family with their Mafia friends tracking him down, so he took another child to throw off the police and the family.

His voice lowered and he was almost whispering, "You did not hear this from me, but I just got word from a very reliable source that the mayor's office has also been leaning very hard on the police task force. My guess is that someone else is leaning on the Mayor. If they don't turn up something soon, some heads are gonna roll. And I don't mean lower-level-nobodies. This will affect some very highly connected people."

Peg's head was throbbing. Caitlin lost — a random act done by a child molester or taken as a decoy. Either way, in the end, two children lost in the worst way possible. Maybe her daughter would still be with her today if they had found little Angela's killer; or was she just grabbing at anything that might give her an answer? The thought caused a sharp pain in the center of her chest — Morelli? She wanted to see him again to find out what he knew. She knew how frustrated the Morelli family also must feel.

"I'm so sorry, Peg," knowing that there was nothing left to say.

"Thanks, let me know if you think of anything at all."

"I will," Craig promised.

Peg went back to her desk, collected her purse, and headed out the door. She walked out into the parking lot, oblivious to the rain that poured down on her, mixing with her tears. Her mood was a perfect match for the dreary, rain-soaked day. Depression had come out of nowhere and enclosed her in a lonely cocoon. She drove home in a trance, stripped off her drenched clothes and went straight to bed.

CHAPTER TWELVE

Every day for the next week, Peg called in sick, telling Bill that she had caught a flu bug. Peg stayed in bed all day, but she couldn't eat or sleep. Her mind was spinning with thoughts about what Craig and Vincent had told her. She was in a state of limbo and wasn't sure what it would take to lift it.

Over and over, she heard Craig saying, "If they don't turn up something soon, some heads are gonna roll."

But the pieces weren't all there. No one knew for sure if the killer was the same person. Although, it seemed that Morelli was thinking along those lines, too; maybe that's why Morelli was so interested in her. Could he think she knew something that could help solve his daughter's case? Was that why he had checked her out and had approached her?

Was he having her followed? She shook her head at her paranoid thoughts. So many questions, and it was so confusing and too much for her mind to handle all at once.

Somehow, it didn't quite fit. Why would the killer go to all the trouble to take another child? It seemed like it would just increase the odds of getting caught. And what are the odds that some kidnapper would back out after accomplishing the grab?

If the killer was looking for a child to take, how could it be that it was from one of the most famous and rich families in New Orleans? The killer was either a calculating, but inexperienced kidnapper going for a ransom, or a degenerate child molester after his prey. But why would he just happen to pick one of the richest families in New Orleans — and then Caitlin?

One scenario seemed as unlikely as the other. Suddenly, it didn't matter. Her depression was again being replaced by anger. She had to do something.

Either way, she thought, someone took my Caitlin and the other little girl and he is still out there. I've got to talk to Vincent. He's holding back something.

"Maybe it's time I go to one of those survivor meetings," Peg mumbled out loud, as she pulled herself out of bed and headed for the phone and her address book.

CHAPTER THIRTEEN

Peg drove to the Monteleone Hotel, parked her car in the dingy underground lot and took the elevator up one floor to the lobby. The elevator and the hotel were both charming but ancient in appearance. As he had promised, Vincent was standing in the lobby at 2 o'clock, waiting for Peg next to a huge hand-carved oak grandfather clock. Vincent was wearing a dark blue silk suit with a crisp white shirt. He straightened his tie and walked over to her and grabbed her hand. She felt an instant attraction for him — a soft tingle of electricity where his fingers enclosed hers.

She had hoped what she had felt that day at the restaurant had been a fluke brought on by anxiety and stress. Now she was certain it was just Vincent. Women seemed to be drawn to him, following him with their eyes as he passed. Apparently, she was not immune to his charming good looks. She quickly withdrew her hand.

"It's great to see you, Peg, I'm so glad you made it. I was afraid you might change your mind."

Vincent put his arm around her waist, giving her a soft squeeze. Peg found the color rising again in her cheeks, and immediately put her cold hands against her face to try to remove the red. He was doing it on purpose. Why was she letting him get to her? Again moving away and putting distance between them.

"No, I wanted to come. What could it hurt, and maybe I can find some answers," she said gathering her composure. Avoiding his gaze she looked up at the four crystal chandeliers that hung from the lobby's ceiling. It was beautiful how the shimmering light danced its diamond reflections from the ceiling, across the walls and suddenly she was again looking into his eyes. How did he do that? This time she couldn't look away.

"Yes, Peg, we all need answers, don't we?" he said, gazing into her eyes. The elevator chimed, breaking the spell.

On the elevator ride up to the hotel room, Vincent briefed her on the meeting's agenda.

"Now you don't have to worry about anyone knowing who you are. When we walk in we are given name tags so that we can identify each other for the meeting. Of course, we use pseudonyms. We feel it is very important to protect our privacy."

"So, Vincent, what is on the agenda for this afternoon?" Peg was starting to feel nervous and would have sent the elevator back to the garage if Vincent wasn't standing beside her.

"We generally update on the latest events, you know. If there has been a recent picketing or a lawsuit that we are witnessing in as friends of the court. We always begin with a testimonial."

"What's a testimonial?" Peg asked, suddenly certain she wasn't going to like his answer. This is why she wasn't a joiner. Some people seemed to have an emotional need to share their private thoughts and feelings with others. The thought of doing that with a group of strangers was the last thing on her "to do" list.

Vincent was sensing Peg's misgivings and decided to quit trying to explain the group. He would let her form her own opinions.

"Let's just hold off on some of these explanations, until we get to the meeting. It will make more sense than me trying to explain it on an elevator ride."

Vincent escorted Peg to the hotel suite. A tall, striking brunette, wearing a navy blue pantsuit, stood at the door; her face was open and friendly; her smile lit up her face. Peg liked her at once and relaxed a little. Maybe this would be good for her. This woman seemed to be doing okay and she seemed happy.

"Vincent, I see you have brought someone new."

"Yes, this lady is very special. I think you will all enjoy meeting her. This is Caren. She is like a mother to our group, and can also help answer any questions, or concerns, that you may have."

"Welcome to our meeting," she said, closing the door behind them, and turning the lock.

The other members of the group greeted Peg warmly. It was an odd mixture of people. Two black women were sitting on the beige sofa having a conversation. Near the bar were two more women, standing with a gray-haired man with a beard. One of the women was very young, maybe 19-years-old, and the other was closer to Peg's age.

In a raised voice, Vincent announced that the meeting was going to start and asked that everyone be seated.

"As you all can see we have a new addition to our group. It would be nice if someone would begin with a testimonial; any takers?"

The large woman with light brown Creole skin, who was sitting on the sofa, raised her hand.

Vincent simply nodded, and the woman began to speak.

"I'm Leticia," said the woman, with a strong Creole accent.

My sona bitch husband use to slap me around, ya know. He'd get so drunk and then he goes around the house tearing things apart, putting his fist through the walls and kicking over de flowerpots. My lil' boy was terrified. So I throwd that husband o' mine out. I had not heard from him in months and then one day he called me at work and tol' me he was gonna get me and that I'd better be watchin out.

"I called de police and the social service and all those women's help lines. Nobody could do nothin about it, so I got myself a gun for protection.

"One day I gets a call from der school asking about my lil' Jacky. The school thought he was sick, and they was a callin because I was suppose to let dem know if he wasn't coming in."

"Jacky ain't sick, I sent him on the bus today."

"'No mam' they said, 'he never made it here.'"

"And fact of matter was, he never made it anywhere after dat day," said the woman, who abruptly broke down in tears, and for the next five minutes, cried and wailed, while her friend next to her joined in, and soon there wasn't a dry eye in the room. Finally — with huge tears streaking down her face, her mascara-smeared, eyes large and luminous in her face — she continued.

"As you guessed, he took Jacky with his doper friends. Deh starting giving Jacky booze and he ended up dying of alcohol poisoning. Ma baby dead and he was only eight-years-old and skinny as a stick, and so sweet. He loved his momma. He'd say 'I'm gonna take care of you momma, don't you worry. I'll get a good job and we'll be fine. I'll always take care of you momma.'"

"And I'd say, well, for now, it's my job to take care of you. I'd say, 'go play and quit worrying, we'll be just fine.' I was suppose ta take care of him. But I failed; I failed my baby."

It was at this part in the story that tears silently started to slide from Peg's already moist eyes. She was remembering her Caitlin, and how she should have held on — she should have held on.

"The police locked my husband up for a few hours and they sent him to a detox center. I went to visit him and brought my gun. They was no guards. I face him and tell him he kilt my boy, ma baby. He looked at me and told me it was my fault cause I treated him so badly. I shouldn't have made him so mad."

"Ya know what? I agreed with him in my head: I says to myself, 'self you done married yourself up to this loser and now it is time to fix the situation.'"

"I go up to the bed, where he lay sweatin and smelling from the poison coming outta him, and I say as sweet as pie, 'why sugar, you right, let me fluff your pillow. I take that pillow — he smiling all the time — and I pretend to fluff it. I stick the gun behind it and when I goes to arrange it behind his head, I pull the trigger. I will never forget his expression, his lips still smilin, but his eyes was big and round, kind of surprised happy expression.

"But me, I'm cold, cold as the grave where my baby is buried. The hate done gone — for the first time in weeks — but I was empty inside, blank, like a chalk board that been done wiped clean off, and left in the dark after the lights have been turned off.

"Then when I get home and I seen Jacky's toy cars all set for play racing in the corner, the pain, oh de pain, it is blinding and I wanted to die. I takes that gun and I points it at my own head and I pulled that trigger, all the while praying that the Lord would accept me even tho' I kilt myself. All I heard was a click and then I realized: no more bullets. The Lord was trying to tell me something — that he has more for me to do. Then I found my friends here and I am helpin, doing God's work for my lil' Jacky — my angel.

"They's lots more details, but the bottom line is the police still don't know where I am. I was able to find help with my good friends here, and I expect the law will eventually give up. I know they was glad I kilt him. He was no good, never was, never would be. Now he's down in hell, with his own shit butt in the fire. And maybe the Devil's poring poison down his throat. Praise the Lord!"

Peg's eyes went wide with shock. She realized she had been kind of mesmerized by this woman's wild tale as her mind traveled back down her own road of sorrow. Her loud "praise the lord" brought Peg back to the room and the reality of her surroundings. This wild woman's raving was almost too much to take in. The woman herself was overtaken by emotion, as she finally folded her head down on her lap, weeping, "Oh Lord, Oh gracious Lord."

Several of the others gathered around her. It reminded Peg of some evangelical healing ceremony for holy rollers. How could Vincent have brought her here with a bunch of loonies, loonies with guns, no less?

Peg was breathing heavily and wanted to get out of there, quick. Her own feelings were still so raw. She was being pulled in by their unspoken offers of comfort, but then her own will and self-reliance kicked back in. She didn't need this group of hoodoo whackos — all they could bring her was trouble... better to pursue the search on her own. Then again, they did have connections that she probably did not. Maybe she could use those connections, without becoming too entwined in all the drama of the group's mission.

She took a deep breath and decided to ride it out rather than run for the door, as her instincts were screaming at her to do, immediately. She did feel a certain kinship with the woman who told the story. While their stories were very different, she knew what the woman was talking about, as she described her grief and anger. She was very confused.

Vincent went to the wet bar and poured a glass of water for the bereaved woman, who was still weeping.

"Here dear, have a sip of water," he said in a calming voice.

The woman, using a tissue to wipe her tears, looked up at Vincent, as if he was her guardian angel. He was the most handsome angel Peg could imagine even if his dark, good looks were more likely to remind you of a devil, instead.

"Oh, thank you Vincent," she said, leaning back in the soft pillows on the sofa. "I'm all right. It's good to get it out. I'm sorry if I shocked anyone, especially our newcomer sitting over there," said Leticia, who was breathing easier and appeared more relaxed.

Peg's face turned red again. Vincent gave her a smile that said without words, he knew she was blushing again and he liked it; he liked her. She tried to speak, but couldn't think of anything to say, the words wouldn't form.

Then suddenly Vincent pulled up a chair next to Peg, and whispering in her ear, said, "I know this may not be what you expected—and don't get the wrong idea —we all have our ways of grieving, and some are, well, more active than others. Revenge is not the only form of healing. That man," said Vincent, pointing to the bearded gentleman still standing by the bar, "has turned to faith in a higher order. He found solace in the teachings of Buddhism. He forgave the man who destroyed his life. And he believes his daughter lives on in another person, another little girl who he may someday find. Maybe next time we will ask Bruce to give the testimonial."

His words caressed her ear and when he pulled away she felt herself longing to hear him again. Suddenly, she realized she was staring off into space. Good God, what was wrong with her! She wasn't much of a drinker now, but a scotch sounded real good right now just to calm her nerves.

Caren was standing at the door, but then walked to the couch.

"Dear, you will find that there is higher power: God, who will give you the strength to face life's tribulations. Our job is finding our own path to healing and forgiveness. We have a shared grief; all of us here. This group is not about judging. The fact that you are here today means that you believe in yourself and you are grasping at a hope that your daughter will be returned to you. Let us give you the strength to fight this devil."

She could sense the bond between Peg and Vincent; she knew their pain was linked and they were obviously attracted to each other, but would that be enough?

Peg could see she would have to reveal some of herself in order to get any information or help from the group.

In a low voice, Peg said, "but I don't know what path I'm supposed to take. I only know that I have to find out why my baby is gone and who did it; that's all I can think about."

"Well then," Caren said. "That's a start. We will work on that, won't we Vincent?"

"Yes, we certainly will," said Vincent turning to Peg. "We'll start with that, and then see where it leads."

Vincent reached over and grabbed Peg's hand and held it in his firm, warm grip.

The next part of the meeting was focused on the group's proactive efforts in New Orleans and the surrounding suburbs. It seemed the group had a database of known child molesters that was rivaled only by the F.B.I. In some states, laws allow the names, addresses and pictures of sex offenders to be printed in local newspapers, or on police web sites; but Louisiana lists only the names along with the offences. The addresses are kept confidential and known only to the parole officers.

Peg was pretty sure the Buddhist man, Bruce, was responsible for supplying the addresses. On closer inspection, Peg had no trouble imagining a Police or F.B.I. identification badge, hanging from the pocket of his dark blue suit. Her suspicions about the link to their classified information were confirmed when she saw Vincent give a brief nod of thanks towards Bruce as the newest entries were discussed.

Each week every member was responsible for distributing a flyer in a neighborhood where a known sex offender lived. These were called "NABS" or Neighborhood Awareness Bulletins. NABS listed the offenders names and aliases, address, physical appearance, age, date of birth, charges against them, and time served. The group was very careful that no link to them appeared in the flyers. They knew they had to stay anonymous in order to be effective. After all, they were breaking the law. Peg was impressed with the group's organization and solidarity. She could see how comforting and compelling this would be to someone lost in grief.

But she could sense that this was more than just some self-help group; it radiated strength and Peg could tell they had strong loyalties – and secrets of their own –maybe this was also one reason why the survivors didn't give their real names.

Last of all, a "Top 10" list was circulated, around the room. It contained the names and address of the sex offenders considered most dangerous, and likely to re-offend in the New Orleans area.

Vincent was the last to get the list. He placed it on the table. As they discussed the focus and location of the next meeting, Peg picked up the slip of paper. She looked it over carefully, attempting to memorize names. Vincent rose from his chair and took a phone call in the next room.

While the rest of the group chatted among themselves Peg began folding the paper into smaller and smaller squares, until she nonchalantly slid the small square of paper into her pocket. She was surprised at how steady her hands had become, since she was so jittery earlier in the evening.

After the meeting was over, Vincent followed Peg to her car.

"I hope you know that we are very sincere in wanting to help you. I have some information about the two kidnappings from the police department. There are some leads in the case, but they are keeping quiet about them. You are entitled to know about it. Can I call you on Monday?" Vincent asked as they reached Peg's car.

Her '95 Nissan Pathfinder seemed out of place next to the Jags, BMWs and Mercedes that filled the softly lit garage of the Monteleone.

"Yes, I really have to know, Vincent. I will never rest until I know what happened to Caitlin."

"What is the outcome you seek? Have you ever thought about what would happen if you did find Caitlin's abductor? Would you want the police involved? Would you want the person dead or in jail?" asked Vincent, with his eyes locking onto hers.

"I want what little Jacky's mother wanted. I want him stopped for good. I don't want another parent to have to feel this pain because of him."

Finally, the words she struggled over came out in a rush: "I'd want to know what happened to my daughter, no matter what it takes to find out, and then I'd want him dead!"

Peg pulled out her keys and unlocked her car, suddenly feeling guilty for the words that came from her heart, but she knew she would never withdraw them, even if she could, for they were the truth, her truth, no one else's.

That was the one thing she liked about the group. They didn't impose their morals on anyone else. Everyone had their own truth and the acceptance of that truth is hard to find.

Vincent grabbed her hand again, and turned her towards him, making direct eye contact. "We both want the same thing. I do understand. Perhaps, I am the only one who ever will, or could; remember that."

Vincent could tell his directness had startled Peg. He pulled her in closer, but softened his grip. "I don't want to rush you into this Peg. You have to go at your own pace, because I can tell you from my own experience, it's heart wrenching to be continually bringing up the memories of the last hours, but those are often where we find the best clues. The next step will be to go over everything you can remember. But not tonight," said Vincent, who leaned over and softly kissed her cheek.

She pulled back, surprised at the feeling of tenderness.

"Why did you pick me to join the group, Vincent?"

She needed to know what he was thinking, not just what he was feeling. She hoped he might let down his guard and answer honestly.

"We have much to talk about. Of course, it was your tragedy that first drew my attention. I hope I won't upset you by telling you I ran a background check."

"We require it on all new members. I know your father, Stuart McGregor, was a highly decorated cop in Baton Rouge. Your mother died when you were twelve. You worked with your father for a while on the force, until the incident occurred that forced you off the job. You moved here and finished your journalism degree, and got a job at *The Times Picayune*, never been married and somewhere along the way you've had a daughter," finished Vincent.

Peg's mouth hung open in surprise and her anger kicked in.

"Well, it looks like you know things that even I have chosen to forget. Now when do I get to know all about you — turn around is fair play," she said sarcastically.

She was upset that he had violated her privacy and dredged up a past that she wanted left behind.

"That part of my life died over six years ago and I don't ever want to discuss it, or even think about it. I'm sure you have more than one skeleton in your family's secret closet, Mr. Morelli. Perhaps, I should send my own little team of PIs and investigate," Peg finished with a hard smile.

Vincent watched silently as Peg got in, slamming the car door angrily. She pushed the keys in the ignition and the car roared to life. Vincent put his hands on the glass and looked at her as if he could hold her there, with just the force of his will. He spoke through the glass of the window.

"One last thing before you go. Lt. Hopper and my family have a history. He's a straight arrow, Peg. Unless you don't have anything to hide, I suggest you think twice before trusting him," Vincent warned.

"You know what? I don't think I trust anyone right now and I don't have anything to hide — not that it's any of your business," she shouted back.

Peg threw the car into gear, but Vincent was firmly planted. She was afraid she would have to run him over to get out of there. What was wrong with him? She glared at him. Any traces of the earlier attraction she had felt were gone.

"I am sorry if I upset you. I didn't mean to hurt you. I told you, because I want to always be honest with you. I want you to know I think you are a very courageous woman. Please forgive me. I had only your's and the group's interests at heart. They depend on me to keep them safe."

And then she watched speechless, as he stepped back, turned around and started walking away. Peg didn't wait to see if he would look back. She hit the gas and the tires squealed, as she reversed and slammed on the brakes, and then threw the car into drive.

She had not thought about her family or her life in Baton Rouge in years. It always made her feel bad and a little scared. She instinctively buried the memories away. Her head had started pounding, but she concentrated on negotiating the parking garage.

Vincent could tell that he had hurt her — and got her temper going. He wished he had not been so direct. A sadness washed over his face as he turned and watched Peg's car disappear out of sight, round the dimmed, echoing, spiral parking lot. He longed to be next to her, to touch her and make her forget the pain.

As Peg got to the ticket booth at the top of the tunnel, the outside sunlight blinded her vision. She rolled down her window and scrambled for her ticket. Finally, she found it on the dashboard and handed it to the man in the booth. She opened her purse to retrieve the three dollars, reaching out to hand the man the money. She was angry that she knew nothing about this man; yet, he knew more about her than some of her closest friends.

"Thanks very much ma'am," said the man, grinning wide, showing his crooked, coffee-stained teeth.

Peg turned right from Royal onto Bienville Street, her anger ebbing slowly away as a fresh, soft breeze rushed in through the rolled-down window, cooling her cheeks.

CHAPTER FOURTEEN

The next day Peg placed a call to the police department. "This is Peg McGregor. I need to talk to Lieutenant Hopper."

"Hold on," replied a women. "I'll get him."

"Hello Peg," said Lester, in a cheerful voice. "It's great to hear from you. How are you?"

Peg ignored the greeting, instead getting straight to the point of the call.

"I've got to talk to you about something that has been on my mind for a while."

"That's fine, Peg. I can always make time for you."

Lester hoped she was doing better. He heard she had returned to her job at the newspaper. So many times he had driven past her house and wanted to stop, but couldn't. What would he say?

"Is it alright if I come by the station after work, say at about seven?"

"I'll tell you what, why don't I come by your house. This station is a madhouse, and I can tell by the tone of your voice that you have something important on your mind."

Lester also didn't want any distractions. He wanted to be able to see for himself that she was okay. He had thought about her almost daily. Now that he had a chance to see her again, he wanted it to be away from work.

Peg made a fresh pot of coffee and was sitting on the sofa, next to the front window. She peered anxiously out between the Venetian blinds, waiting for Lester.

Her mind was filled with memories of when he came to tell her that a tiara had been found and they wanted DNA samples to provide a match. She broke down horribly and he held her, made her tea. No wonder he wanted to come here. He probably was afraid she would become hysterical and create a scene at the station.

No, that was wrong, she knew he was kind and caring, but she still had suspicions that he was hiding information. She couldn't believe the police hadn't found a single clue, with all the investigators on the case.

She spent hours investigating the group's Top 10 wanted list, even researching information on the first few names. She was toying with the idea of showing the list to Lester. She thought he might help her if he knew she could offer some clues in the kidnappings. She wouldn't though, because some of Vincent's words had hit home, and she knew he was right about Lester. He wouldn't do anything to compromise the law. He would want to know where she got the list, and when she couldn't tell him, he would start investigating, and that might lead him to the survivors. The group was her only real lead to finding answers. Plus, a part of her didn't want to ruin Vincent's trust and sever their connection.

Her mind conjured up Vincent's face, but then Lester's sympathetic face replaced it. She remembered Lester as he had stood in her kitchen that day. It seemed like ages ago, but she instinctively knew he would not understand her need to work with Vincent's group. Vincent was right about Lester. Lester's world was black and white, whereas, Vincent could see the shades of gray hidden in between.

If she confided in Lester and showed him the list, she would hurt the group; maybe even cause them to disband. She would also break Vincent's trust. As much as she wanted to believe in Lester's abilities, Peg felt sure that Vincent and the group would be her best hope at finding her daughter's abductor. Her mind was made up and with a sigh she refolded the list and returned it to her file cabinet in the spare bedroom she used as an office.

Lester was driving an old rust colored sedan. Peg watched him get out of the car, grab his jacket from the front seat and put it on. He straightened his tie as he walked up to the porch.

She would have to be careful. Lester was someone with whom she felt instantly comfortable, and she found herself wanting to confide in him. He was one of the rare people that you meet and immediately feel as if you had known your whole life. Her heart lurched, as she remembered his last visit and the feel of his hand as it enclosed hers.

Peg opened the door before he had a chance to knock.

"Hello, Peg. I hope I'm not late."

"No, I'm just rather anxious; come on in. I made a pot of fresh coffee. Do you like chicory? And remember, it's Peg, not Ms. McGregor."

"Right, Peg…and yes, coffee sounds great. I drink it black."

He followed Peg into the kitchen. She filled two mugs with coffee and handed one to Lester.

She led him back into the living room.

He had a chance to observe her, as she settled on the couch and put her cup on the coffee table. She was dressed casually in faded jeans and a T-shirt, but she looked very feminine and attractive. Her blond hair was cut so that it fell just below her shoulders and delicately framed her face. She looked fresh, rested and years younger than the last time he had seen her. Her blue eyes were clear and dry.

"I guess you want to know if we have any new leads?" Lester said.

Good grief, he was not one to beat around the bush. It was as if he could read her mind. Suddenly, Peg was not feeling quite so self-assured.

"Well yes, but there is a question that has been bothering me. It was something that came up after I talked with a man named Vincent Morelli. His daughter was also kidnapped and found murdered. He thinks the two kidnappings might have been done by the same person."

She watched the surprise and concern float across Lester's face.

"Whoa, wait a minute. When did you talk to Vince Morelli? I didn't know you knew him," said Lester, suddenly not liking the idea of Morelli alone and talking to Peg. His eyes lit up with anger.

Peg was surprised at Lester's reaction. He was obviously upset that Vincent had spoken to her. Maybe he was keeping things from her after all. She went on as he continued to pin her with his gaze.

"He called me one day, telling me he needed to talk to me. Obviously, we have some things in common and I was impressed by the way his family coped with Angela's death. You know he and his father were the ones who brought the alert system to New Orleans. I only wish it had worked for Caitlin. He is still very active in a victim's support group. He told me I should go, too; he said it would me help get through this."

"That's absolutely true. You should get help. No one could possibly go though what you have and survive without some counseling, but not from him. I have to warn you, Vincent is not a person to be trusted. His family is full of crooks; they are into loan sharking and gambling big time. You know, his wife committed suicide. At least, that was the official ruling. The coroner is in Pops Morelli's back pocket. Did Vincent tell you he and his wife were having problems before the abduction and that his wife had been taking antipsychotics? And there were rumors that he was fooling around."

Lester's words kept spilling out and Peg could tell that she had hit a nerve. He was telling her things he shouldn't, but was desperate to convince her that Vincent was no good.

"No, he didn't tell me all that," said Peg, suddenly flustered and put out that she was having to defend Vincent.

"And I don't care about rumors. It is none of my business. I don't plan on dating or marrying the man. He has offered his help, which is more than I have gotten from the New Orleans PD in over two months!" Peg's face was flaming.

"Which leads up to what I wanted to talk to you about? Do you think it's possible that Angela was kidnapped for money?" asked Peg quickly, trying to regain her composure.

"Why would you think that?"

Lester's own anger dissolved as soon as hers surfaced. God, she was pretty and her blues eyes sparkled and flashed when she was angry. It made him smile, without thinking how this might appear to Peg.

"Why wouldn't I? Like you say, the family's rich."

Peg thought to herself, "look at him, sitting there smiling at me."

She suddenly wanted to clobber him with the nearest lamp.

"Yes, but Peg there never was a ransom note."

Lester watched her eyes move between him and the lamp. Their eyes met and locked, and suddenly they were both laughing together.

"You were thinking about doing me bodily harm with that lamp over there, weren't you?" Lester said, still chuckling.

"Oh, you made me so mad, no I'm sorry; I have just been on edge lately and dwelling on all the possibilities. I just couldn't take it if you think I'm crazy. I'm not crazy Lester. I still believe my daughter's out there somewhere and she's waiting for me to find her. I can't give up even though it appears everyone else has, even the police department."

Lester moved over to sit beside her on the couch and put her hand in his.

"Peg, I am so glad to see you this way – fighting back. I was so worried about you, but I have never thought you were crazy," said Lester, who gave her hand a quick squeeze, before letting go and walking back to the window.

Just touching her hand brought forth emotions that he struggled to control. He needed to keep some distance between them.

"But could it be possible that the kidnapper botched the kidnapping and covered his trail by taking another child, trying to make it look like he was a child predator?"

"Peg, are you saying that you think Caitlin was taken by the kidnapper just to cover his tracks?" said Lester, shaking his head.

"Is it possible? Because if it's not, then isn't it just as unlikely that the killer picked Angela at random not knowing who she was?"

"It's strange that a child molester would, by chance, take the richest child in the city," agreed Lester. "But you are right; that it is possible the two kidnappings were also random. And the evidence shows that the Morelli girl was sexually assaulted. We don't know about Caitlin. And we may never know," said Lester, as he lowered his eyes, not able to look directly at Peg. He couldn't bear looking at her pain at that moment.

Tears rose in Peg's eyes. He desperately wanted to go back to the couch and comfort her, but he stayed where he was. "Peg, I'm so sorry."

Lester wished things were different and that they could go back and wipe away this tragedy. He wished that he could meet her under different circumstances.

A shrill beep sounded three times from the pager attached to Lester's belt.

"Damn, I guess that's me again. I hate to leave you like this. Can I get something for you? Is there anyone I can call?"

After he said it, Lester realized that the last time he was here, he had left her this way.

"No, I'll be okay. But you have to let me know what you find out," said Peg, regaining her composure.

"I will, but you need to stay away from Morelli. Please Peg, that guy is bad news. The family is dangerous, the worst of their type. Promise me," demanded Lester.

"If you get sucked into their world, it will be very hard to get back out. Nobody has ever gotten close to them and come away in one piece," he stressed, as he pinned her with his eyes, willing her to listen and pay attention to what he was saying.

"Promise me," he said with an edge to his voice.

She had only nodded yes and he was out the door.

Watching Lester disappear into the early evening gloom of that Friday night, she wondered if it was a promise she could keep. Memories of Vincent's gentle touch and dark eyes swirled around in her mind.

Peg shut the door and collapsed on the couch. She was exhausted. Her head had started pounding and she felt a killer migraine beginning in her skull. The throbbing started at her eye sockets and moved to encircle her head in a vise-like grip of pain.

Slowly, she staggered to the bathroom. She still had the medicine given for her migraine attacks, which had begun to intensify and occur more frequently. She hadn't had any attacks this bad since she was a kid. She knew it was stress and hoped they would gradually get better over time.

The bottle was on the shelf among her other pills. She shook two out and swallowed them down with a glass of water. Peg walked back into the living room, locked the door, turned out the lights and laid down on the couch. The pain from her head was now throbbing worse than ever. She put a pillow over her head. She could tell this was going to be a real doozy.

CHAPTER FIFTEEN

The cold of the cement wall pierced through her black jump suit, except for where the Kevlar vest encircled her chest. She ran the length of the alley and was pressed up against the wall, trying to still her labored breathing.

She had trained thoroughly for this, and it was not physical exertion, but the emotional turmoil that made her heart race; her breath coming out in short, controlled puffs.

The alley was dark, except for the strip on the north side that the full moon illuminated. She was pressed into the shadows of the south wall.

Her earpiece hidden under the black knit cap came to life.

"T5 in position," said the voice floating through her head.

"T4 in position, T3 in position."

"T2 in position," her own voice whispered to no one in the dark alley.

"Objective in range in T-minus 5 seconds."

She gasped as she recognized her father's voice.

"Dad, Dad, don't go in, don't go," she tried to call, but her body would not obey the signals and commands she was sending.

She watched herself leap up and grab the pull-down ladder hanging above her head. Effortlessly, she scrambled up the ladder. She was standing outside a full-body length double-hung window that had been painted black from the inside.

"T2 set," she heard her voice again.

"Initiate," said her father's voice solemnly.

All she could do was watch helplessly as her body went through motions already defined and orchestrated in another time and place. She was filled with dread and dejeuve, but unable to stop the events as they progressed like an automated machine that runs on and on without an operator at the controls.

Expertly, she attached the large black suction and swung the tracer's edge around the outside circle. One slight pull and the suction came off with the circle of glass attached. She reached in and flipped the lock, raised the lower panel and slid through in one fluid movement.

She was immediately enveloped in quiet, heavy darkness. She could feel it pulsing around her as if it was a living thing. She waited for her sight to adjust to the blackness. Slowly, she was able to distinguish doors and the cracked and eroded tiles that lined the hallway of the decrepit building.

She jumped as she heard the loud banging beginning on the south side of the building's first floor. Avon was calling whether anyone was buying or not. She had to hurry.

To her right was the stairway, just as they had expected; but there was no door. It had been removed at some earlier time and now the stairway lay exposed to the dim light of the hallway.

She headed for the opening and raced up the stairway using both hands to press against the walls to keep from falling in the pitch darkness. She prayed there would be no missing steps or holes, because she had thrown caution aside in her need to emerge from the closed-in darkness of the stairs.

Before she knew it, she was on the fourth and final floor; her feet sliding to a stop as she almost ran into the closed door. This one was still intact and groaned loudly as she pushed it open.

She swore under breath as she caught the door and squeezed through.

At first, she was thrown by the size of the open area. There was a bank of windows along the north wall but they had all been painted black. The room's only light source was two large skylights set into the rooftop. One was propped open and the other had several panes broken. The cold night breeze swept down and flowed through the room. It felt good against her hot cheeks, and turned the sweat running down her neck into trickles of ice. She shivered.

She made for the square structure in the northwest corner of the room. Just as she reached the outside knob, a voice crackled through.

"Maggie, wait, go slow. We're in and no one's here. The basement's empty. The drop's been made and they got two in custody, but there's no sign of Larson."

"I'm on the fourth floor. It's quiet. I don't think he's here, maybe he bugged out. It's an open loft with one small room in the corner. I'm gonna check the room."

"Maggie, wait, we're securing the first floor, Mac and I are on our way up."

She heard the worry in her father's voice. She knew he sent her on this part of the job because it should have been less dangerous. Their objective was supposed to be located in the basement of the old abandoned building. She crept up to the door and listened with her ear against the panel. She could hear a heavy wheezing sound coming from the room. Someone was in trouble. She braced herself and slanted her revolver away from the sounds in the room, as she blew the lock and threw her shoulder into the door. She came through, dropped and rolled, and ended up against the far wall at the foot of a queen-sized mattress thrown on the floor in the corner of the room.

Tom Larson heard the shot as he climbed up the hidden passageway at the back wall behind and right below the room she had just broken into. Too late, they were already here. He was consumed with rage, as he crawled the last few feet to the top of the trap doorway that would swing him into the room.

A small lump on the mattress was heaving up and down with each tortured breath.

"Oh God, I've found him and we need an ambulance," she transmitted as she rushed to the mattress, after confirming the small space was empty, except for the mattress and its occupant.

"It's on the way," said her father, as he and Mac came through the doorway, breathing heavy.

They must have flown up the stairs from the basement level. She set her revolver beside the mattress and immediately pried at the tape across the small mouth of the little boy. The little face was slick with tears.

"You got his inhaler?

"Right here."

She reached for the medicine and propped up the small body; his mouth free, his breath came in huge wheezing gasps.

She shook the medicine and held the mouthpiece up to his mouth and pushed. The medicine rushed out and was inhaled by the wheezing boy. Two more puffs and the wheezing was a little better; she could hear him start to cry.

Mac pulled the chain hanging from the single bulb in the middle of the room. A sickly yellow glow helped define the starkness of the dirty little room. The old mattress was yellow-and-gray-striped, and was full of large brown stains and ripped places. The small child still had on his Geranimals tan and red pants and matching top. Though they were also dirty and ripped after nearly three days in captivity. There was one sock on his foot, but his shoes and the other sock were nowhere in sight.

Mac and her Dad were working on the chain and stake driven through the mattress and anchored into the wood floor underneath.

The chains were attached to cuffs around his small ankles.

"That sick bastard. I wish we would have found him. The kid could have died before we found him," whispered her father so the boy couldn't hear.

"That's what he intended," she said, as she rocked him in her arms, whispering that he was safe now. It was all over and his mommy and daddy were waiting for him.

Jake Langly was the 5-year-old son of Martin Langly of Langly Industries, a multi-million dollar digital communications company. His family was the target for an experienced band of kidnappers. Tom Larson was suspected in two other high profile kidnappings. After the ransoms were paid neither victim was found alive.

This was the first time he had taken a child and it had mobilized the Children's Protection Division of the Baton Rouge Police Department. Maggie studied criminal profiling and criminal justice in college and as a recent graduate joined her father's division.

"There, it's loose," said her father as the chain went slack.

As she looked up, the ceiling suddenly opened up and a large shape loomed into the room.

"No!" she screamed and this time she knew she was screaming in unison with the events.

She saw Mac and her father turn from the mattress, her dad already pulling out his revolver as he spun around.

Too late — bullets pounded through Mac and then towards her father, driving him against the far right wall with a thump. She watched his body slide slowly to the floor.

She was not even aware of how the revolver got into her hand, but she had it raised as Larson spun around to shoot her and the boy. The first bullets hit Larson in the chest and shoulder, which drove him flat on his back and caused his gun to fire uselessly into the ceiling. Plaster and sheet rock rained down in chunks and fine powder.

Still, she kept firing. She could hear the boy wailing in the background. Larson had tried to rise and blood spurted from his throat and chest. He finally pitched to the floor at the edge of the mattress.

She was aware of a clicking noise and she realized her finger was still pulling the trigger of the empty gun. The rest of the team burst into the room as she sunk to the floor.

"She's shot; tell EMS we need more stretchers and hurry. We got officers down…repeat…officers down."

Peg shot up off the couch. Sweat poured off her body. "Daddy, Daddy" she sobbed aloud remembering the vivid nightmare.

Then she sank back down and was out again.

She finally woke Saturday afternoon around 2 p.m. She was still on the couch. Sometime during the night she had put on her sweat pants and she vaguely remembered going in the bathroom and flashed on changing clothes.

God, her whole head felt numb. Whatever she took knocked her for a loop, but it also took care of the terrible migraine. She tried to sit up, but her whole body ached, probably from crashing on the couch during all those hours. She had a burning thirst. Her mouth felt like it was packed with cotton. It had to be an after-effect of the medicine she took and the nightmare.

She made her way into the kitchen and gulped down some milk right out of the carton. She remembered the terrible dream, her father, Mac. She couldn't think about it now…too terrible.

Her legs felt like lead; She was still so bone tired, but managed to slowly shuffle back to her bedroom. This time, she crawled into bed and immediately went to sleep.

CHAPTER SIXTEEN

Westwego, La.
Cadre St.
12 Midnight

Ten-year-old Lisa Marie lay very still and quiet in her twin bed. Her little sister Callie slept in the other twin bed directly across from her. She could hear her sister's steady, rhythmic breathing and knew she was fast asleep.

She could also hear pacing footsteps on the hardwood floor of the living room and knew it was not her mother. Her mother had gone to bed at ten, early for a Friday night. She said she was very tired from her job at the hotel downtown.

Her mother, Laura, was the supervisor of all the maids at the big downtown Marriott. When several girls would call in sick, her mother covered for them, which meant she did twice the work of a regular maid, with not much more pay. Her mother said every little bit helps when you're raising two children as a single mom. Their dad left when she was barely three and Callie was just a baby in her mother's tummy.

When her mother met Jeff, it seemed like a miracle. He was so sweet and kind. Every time he came to get their mother, he would always bring something for her and Callie. He once brought her a beautiful china doll with a blue satin dress, curly, long brown hair tied with pink ribbons. She was beside herself with joy. She had never seen anything so beautiful – and it was hers! She threw her arms around his neck and hugged and kissed him. She remembered he squeezed her very tightly, gently rubbing her back in a caressing way and patted her bottom. As she took the doll to her room, she had an odd unpleasant feeling that she couldn't place, but each time she looked at the beautiful china doll, she burst with happiness.

Her sister, Callie got a soft, huggable baby doll, and their mother got a sparkly ring. One month later Jeff and Laura were married. It wasn't long after the wedding that Lisa Marie started to avoid Jeff. Every chance he got, Jeff would touch her or kiss her in ways that made her feel bad – and he was always there. He told her it was her fault, because she was so beautiful and he loved her so much. He told her if she told her mother, she would hate Lisa Marie.

He said the real reason her daddy left was because of her. He said her daddy loved Lisa Marie, but she wouldn't love him back so he left. She was only three when he left. Was this true? Did her mother think she made their daddy leave?

She couldn't ever tell her mother. Instead, she did her best to avoid him. It was getting harder and now he was hugging Callie, too. Her mother had to work this weekend and they would be all alone with Jeff. Her mother was sleeping over at the hotel Saturday night because of a big convention. She was so worried; she couldn't sleep. She never slept until he left.

Jeff worked the third shift at a factory across town. Lots of times she heard his footsteps stop outside the door and she would always hold her breath, until they retreated. Now he "loved" Callie too. What was she going to do?

She got down on her knees beside her bed and prayed to God to help her and Callie. She once asked her mother why she had to be on her knees to pray: Would God hear her better? Her mother said it was a sign of respect and love, but that God always listened, no matter where you were when you prayed. Lisa Marie was taking no chances. She knelt and poured her heart out to God, and then she climbed back into bed. She heard the door slam.

Quickly, she got back out of bed and ran to the window, and pulled up the shade. She saw Jeff walking to his car parked in the street in front of their house. Just as he reached the end of the driveway, he seemed to stop, as if he had run into an invisible wall, then he slowly turned and looked towards the house. Lisa Marie felt like he was looking at her, but she couldn't look away. Next, he slowly slumped to the ground. What was he doing? Was he trying to get her to come outside? She heard the bushes scrape against the house right beneath her window.

Suddenly a black, crouched shape darted across the yard, heading straight for Jeff. She tried to scream, but no sound came out. She could feel the air rushing out her mouth; but there was no sound. Her heart was pounding, as she watched the black thing hover over Jeff, and then it was off and running, still bent low like an animal, down the sidewalk till it disappeared past the Johansen's big hedge. Jeff did not move.

Somehow, she knew Jeff would never move again. Slowly, Lisa Marie backed away from the window, bumping into Callie's bed. She crawled in next to Callie and hugged her warm body. Her mind was numb and her thoughts all jumbled up. Then finally a deep dreamless sleep claimed her, which was how Laura found them the next morning, curled up together, sleeping soundly. How sweet and precious her girls were. She was so lucky.

Outskirts of Westwego
River Road.
2 a.m.

The sleepy street lay still and silent, except for a gentle breeze that slowly rifled the trees and aimlessly turned the pages on a child's abandoned coloring book that lay among a few scattered and broken crayons on the sagging, wooden porch.

No children lived in the house, but there was evidence that children had visited the house. A rusted tricycle, an abandoned doll and several broken toys lay scattered throughout the yard. Anyone glancing at the house in passing would assume children belonged there. If a person studied the house day after day, week after week, they'd realize it was tainted and represented evil at its lowest and vilest form. Looks can be deceiving.

Evil has many faces. Deception is a predator's best trick and the young and innocent were so easily deceived. There are only two choices to make when dealing with such evil – look away or demand retribution. Retribution had finally come to awaken the sleepy street.

The gentle rustling in the thick bushes next to the porch was not the work of the wind. Away in the distance the silence was broken by the sound of a car crunching its way up the dirt road. The rustling of the bushes increased as a dark shape rose from ground level. Retribution was at hand.

Kent was drunk again and trying to get home without crashing his car into a tree or some other stationary object. He didn't even worry about possibly hitting a pedestrian. Fuck them, if they couldn't get out of the damn way! Hell, he was going slow enough!

No one ever did him any favors. Everything that was wrong in his life was caused by others. He had been wronged since birth and he felt it his duty to pass that on to others, "educate em" at an early age to what a shitty experience life could be. Especially, the dirty little snotty-nosed kids, the little brats who were lucky to be alive, "should drown em all like kittens." That's what his daddy would say.

He was one of the lucky ones all right, the only one of his ma's five children to make it to adulthood. It was his right to pass on the "education." His education had cost him one eye, the hearing in his left ear, several broken bones and a collapsed lung, but he didn't cry about it.

He was spared to carry on the special mission of education. Hell, kids were way too soft these days. One bloody nose and a few loose teeth, all from one quick slam into the wall, was enough to put out their lights. Ya had to be tough to survive in this world and Kent was a survivor, his mission was to educate those less fortunate.

His mood restored, Kent was smiling and whistling drunkenly to the tune of the "Andy Griffith Show." Now there was a child that needed "educating." Kent wished he could have had a crack at whipping lil 'ole Opie into shape. He could also easily break that wimp Barnie into kindling wood, but not before having a little fun with him. He bet ole' Barnie could sure holler loud. As always the thought of "educating" the weakest gave him an almost orgasmic high.

Kent was softly chuckling to himself, as he stepped out of the old rusted-out Chevy Nova. The chuckles were abruptly cut short as a single, silent bullet pierced through Kent's blind right eye. A small trickle of blood drained down his face, as he fell with a "whump" to the hard-packed dirt of the driveway.

Silence descended once again upon the sleepy street. The dark form slid from the bushes and quietly walked over to the fallen man.

A black-gloved hand slowly lowered and placed a dark odd-shaped object on the chest of the dead man. The dark form moved silently down the street. Faintly, as if from far down the block, the gentle night breeze carried the whistled tune to the "Andy Griffith Show," and then silence descended again for the second time that night.

3 a.m.

The same night

Bayona Ave.

Old Algiers Pointe

Phillip Winston was a 32-year-old white male, 6'1" and weighed in at 180 pounds. He had brown eyes with long brown hair tied in a ponytail that hung in a tangled greasy mass down his back. He was easily distinguished by the many tattoos that decorated, or as some would say "desecrated" his body. His collection included striking snakes, laughing skulls, a bar code on the back of his neck and bands of barbed wire encircled his large biceps. A multitude of white supremacist symbols liberally filled in most of the other empty patches of skin. Nothing marked his face, which was unremarkable in its commonness. It was a face that could easily disappear in a crowd if the hair and tattoos were hidden.

Phillip was also a registered sex offender well known to the New Orleans Police. His first rape and assault was on a 13-year-old girl. He was found guilty and received five years probation. He had immediately raped two other young girls and was not caught again until he had broken into the home of a 33-year-old woman whose husband just happened to catch him in the act. He tried to convince the guy that the wife had invited him in. The husband called the cops, but not before he turned Phillip in to a punching bag and beat him to a bloody pulp.

It was the one time Phillip was glad to see the cops show up. He got six years for that offense, but was released early for good behavior in January. He learned his lesson and would be extra careful in his future choices. The solution was simple: no more older women who may have husbands or boyfriends, no witnesses and no convictions. He had come close to killing his victims many times before and from now on he would make sure he finished the job.

Just thinking about his next encounter made his blood rush through his veins. It wasn't the sex. He could easily get sex, willingly, from a multitude of women he had come across in the sleazy bars he frequented. It was about the power he felt when he saw their fear, and the control he had over everything that happened. The younger the better; he preferred them anywhere from 12 to 17-years-old.

It was a high that even drugs could not match. He smiled and unconsciously licked his lips in anticipation. He was one of the last to leave the decrepit bar, Cajun Joe's, and quickly crossed the deserted parking lot. He decided tonight was the night. He had been watching her for two weeks now. Last night, he could barely pull himself away.

She was probably about 16, a very pretty redhead who always shut her shades when changing clothes, but stupidly left her window open on the humid and hot New Orleans nights. He had also been able to pinpoint which nights her mother regularly stayed at her boyfriend's house, usually not returning until 5 or 6 a.m.

Phillip got into the only vehicle left in the lot, a white 1984 Ford F150. The Confederate flag was proudly displayed in the back window and bumper stickers that said "My great, great, granddaddy shot Lincoln" and "Rebels Never Die" glowed in the light from the single lamp post that dominated the middle of the lot.

The only things missing were the rifles that used to adorn the empty gun rack that still hung across the back window. He had to store his guns in a long metal box attached to the underbelly of his truck bed. It was a shame, but necessary, since he was a paroled convict and could not legally possess them. He also had a handgun hidden in a secret compartment behind his dashboard. Hidden in his right boot was a 9" Bowie hunting/survival knife with a deadly serrated blade that he kept sharp enough to slice paper. They would never take away his right to bear and possess arms. A man had a right to protect himself, didn't he?

Phillip pulled the crumpled red and white Winston cigarette package from his right front shirt pocket and shook out a cigarette from the almost empty container. He thought it was cool to smoke cigarettes that shared his last name. He sometimes had delusions that he was a long lost heir to the Winston tobacco dynasty. He had, in fact, used the story in bars to get free drinks. He was surprised how often it worked and did feel sorry for the Winston tobacco people. He felt a certain kinship, if not by blood, what with all the bad rap the press and health fanatics gave them and everyone suing them, left and right.

He understood their pain and had written them many letters offering his support as a spokesperson to support "Constitutional Rights" to smoke. He knew he had not heard back because his letters were being stopped from reaching the company by the controlling federal government. The government was behind all his misfortunes. He was going to a meeting next weekend in Savannah and hoped to join a local group who thought like he did.

He pushed in the truck's lighter. The lighter popped up as he started the Ford's engine and turned on the headlights. He lit the cigarette, now dangling precariously on his lip, took in a deep drag and headed for the exit onto the bridge.

As he turned the corner, he thought he saw another set of lights pull out of the parking lot behind him. He waited for his exhaled smoke to clear the cab, and when he looked back again, they were gone. Trying to spook himself, that's all it was. Tonight was definitely the night. He was too pumped up to give up that easily. He switched on the radio and pushed a CD into the disk player that he had installed himself just last weekend. Immediately, a German band's techno vibes bounced around the interior of the truck. He lost himself in the music's pulsing rhythm, as he drove without thinking toward the house of the sleeping 16-year-old beauty.

Minutes before the pickup circled the block and parked down the street; another car had also circled the block and parked around the corner. The car was now dark and the interior empty. The soft pinging of the still warm engine floated on the night air.

Phillip donned his black ski cap, grabbed his duct tape and put out the glowing cigarette before stepping out of the pickup. He followed the same route he had been taking for the last two weeks, until he was just yards from the girl's window. His luck was holding true and her window was open. He could see the lace curtains moving softly as the gentle night breeze blew them back into the interior of the room – piece of cake.

He took a deep, calming breath as his excitement was mounting to a fevered pitch. He moved to the window and carefully and expertly removed the wooden-framed screen. He placed his hands on the windowsill and boosted his feet off the ground. As he brought one knee up onto the window's ledge, a bullet tore through his left shoulder and entered the window's casing. The only sound was a slight cracking noise as the bullet split the wood.

When Phillip's head jerked up involuntarily, the bullet passed through him, its force causing his face to smash into the top half of the raised window. His arms cart wheeling like a circus clown, he teetered and then tumbled backwards to the ground. As his back hit the hard-packed earth, he felt the air rush from his lungs.

Still not registering what had occurred, he desperately tried to pull air back into his empty chest, as he clawed off the cloying knit mask. Immediately, he felt something cold and hard pressed against his forehead and then everything went dark.

Inside the room, young Sandra, stirred and turned over in her sleep. One slender foot with its small, silver metallic decorated toenails, escaped the confines of the white flowery cotton sheets. A gentle breeze blew against her pale sleeping face, as she slumbered peacefully, oblivious and in stark contrast to the scene right outside her window.

The lower half of the window slid silently down, until the doubled-paned glass muffled the sounds of the soft New Orleans summer night.

CHAPTER SEVENTEEN

Saturday morning Detective Pierre Martens was leaning back in his black leather chair, peering out the window as he watched the barges chug down the Mississippi River. The French Quarter police station was on the second floor of the restored old Jax Brewery building, which provided a clear view of the river bend.

Pierre never wanted to be too far from the sight of the Mississippi. It kept him close to his boyhood.

Pierre was born only a few blocks away from the brewery, on the outskirts of the French Quarter, in an apartment on Esplanade Avenue. His father Gerard, a Creole, made a living as a barge ship captain and was often gone for months at a time. Young Pierre would stand with his mother, Marquette, on the wharf, waving goodbye and watching the barge ply down the river. Once it was out of sight, they would turn and head back home. Sometimes, they would stop for an ice cream, in celebration of the unspoken happiness they felt knowing they would be on their own for awhile.

Pierre inherited his mother Marquette's brown coloring and delicate bone structure. His father took every opportunity to "turn him into a man," while his mother wanted him to learn the finer things in life, such as an appreciation for music, art and theatre.

Marquette's mother, Quanah, was a mulatto mistress of a white European aristocrat, which made Marquette a mix of Creole and white blood, or a quadroon. The father, Eduardo Saxon, never married Quanah, but he supported Quanah and paid the tuition for Marquette to attend Sacred Heart Academy in the uptown Garden District.

Pierre felt torn in his efforts to please both his parents. He soon learned how to be one person for his mother and another for his father. But his heart truly belonged to his mother; she was the center of his world.

Thus, while Pierre ended up appearing to be weak and non-threatening, he was a very skilled and fierce fighter. This had surprised many criminals who laughed out loud when he was called to make an arrest, but they weren't laughing later while they nursed a broken nose and missing teeth, sitting in a smelly jail, wondering what the hell happened to them.

Pierre spent most of his childhood helping his mother, who worked at the French Quarter fish market. Pierre would make the deliveries of shrimps, crawfish and snappers to the local restaurants. The chefs always rewarded Pierre with samples of some of the best cooking in the country. In those days, life was a parade of culinary delights for Pierre. Each day brought a new delivery, a new tasty adventure of all the latest cuisines.

His daydreams of childhood were jolted away with Lester's bellowing voice. "Any progress on the Keaton, Peyton and Winston murders?"

"Ah. Right. No," said Pierre, his mind shifting gears. "No motive, no fingerprints, no nothin', just three dead bastards. One was holding a stuffed teddy bear, one with a yellow rubber ducky swimming on his chest, and the last one had a bright green frog hand puppet sitting on his face.

"Kind of sweet, huh, and very weird...I could understand a dead chicken, a black cat, maybe one of their own body parts, but a cute teddy bear, a kid's best bath time buddy and a frog puppet — can't figure it. There's nothin in the crime computer to match it to.

"The Keaton guy was a loner," Pierre added. "Records show he had served some jail time. Assault and battery was his specialty, usually kids, ya know, friends and family. We don't have any information from the family. They seemed to think his passing was good news. No one has seemed too concerned about finding his killer.

"Now the rubber ducky guy, Jeff Peyton, is a whole different story. He has quite a sheet — seems like he slipped away from his parole officer in Texas. His specialty is to target single mothers, so he can molest their children. He was currently married to one Laura Peyton, who just happens to have two little girls.

"The wife was totally unaware of his past," Pierre continued. "And just getting over the shock of finding him dead in the driveway; then being told she married a monster has been a little too much for her."

Lester's face got more somber as he listened, "What about the girls? I hope no one was stupid enough to question them without a psychiatrist present."

Pierre just shrugged his shoulders in reply.

"For God's sake no one else questions those kids until I talk to the resident psyche and legal," grumbled Lester.

"The last guy, Winston, was a convicted rapist and it looks like he was clocked out just before he could score another victim, a sixteen-year-old female. He was sneaking into her window when he got shot, once in the shoulder and then a bullet to the forehead," said Pierre shaking his head in disgust.

"These are obviously connected and done by a professional. I'm thinking the same guy."

"I'll start looking harder into their backgrounds and see if I can come up with a common link: why one person or persons would want them all dead?" Pierre said.

"Okay. That's a start, but I have a funny feeling this is just the beginning," said Lester. Pierre turned to look at him and changed the subject.

"How bout you, anything new with the Morelli kidnapping, any leads?" asked Pierre, knowing that there probably wasn't anything new, but he wanted to make Lester admit that he hadn't made any progress in solving the case.

"Nope, the father has offered a reward that matches the grandfather's, but I don't expect anything to come from it."

Pierre whistled, "Boy that's some serious money, five-hundred grand. We're gonna have tons of leads with every Tom, Dick and Harry rushing to collect that reward," said Pierre thinking about what he could do with half a million. He certainly wouldn't stay on the force.

"We're putting the McGregor and Morelli cases on the back burner until we get a new lead."

"These triple killings take priority for now and we better make sure the press doesn't find out about the toys. At this time, as far as we know, none of them are linked.

"Got it, boss," mumbled Pierre. Damn, he was looking forward to the big wad of cash the hot tip about the toys linking the killings would bring him from his news contacts. He knew that it would be career suicide to even breathe a word about it right now.

He had never seen Lester so wound up. He wasn't going to be the one unleashing Lester's pent up anger and frustration. These cases all involving children were really getting to Lester. Then the mayor's office was pushing pretty hard for answers on the Morelli kidnapping case. The mayor wouldn't like the case being put on hold. Some heads were sure gonna roll soon and Pierre didn't want to get caught on the chopping block. Maybe Pierre should make an appointment to talk to the police psych officer, just out of his concern for Lester. The thought of talking to the psych officer made him uncomfortable. On second thought, he would let it ride for now.

He realized he was still staring after Lester who had long disappeared from the doorway.

CHAPTER EIGHTEEN

Dr. Kitchen was a well-known child psychiatrist in New Orleans, having practiced for more than 40 years. He had a kind face, silver-gray hair and wire-rimmed glasses. He had been told he resembled Jimmy Stewart. He took that as a compliment.

Maybe that explained his success with children. They instinctively trusted him and were right to do so. He was an expert at helping emotionally shattered children. His secret was simple: He cared and truly loved each child he counseled and would never give up, even if the children's own families did. Many clients who had long ago reached adulthood still visited him. He never made time for a family of his own, as he was in constant demand. It was a sad fact that there were so many abused children living in New Orleans.

But he had a family; he had hundreds of children who loved him and this is what fulfilled and drove him even past retirement.

Dr. Kitchen eyed his latest challenge as she walked into the room. She was clinging to her mother's hand and sucking her thumb, which he would guess was a recent behavioral change. He had read her file. She was slender, with long brown curly hair and big expressive brown eyes. She had a waif quality to her features. Dr. Kitchen gave her his most disarming smile and her eyes seemed to loose some of their fear, to be replaced by curiosity.

Children were such wondrous creatures, their minds so open and honest. He knew that, even before speaking or treating her, she would be another success. "Hello, Lisa Marie, how are you today?"

Lester, Pierre and Laura, the girl's mother, watched the session through the one-way glass mirror. It was a full 30 minutes into the session before Dr. Kitchen drew Lisa Marie back to the night at her house when Jeff was murdered.

"Now Lisa Marie, tell me what you do before going to bed each night. Do you have a routine?" asked Dr. Kitchen, careful to keep the same light friendly tone Lisa had come to know. She liked his voice: it was smooth and silky and reminded her of the way chocolate feels all smooth on your tongue, as it melts slowly in your mouth. Dr. Kitchen made her feel safe; she already trusted him, and was talking freely, uninhibited.

"Callie and I always put on our pajamas and then brush our teeth. Momma comes and reads to us. I love that because momma pretends like she is the people in the story. It's funny when her voice changes, it makes Callie giggle like crazy. Then we say our prayers and ask God to watch over everyone we love. Then momma kisses us and we go to sleep," said Lisa Marie, a little breathless after her long speech.

Back in the booth, it had become very quiet and Laura had tears standing in her eyes. She stood straight, her back rigid in front of the mirror with her hand clamped tight over her mouth. Lester walked over beside her.

"Are you sure you're all right, ma'am?" he inquired.

In reply, she just nodded her head up and down, not trusting herself to speak. Lester inhaled deeply and stepped back away from the glass.

"Now Lisa Marie, did you follow your bedtime ritual the night your stepfather was killed?" asked Dr. Kitchen in the same tone of voice.

"No, mamma was tired and she asked Jeff to put us to bed but I said I was a big girl now and I would put us to bed," said Lisa Marie, a defensive note creeping into her voice.

"Did you not like Jeff putting you to bed?"

"No"

"Why?"

"He made me feel bad, his love was bad. He said he loved me and Callie, but it was bad love."

"How do you mean bad?" asked Dr. Kitchen.

"Well, like when my mom buys strawberries sometimes for a treat. I love them, they are my favorite. But if they stay too long in the package, they get all slimy and fuzzy and icky. Then they are bad for you; sometimes things you love can become bad for you. Jeff was bad, but my mom loved him and Jeff said I would hurt her," finished Lisa Marie, a sob catching in her throat."

"You won't tell her will you?" she said, suddenly afraid.

"Lisa Marie, your mother loves you and Callie more than anything in the world and Jeff was a bad man. He fooled your mother and you and your sister. He has fooled many mothers and their children. It is not your fault. Your mother knows that and she only wants for you to be happy."

"She knows Jeff was bad?" asked Lisa Marie.

"Yes, she knows he was tricking her. He was a bad man."

"I think I killed him," she said slowly.

Dr. Kitchen was startled by her reply. He paused for a moment to gather his thoughts before he asked, "Why would you say that? He was shot with a gun. Do you know about guns?"

"Yes, but I didn't pray for him that night. I prayed God would take him away. Right after I prayed and jumped into bed, I heard him leave."

"Did you look out the window?" asked Dr. Kitchen very softly, relief flooding through him. He had counseled children who had turned to murder to relieve their torment. He was glad Lisa Marie would not have to carry the burden of murder for the rest of her life.

"Yes"

"What did you see?"

"I saw Jeff walk to the end of the driveway, and then he turned and looked at me, I thought, and then he fell. I heard a scraping noise and I saw a black thing come out of the bushes and go to Jeff. It took him to hell where the Devil lives, because he was bad and because I asked God not to watch over him."

"Why would you think that?" asked Dr. Kitchen, stunned by her revelations. She was a very deep thinker for such a young child. He had not been caught off guard in a long time. He was intrigued by her ability to process information on such a mature level and was sure she had a high I.Q.

"I saw it on TV. My momma said I couldn't watch, and put us to bed, but I crept down the hallway and I saw the scary black things take the bad man and drag him down below the ground. It was really scary. I couldn't ask momma about it because I wasn't suppose to watch, and I would get into trouble. But I was pretty sure they were taking him to hell. He was screaming."

"Oh God, she's talking about a scene from the movie *Ghost*," said Laura. Tears were now running freely down her checks.

"Oh, yeah, the one with Demi Moore and that other guy, what's his name?" said Pierre.

Lester shot Pierre a hard look and he shut up quickly.

"Where did the black thing go?"

"It ran away and I'm afraid it will come back," said Lisa Marie, tears suddenly appearing. "I'm bad now too, aren't I Dr. Kitchen? It's going to come back for me now?"

"No, no, you are a very good girl. If I tell you something, will you believe me and know that you can trust what I say, because I will not ever lie to you?"

"Yes, I trust you."

Dr. Kitchen went through all the events Lisa Marie saw and described them to her, slowly pointing out everything she imagined and explaining the real happenings.

Lester and Pierre left the room soon after Dr. Kitchen began his explanations.

About an hour later, Lester and Laura met alone with Dr. Kitchen.

"First I want to tell you that we are all very lucky. Wait, wait…I see the look on your face; I meant that I'm positive neither of the girls was raped. I think he had only had a chance to pet and fondle, but ultimately, he would have raped them. I want to see them both in my office, twice a week, and continue with the healing.

"But, I can't afford that kind of treatment," said Laura, with a mournful look on her face. "In fact we'll probably lose our house. I can't afford the rent on my own, and we gave up our subsidized housing when I married Jeff. It will take months to get back on the list."

"Not to worry," said Dr. Kitchen, smiling broadly at Laura. "There is a victim's assistance fund. I will contact them myself today."

Laura visibly relaxed and sighed with relief.

"Laura, you might check with Jeff's employer. He may have had a standard company life insurance policy. Usually the spouse is automatically listed as beneficiary," said Lester.

"You and your girls could have a second chance."

"Let's go see what the girls are up to," said Dr. Kitchen, as he put Laura's arm in his, and headed back down the hallway towards the lounge.

After they were gone, Lester turned out the lights and went out into the hallway where he encountered a quiet and brooding Pierre.

"Well the kid's story clinches it, poor little thing, it was a professional hit: dressed in black, silencer, and an excellent shot — one in the back the other straight between the eyes," said Lester, shaking his head.

"I forgot to tell you that the ballistics came back on the bullets: all three murders were done by the same gun. You sure we should keep this quiet? Maybe, if we alerted the public, someone might turn the shooter in. We could offer a reward."

Pierre's face lit up as he imagined the amount of TV coverage the announcement would bring.

Lester shook his head in dismay, as he considered Pierre's foolish idea. He decided to drop the niceties and lay it on the line.

"Well, Pierre, he was a busy guy. First, he shoots Peyton and then goes straight to Keaton's and finishes off Winston last. We have to find the connection. We won't find the connection by scaring the public. Again, I want to stress keeping the kids' toys thing out of the press – they are a major clue – I can feel it. Do you understand?" said Lester, looking pointedly at Pierre.

Shit! thought Pierre, maybe he's on to me. No, he must just suspect, till then he would play it cool.

"You're the boss," he said, as he smiled, turned around and headed back down the hallway towards his office. Pierre walked over and stared out the window, suddenly needing to see the river very badly; it always calmed him. His face was burning, sweat had gathered under his arms and he could feel it trickling down his sides.

Another detective started to walk in, but seeing Pierre's intense mood, decided it could wait for a better time.

"Damn! Damn! Damn!" Pierre muttered under his breath, as he gazed out at the window, watching the latest round of weekend tourists following the river's levee, heading to the Café'du Monde. He turned away, disgusted.

CHAPTER NINETEEN

Vincent picked up his two hunting rifles with one hand, and grabbed the ice cooler with the other. He was heading out the door, when he heard the phone ring. He turned around and set the guns and cooler next to the desk and flipped open his cell phone.

"Vince, dear, don't forget the chicken necks, you know Carole's counting on going crabbing."

His mother's timing was impeccable. One minute later and he would have been out the door.

"Chicken necks, right mama, I'll go back and get them," he said, chuckling into the phone.

It was the 4th of July weekend. The family was gathering at their country lake house in Covington, located about 40 miles outside New Orleans. The holiday weekends were usually spent trolling for catfish, crabbing and duck shooting.

He remembered how Angela and her cousin Carole always loved to go crabbing. They had the ritual down: first tie the chicken necks securely onto the center of the nets, find a comfortable spot on the pier, and gradually lower the net into the brackish waters of Lake Pontchartrain.

"I got one, I got one, Dad!"

He remembered her squeal like it was just yesterday — as if she was really there. He could almost believe that his little Angela and his wife Elizabeth were waiting down at the house with momma, poppy, and all the rest of the Morelli clan.

But of course, they weren't there at all, and never would be again. His heart sank, and for a second or two he pictured himself swerving off the long bridge with his shiny gray Lexus. The 24-mile bridge connecting New Orleans to Covington was the longest bridge in the world, but the barricades were made of thin aluminum, and would never withstand the impact of a careening car.

He rolled down the electric window and let the lake's salty breeze stream into the car. The sky was crystal clear and the water of the lake shimmered like glass. The breeze felt good against his skin. He knew later in the day it would grow hot and stifling, and decided to leave the window down.

As a further distraction Vincent turned on the radio. The blaring sounds of the commercials helped focus his senses away from the momentary insanity that crept up from time to time, especially during family gatherings when he missed his wife and daughter the most.

Vincent tuned into "Troy Talk." Troy was opening his program to callers who wanted to discuss the triple murders. Vincent had put out his own feelers on this one, since his contacts told him the police suspected they were "hits" by the same person. All his checks had come back with a big zero.

Vincent turned up the radio.

"It seems that three men, seemingly unrelated, were gunned down, execution style by the same gunman," Troy said. "The catch is all three men were convicted child predators and were currently out on parole. I want to hear your thoughts, listeners. The call-in lines are open."

"Yes, caller."

"Hello, I'm a teacher in the New Orleans Independent School District and I want to say that many abusers were themselves abused children and we should be tolerant and find ways to help them, instead of cheering their murders. What are we? Barbarians?"

"Well, thanks for your opinion" Troy said dryly.

"Okay, I have been informed we have a special caller on hold. It seems we have a relative of one of the murder's victims.

"Go ahead, Christy."

"Hello, I want to say first off I am not a relative of the victim. A close friend of mine and her family were the victims of a man who targeted single women in order to molest their children," said Christy, her voice growing angrier with every word.

"The person who saved her girls from this man should be thanked. I don't care who you are or what kind of person you are. To us, for that moment in time when you removed that evil man from their lives, you were an instrument of God, our knight in shining armor, and we will be forever grateful," said Christy, her words rushing out at the finish, the sound of tears evident in her voice.

"Thank you, we are all sorry for what your friend and her girls went through and are relieved that they are all safe. What are their plans for the future?" Troy asked.

"Well Troy, I'm not sure. The company that he worked for is refusing to pay the life insurance policy."

"What company is that Christy?"

"New Orleans Crescent Steel, they said the jerk lied on his application about having a conviction and being on parole, he lied to everyone, so his benefits are revoked."

"So your friend and her girls are made a victim twice. That sounds like something that needs to be investigated. Maybe we could help?"

"Thank you, Troy. You are the greatest! I always listen to your show. I know you care about the people of New Orleans. Thank you. Bye."

"Well listeners, there you have it: human triumph in the face of adversity. It seems like we have either a saint or a knight in shining armor, who might be starting a crusade – you decide."

"Let's take another caller."

"Yes, this is Bubba and my heart just cries out for that little lady and her babies. I want to send her a donation; it's not much but I want to help. I also want to say that the guy that took them out is a hero, just like you said, a 'Crusader,' and I would like to buy him a beer. So Crusader, if you're listening, come by "JC's Beer Barn" at 10 p.m. and we'll celebrate."

"Why thanks, Bubba," said Troy, laughter in his voice. "I'm sure he'll be there. It seems like we have a name for our knight in shining armor, 'the Crusader.' If you are listening, Crusader, we would love to hear from you."

"Okay, next caller..."

Vincent gave a half chuckle. "Crusader indeed, now that's pretty good."

The talk show had lifted his gloomy spirits and by the time he arrived at the lake house, he was ready to shoot up some birds himself and help little Carole tie those bait necks to the nets and catch some crabs.

At least it looked like the press would make sure the heat stayed off the Morelli family. It would hurt business if they decided to lean on the family about the murders. Trouble, he didn't need right now.

Vincent could see little Carole's arms waving wildly. As he approached the lake house, he slowed down, rolled down his window and waved back. He could hear his wheels grinding down on the gravel road, a familiar sound of coming home.

"Get out of the way mi amore or I'm going run you down," he teased.

Her excitement drew her even closer to the car.

"What took you so long Uncle Vincent? We've been waiting all day for you. Gramma's already got most the food laid out on the table and it's about to get cold," she screeched.

"Oh well, we can't have that can we? You run tell her Uncle Vincent's here and he's got a big appetite."

"After dinner, will you come crabbing with me?" she whined.

"Why, you know, other than those andouille stuffed quail your Gramma makes, there's nothing else I enjoy more."

The small framed eight-year-old grabbed Vincent's hand and led him up the walkway. Vincent opened the squeaky screen door of the patio wide enough for them to both walk in together.

"That must be Vincent I hear," said his mother.

She ran out of the kitchen to meet him. She wrapped her arms around him, squeezing tightly.

"Oh, I'm so glad you made it here. I miss you all the time."

"I miss you too Mama. What smells so good?"

"Let see. Could it be the crawfish stew or maybe it's the brownies that Carole's got in the oven."

"Now that's an interesting combination," said Vincent laughing.

"And so are you two," she quipped.

Vincent looked at his smiling mother. She was only 5'5", but her dark flashing eyes and beautiful big smile were legendary. When they were young, his father went all the way to Italy to propose and subsequently marry her, after having only known her as a child, and not seen her again until he proposed.

Vincent had asked his father how he could do such a thing after so many years. His father had laughed and said, "Vincent I am not stupid. I was prepared to run, but the moment I looked at your mama, it was fate."

After dinner, Vincent kept his promise to Carole. They headed down to the lake. Vincent and Carole walked gingerly around the loose boards of the pier.

"Careful love, I believe this termite-infested pier could crash down into the lake any minute, and we'd be swimming down there with the crabs and crawfish, too. Maybe they'd decide to have us for dinner!" he joked.

Carole burst out laughing, as she bounced along beside him so full of energy she seemed to glow. Vincent wished he could bottle up the energy of a child like Carole – that would be the real fountain of youth.

As he had predicted, the day had grown hot and muggy. He could feel the first trickles of sweat run down his back beneath his shirt. The lake was still smooth as glass and reflected the midday heat. Vincent wished he had remembered to bring his fishing hat.

They sat down at the edge of the pier and began the ritual of crabbing. Carole separated the three nets, while Vincent took the slimy chicken necks out of the baggie.

"I want to tie them on myself," she insisted. "Oh, they're so gross," her disgust followed by bouts of the giggles. It was infectious, and soon Vincent found his already large grin had also dissolved into chuckles. He thought it would be painful to be around little Carole, but it was just what he needed and he felt really good for the first time in weeks.

"Just tie them on good, so they don't get gnawed off the first time we drop them down in the lake."

Vincent watched as Carole dunked the nets in the murky lake. She kicked her legs back and forth, waiting for a bite. She was unable to stay still for even a second.

Vincent peered out into the horizon and his mind began to wonder. How long ago it seemed since he was Carole's age. His own memories flooded in. The house was used as a vacation resort. Summers were spent circling the lake in their motorboat. Vincent and his brother would take the motorboat out by themselves and fish for hours.

Not all the memories were so blissful. He remembered the summer when the innocence of his childhood was shattered. It was the day he realized the rumors of his family's Mafia connections weren't just rumors.

It was a clear hot day, just like today. The lake was smooth and the wind was still, perfect for fishing. He and Johnny had taken the boat out to the far end of the lake, near a brushy area. As they approached the bank, the boat suddenly swerved. They looked down and saw a large plastic bag, bobbing up and down from the currents of the boat. The boys poked the bag with their fishing rods, until they had torn a hole. He can still remember the feelings of shock and alarm as they suddenly realized what was in the bag.

Vincent's stomach had turned; He went to the side of the boat and puked.

Johnny quickly pushed the grisly package away from the boat.

"Let's get the hell out of here," he remembered Johnny saying, as he gunned the motor to top speed and headed back across the lake towards the house.

When they got back to the house they told their father. He and his mother were sitting on the veranda, having lunch.

"Boys, what's going on?" asked his father.

Vincent couldn't speak. Johnny blurted out,

"We found a dead body in the lake. Actually, I think it is just a head in a trash sack, Papa."

"Oh, God, no!" his mother cried.

The police were called, but only after Vincent's father made a few phone calls of his own. Vincent and his brother were hushed away to the upstairs with their mother. But he could still hear his father on the phone screaming profanities.

"Those stupid sonso bitches. My own boys found the motherfucker's head. You idiots, where's the damn body, you fuckin moronic shitheads?"

Suddenly, Vincent was pulled back to the present.

"Crabs, crabs, look I got three in my net, all at once." Carole's screams jolted him out of his dreamland — or nightmare.

"Why, yes you have three alright; let's get them in the bucket."

After catching another nine crabs, an even dozen, Carole was ready to head back to the house. The late afternoon sun was now blazing down on the pier and heating the planks. It was definitely time to go inside and cool off.

Vincent felt like he could down a whole pitcher of his mother's flavored ice tea.

As Vincent drove back to the city, back across the causeway, his thoughts returned to his daughter and his wife, Elizabeth. The mystery of the kidnapping continued to haunt him. Could his daughter have been the target of a payback hit from one of his family's mob enemies? Or was it his family's wealth they were after?

He also remembered the strange circumstances of his wife's death and her odd behavior weeks before Angela was taken, and the two strange bags of herbs that she put next to the bed. Then the suicide note, "Vincent, I'm so sorry, it's my entire fault, I conjured the Serpent Cross and he took her."

He figured that the shock of Angela's death, combined with the strong tranquilizers, caused hallucinations that must have driven her over the edge to insanity.

Vincent had to drown those memories, to keep going and, like Peg, find the bastard that killed his daughter and drove his wife to commit suicide.

His mind focused on the next step: He had to find out more about the other abduction, Peg McGregor's girl. Even though they hadn't found her body, Vincent felt sure she was dead.

Were they related? He would call Peg when he got back. The tracks of the killings might become more visible if they are both looking for them together. He also found himself very much drawn to the pretty blond with soft blue eyes. She was different than the women who he was used to, and he found himself thinking about her at the oddest of times.

He knew any kind of romance was useless. It never worked to bring an outsider into the family and there was plenty of history to prove it. He knew Peg was not the kind of woman who would allow herself to become involved in a relationship that had nothing to offer but physical pleasure, but he wanted more than anything to have her in his life. There was something about her, a depth that he couldn't quite fathom. She was holding back. She had secrets of her own. As someone who had kept secrets for too many years, he could see what others could not. He had patience and he would find out the answers; and then he would decide where it would lead him.

On Monday morning after Vincent had his second cup of coffee, he resolved to call Peg and invite her to another meeting of the victims' group. Perhaps in an emotionally protected place, she might reveal some information that the police might have told her to keep to herself.

If his decade-long career as an attorney had taught him anything, it was that police often kept vital clues of the case to themselves. He, like Peg, was of the same mind in believing that the two abductions were connected. There must be way to find out.

Despite his recent separation from his family's shady business dealings, Vincent was still a Morelli. He could only get so much through his cash informants, and then there were others whom he could tap for information, but he would owe favors. He didn't like owing favors. The police weren't going to hand him any favors, but Peg might.

The drive to find Angela's killer was now the only thing keeping Vincent going. He had totally given up his career ambitions and any thoughts of running again for district judge. Right before his daughter's death, his family and business associates had raised enough money for Vincent to enter the upcoming election. His chances looked good. There were only three other contenders and Vincent was in the lead. His father was furious when he withdrew.

Vincent was raised in the luxury of money and power but his family kept pushing for more political clout. The only way to gain more control of Louisiana politics was through the judicial system. Vincent was handsome, polished and smooth talker. His dark Latin looks and wide smile charmed the women.

Vincent was happy to go along. At first he lacked a certain confidence, but it was a characteristic that worked in his favor. He began to like the attention and the excitement of the political scene in New Orleans. He could walk a political tightrope, and was comfortable entertaining the Republican Women's club luncheon at a snazzy restaurant on St. Charles Ave., and then skipping across town for dinner at the Lion's club.

He knew the last few months of the political campaign had caused some friction with his own family. His wife, Elizabeth, had given up her teaching job at the elementary school to raise Angela. At first, she was happy to be at Vincent's side during the parties and dinners, but after a few months, she grew tired and became more suspicious that Vincent's family would be using his position for their own ends.

She had wanted to live out in the suburbs, in Metairie, but Vincent's father insisted that it was better that they live in the ancestral home in the Garden District.

Vincent thought about Elizabeth, and her fears that the family was exposing itself too much. The mafia in New Orleans kept a low profile; paying off politicians, not becoming one. The Morelli's were taking a chance, but they had their golden boy and figured having Vincent as judge would give them unprecedented power over their enemies and the police department… and beyond.

Vincent didn't want to let his family down, so he accepted his new destiny, and tried to convince Elizabeth that everything would turn out fine.

In early October, Vincent remembers sitting at the desk of the New Orleans World Trade Center. His office was located on the 17th floor, which provided a panoramic view of the river and French Quarter. He had just received a call from one of his father's friends, his campaign manager, who was just wrapping up a few loose ends for the big fundraiser reception scheduled for Saturday. It was to be held at the Columns, a century year old mansion on St. Charles Ave. that was often used by the New Orleans debutantes for their coming out parties.

Over the last few months, Vincent's campaign had shifted into full gear. There wasn't a street in the Garden District that didn't have at least one "Morelli for 2nd District Judge" sign.

But for him, everything came to a halt that day, when he received that hysterical call from Elizabeth, saying that Angela was missing. He didn't care anymore about political ambitions and he found it too hard to pretend.

CHAPTER TWENTY

Vincent knew more than anyone else what it was like to feel dead and then, somehow, face a reawakening. Once the intense mourning is over, the body becomes refocused. A new sensitivity, a new drive for living takes over. Vincent might have gone along with Elizabeth, taking a bottle of pills; but something was keeping him going.

After he got over the shock of Elizabeth's death, he decided to find out about the strange bag underneath the bed. The police had identified it as a gris gris, a harmless bag of herbs used in voodoo to bring good luck. Vincent knew it had come from the old woman at the Sweet Shop, where they had stopped every Wednesday.

The voodoo lady immediately recognized the bag. When she saw Vincent, she burst into tears.

"You must be de husband. I am so sorry. I didn't know. You must give me de bag, and I will take away the evil. You must go away and find de good, from the bad. I know a lady, she can help."

The shop lady gave Vincent a card; it listed an address on Privy Street. The paper had a strange insignia: a golden cross with a purple serpent wound around it.

"Der will be a voodoo ceremony on Sunday, go there. You will find dey way out of your grief. The snake is winding around you, de cross, and you are its beginning and end. You will become de great Dr. John man, who has the flaming baton and will take de good back from de evil."

At first Vincent was stunned. Then he wanted to laugh at the ridiculousness of the whole situation. Why in the world was he doing this? He wanted to turn and walk back out the way he came in but something held him back so he stayed and listened.

He had heard of voodoo ceremonies that take place on the outskirts of town, near the old projects. He thought they were just displays for the tourists. This woman seriously believed everything she told him. Vincent was pretty sure she was crazier than a mudbug, but he also was too curious to turn down an offer to attend a voodoo ceremony.

All her talk about him conquering evil and his destiny made him a little uneasy. He had spent months working with private detectives and the police, with no solid leads. How could it hurt to try something, well, more primitive?

"But I came here to find out about my wife; what did you tell her?" He demanded.

"I cannot say and never will; but I will try to help you in oder ways. Please go to de voodoo ceremony."

"Will you be there?"

"Yes man, but I don't talk to nobody during ceremony. We contact only to de spirits."

So Vincent had drove to the address the old woman gave him and parked his car near an old oak tree that had Spanish moss draped like cobwebs over its branches. It was a moonless night, everything blanketed in complete darkness, except for a few kerosene lanterns that lit the street so all that was visible was the wildly painted faces of the men and women dancing in a circle around a headless chicken.

He felt something tickle the back of his neck and when he turned to look a strange black woman had materialized out of the darkness. The woman told Vincent she knew who killed his daughter, but he must first help others. He must wash away the evil of his family. Her voice was smooth and seductive.

The woman gave him a yellowed slip of paper with an address scrawled in red ink. He had to flick his lighter to read the numbers. Vincent recognized the address. It was the Monteleone Hotel.

"Go der on de first Wednesday of dey month. Room 38."

He put the slip of paper in his pocket and turned to ask the woman about the strange dancers, but she had disappeared. A Creole lady, who was wearing a shiny crucifix, was shaking to the Mambo, with a snake draped around her neck. She was leading the tribe in circle dance, and they were all adorned with head feathers. Their painted faces hid their identities.

Vincent squinted his eyes; he was trying to see if she was the same woman who only seconds ago spoke to him. Watching her dance with the snake, he remembered the strange feeling on the back of his neck and gave an involuntary shudder. He hated snakes. He laughed at his own jitters and walked back to the car. He remembered the odd sensation had stayed with him, until he reached his own driveway and then it faded like a dream.

Vincent had been to the Monteleone many times, for dinner, and to entertain out-of-town visitors. It was one of his favorite hotels. But this time, when he approached the lobby, he felt like he had never been there before. He was anxious and wondered whether the meeting would be another freak show.

When Vincent walked into room 38, a small woman, with dark green eyes and short red hair, greeted him. She seemed normal.

"Welcome, we knew you would come."

Before he knew it, Vincent was coming to the meetings on a regular basis. The group called itself the Survivors. They were parents of children who were missing, kidnapped or dead. He never saw the snake woman at any of the group meetings; when he asked about her everyone just looked blank and smiled. He soon learned that one major rule was to never speak about how you learned of the group. He felt comfortable among the group. The groups' atmosphere of secrecy was similar to that of his own family and their connections. He was used to working in a vacuum, sharing thoughts and feelings only with those directly involved.

He soon became a valuable member of the group and held a position of leadership, along with another older member he suspected as FBI. In the group, one's outside affiliations came second to the mission of the group. There was complete trust among those who shared the greatest pain. No outsider would have ever believed a high level Fed and a top member of New Orleans notorious crime family had formed a bond of friendship on such a basic level.

The group helped Vincent focus on something positive. He thought it might help Peg, too. She was his first inductee and he was eager for her to become more involved. He thought she needed what the group had to offer even more than he had, when he first joined. He would be persistent but also patient and he would definitely leave out the part about the voodoo.

He had called several times in the last few weeks and she had turned him down. Yet today, she sounded almost anxious to go.

"Shall we meet at the Monteleone Hotel, again?" asked Peg.

The meeting is at the hotel, Wednesday and starts at 8:00 p.m. I'll need to be there at 7:30. Instead of meeting there, how about I come by and pick you up?"

Peg didn't want to accept, but couldn't think of a quick reply that would gracefully get her out of the offer.

"That's fine."

She gave Vincent directions to her house, cringing inwardly at what Lester's reaction would be to her evening plans.

"Great," said Vincent. Of course, he already knew where she lived and had pictures of her house in his files, but after her last reaction to his snooping he kept his mouth shut.

"I have to go now. I've got another call coming in. I'm on deadline."

Peg hung up the phone, angry with herself. Why did she always go brain dead whenever she talked to Vincent? It was like he had cast a spell on her. Her instincts told her she was playing with fire and she should call him back and cancel. Her ego wouldn't let her admit he had the power to rattle her. She would keep the date.

Peg was still touching up her lipstick, when she heard the doorbell ring. It was 7:15, Vincent had arrived early.

She rushed to open the door.

"Hope I'm not too early, traffic across the bridge wasn't so bad, so I made good time."

Vincent smiled and held the screen door for her as she turned and locked the door. They walked to the car. Vincent followed her around the car, and opened the door for her. It felt strange to be in a car with another man, especially with someone who was as attractive and attentive as Vincent.

"How have you been? Not working too hard I hope."

Vincent was consciously trying to keep things light. He didn't want to upset her again.

"No, not much going on, except for the homicides," she replied. "What about you? You seem to know an awful lot about me, and I can't think of much that you have told me about yourself."

Peg decided to take the offense from the very start.

"Alright; what do you want to know? I don't have much to tell. I practice law at the Hillman law office downtown, mostly transportation law. I've lived in New Orleans my whole life, except when I went to LSU. Last year, I tried to make a run for District Judge, but that's a whole other story."

Vincent smiled and waited for further questions.

Peg wanted to ask Vincent about his family, but didn't have the nerve; instead, she filled in the conversation with small talk about the news and the newest bunch of elected officials on trial for the umpteenth time for alleged illegal activities…bribery, etc.

"Do you think any of them will go down this time?"

"Not a chance, they've got a few officials in his pocket, I'm sure," said Peg, who suddenly realized that Vincent's family may also have a few on their payroll.

They arrived at the Monteleone Hotel early, and Vincent suggested they sit at the nostalgic carousel bar and have a drink.

Vincent was dressed more casually this time. He wore a stripped cotton shirt and trim fitting brown slacks. He held his arm tightly around her waist, leading her into the elegant bar. The bar was built to resemble a real old time children's carousel, though there was a marble bar top and chairs to replace the colorful horses that usually grace a carnival carousel. The bar slowly revolved.

"This is beautiful," said Peg, while wondering how many people sat there, got drunk and fell off their chairs, while the bar's movement affected their alcoholic equilibrium. She was tempted to ask the cute young bartender. She studied Vincent as he turned to talk to an acquaintance. God, he was handsome. Out of all the interesting men she had met in New Orleans, she never before had a problem being professional or detached. She hadn't felt drawn to any man in years.

Since Caitlin's abduction her emotions had been out of control and against her own wishes, she felt herself drawn to two very different men.

He turned and caught her staring, lost in thought.

"What would you like to drink?" he asked, gazing into her eyes.

"I would love a glass of Chardonnay."

His intense gaze made her feel uncomfortable.

The waiter approached and Vincent ordered their drinks.

"Are you looking forward to this evening?" Vincent asked.

"Yes, I'm curious about what may happen, and now I feel a bit more relaxed about going. I can see how a group like this can be valuable to people like us, who have lost so much. No one else can really understand it," said Peg struggling to stay detached.

"You are so right."

Peg looked in Vincent's eyes and tried to see the loneliness that must be hiding in their chocolate depths. He seemed sad tonight. Normally, he smiled and played the role of protector. He was there for her, but at this moment, it seemed he was allowing her to see a glimpse of his true emotions. So much for trying to stay detached.

"We have time for one more glass," he said smiling again.

He saw her concerned expression. She was seeing the face of a man who was still living with the sadness of past memories, when his wife was with him.

"I'd love one," said Peg, thinking that Vincent might need one as much as she did. She turned away and focused her attention on the elegant furniture store visible through the window. She needed some time to think. But all her thoughts were questions and she had no answers. What was she doing here? Where did she think this was going to go? She was tempted to get up and run from this man and this room with the strange sculptured hands that sprouted from the walls and held softly lit candles. The whole place was surreal, like a dream.

They finished their second drinks more quickly and walked to the meeting. Peg was feeling lightheaded and subdued. Vincent led her to a large blue velvet armchair.

"Just relax, we'll call the meeting to order in a few minutes."

Vincent's previous sadness had lifted and he was flirting with a woman standing by the window. He had a spark that lit up the room and a reassuring smile that made women feel they could open up. She figured those skills must make him an excellent attorney.

"Let's get started. Who wants to go first?" Vincent's voice cut through the chatter in the room.

A slender woman who had been standing by the window spoke first.

"Hello, everybody; I just wanted to let you all know that we have made some real headway in lobbying Congressman Tolerio. He may be our best chance at getting the parole laws changed for sex offenders. As you know, we have had two in the last month who were released on "so-called good behavior," and they went back on the streets, only to commit their sick crimes again.

"We can't fight this battle if the courts won't help. And we are still not giving up on getting the laws passed that will allow addresses of sex offenders to be posted in the newspaper. What good does it do to show names without addresses? People won't know if the sex offender is living right across the street. That's the whole point, to protect the children. Several other states, like Texas and Kansas, have laws that allow this; we have to try to get this passed in Louisiana.

"I have petitions that I would like you all to take with you tonight about the laws. Take them to work, pass them around. We have to keep plugging away at this. Next week we will take them to his office."

Vincent spoke next: "Thanks Matty, this is what this group is all about. Would anyone else like to speak tonight?"

Peg cleared her throat, and raised her hand.

"Go ahead."

Vincent seemed surprised that she had decided to talk.

"I'm glad I came here tonight, because I really feel what you are all doing is wonderful. At first, I was resistant. I usually like to get through things on my own, but seeing how much you all really care has made me realize what I have been missing."

Peg stopped for a moment to gather her thoughts. She didn't intend on giving a testimonial, but rather say just enough to gain the group's trust. She still didn't trust herself to talk about her daughter's abduction in public.

"I am still not ready to talk about my own loss, but just knowing that you are all here for me will make it easier when the time is right. What I do want to say is that anyone who hurts a child is evil. I have heard many people call it a sickness. Those who view these people as sick are holding back real justice for these perpetrators. It's not a sickness; it's evil at its purest form. Unless we start educating the public and pushing for legal reforms, these criminals will go unpunished in the courts."

As Peg finished, real tears glistened in her eyes and made her words ring true. She was a little rattled at her vehement speech, but the group wholeheartedly approved as they all clapped and several "amens" filled the air. But as Peg had feared, just considering talking about Caitlin brought a deep depression upon her. She was ready to go home.

Caren came over and placed her hand on Peg's.

"That's fine dear. Everyone has a different experience. You'll know when the time is right. You obviously share our own views and that is enough for now."

The group all nodded and small conversations broke out.

"I think it's time for us to go."

Vincent held his hand out to Peg. He could tell that she seemed uncomfortable. She placed her hand in his and allowed him to walk her out the door.

They walked in silence to the car and Peg regained her composure.

Vincent could tell Peg felt embarrassed. Before opening the car door, he put his arms around her, squeezing tightly. After making sure she was seated, he gently shut the door.

During the trip to her house, Peg looked out at the glittering lights on the bridge and the full golden moon that reflected off the river. When they arrived at Peg's house, Vincent stepped out and opened the door, leading her by the hand up the sidewalk. Even with the small porch light above the doorstep, the house appeared dark and gloomy. When they arrived at the front door, Peg turned around, speaking for the first time since they left the hotel.

"Good night, Vincent," she said softly, slowly placing both arms around his neck and giving him a gentle hug. He really had been a gentleman tonight and very sweet. She meant to release her arms, but they drifted down to his shoulders. She turned her head sideways, closed her eyes, and leaned against his solid muscular chest.

Though barely touching, she felt his warmth and strength in the gentle embrace. As she pressed harder against his shoulders and chest, she let go of herself. For a brief, restful moment, she felt peace.

The darkness brought a stillness and comfort that she had never felt before. Moments later, she reluctantly released herself, opening her eyes, looking up to Vincent with a faraway expression.

Vincent's face softened and he leaned forward toward her, closing in for a kiss. Peg was surprised at first, but then felt drawn to him, and so she turned her head upward and closed her eyes. Just before their lips were to meet, she suddenly got scared and pulled away. What was she doing?

Seconds later, she felt a soft kiss land on her right cheek. She opened her eyes, feeling relieved. Vincent took her key from her hand and unlocked the door for her.

"Goodnight." Peg said, feeling confused.

Should she ask him in? Before she could decide, he had ushered her through the door, handed her the keys and without saying a word, smiled at her, pulled the door shut, and walked back to his car.

That night, as she relaxed in her bed, her thoughts returned to Vincent. It felt good to be close to Vincent, to be in his arms, to have someone strong to lean on. Still, she regretted having been so vulnerable, so needy. She was embarrassed that he saw her fear and confusion.

But she had seen something new in him. He had not seemed as sharp as usual. In fact, he seemed moody and sad. There was a gentleness that had shown through, a vulnerability that she hadn't seen before. He needed the closeness as much as she did. But she couldn't allow her feelings to get in the way of the investigation. If they became lovers, she would lose her grip. She might really fall for him. She had to stay an arm's length away, and no more glasses of wine!

She was happy about the meeting. They liked her small speech. Actually, she only said what was truly in her heart. She startled herself at the intense feelings that had suddenly gripped her. She was filled with conviction. Next time she would try to make a personal connection with some of the members of the group. To do that, she needed to distance herself from Vincent. He could read her too well and would probably see right through her future efforts.

CHAPTER TWENTY-ONE

Peg was feeling rejuvenated and had no trouble keeping busy at work. The editorial staff had all their resources focused on the triple homicides. Peg was pulled off her health beat to follow up on some leads. She got quite a jolt that night when she went home and realized what she suspected was true – all three of the murder victims were on Vincent's top 10 list that she retrieved during her first Survivors' meeting.

In fact, the three men killed were the first three names on the list.

Peg spent the rest of the evening mapping out the other seven's addresses on a city map. Could one of the ten criminals on the list be the one who abducted Angela and Caitlin? Tomorrow, she would start researching information on the remaining seven. She had a hunch one or more of them would be the next to die. If they did, that meant the group or one of its members was somehow implicated.

She pinched the bridge of her nose with the thumb and forefinger. She was bone tired. It had been a long day. Her boundless energy was finally running dry.

She decided to go to bed; maybe sleep would help her think more clearly in the morning.

As she hovered on the edge of sleep, she flashed on Vincent and Lester's faces. They both kept popping on top of each other as her mind struggled to decide on which one to focus.

That night she again relived her father's death and Caitlin's disappearance, only this time they were intertwined in her dream world. She was running and running, screaming for Caitlin. Mac and her father were there with her, helping her.

She could hear them calling along with her. Then she was in that warehouse again and shots were going into the ceiling. Instead of plaster, Mardi Gras beads and coins rained down on her. She could hear Caitlin calling, "look Mommy, a pink one."

She awoke in a cold sweat. The alarm buzzing her 7 a.m. wake up call. She felt like she had not slept at all. She dragged her tired body out of bed and hoped a hot shower would revive her.

CHAPTER TWENTY-TWO

Pierre slung one arm around the pole of the streetcar to steady himself, while grasping the playbook in the other. He had been putting in so much overtime at the station – with the triple murders – that he fell behind in learning his lines for the play.

He had the male lead, the art teacher and paramour, Teddy Lloyd, in "The Prime of Miss Jean Brodie." Muriel Spark's play about Miss Jean Brodie, an eccentric Edinburgh schoolteacher from the 30s, was one of his favorites.

Really, it was not so much the play, but one of the great lines that Pierre loved. He looked at the words, but he knew them by heart. And he had no trouble with pronouncing them with the proper Scottish brogue inflections.

"A teacher, a leader, a prophet-like figure – the dangerous Miss Brodie and her troops. Well, where you lead, Jean, I will not follow!" Teddy says sternly, then turns away and storms out of her lecture room.

It was one of the most dramatic lines in the play, delivered to the self-righteous and delusional Jean Brodie. Teddy Lloyd, weakened by his years of unflagging love for Brodie, had just found out that one of the "Brodie set" girls, Joyce Emily, who had secretly enlisted in the Spanish Civil War to please her teacher, had been killed in a train accident.

Brodie's response to the tragedy was harsh, saying that the girl, too spoiled and stupid to ever have a prime like she, but now was a hero. Teddy Lloyd had spent many years enraptured and taunted by Miss Brodie's charm and beauty.

She called him "the love of her prime," but in the end, Teddy finally untangled himself from her, realizing that Brodie's fanaticism had sent the young impressionable girl into battle and early death.

Brodie and her "prime" had turned sour and gone too far, even for the devoted Teddy. It was "prime time" for Teddy to unreel himself from her hold.

"Where you lead, I will not follow!" said Pierre, mumbling the final words out loud, this time with his own Cajun accent…and in his own defiant chant against women and others who had tried to stand in his way. One woman on the streetcar turned and starred. But Pierre just stared back more intensely.

He felt strong and invincible when he said those lines. He found himself saying them at the oddest times, especially when he was around Lester.

"I will carve my own path, and I will be the hero and all the rest of you can go to hell!" he said again out loud. Those weren't the lines in the play, but that's how he felt in real life. He looked up to see the woman had turned and was pushing her way to the other end of the car. Pierre laughed out loud, his sense of humor restored.

"Stupid bitch," he muttered to himself.

After clapping its way down the avenue, the St. Charles streetcar stopped at the end of the line on Canal. Pierre briskly walked the five blocks down to Chartres, heading to the Le Petite Theater, his heart still racing from thinking about the play.

Pierre had dreamed of being a professional actor – Broadway bound. In school, his elocution talents won him prizes in the citywide speech and debate tournaments. His high school speech teacher, Mrs. Fry, had encouraged him and used her connections to get him a part in the play, Oklahoma, at the Le Petite, the small community theater in the Quarter.

During high school, he continued to try out for plays, often securing the male leads. After graduation, Pierre planned to study acting at Tulane University, but it was the year his father had a stroke, so he stayed behind to help his mother.

He got a job as a waiter at Galatoire's in the French Quarter. He had little time to take on parts at the theater, and lost the momentum in acting, even though he was a favorite at Le Petite.

His father's illness drained the family, so Pierre was forced to look for a new direction. It was his mother's idea for him to be a detective as a new career.

"You are so clever, and you understand people," she would say. "And it is a noble cause. The filth and low life in the city are ruining it. Those Italian sharks are taking over this town. Your father would be so proud. You would be our hero."

Pierre had a few old school buddies who were cops. Perhaps it wasn't such a bad idea. He could stay close to home, help his mother and solve crimes. There would still be many opportunities to pursue acting and his other interests.

But it didn't work out the way he planned. After his father's death, his mother had a heart attack and became frail and clingy. He felt he could not breathe; he was suffocating. And when she finally died, he still felt like he was trapped in someone else's life. Now he was nothing more than Lester's grunt and slave...some career.

Pierre pushed down on the small round doorbell located to the left of the wooden door of the theater. A young girl, who played Sandy in the play, opened the wooden door.

"Hi Pierre, we're just getting started," she said cheerfully.

The inside courtyard of the antiquated theater was decorated with ceramic pots of boston ferns and begonias. The walls were painted a soft melon color and the doors to the backstage of the theater were hunter green. A large marble fountain sat in the center, adorned with two fallen angels spouting water from their horns. The inscription read "Le Due Devil."

The rehearsal went well. Pierre delivered his lines with the usual competence and flair of someone who was more himself on stage than off. He easily shed the roles of the poor boy running errands for his half-breed mother, waiting tables for the fat cats, or Lester's sidekick. Today, he was the amorous Mr. Teddy Lloyd; next season, he might be Shakespeare's King Lear.

After rehearsal, Pierre walked down from the Le Petite to Decatur Street, heading toward the Central Grocery to get his weekly muffuletta sandwich. He sat at the counter, watching the tourists across the street at Café du Monde.

The city had changed so much since his boyhood. There wasn't a fish market anymore. Morning Call, a café located at the end of the market, had closed. The café had ornate mirrors in front of the barstools, so you could watch yourself eating the sugar-powdered beignets.

Now strange cement sculptures of modern artworks, tacky marble fountains and trinket stores filled the streets where the fish market and colorful vegetable stands used to be. The French Quarter was cluttered with the sights and sounds of unruly children trying to grab the shiny quarters out of fountains. Their parents fought to get tables at the café and the Vietnamese waiters scurried around the tables, filling orders at fast as they could. More store owners were cashing in on the new Big Easy, and "let the good times roll."

Pierre hated the place now. He began to understand how his mother and father felt when they first arrived in New Orleans. The city was at its finest in the early part of the century. But each year, the greed and commercialism was chipping away at the city's charms and mysteries.

The muffuletta he was chewing, with its layers of Provolone cheese, ham and salami, drenched in an olive salad and served on a round loaf of crusty bread, was one of the few traditions left untouched. It didn't even matter that it was from the Italian grocery.

Even the river road had changed. The graveled levee that he could walk from the Quarter to Tchoupitoulas street now was lined with a fake streetcar. And the real horror was the new five-block-long Convention Center, Riverwalk and adjoining mall.

It got even worse.

The city had torn down the old Godchaux's and Maison Blanche department store buildings and built "Canal Place," a block-long mall with designer stores and even a movie theater. Other midtown shops and cafes were converted to condos with rooftop swimming pools. The Superdome, which looked like a flying saucer that had landed in the middle of the city was also hideous.

Pierre learned that the best way to keep his spirits up was to confine himself to a few pockets of the city: his old house on Carrollton Ave, the police station, Le Petite and a few favorite eating spots, like the Upperline, that still exuded the old-city charm.

The theater had given Pierre an opportunity to be the hero on stage, but it was his ambition to become a true hero that kept him focused on his police work. As he sat on the bar stool, he imagined himself as New Orleans's hero cop, finally being able to prove himself better than all the others — even Lester. He had decided he needed a boost to get him on the route to stardom. Since he had let the years of his youth pass by, he would need some kind of spotlight to introduce himself to the world.

These days all it took was to get on national TV and the world was your oyster. A nobody from nowhere could live on an island through a reality TV series and not even win the grand prize and still win a movie role. Exposure was the key and it had to be positive exposure. None of the stupid teenagers shooting up their schools would ever have anything but a moment of fame. The minute they were locked up, the world forgot them. Pierre wanted his moment of fame to propel him up the ladder of success. He saw the current killings his big break to make a splash. Yes, the hero cop going to Hollywood looking for a break — what a story that would make! He was sure he would be showered with offers. Once Hollywood gave him the opportunity, he knew he had the talent to succeed.

To get that opportunity, he had to figure out a way to beat Lester and be the first to solve the triple murders. Perhaps there was something he could do to speed things along. Instead of heading back toward home, Pierre decided to walk back to the police station and check the files once again to see if there was anything that had been overlooked, or if Lester might be hiding something.

When he walked into the station, a band of junkies, drunks and degenerates were sitting along the benches. Some of them — teenagers — had sobered up from the night before and were slouched over, trying to grasp on to the reality of daylight. Pierre gave a quick and sneering glance at the motley group and kept walking back down the hall to the office he and Lester shared.

He unlocked the door and walked over to the file cabinet. He quickly eyed the file on the triple murders. Any idiot would know that the MO was the same, but the question was why would one person want to kill these losers? Find the motive and you find your man. Pierre knew he could figure it out; he just needed to focus, and maybe call a few of his "friends" on the street. Lester had the sharper mind, but Pierre had other advantages: his connections with New Orleans street life. Pierre also had a gift for analyzing people and getting them to tell him things that they might not ordinarily reveal to a cop. That, along with not being above beating it out of them, made him feared among the lowlifes. They could see that he was a wolf in sheep's clothing.

He liked being what others did not expect when they looked at him. As his father always said, "never judge a book by its cover." Pierre loved that moment when he looked in someone's eyes and the person realized he was not who they thought he was. That was what made him such a good actor. He had refined those skills in his everyday interactions.

Pierre opened the file on the Keaton murder. The officers at the scene had filled the file with snapshots of Keaton, his body framed in driveway gravel with a perfectly round hole in the middle of his forehead. Too bad for the loser – the bullet didn't make as small a hole coming out. The autopsy photos showed the corpse was missing the entire back of his head. Nothing unusual – except, of course, the teddy bear next to his body and that he was the second of the triple murders that happened all in one night.

Pierre suspected that the murders were related to a drug deal gone badly. Maybe some local ring of dealers tried to stiff the big guys. He was sure he could find the connection. They all had records – maybe they served time for sex offenses in Angola together. Or maybe they grew up in the same neighborhood in Westwego. Hell, maybe they were drinking buddies. Pierre laughed out loud at his own joke. Whatever the connection, these guys really pissed someone off big time.

Pierre found the Keaton address, 1019 First Street, Westwego, and decided to check out the neighborhood himself. Since Lester was the one on duty the day of the investigation, the Captain had put Lester in charge. Pierre was also pulled in on the case after they had run short on manpower investigating the first two murders. He read all the reports of the three crime scenes, but never had been to the Keaton house.

"It's a nice day for a drive down to the swamps, don't you think baby doll?" he said to Margie, a plump brunette who worked the Sunday shift.

"Whatever you say handsome. Have fun," she replied with a grin and wave.

Pierre drove across the Mississippi River bridge, exiting onto the ramp connecting to the Westbank expressway, passing the malls and fast food restaurants. After another five miles, the expressway narrowed to two lanes. The sights on the road changed considerably. Small bait and tackle shops dotted the highway and wild waving swamp grasses crept along the shoulder of the road. The highway became a bridge over a bayou, surrounded by rows of cypress trees draped in nets of Spanish moss.

Finally, when Pierre saw the signs posted along the road, advertising the "Swamp Tours," he knew he had arrived in Westwego. Westwego was located on a small lake – really a large bayou that fed into 'papa' lake Pontchartrain. Cajun fisherman staked out the swampy area as their own years ago, and gradually built up a thriving shrimping industry. For about 50 years, not much changed in Westwego. Then when the tourists decided that they were bored with the "Mark Twain" paddleboats and glitzy riverboat casinos, they found a new thrill: the swamp tour. For the cost of a cab ride across the river to Westwego, and 15-dollar boat ticket, a person could get a seat on the Swamp Boat and see real live alligators on a bayou boat tour. As long as the marshmallows held out, the gators were up for the show. Who would have guessed that the bait of choice would be a marshmallow? Perhaps some stupid Cajun was going shopping one day and figured that those little round things called "marsh" mallows might tame the beast of the marsh.

The marshmallows are dropped one by one behind the swamp boat. The gator follows the trail until the creature is close enough to the boat railing for the Captain to pull out a bigger and more tempting bait – such as a dead floppy chicken tied to a stick. It is held over the side of the boat, and the alligator jumps in the air, wiggling, twisting — and with swift movements, opens its toothy jaws and clamps down on the chicken, devouring it in one bite. The men on the boat gaze in silent horror, while the women and kids shriek with terror.

"Now ain't this fun," chuckles the Captain "Did you see dose teeth?"

Then the Captain tells bayou stories in characteristic Cajun accent over a microphone. "See that place over der? Miss Jolene lived there and raised her ten kids. All dem kids would swim in this bayou with the gators. Course they knew that it was important to swim in afternoons, when the gator had already had der breakfast."

It didn't take much to get laughs from the tourists, who were usually loaded on the free Dixie beer pumped from a barrel. Just thinking about the swamp boats made Pierre's stomach churn. Now even the legends of the swamps were up for sale. A city, whose French Quarter artists drew caricatures of the tourists, had become a caricature itself. The Big Easy had become the Big Joke and a big stinky swamp to go along…

Pierre was so overtaken with his disgust for the city that he almost missed the turn on First Street. The houses on First Street were not as shabby as Pierre had expected. The single-family cookie-cutter homes had brick façades and wooden shutters. The small community mirrored many others that had become a new suburbia, where middle class residents could find affordable housing.

Algiers and Terrytown were the upper class communities that had first spouted up on the Westbank in the 60s near Oakwood, the new shopping mall. Since that first wave of growth, the area had now become prime real estate. New Orleans kept on stretching its borders into such unlikely places as Westwego.

Except for the peeling turquoise paint on the shutters, Keaton's house wasn't that different than the others on the block. He parked his unmarked cruiser along the curb and walked up to the house. Several flowerpots were on the porch. The plants were long dead. However, it looked like someone had recently mowed the lawn. Pierre walked around to the side of the house and opened the gate. The backyard had an old rusted grill on the small concrete patio. A cluster of banana trees were growing along the back fence and large ferns filled the side flowerbeds.

Pierre was walking around the yard, when suddenly he heard a woman's voice shouting.

"Are you the real estate agent?" called the woman from the backyard of the next house. A small boy, with fine brown hair, maybe 4- to 5- years old, was trying to jump on the chain-linked fence to get a better look.

"Get down Roy, you're going hurt yourself," she yelled. The boy pretended he hadn't heard her and kept jumping on the fence.

Pierre smiled at the child, and walked up to the fence.

"Well, not exactly ma'am, but I am interested in the house. Did you know the neighbors very well?" asked Pierre pouring on his best good o'boy charm.

"Neighbor, not neighbors, there was just one man living here. He was renting the place," she said.

As he drew closer, the woman realized he was not as small and skinny as he appeared from afar. In fact he was very handsome — not rugged — but with picture-perfect magazine good looks. He had a boyish charm reflected in the dimple, which appeared as he flashed a toothy white grin at her. His hair was dark brown, almost black and curled at the ends. He had brown eyes that sparkled with golden tints. She felt her heart flutter and miss a beat as he focused those gorgeous eyes on her.

"Oh really, so when did he move away?" Pierre smiled and winked at the woman. He knew she was checking him out and apparently liked what she saw.

The woman was about to answer, and then suddenly flustered, she told Roy to run get a soda.

"I didn't want to talk about it in front of Roy, but you know, this was the guy killed in the 'triple murders.' It's been all over the news. I even was interviewed by Channel 4 News but I guess they decided not to show it.

"I tell you we were just so shocked by it all…this man living right next door. And you know I was home that night and I never heard a thing. I don't wish an early death on anyone, but I tell you what, I'm glad that man is not living there anymore — or anywhere for that matter."

"You know he was a child molester, let out on parole and we didn't even have a clue. He could have come after my Roy. I just can't imagine that anyone could be so sick as to hurt a child like that. What was the police thinking about? It seems the police are never around when you need them."

She rattled on at a dreadful pace, fluttering her eyelashes trying her best to convey signals of her attraction to Pierre. He decided he could stand no more of her prattling when she started trashing the police department. Good God, why couldn't that idiot Keaton take out this crazy bitch before he was offed? Pierre smiled at the woman the whole time, as he was wishing she would fall off the face of the earth.

"So no one had any reason to suspect that this guy was a sexual predator?" asked Pierre. Now that he had her hooked, he decided to pump her for more information.

"Well, actually, there were flyers that were distributed several weeks ago warning about child molesters living in Westwego, but you know, I figured they were talking about some other areas, you know, down in those slum areas. Who would think someone like that could be living here?"

"Yeah, who would ever figure that," Pierre replied with a sarcastic tone. "Just what kind of flyers are you talking about?" asked Pierre, his interest sparked for the first time.

"Oh just regular flyers, wound up by a rubber band and put on the door-knob. I may still have one. Would you like to see it?" she said.

The woman, who seemed excited to have such a handsome man to talk to, dashed into the house. Seconds later she came out and handed Pierre a yellow piece of paper.

In large bold type the words "WARNING – THE CITY OF NEW ORLEANS HAS PAROLED SIX SEX OFFENDERS THIS WEEK. THESE SEX OFFENDERS WHO PREY ON CHILDREN MAY BE LIVING IN YOUR NEIGHBORHOOD. PLEASE WATCH YOUR CHILDREN AND INFORM THE POLICE IF YOU SUSPECT CRIMINAL BEHAVIOR.

"May I keep this?" he asked the woman giving her another toothy smile.

"Oh sure," she said. "You know this really is a nice place to live."

"I'm sure it is," said Pierre. "I'd better be going now. You and your boy take care."

"Hey, would you like to come in for a cup of coffee, or maybe a beer? It's such a hot day out," she stammered, realizing he was about to slip from her grasp.

"You never did tell me your name," she said, surprise making her voice shrill, as she realized she had just told a complete stranger everything she knew about her reclusive dead neighbor.

"It's not important, maybe I'll come back by and get that beer another time. I never drink till the sun goes down."

Pierre grinned at the woman over his shoulder as he headed for the gate. Something in his look made her turn around and rush back into her house.

Pierre laughed as he made his way back to the car. Stupid woman; he had just taught her an important lesson about talking to strangers. She wouldn't even know the favor he had done her.

He couldn't believe how desperate some women were for an attractive man's attention. Why if he had been a criminal she would have led him right into her house and he could have taken anything he wanted. That's why Ted Bundy had been so successful for so long. Women just didn't expect a handsome man to be bad—another one of life's little surprises.

Of course, women had used the trick of deception much more often than men. Beautiful woman had been fooling men for ages. Pierre thought once in a while, turn about was fair play.

He felt sorry for the little boy. He knew what it felt like to have a mother who put a man before her own child. He scared her on purpose for the sake of the boy. She was pretty empty upstairs. Or as his beer buddies used to say, "The wheel's turning, but the hamster is dead."

She would probably be offering coffee or beer to the mailman or plumber next week if they smiled at her just right.

Pierre shook his head as he looked at himself in his rearview mirror. He brushed his sweat-dampened hair from his eyes.

"You are a handsome devil," he said as he grinned at his reflection and started the car.

CHAPTER TWENTY-THREE

Pierre walked into the police station with the flyer tucked in his front jacket. He stood next to Lester and pulled the paper out, unfolded it and placed it on the desk.

Lester was leaning back in his chair, sipping his cup of coffee.

"What's this?"

"Just read it." Pierre had a smug look on his face.

"So, what's the point?"

"The point is," said Pierre, getting huffy, "I got this from Keaton's next door neighbor. Someone's going around neighborhoods with these flyers. That same person may be our vigilante. Get it?"

"Alright Sherlock, I get it. Now we just need to get our hands on who is distributing these flyers."

"Right, you got any ideas?" Pierre was looking smug again.

"Maybe we will have a solid lead if they show up in the other neighborhoods. All right Pierre, you get the gold star today," said Lester. "Now, we can finally get started on a plan to find our serial killer, or killers."

"And what plan is that?" said Pierre, who seemed more ready to take a break and celebrate the lead he had found, than to try to figure out what the next steps should be.

Lester's mind was already moving forward. "We've got to go to the Winston and Peyton neighborhoods and find out if these flyers were sent around there. Since this was your lead, I'm sure you want to see how it plays out. I know it's close to quitting time but the sooner you check it out the better."

"Oh right, of course," said Pierre, nodding. Shit, how did Lester do that? He always managed to turn the tables. Now he would be working late and Lester made it impossible for him to refuse.

"I'll take a couple detectives out to the Winston place in Algiers and then go to Westwego and check out Peyton's neighborhood."

"Great. We got a meeting with the Captain in the morning and we'll hopefully have something positive to tell him."

The next morning Lester and Pierre were in Captain Jackson's office. The flyers were found in the other neighborhoods.

"The strange thing here is that they were distributed in exactly a two-mile radius from the addresses. It was like someone had already pegged these guys. A target you might say." Pierre was really enjoying being the center of attention.

"What about the Keaton house? Was the distribution the same?" Jackson looked at Pierre, totally ignoring Lester. Pierre was literally glowing.

"Haven't had a chance to check that out, but something tells me we would find the same pattern."

"So what does this all add up to?" asked Jackson.

Lester jumped in as he noticed Pierre, floundering over the Captain's last question. "We aren't sure. Don't expect us to figure this all out in a day. We need to sit on this awhile."

"Don't ponder too long boys or we might find ourselves with another handful of flyers — and dead bodies to go along."

Pierre looked pointedly at Lester, and then back to the Captain, "well don't you worry sir, I found the link and I'll find the killer," he said, as he turned and walked confidently from the room.

Jackson looked at Lester. "What's up with him?"

Lester just smiled. "He's just looking for glory. Don't worry; I'll keep an eye on him."

"Good. Never know what that boy's up to from one minute to the next. I swear he's got a loose connection somewhere."

CHAPTER TWENTY-FOUR

Peg stared at the computer screen, trying to come up with a lead for her story. Since there hadn't been any new information on the serial killings, she and others at the papers were put back to working their regular beats.

Peg was writing her second of a series of articles about the contaminated fisheries. The city was up in arms about having another year of rotted oyster beds. Wholesalers were being forced to import the seafood from the northern coast or overseas to sell to the local restaurants. She was following a tip that an oil refinery in Lake Charles was contaminating the waters.

She was having a hard time concentrating on her writing. She found herself daydreaming about Vincent. She felt waves of fatigue whenever she sat down to work. A sharp ache in her shoulders made it hard to type. Her neck stiffened when she turned sideways.

Last night she had trouble sleeping again. She would find herself staring at the TV, in a daze, only slightly aware that she was watching a movie. Her body was exhausted, yet her mind kept reeling with patchwork memories of Caitlin. She relived those early fears, when she found out she was pregnant. She knew it wouldn't be easy raising a child alone. But she didn't have any choice. After her father's death, loneliness consumed her. She made the mistake of falling for a married man, a handsome blue-eyed reporter with the Baton Rouge Advocate. He stood out from the other newspaper journalists. He was a sharp reporter, but had a soft nature. She was a rookie cop and he covered the crime beat. One night they found themselves in a bar, tipsy from too many shots of tequila. They laughed and shared "war" stories. Both felt the mutual physical attraction which neither could resist and ended up in her apartment for the night.

Peg slept with him only once, but that was all it took. When she found out she was pregnant, she checked him out through the records files. He was married. She felt so stupid; but maybe this was fate's way of pulling her out of the rut into which she had become mired.

She knew there was only one choice: find a new home. Peg's friends tried to convince her to stay. They would help her raise the child; but she couldn't stay. She could never let Caitlin's father know that he had a child. It would destroy his marriage, but the truth is, she didn't want the baby to be a connection between them. She didn't want to share this baby with anyone; better to leave town. Besides, after her father's death, she had been living in a dream, floating through life and drinking way too much.

By pulling a few strings, Peg's Captain was able to get her a position on the New Orleans police force. But after a few weeks on the job, Peg realized that she needed a desk job. Her back couldn't take the physically demanding work, not to mention the long shifts.

She also moved too slow. Police work and child rearing was not a good mix. Besides, when her pregnancy started to show physically, she would be expected to resign or take on some mundane task like being a meter maid or paper pusher. She knew after all the assignments and exciting cases she had worked on, doing anything else less challenging would drive her crazy. Peg decided to try something new.

Reading was her passion and she had a natural talent for writing. If not for her dad's influence, she might have followed a different career path — journalism. Perhaps it wasn't too late.

It was a struggle at first. Peg enrolled in night classes at the University of New Orleans. She got a lucky break, when one of her journalism teachers, who worked for *The Times Picayune*, decided to publish her article on the healthcare of prison inmates. Peg had impressed her teacher by her willingness to go to the prison and interview one of the inmates who had AIDS. Peg remembered what her teacher told her; always write about what you know. It seemed to work for Peg.

With the recommendation from her teacher, and a few published articles, Peg was able to secure a part-time position at the paper, first writing obituaries, and then some feature stories. Finally, a position opened up on the healthcare beat and Peg was given the full-time job. And now here she was, six-years later, still writing the same public healthcare crap. Peg gave up and turned off the computer. She headed out of the newsroom and walked past the receptionist desk, her eyes staring blankly ahead.

"Leaving already?" said Andrea, checking her watch.

"Yeah, I've got to get some air. It's stifling in here."

Peg stood on the pavement, only to be blinded by the bright morning sun. She decided to go to the Acme Oyster House on Iberville to get a drink. It was still early morning, but she needed something to tame her mood. Normally, Peg wouldn't have thought about alcohol this early, but her nerves were shot and booze seemed to be the only thing that would stop the twitching of her right hand.

At first, she thought the muscle spasm was a type of carpal tunnel syndrome, and added it to the other list of aches and pains that had recently developed. But she found that it was beginning to twitch in the middle of the night. Was this what middle-age felt like? She also woke up feeling exhausted, reeling from jumbled dreams of flashing lights and sounds in the darkness. She thought maybe it was the nightmare of her father's death starting up again, but the next day she didn't remember dreaming about anything.

At this point, she didn't really care. She just wanted to relax, to forget, and to stop shaking. Maybe she should take up smoking. Hell, if she was going downhill this fast what would it hurt?

She looked up and realized she was at the door to the bar. She found a table near the window. The Acme was right between Royal and Bourbon streets and tourists often stumbled along the sidewalk with their Hurricane glasses from the ribaldry of the night before. Their hangovers made Peg feel a little better about herself, and for a while, took her mind off everything that was happening.

She needed to stop worrying about Vincent and Lester — she needed to put them out of her mind. They seemed to want to save her, protect her. But how could they? They didn't even know her. She was a victim to them, to be pitied, but she didn't feel like a victim. She felt more like a boiling pot, with the lid banging around from the force of the steam. She felt like she was about to explode.

She found herself looking critically at every man that passed by. Each face could be the face of a killer or abductor. Why was it that the male sex could be so perverted? How many women kidnap children and commit murder?

Women, she thought, weren't much better though: they are weak. They let men rule their emotions — from love to hate. Why aren't women capable of standing up and fighting back?

Tears gathered in her eyes. She was trapped just like every other woman, unable or untrained to be strong and allow the primal force to erupt. A man with this kind of rage would have stood up and punched the first person he saw or thrown something across the room.

But Peg could only wipe her tears and down another Bloody Mary. She hadn't remembered drinking so heavily since the days after her father died. Of, course, there was that one time when drinking had actually helped her. It had let her open up to another person, and she had been given Caitlin.

"Caitlin," she whispered. "What would you think of your mommy now? You trusted me to keep you safe and I let you down. What terrible things are you suffering?" Again she felt the soft plump fingers slip through hers.

It seemed the more time that passed, her hope faded further away. Bitterness and anger were making her miserable but she didn't know how to turn it all around. Every night she fell into bed exhausted but sleep eluded her. How long would this continue. She was burning out fast.

She grabbed her glass and downed the contents.

"Another double," she said to the bartender, as she placed her empty glass on the bar.

CHAPTER TWENTY-FIVE

Troy continued his "child abduction" theme that had been the subject of some great morning drive-time shows. The station was leery of the controversy but they shut up when advertising rates went through the ceiling. They gave Troy carte blanche to pursue the subject as he saw fit. They even had an inquiry from the "Oprah" show.

Just as Troy was beginning to go on the air for his morning radio talk show, the phone rang. The number on the caller ID was James, the front desk receptionist.

"James, don't you know I'm fixing to go on the air in two minutes?" said Troy, his voice revealing irritation.

"Oh, yeah, sorry, but this letter arrived this morning. Someone put it on my desk when I was in the men's room. It seems rather mysterious. I thought you'd want to see it right away."

"It'll have to keep, but bring it up to the office and give it to Sue."

"Sure thing. Sorry to bother you boss."

This morning Troy was going to interview the coach of the Saints. After 20 or so years, the New Orleans team was finally proving itself to be a winner.

Troy didn't much care for sports, but there had been some rumors of drug use among one of the top players.

The coach was coming on the air to squash the rumors.

The letter waiting to be opened was tugging at Troy's concentration and he was glad when the show was over. Sometimes, even talk radio can get tedious.

It was 10 p.m. before Troy got a call back from the police station. He had placed a call to his friend Detective Pierre Martens soon after reading the letter.

"Hello Troy, what's going on? You gonna ask me to be on your radio show," he chuckled.

"No, it's a little more serious than that. I got a letter today that I think you might be interested in reading."

"Oh, not another love letter," Pierre said, continuing his ribbing of Troy.

"It's obvious you aren't getting the message," said Troy, raising his voice. I'll put it to you straight; I think this town's got itself a vigilante. Those series of killings, you know, the Westwego guys, and then the one in Algiers, in the same night under the same strange circumstances may not be a coincidence. This letter is very strange and could provide some leads."

"Better let me see that letter. I'll be right there," Pierre said, with a sly grin on his face.

Troy unfolded the crinkled letter and read it again. He couldn't believe it. Why would the vigilante send the letter to him? Perhaps he was supposed to read it on the radio show? Was it a warning? He made himself a copy of the two-page letter for safekeeping but would hand over the original to the detective.

Troy planned to try to use the letter to bargain with Pierre for more information about the triple murders.

Pierre arrived about thirty minutes later. Troy brought him into the back office where they could have some privacy.

"Come on Pierre. I need something to keep the public interested. Give me a new lead or let me use the letter and flyer on the air. The station manager is chomping at the bit for me to keep this going. Our ratings have been through the roof," Troy said with excitement.

"Listen Troy," said Pierre sternly, "I know we have a history of working together, but if Lester found out about this he would throw me to the gators."

"Maybe I was never here today. You go ahead and use the letter on your show and I can storm over here after the broadcast and confiscate it, and then we both win," said Pierre, smiling.

"Of course, a little cash to send me out for a nice dinner tonight would help."

"What's this crap, Pierre? Come on, I could have done that instead of calling you. Give me something else and I'll buy your dinner for the next two weeks," Troy pleaded.

Pierre's natural greed overcame his better judgment.

"Okay, but this will cost you two grand."

"It had better be good then."

"They do have a perp's viable DNA evidence from the Morelli girl and are calling in anyone they can think of for testing. They are starting with all known paroled offenders. The three guys killed by your Crusader were brought in several weeks ago and cleared," said Pierre with a grin, knowing he was pretty safe with this bit of information, because the coroner's office was full of leaks and they would be targeted as the source.

"Remember, I was never here."

"I'll have your dinner covered by tonight; same M.O. as before?"

"Suits me fine."

After Pierre left, Troy studied the letter more closely.

The letter began with the words, "I am the Crusader. This is my warning for when I will be in your neighborhood. Beware!"

Enclosed with the letter was a yellow flyer that said "WARNING – THE CITY OF NEW ORLEANS HAS PAROLED SIX SEX OFFENDERS. THESE SEX OFFENDERS WHO PREY ON CHILDREN MAY BE LIVING IN YOUR NEIGHBORHOOD. PLEASE WATCH YOUR CHILDREN AND INFORM THE POLICE IF YOU SUSPECT CRIMINAL BEHAVIOR."

The letter that accompanied the flyer was a piece of white notebook paper with words taken from a magazine cut and pasted to form the warning sentence. It looked like something a kidnapper would piece together to send his ransom request.

"Weird," Troy said out loud.

Then, as if he just realized his pants were on fire, he jumped out of his chair and headed to the station manager's office.

CHAPTER TWENTY-SIX

Pierre was practically skipping down the sidewalk to his car. He never dreamed Troy would actually call him about the letter so quickly. Now, he didn't feel so bad about the two hours he spent cutting and pasting all those damn words while wearing rubber gloves. All he wanted was to get that flyer out to the public, where he felt sure someone would eventually call the station with some information. This was just the bait that he needed while also generating a little personal cash flow.

Pierre was still fuming about how little attention Lester had given his important find. Lester even managed to turn it around, so that he looked stupid for not already checking out the other two neighborhoods.

Pierre decided he would also call a couple of TV reporters he worked with frequently. The more TV stations covering him picking up the vigilante letter would better ensure that all of the people in New Orleans would know that he was the one who tracked a major lead.

With his new windfall maybe he could go ahead and get those Bruno Magli shoes he had his eyes on. Yes, everything was falling into place. Tonight when he meets Troy at the Blues Café, he will be two grand richer. He was sure more cash would follow. It was about time he got a break.

Pierre was daydreaming about being promoted to Captain and ordering Lester around, when he realized the car in front of him had stopped unexpectedly. Pierre slammed on his brakes and his half empty coffee cup rattled in its holder and splashed cold sticky coffee all over his crotch area.

"Shit, sonofabitch!" Pierre shouted through clenched teeth.

He felt the cold coffee trickling through his freshly starched Dockers and soaking through to his Polo briefs. He plucked at his crotch area trying to pull the wetness away from his body. Every time he thought things were turning around something would always happen to bring him back down to earth.

"Pic kee toi! Pic kee toi merde!" Pierre yelled loudly at no one, as he turned on his blinker and headed for his house instead of the police office. When he was really angry he sometimes resorted to Cajun swear words. He heard them often enough around the station and out on the streets. It basically meant "fuck you, fuck you, shit."

When Pierre pulled up to his house, he was shocked at how unkept the place looked. Pierre's packed schedule had left little time for yard grooming. The honeysuckle and ivy covered the small rotting picket fence, almost making it impossible to pull open the gate.

"This place looks like merde," he said out loud, yanking the ivy off the gate.

As he walked up the steps, he almost tripped over a small baseball.

"If it ain't bad enough that I have to live next door to these pic kee toi welfare trash, now I have to pick up after them," he mumbled to himself.

Pierre hurled the mud-caked ball back over the fence, brushed the dirt from his hands on his already stained pants and kept walking.

The inside was just as messy and unkept as the yard and reeked of mildew. His housekeeper had been sick the last two weeks and Pierre hadn't time to keep the place clean. If the truth be known Pierre didn't care anything about his surroundings. He preferred spending his money on clothes and toiletry items.

He was very self-centered in his spending and since he never, ever, invited anyone he knew to his house, he could care less how old or worn-out his house or furnishings became. Even Lester had not ever set foot in Pierre's house.

Besides, it was easier to maintain a crisp, elegant image if his money didn't have to stretch beyond his personal exterior. On his pay, it was hard just to keep his head above water with food and utilities. Sorry mess that it was, at least the house was paid for. He had inherited the house after his mother died, so he didn't have to worry about rent or a mortgage.

The only thing he did keep up was the insurance policy. He planned to burn the place to the ground if he ever got really desperate. He knew how to do it where it would be ruled accidental.

Without his extra side income he would be walking around in thrift shop rags instead of designer duds. Not that any of those idiots at the department would notice the difference between an Armani shirt and a Wal-Mart knock-off version. Maybe that was for the best, laughed Pierre. He wouldn't want anyone wondering how he could afford to pay for those expensive items. He was smart enough though not to stretch his luck by wearing his gold Rolex watch to work.

He opened the old style pull handle Norge refrigerator and grabbed a beer and some leftover red beans and rice. He placed the bowl in the micro-wave and zapped it for two minutes. A few drops of Tabasco and dash of salt brought the beans back to life.

After dinner, Pierre was feeling more relaxed. He stretched out on the sofa and turned on the TV to watch the evening news. He was slowly drifting off to sleep, when suddenly he heard the mad crackling sound of the cicadas. He jumped up and grabbed his pellet gun that was leaning against the television set.

"I'll shut those fuckers up once and for all," he said, as he dashed out the door into the early evening gloom.

New Orleans was having one of the worse years with the cicadas. Every evening at about sunset, they would nest in the trees and sing in a maddening screeching chorus. Pierre's large weeping willow in his front yard was loaded with them. He stormed out the front door like a madman, firing pellets wildly into the tree. Handfuls of the prehistoric flying beasts dropped down after each round of shots, amid a shower of Spanish moss that hung from all the trees on his street. It was a somewhat gratifying experience.

Suddenly, Pierre's attention was drawn away from the tree to the loud shrieking yaps of the neighbor's chow. The gun had set the black fur ball into a barking frenzy. Pierre turned his body to face the picket fence, where he could barely see the dog, jumping up and down on its hind legs, barking wildly.

God, he hated that damn piece of shit dog. He swore the damn thing slept all day so that it could bark all night. It was a damn vampire dog and he wished he could drive a stake through its yapping heart. Instead, he aimed the gun and pulled the trigger. The dog let out a short yelp of pain and retreated to its usual position, under the neighbor's rickety front porch. Pierre could hear a low growl as he squinted toward the neighbor's porch. The gathering darkness made it impossible to try to see if he could get off another shot.

"Forgot your last lesson didn't ya, stupid, little, shitty-fucking dog. Come back any time for another lesson!" yelled Pierre, smirking and wishing he could use his real gun and put it out of its misery, but that wouldn't be neighborly, would it? At least tonight he had finally hit his target.

Pierre was grinning, as he turned back to the willow tree and blasted out a few more shots, turned around, walked back inside and plopped back down on the sagging, worn sofa.

As usual firing a gun always brought back memories of his father. When Pierre was a young 8-year-old boy, he was delighted to be in his mother's company, visiting art museums and going to plays. He had no desire for guns or any of the things his father loved.

His father tried to take him hunting and it was a disaster. Young Pierre refused to fire the gun and cried when his father shot a deer. His father was so angry that when he got home he had a terrible fight with Pierre's mother. He said she had ruined Pierre. Turned him into a "cowan" a "pussy," a fag. Pierre was too young to understand what a fag was but he knew it was not a good thing to be.

The worst part was when his father had stormed into his room and told Pierre that if he wanted to be a baby then he would dress like a baby. He took off all of Pierre's clothes and pinned a white pillow case around him to look like a diaper and shoved Pierre out the front door saying, "There, baby go out and play with all the other babies."

Pierre was locked out of the house for the rest of the afternoon. He remembered his mother waving pitifully at him from her upstairs bedroom window. Pierre spent the rest of the afternoon crying and hiding in the hot and smelly garden shed. Why didn't she let him back in the house? How could she let his father do that to him?

Pierre never forgot the burning humiliation of that day or the hatred he felt for both his mother and father. His father for his obvious cruelty, but he hated his mother even more for her weakness and unwillingness to rescue him from his father's crudeness. He thought she had loved him above all else but it was a sham, a lie, a game.

The next week when his father took him hunting he shot two deer, three unfortunate birds and one rabbit. Each time he sighted an unfortunate creature he was reminded of his humiliation and it was easy to pull the trigger. In fact, causing pain and death was like a salve to his crushed and bruised self-esteem. He had power over life and death. His father had given him that power. His mother only gave him shame.

He felt great riding home in triumph. His relationship with his father was never again strained after that day. He became the son his father wanted him to be. Pierre learned how to act the part, and his life had become a play, in which he was just a player, perfecting the role of the ideal son to both parents. It was the only way he could cope with the loss of the myth of his mother's love.

His mother and father were also just playing a part in his life and it was now time for him to join the show. To Pierre life had now become a series of parts in a multitude of plays, some onstage and some off. There was always a villain and a hero and Pierre was adept at either part. But if he was honest, the villain was usually a more challenging and fulfilling role.

Pierre preferred powerful roles. Maybe that was why he enjoyed being a police officer so much. He drifted off to sleep with a smile on his face. His gun, leaning against the sofa, stood ready for some more nighttime action.

CHAPTER TWENTY-SEVEN

At the same time across town, Lester was stretched out on his brown leather Lazy Boy recliner, watching a rerun of the Tonight Show. He had two more beers left in the six-pack of Miller light. He couldn't remember what had started this binge, but he was in a rotten mood. He popped the top on a fresh can of beer and thought about how much he hated being a cop.

Babykitty was busy purring away in her nesting spot on his lap. He absently stroked her soft silky fur and rubbed behind her ears. Lester had come a long way in 15 years. When he first patrolled the streets of New Orleans, he had just turned 23. A young stud, he was ready to make his mark on the city.

It didn't take long for him to see that his hard work, honesty and dedication would not get him far in the New Orleans PD. Corruption was rampant in the department. The top brass regularly turned their heads to ignore the kickbacks, payoffs and bribes that took place on a daily basis. Hell, who was he kidding the top brass were the ringleaders!

After only six months on the force, he was fed up. Lester decided to apply for the Bomb Squad. It was an area that interested him and he felt he might be able to actually make a difference, which is why he became a police officer in the first place. One thing was for sure, he knew if he stayed on the track he was on, his temper would eventually get the best of him and he would say how he really felt to the wrong people.

If the cops he worked with and depended on to cover his back thought he was against them, he wouldn't last long on the streets. He would find himself nestled in a pine box six feet under before he could celebrate his next birthday. So, by the age of 24, he was a trainee in the New Orleans PD Bomb Squad. He learned fast and had a natural talent for getting into the way a criminal's mind worked, and soon earned quite a reputation as one of the best at finding and diffusing all types of bombs, from your average pipe bomb, to the home-made fertilizer variety, up to the newly popular military grade C4.

They sent him to a month-long course in Alabama to earn his certificate. He learned beside dozens of other recruits from across the country just how many weapons of mass destruction really existed. It was a scary eye-opener. He thought he was cooked, after the second day, when he blew his first test. He hated taking tests. The instructors were really good and they worked with him and after his fourth test in two weeks, he finally got over his test-taking phobia and breezed through the rest of the class work. They literally tested him to death. Too bad they didn't try that method in high school. He would have raised his grade point average for sure.

The last part consisted of fieldwork. He really excelled in the hands on lab and field portion of the training. When he finally came home, armed with all his new gear and knowledge, he felt ready for anything.

Of course, most of the time he was busy blowing up harmless stuff that was suspected to be a bomb. He had blown up a lunch pail, many unsolicited packages of advertisement items, and even a belated birthday gift that was an expensive clock.

He was also great at reading a crime scene and soon was regularly called in on cases that didn't even involve an explosive. After ten years on the Bomb Squad, at the age of 35, he was tapped for the Lieutenant's position and supervisor of the Criminal Investigations Division. In his new position Lester had to deal with a little bit of jealousy, since he totally bypassed the usual stint as Sergeant. As Lieutenant, Lester tested for and received a *Certified Senior Crime Scene Analyst* certificate.

Now at 38, and fully entrenched in the position, Lester finally felt like he could help tackle some of the in-house corruption. Though in the last ten years, a lot had been wiped out by the demands of the unhappy citizens and the national spotlight shining on the City of New Orleans. The Mayor and the newly elected Chief of Police realized that to stay in office some things would have to change. So far, both men had shown themselves to be very adept at walking the tightrope between both groups. Lester was always trying to shake the rope and see where the politicians would fall. New Orleans was ripe for some changes, maybe this time the good guys would win.

Thinking about the rampant corruption always brought Pierre to mind. Lester knew Pierre thought he was oblivious to his fancy clothes and the money that he regularly took for confidential information. But that was one of Lester's finer qualities. He may not act like he noticed such things, but if the truth be known; nothing escaped his line of vision. He had been watching Pierre for months, trying to decide how to handle the situation.

Pierre was well-liked and known for his dedication. He wouldn't move on any of his evidence until he had something really big. Every day, Pierre got more reckless. His thoughts drifted back to Pierre, over and over, wondering if the evidence from the murders would find its way, via Pierre into the press. If it did, then Lester was ready to take Pierre to the mat, if he didn't kill him first. This case was high on his mind and he wanted it solved more than he had wanted anything in a long time.

Even after his fifth beer, Lester still couldn't remove his mind from the week's events. Something just didn't seem right about the "new lead" from Pierre. Surely a "Crusader" who was as good a shot as this guy was, wouldn't be so stupid as to advertise the hits.

Lester still believed that the Morelli clan might be behind the three slayings. He hated the Morelli's and all their mobster clan. As for the flyers, who knows? Could be some community activist or some overzealous neighborhood crime watch group? It could be a coincidence that the flyers were found in the same neighborhood.

He knew there had been trouble across the country, ever since people had pushed for stricter pedophile laws and methods of tracking and notifying communities of a registered offender living in their area. Maybe that's why New Orleans was taking a watch-and-see position about the notification system.

There were plenty of reports of mobs of angry citizens, picketing registered offender's houses, throwing rocks, garbage or anything that might make these guys leave their town. He even heard of children carrying signs with a picture of a coffin that said, "get out or get in."

In a way he couldn't blame them. Letting a high-risk offender live in a neighborhood full of children was like putting a fox in the hen house. It was only a matter of time before the fox ate the chicken. This was what he hated about being a cop. He could do nothing until the offender had reoffended. How many children were sacrificed yearly to make sure these criminals got their "due process" in the law's eyes?

Lester unconsciously popped yet another beer. He felt the anger and hatred rising. He used the beer to take the edge off. As a cop, he was supposed to pursue vigilantes; even so, he could understand their motives and anger.

He didn't even want to think about what he would do if a child of his lived next to a ticking time bomb. Instead, Lester pushed the vigilante thoughts away and thought of Morelli, and took another gulp of beer.

"I know it's gotta be the Morelli's. They have the motive, and took these guys down. I just have to figure out a way to prove it," said Lester, thinking out loud. Babykitty looked up with sleepy eyes, yawned, showing her sharp teeth and then settled back to her nap. Lester absently rubbed her ears while she purred, oblivious to how subservient he was to the small mound of fur.

He could deal with the Morelli's. He didn't want to think about dealing with a vigilante. It would be a no-win situation.

To top it all off, Lester had been working part time with the FBI on an undercover sting, some couple running a child pornography web site. It was all coming to a head and he was assigned for the big take-down tomorrow.

He was finding himself requested more and more for these kinds of cases and it was beginning to interfere with his regular job. When he mentioned it casually during a recent briefing, Agent Kyle said he should freelance. He said the FBI could be counted on to keep him busy, either as a consultant or a full-time agent. Kyle offered to pursue the offer on his behalf. Lester, surprised by the offer, had just shrugged and said he needed to think about it.

It seemed like the offer kept popping into his head, no matter what he was thinking about. The more often he thought about it, the more appealing it became. He supposed some of the corruption that ran rampant in the department had rubbed off on him. For the first time, since becoming a cop, he was thinking selfishly about his future and where he wanted to be when he retired.

He had even toyed with the idea of being a private investigator, but he knew the lack of interesting criminal cases would drive him crazy. He just didn't have what it took to stake out cheating husbands or wayward housewives. But, to consult with the FBI would be a dream job for him. He would be involved in some of the most interesting and complex cases and not have to worry about punching a daily time card. He had already taken a quick trip to Mexico on this current case and he was sure future assignments would involve travel.

As Lester drained the last of the beer from the can, he decided he would ask Kyle to put in the inquiry for him. It was time to get out. The latest problems with Pierre had helped make his decision. He knew once he lowered the boom on Pierre, the rest of the guys would be on guard around him.

He was tired of playing the hatchet man, even if he was getting rid of bad cops. He was smart enough to realize his popularity was running thin. It seemed he couldn't enter a room without all conversation ceasing the minute his presence was detected.

It was time for him to go. Let someone else take up the cross…he was through. With that final thought ringing through his head, Lester banged the empty can down on the table and Babykitty flew from his lap, turned and looked at him like, "hey, what the hell." "Sorry girl" Lester said and headed in the direction of his bed and some much needed sleep.

The next morning, Lester's job plans were put on a back burner. He needed to focus on solving the triple murders and the child abductions. He knew he couldn't think about leaving until these last two big cases were closed. Lester called in four of his best cops. They listened as he outlined what he wanted done.

"We are going to put a 24-hour tail on Vince Morelli. Morellis' are the connection and there has to be some record of a payoff. These guys hired a professional hit man who killed three men in cold blood. They must have found some information on their own about their daughter's kidnapping that is connected with the targets of the vigilante. Somehow, they have gotten a step ahead of our own police investigation, but now we are going to catch them. We're going through our files again and again until we find this hit man."

He assigned two men to stake out Morelli, and the other two were to tackle the files and run down the most promising leads. He thought taking action would make him feel better, but as the men left his office, he kept thinking something crucial was missing.

These last cases were gonna drive him crazy, he thought, while heading down the hall for his fourth cup of coffee.

CHAPTER TWENTY-EIGHT

Friday Night

8 p.m.

City Park

Tim Landers sat on the chipped and peeling wooden bench at the edge of the new children's play area. His obese form filled the entire bench the same way a glob of Jell-O will slowly flow to the edges of your dessert plate on a hot day. His clothing even seemed ready to explode under the oozing strain. As a matter of fact, he simply had not changed the mental image of himself of three years ago, when the clothing was still snug, but basically the correct size.

Every seam on the overloaded polyester pants, shirt and jacket were strained to their limits and ready to explode. As a consequence, the globs of flesh that could not be restrained bulged out in awkward places, resembling strange growths and protrusions. His legs were like knobby Samoa tree trunks, encased in dirty brown pants.

The sweat ran in small rivers down his face that he mopped every few minutes with a dirty and stained handkerchief, for the sole purpose of keeping the stinging sweat from dripping into his eyes. Lately, every small movement was an effort that demanded his full will.

Almost forgotten on the small portion of wooden bench, not occupied by the mountain of flesh, lay the picture of a small, curly-haired, black dog. The dog or puppy looked like a cocker spaniel/poodle mix, known as cock-a-poo in some dog circles.

Tim had given up calling "here lil' puppy, puppy," over an hour ago, and was now just gathering his strength for the journey home. His pitiful cries had largely gone unacknowledged, except for drawing suspicious glares or stares of pity from some of the parents who watched their children play. He had not even had a nibble of interest from a child.

The oozing man, who had become an almost daily fixture on the sagging bench at the outskirts of the newly renovated park, was a scary creature to the children who played there. Unknown to him, they called him "the blob" and fired their pretend guns and flame throwers his way, as they guarded the wooden fort-like structure that dominated the new play area in the bark-filled enclosure. They would not even have dared to go near enough to actually see the picture of the cute little lost puppy dog.

Tim watched with frustration, while they swung on ropes from one wooden platform to another, or climbed the rope ladder that stretched from the main structure to pegs buried in the carpet of bark chips. Their laughter and cries were mingled and muted enough, so that when the sound reached his ears, it was a strange singsong noise. In the last miserable half hour, the singsong noise had become an annoying buzz with sharp crescendos that crashed through his head.

Tim's head throbbed and his tongue was stuck to the roof of his mouth. The sun had broken through the trees in the late afternoon, and he deemed it too much trouble to move to another bench that was still shaded. The heat from the direct sun had pounded against him and he had literally melted and dripped like a glass of iced tea at an outdoor cafe. His only relief was to think about food.

Umm – "Lucky" dogs, a big plate of boiled shrimp, a fried oyster Po' Boy, fully dressed, a large piece of pecan pie loaded with ice cream and assorted pastries swam through his pounding head.

Tim's passion for food fought against his passion for small boys. Unfortunately, for Tim, he had gained 200 pounds, since his last stint in prison for molesting his neighbor's 8-year-old son. He had been assigned to the prison kitchen, and being a man of severe addictions combined with crafty intelligence, he had spent the last two years replacing his sexual yearning with stolen food.

Some of the guys in prison said he had "dickdo disease," and they laughed as they pointed out in the showers, "Hey Tim, your stomach sticks out further than your dick do!" This was always followed by gales of laughter. Tim ignored their taunts as he huffed back to his cell and gorged on stolen hohos.

Now that he was out of prison, his other passion would not be so easily pushed aside. But his food addiction had turned him into an obese freak that children avoided. He realized the picture of the lost pooch was not going to work. In reality, the dog really was lost. He pulled the picture off a community bulletin board at his neighborhood drug store, a 40-minute bus ride from the park.

As he sat lost in thought, the park had cleared out and only a few stragglers remained to play in the last traces of murky sunlight that signaled the end of evening and the beginning of night. Thankfully, the sweltering heat had also retreated with the sun. He finally felt some relief as an evening breeze cooled the sweat on his face and body.

Slightly revitalized, Tim watched a small, slender and dark-haired boy climb up the rope ladder and swing to the ground. He turned and waved to his friends who were leaving in the other direction with their mother.

"Wait a minute," said Tim aloud, as he watched the small boy cross the street and run up the porch steps to the light blue wooden framed, two-story house across the street. He waited, his breath held, as he watched to see whether the boy went in, knocked or "yes," seemed to be reaching in his pocket and then opened the door.

"Yes," what a stroke of luck! A 'latch-key' kid had been thrown in his lap right in his hour of defeat. He sat intently watching the house, as the porch light went on and then a window on the second story. He could have jumped with excitement, but settled for a small bounce on the already strained bench. His stomach growled loudly and reminded him that he had not eaten since before lunchtime.

The park playground had retreated into darkness and the sidewalk leading to the bus stop was illuminated only by a single streetlight.

"Tomorrow," Tim groaned, as he pushed his large form up off the bench. When he stood up, he suddenly became dizzy and had to grab the back of the bench as he struggled to breathe. After a few moments, the dizzy spell abated and he slowly lumbered through the darkness, his feet unsteady on the soft grass as he headed towards the sidewalk.

The picture of the small dog lay forgotten on the edge of the bench and the night breeze soon carried it away to the grass beyond.

A stretch of dense thick trees and bushes wound its way from the play area to the sidewalk. Tim became aware of a sudden rustling sound somewhere behind him in the darkness. He stopped and tried to listen above the huffing and puffing sounds of his labored breathing.

He could hear a whining sound, almost like an animal in trouble or scared. He didn't know whether to call out or not, his voice was strangely frozen in indecision. Suddenly, he heard a very menacing low growl that slowly and gradually gained in volume and intensity.

Tim felt his heart pound in his chest, as he looked towards the street and the softly lit sidewalk, a quick sprint for a healthy person but a good five-minute huffing walk for him. The growl grew in volume and he felt something coming closer. He heard the bushes directly behind him start to shake and rattle.

At once he was in motion walking as fast as he could. After five paces, his breathing was huffing in and out, and a loud rasping wheezing noise filled the night air — his open mouth resembled a fish out of water struggling to breathe. The bushes exploded somewhere behind him and the growling seemed to be at his heels. Terror grabbed at his heart and spurred him into a shambling run. He dared not look behind him.

With each step, he felt his mounds of flesh bouncing and swaying hideously. Adrenaline coursed through his body, but his heavy legs seemed stuck to the dirt.

What was behind him? He was too afraid to turn and look and risk losing precious time. Instead, he shambled on, anticipating the threat of sharp teeth ripping into his ankle, leg or thigh. He didn't even know how big the dog was, or even if it was a dog. It sounded very big from the crashing noises coming from the bushes closer and closer behind him or was it now beside him?

An uncomfortable pressure and fullness squeezed at his chest. Sharp pain spread rapidly from his heart to his shoulders, neck and right arm.

Still far enough from the street and totally shrouded in darkness, he tripped over his own feet and landed in a heap. He couldn't seem to catch his breath as the nausea hit him and he thought he would throw up or faint. His blood pounded loudly in his ears as he struggled to hear what was following him, while bracing for a mass of flying fur and teeth to come crashing onto his back. In vain, he tried to rise and cried out in frustration.

"Help, help, someone please help me," his voice barely louder than a whisper.

Someone was beside him in the darkness and a dog was panting, growling. The dog seemed to be held back or he was sure it would have already been on him. Too dark to see for sure. He wanted to roll over but then his huge stomach would be exposed and the pain in his chest was staggering. He sensed a presence very close now.

He inhaled sharply and attempted to roll over. "Please, keep your dog away and call an ambulance, I need help," he pleaded, hoping whoever was there would take pity on him.

As he rolled onto his back, another severe pain struck, squeezing a tight band around his chest, until he couldn't breathe. A red haze blocked out all thoughts and his clutching hands found only grass.

A loud click sounded and the sounds of the growling dog abruptly ceased. The recorder was slipped into the pocket of the stranger.

After several minutes passed in silence, a gloved hand reached for the fat man's neck to check for a pulse, but before the glove could meet flesh, it pulled back. Instead, the barrel of the silencer settled on his forehead, as one round left the chamber with a small flash and hardly a sound. A black, fluffy, stuffed dog was placed on the fat man's still chest, before the silencer and its owner vanished into the stretch of trees.

Midnight
Lakeside Drive

Don Hart sat hunched over the computer desk, his eyes locked on the screen. Somewhere in the background, he was aware of his wife, Staci, banging pots and pans around, as she cleaned up the kitchen after dinner.

Recently, they had been eating later and later, since they had basically become second shifters. They never awoke until around 1 p.m. and didn't turn in for the night until around 4 a.m.

Don was 55-years-old and was a dead ringer for the self-made business-man Ross Perot, except he lacked the large ears and all-American morals that were a trademark of Perot. Like Perot, Don was steadily amassing quite a fortune, but unlike his look-alike, his money was made through the suffering and exploitation of others.

Don met Staci in a club on Bourbon Street just three years ago. He was down on his luck, after suffering his first arrest and conviction for what he thought and argued unsuccessfully in court, was his right guaranteed by the American Constitution: the freedom of speech.

He was arrested for helping to set up and run a child pornography web site. He served one year and was just starting to serve his five years probation when he met Staci. She was a dancer and also available for "dates," if the price was right. Don, always attracted to the finer things in life, decided he had to have her. Don convinced her to marry him by telling her that within two years, they would be wealthy beyond her wildest dreams.

True to his word, they had just moved into a new home in an exclusive section of New Orleans near the lakefront. The home was located in a gated community that boasted its own security guards and Creole maids. They could certainly afford the live-ins, like so many of their neighbors, but that was too dangerous. Instead, they used the maids only twice a week for regular cleaning.

Don and Staci ran several very successful businesses on the Internet. At first they only handled credit card and billing transactions for several online companies dealing in porno. But greed had gotten the best of them; it wasn't long before they were hosting their own sites.

Staci who was 35 years old and still had a well-maintained body, voluptuous but lean, was the star of their first site. Soon her pictures were bringing many paying customers to the site. She thought it was a lot of fun, until she began getting death threats from some of the stranger customers. She demanded that Don take the pictures off and host another girl on the site.

It was on the trip to Mexico, his way of calming her frayed nerves, that they discovered a way to make more money than either of them had dreamed. It was very risky and very illegal. He had no intentions of ever going back to jail. Soon after their new venture, Don began transferring large amounts of money to an account in Switzerland. Always a man with a backup plan, he had purchased fake identification in case they had to make a quick get away. That was two years ago and so far there seemed to be not a whiff of suspicion. Even so, he felt better knowing they were covered, especially since if his business dealings were ever to become public, he would be very unpopular among the American public.

In fact, they would be outcasts, hated and more than likely thrown out in the street by their snobby neighbors and fellow country club members. It wouldn't matter how much money they had, their life would be ruined, that is, if they found a way to stay out of jail.

It was on the trip to Mexico that Don and Staci met a seedy, beady-eyed man named Carlos. While they were looking for fun in the small border town of Matamoras, they had been drawn to the poorer section that sported the bars that were clearly not for the average tourist. It was outside one of these establishments that Carlos had offered them the services of a young Mexican girl. The girl could not have been more than 12 years-old, but she smiled at them both and seemed eager as she questioned "party" "si party" in broken English.

Don's business mind, always greedy and working overtime, put his arm around Carlos, and offered him $500 American dollars if he could film the girl having sex with another child. Carlos' eyes glowed at the amount offered and it was arranged for the next night. That tape alone had made them a mint, but subsequent trips back had made them filthy rich. But the films had gotten more and more grotesque, as Carlos sought to keep the rich Americans coming back, and many of the recent films were more in the line of bondage and torture, with the participants not so willing.

Don was afraid that Carlos in his greed had started grabbing local children, and while Don's own greed did not give him any guilt about the misery he was inflicting, it was his own hide he grew concerned about. He wouldn't let greed make him stupid.

Staci had stopped going with him after the third trip, claiming it was disgusting. She honestly had no qualms about how the money was made, but she felt better not being an actual part of it — out of sight, out of mind.

Sitting at his computer, Don had decided last week's trip was to be his last. It was getting too risky. He knew he was no longer flying under the radar of suspicion. They were too visible and wealth always brought its own problems, when it became obvious to others.

On the way back from the airport, Don even had a paranoid attack and was sure that he was being watched. When he was going through customs, he actually broke into a sweat — his heart racing and nerves twitching, thinking for sure that he would be stopped. Yes, that was definitely his last trip to Mexico.

What he did not know was that he should have been paranoid. He was being followed. The FBI had been profiling him and monitoring his web sites for months. They were very close to shutting him down...painstakingly, building watertight evidence for the big bust.

They even had the Mexican authorities involved and Carlos had already suffered the Mexican form of quick justice. He had tried to buy his way out of police custody, which would have normally worked, but unfortunately for him, one of his last two abductions had been a niece of the local constable. He was now lying in an unmarked grave. For his crimes, he was gutted and his testicles shoved down his throat. He was still alive as they threw the dirt on his body. Soon after the last shovel of dirt was thrown, he was already decomposing. Hoards of nature's workers were already quickly dismantling Carlos to be used for nobler purposes.

If Don had known Carlos' fate, he would have run straight to the airport, but it would have been a wasted trip. What Don didn't plan for was how to disappear when the heat was on. He never considered that he would be under constant surveillance. The Feds were eager to build an airtight case. They also wanted Don's computers to track and bust his business operatives and customers. This was looking like one of the biggest Internet child pornography busts of the century. Don had certainly moved into the big time with his current operation that had ties into several foreign countries.

The only downside is that they would probably have to make some concessions to the Harts to get them to cooperate, so they could nail their contacts worldwide.

Last week, they brought in a local New Orleans Police detective, some hot shot guy named Hopper, to help gain more information about the Harts and to ensure that there would be no problems when they made the arrests.

Don logged off and rose slowly, trying to stretch the kinks out of his back. As he moved across the room, he looked like a stooped old man. When he reached the hallway, he was finally in a fully upright position. He noted it was 4 a.m. as he passed the grandfather clock at the end of the hallway. As he neared the master bedroom, he could hear the television and knew Staci had probably fallen asleep again while waiting for him to come to bed. They were starting to resemble an old married couple. Maybe it was time to replace her too. A fresh start all around.

The phone rang while he was sitting on the side of the bed, taking off his shoes. Who could be calling at this hour? Don thought as he reached over and picked up the phone.

"Hello."

"Is this Don Hart?" asked the caller.

Don struggled to place the voice, but he wasn't sure if it was a man or a woman.

"Yes, who is this?" he asked with an edge to his voice.

"This is a friend who only wishes to help you."

"What do you mean help me? Help me with what? What do you want? It's after 4 a.m., damn it," he said, anger clearly controlling his voice.

"Don, Don, calm down and listen, if you want to save your ass, and I know you want to save your ass."

Don felt his chest tighten, as the voice took on a slightly menacing tone. He was sure the caller was using some kind of electronic voice disguiser.

"Tell me what you want," Don said again, but without the anger and a little fear beginning to show through.

Staci woke up and was now staring wide-eyed at Don.

"That's better Don. Right, because right now you have about three unmarked cars watching your residence. In the morning, if you are still home, the FBI and New Orleans PD will come a calling. When they do, you and your pampered wife will spend the rest of your days in jail. Of course, not before you are dragged through the mud by the media. You will become much more popular than O.J. Simpson. Or should I say unpopular, if you know what I mean. You do know what I mean, don't you Don?"

"Why are you telling me this?" Don barked out, fear now clearly etched in his voice.

"Don, I am telling you this because I wish to help you. For a price, of course. Pack your bags, and another bag with all your cash and valuables. Don't take your car. You'll have to sneak out the back entrance. I'd pack light because you are going to have to travel by foot for two miles to the boat pier. A boat will be docked there. For the price of the cash and valuables, it will take you to freedom."

"Why should we trust you? Why would you help me?" asked Don. His paranoia rising up.

"For the money and you have lots of it. I know all about you. I've seen your stuff. Your Mexican contact has already talked to authorities; it is only a matter of a few short hours before both your faces are splashed across every newspaper in America. This is your one and only chance to avoid the spot-light. Take it or leave it."

"Okay we're in." The mention of Carlos clenched the deal in Don's mind. He must be talking to a renegade FBI agent, out to make a little money on the side.

"Better hurry then Donny; it's only another hour and a half before sunrise."

Then the line clicked and he heard a dial tone buzzing.

Slamming down the phone, Don quickly threw some things in a duffel bag, while Staci cried and followed him around the room.

"Don, please isn't there another way? I can't leave my house and things."

Staci was sharp enough to know what was said from listening to the one–way conversation. Her world was in turmoil.

"Listen Staci, this is why we put the money overseas. You knew this could happen. We have to leave. We can start fresh over there. We probably should have left earlier. We can start up the site again and make all the money back." He hadn't told her about the off-shore accounts.

As he was talking, he was dumping the contents of the bedroom safe in a separate duffel bag. He grabbed her arm and dragged her down the hallway.

They followed the caller's directions, walking through the grounds of several of their neighbors. As the sky was just beginning to grow lighter, they came upon the small dock with a late model cabin cruiser tied up.

They had been instructed to leave the duffel bag of valuables on the dock before boarding the boat. He looked around for some sign of life, but their contact could be hiding and watching from any of the bushes that lined the lake. He dismissed any thoughts of taking the duffel bag with them, and reluctantly left it in plain view before following Staci down the wooden pier to the boat.

Don untied the boat and threw the rope on the stern, as he helped Staci aboard. He threw the duffel containing their clothes, passports and spending money into the boat and left the other bag on the dock, before climbing aboard.

As he entered the cabin, he noticed a note taped to the windshield.

He read, "The key is in the ignition, bon voyage."

Don crumpled the note and turned the key. Staci, trembling, had retreated to the cabin to chain smoke and cry.

The boat slowly left the dock and ambled toward the center of the lake, headed to where a car was waiting on the far bank. That would be their ride to the airport. Don was wondering why their "friend" hadn't just parked a car at the dock, when his thoughts were forever stilled. The boat was ripped to pieces by an explosion that shook the still, early morning air. Flames engulfed the wreck as it slowly sank into the lake. Burning boards and debris from the blast rained down.

The bag containing the valuables was already in hand and being carried from the dock to a waiting car. In its place, on the edge of the dock, stood two child's playhouse figurines: a mother and a father. The mother was in her blue dress and white lace apron and the father was dressed in his business suit and tie, ready for a day at the office —their plastic faces set eternally in a happy smile as they gazed out at the black, smoky cloud surrounding the burning boat.

Thirty minutes later Sister Helena of the Little Saints Orphanage rushed into the rectory carrying the same gray duffel bag.

"Father Louis, quick, look what was left on the porch."

Father Louis rose from his chair behind the oak desk, as Sister Helena set the bag on top. He pulled the drawstrings of the bag open. They both gasped in surprise at the thick stacks of money and gleaming jewelry. A small folded piece of notepaper lay on top.

"A note. Father read it. It may tell us who this is from," she said, her voice rising in excitement.

Father Louis grabbed the note, pulled out his eyeglasses and squinted to read the words aloud.

"This bag holds the price of freedom," read Father Louis.

"How strange, what does it mean?" asked the puzzled Sister.

"Obviously some poor soul wishes to make amends for past bad deeds. Let us pray for their soul and then we will put this windfall to good use. "

"But Father, it is so much. What could someone have done? Maybe it is tainted and evil?"

"Sister, leave the judging up to the Lord. Just yesterday we were praying for a new roof and more beds. There are so many homeless children. Once again, our prayers have been answered."

As Sister Helena rushed to spread the news to the rest of the order, Father Louis pushed away any doubts. He would pray for guidance and would use the money for the children; No matter its past, it now would be used for good.

CHAPTER TWENTY-NINE

"Lieutenant Hopper, this is Sam from the 8th precinct. I've got some disturbing news. Sorry to call this early on a Saturday, but I figured you would want to know right away."

Lester looked at his clock — 8 am — so much for sleeping in.

"Okay, what's it this time?" he asked, as a beer-induced hangover throbbed in his temples and behind his eyes, which he closed, while he pinched the bridge of his nose with his free hand and waited. His eyelids felt like they were made of sandpaper; they scratched and burned his eyes each time he blinked.

Babykitty was winding in and out of his legs and crying for attention. Lester scooted her out the bedroom door and down the hall with his foot, so Sam wouldn't hear her. She looked back at him from the end of the hall; her tail straightened up and plumed like a feather duster. Her disdainful look said it all.

"It looks like we have another set of triple murders. This time they're scattered: one uptown and two in Metairie," he finished, while almost losing his breath as he tried to get it all out.

"Oh, good God! I'll be down right away. Does Pierre know?"

"No, but I'll call him right away."

"No, wait, I'll call him myself."

Lester hung up the phone and headed straight for the economy-size bottle of aspirin. He popped four in his mouth, crunched them up with his teeth and washed them down with half a beer — now lukewarm — that was left on the nightstand from the last night's binge. He must have stumbled to bed with his last beer still clutched in his hand. He cringed and grimaced at the bitter aspirin taste: it was a habit he had started in his youth. He still held onto the belief that they worked faster if you chewed them up first and a beer chaser couldn't hurt. It was also a good remedy for a toothache or sore throat.

"Hair of the cat that bit me," he said aloud to Babykitty, as he headed for a hot steaming shower. In return, she showed him her furry backside, huffily walking in the other direction.

Thirty minutes later and feeling almost human again, Lester pulled his front door closed and headed for his car. Before he left he made sure he put out some kitty treats as a peace offering to the still offended feline. He climbed in his tired old car and said a silent prayer as he turned the key. He knew he needed to trade the old girl in, but he hated dealing with car salesmen. Most guys he knew were thrilled at the prospect of looking for a new car and the haggling and dealing back and forth that went with it. Lester just viewed it as he would a trip to the doctor or dentist — a necessary evil.

As the engine turned over and jumped to life, Lester pushed the thoughts of a new car to the back of his mind. He would just wait until this one died, he said to himself, pulling out into the morning rush hour traffic. At least the sky was a bright blue and the mist had cleared. The air even smelled fresh for a change. But even the nice weather couldn't dispel the gloom that settled around him as he thought of another triple homicide, and the repercussions it would bring to New Orleans.

He remembered spending last night fighting the urge to call Peg McGregor to see how she was doing, and then going to the refrigerator and downing a cold one. It was odd how her face kept popping into his mind. Before he knew it, he was on his third Miller light and from there on he lost count. He really wasn't a big drinker, but he had been under a lot of stress lately because of this case, thoughts of Peg, and trying to decide whether to leave his job with the New Orleans police force. He was also expected later this morning for an FBI briefing about the Internet couple that were going to be arrested. In fact that was most likely happening right this very minute as he drove for the office. It was all swirling around in his head and causing his mind to work overtime.

He hated more than anything that he couldn't end Peg's grief, by finding the person who had abducted and most likely killed her daughter. He was frustrated that her case was swept aside by some maniac "Crusader" blowing away a bunch of criminals. Hell! He wished he could get a list to the guy. He could think of dozens who he had arrested and somehow ended up back on the street to commit more crimes, usually worse than the original.

If he was honest, he would admit that he wanted to be the one to help Peg. He also wanted her case closed, so he could see her on an unofficial basis.

Who was he kidding? What would she want with a cynical bachelor cop who had seen too much of the dark side of life? She needed someone to bring security and joy into her life. He was stuck at the bottom of a deeply rutted road and wasn't sure if he could climb out, or if he even wanted to.

Lester pushed any thoughts of a future that involved the two of them from his mind. He realized that fantasy was the reason he had started on that first beer last night. He tried to clear his head. He took a deep breath of the crisp air that rushed in the open window and ran his fingers through his hair.

"Damn, was it a full moon last night?" he said out loud, as he suddenly swerved to avoid a slow moving garbage truck.

As soon as he was on a clear stretch of road, he pulled out his cell phone and punched the speed dial for Pierre. He pushed a stick of doublemint gum in his mouth and waited for Pierre to pick up.

CHAPTER THIRTY

The phone rang and Pierre expected the call to be from Troy. Pierre was anxiously waiting to find out the time for his radio station interview. In preparation for the "media event," the night before, Pierre laid out a newly purchased suit and shined his shoes.

"Good morning," said Pierre in an unusually melodious voice, not wanting to sound too exited.

"Pierre?" said Lester from his car phone.

"Of course, who is this?" Pierre snapped back, his good mood gone in a flash.

Then he realized the caller was Lester and immediately his guard came up. He never knew what to expect from Lester. The guy appeared an average Joe, but Pierre knew from experience, that their was always more going on in Lester's head than he let on. It was a constant source of frustration that he had been unable to figure him out through all the years he had known him.

"Lester. I didn't recognize your voice. You sound different. Sorry, I didn't mean to respond so gruff; but I'm waiting for an important call," Pierre said in clipped but softer tone.

"Well, I thought you would like to be informed of the latest homicides and your morning off has been canceled. Get into the station, pronto."

Lester didn't give him a chance to respond as the phone went dead in Pierre's ear.

"Arrogant God-damned bastard!"

Pierre slammed down the phone, pushed off the couch and headed for the bedroom.

Seconds after Pierre hung up the phone, it rang again. He turned around, hurried back and snatched the hand piece from its cradle, resisting an urge to bang it on the table before answering.

"I'm on my way," Pierre gruffed.

"Pierre this is Troy. I was listening to the police radio and heard there were more murders last night — looks like our Crusader is on the loose again. I know you were planning on coming down to talk about the letter, but this is bigger. What do ya say? Can you breeze on by here?"

"Shit no, Troy. I've got to get to the station before Lester blows a gasket, and you want me to be your radio star today? Come on, Troy."

Pierre was impatient to get off the phone, but also couldn't afford to alienate Troy.

"You got a point. But maybe later today, when things calm down."

"Maybe, I gotta go. Lester is probably already at the station, trying to clean out my desk."

This time it was Pierre who hung up without saying goodbye. Disgustedly, Pierre hung his new suit back in the closet and pulled one of his old but freshly dry-cleaned jackets and matching slacks from the closet. He was seething inside about the way Lester spoke to him. If it was the last thing he did, he would turn the tables around and have Lester bowing down to him. His thoughts brightened when he remembered the tension in Lester's voice. He thought about what three more murders would do to Lester's reputation and status if they remained unsolved, or better yet, if Pierre solved them. He was actually grinning, as he grabbed his keys and headed for the door.

Even the neighbor's shitty little dog didn't change his mood, barking and growling from the other side of the picket fence. Pierre just turned and pointed his finger at the dog like a gun and said "bang." He was still laughing as he climbed into his car.

CHAPTER THIRTY-ONE

Peg was stretched out on the sofa, flipping through the movie guide. It was Saturday afternoon, bright and not as humid as usual. It really was turning out to be a beautiful day. The afternoon sun was brightening her spirits.

She spent the morning sleeping off a restless night, trying to push away the nightmares of Caitlin and Mac running together in the dark. It was a recurring theme – bullets flying in the air, Peg, helpless and unable to see the point of origin, unable to block the danger lurking in the darkness.

To escape these thoughts, she needed to keep herself busy. After lunch, she went outside to tend to her neglected garden. When she finished pulling weeds and fertilizing the caladiums and azaleas, she came inside to relax and pour herself a glass of iced tea. The TV was tuned to CNN headline news. She was about to get up to change the channel, when she looked up: across the screen was a news bulletin: "New Orleans Vigilante Attacks Again – Three More Victims."

A tense reporter stood in front on the Cathédrale Saint-Louis, holding a microphone: "It's another tragic night for the city of New Orleans, as two men and one woman are killed in what police suspect is another vigilante rampage of violence. Police have been quiet about the details, but CNN has learned that at least one of the victims was on parole for a sex crime. Two of the victims are a wealthy couple, who allegedly ran a computer consulting business out of their secluded home near the lakefront. And most shocking, these murders follow on the heels of the still unsolved three 'Crusader' killings.'"

Peg covered her mouth with her hand in disbelief. She couldn't believe what she saw next: Lester!

The station cut in with a scene in front of the precinct. The scene showed the crowds of rowdy TV crews, with huge microphones pointed like swords at Lester. Lester stood on the steps, trying not to be distracted by the mob of frenzied reporters. Lester's face was flushed; his features grim and set like stone. He appeared barely able to smother his aggravation and frustration at the hungry reporters who were ready to pounce on him, if he refused to answer their questions.

"We are still investigating the crime scenes and one of the victims has not been identified, so we are not going to release any information at this time. But I assure you that the New Orleans police department is going to put all its resources towards finding the killer or killers. Now that is all I have to say; I have a job to do," Lester shouted.

Peg couldn't believe how forceful Lester was with the reporters. The Lester she knew was soft-spoken, but here he seemed irate as he forced his way back into the police station. Peg jumped up from the sofa and ran to the phone. She dialed the precinct. The line was busy. "Figures, I guess every reporter this side of the Mason-Dixon Line is calling," she thought to herself.

Then she remembered that Lester had given her his card with a private beeper number. Where did she put it? She searched through her wallet and found the card. She punched in the numbers. Lester had promised that he would always be there for her; now let's see if he really meant it.

Ten minutes went by. Peg tried the number again. She paced the floor, trying to relieve her tension. Suddenly, the phone rang.

Before even giving Lester a chance to speak, Peg rushed in to initiate the conversation.

"I've been waiting for your call. Lester, do you think one of these guys is the one we've been looking for? Are they on any of your lists?"

"Peg, this just happened last night. The investigation has just begun. But, yes, they were on a list of recent parolees. I suppose it is no coincidence that the MO matches the other three killings. I'm not giving you this information to use in an article, but I want to talk to you about something else. We need your help. Can you come down to the station, right away?"

"Well, I thought you would never ask."

"And don't bring your little reporter's notebook, this is a personal matter. I'll have a uniformed officer waiting for you at the door to let you in. And be prepared to push your way through. We have a feisty crowd out here," he said more softly.

He was trying hard not to take his bad mood out on everyone else. He was still reeling from his conversation with the FBI earlier that morning. Lester's case against the Harts was just about to reap some fruit and now he would be expected to turn over his files to the FBI.

Peg's voice pulled him back to the present.

"Lester, are you okay?"

"Sure, I just have a lot on my mind. But it will be good to see you."

"See you soon."

Peg rushed to get ready. She realized she was actually looking forward to seeing Lester again. It was crazy because she barely knew him, but yet felt a bond there, a trust. And she didn't trust easily; with her, trust was something that had to be earned.

Lester was right; the station was a mob scene. She elbowed her way up the first few steps. The officer at the top spotted her and waved. Peg headed up the remaining steps, still pushing and shoving all the way to the door. The officer held the door open long enough for them to both walk in and then shut it forcefully and turned the lock. He brought her past the reception area to a small cubicle in the back of the building.

Peg immediately noticed a couple dark suits, whom she suspected were the FBI. They both had cell phones plastered to their heads and were engaged in a heated conversation with someone on the other end of the line. They didn't even notice as she slipped by. What was going on here?

She recognized Anne, the officer who spent that terrible evening with her after Caitlin's disappearance. She smiled at Anne as a twinge of pain encircled her heart. God she never knew where the pain was going to come from. Sometimes, the most inane things brought the pain rushing back. This morning, working in the garden, she could hardly glance at the little bucket of garden tools that were Caitlin's without imagining her walking beside her in the sunshine, the bucket swinging at her side chattering away with the anticipation of helping plant the spring annuals. She broke down and cried a full 20 minutes on the dirt floor of the old wooden shed. Just when she thought the tears were gone for good – when she seemed at last barren and dry – something would trigger the pain. It was as if it all happened yesterday. She honestly didn't know how she would survive if the pain didn't fade away as everyone kept telling her would happen. She didn't see how that would ever happen. Many months later, at unexpected moments, the pain still felt as raw and fresh as that first night when she realized Caitlin was gone.

She tried to never let the feelings come in public places and feared breaking down and crying uncontrollably in front of strangers.

She squashed down the memories and pain, took a deep breath and swallowed the feelings deep down, hopefully, buried for now.

Turning her mind away from the painful memories, she starting running her checklist of questions to ask Lester.

"Peg, it's great to see you. Lester's waiting for you in the Captain's office, straight down that hall, turn right," Anne said, pointing the way with her right hand as the other reached for the ringing phone on her desk.

Peg followed Anne's directions and headed down the hallway. The place was a hotbed of activity. The noise level dropped a little as she reached the end of the hallway and stood in the open doorway of Captain Jackson's corner office. Lester, Pierre and two other officers were gathered around the Captain's desk. They were running some kind of computer program.

The sun was shining from the rear window. A background of the Mississippi River and a spectacular blue sky filled with puffy white clouds illuminated the men. The twin cantilever bridges were highlighted and shined over the water. Peg felt an urge to walk to the window and gaze at the picture perfect view.

"That's our guy, recently out on parole for sex violations. What a surprise!" said Pierre.

Suddenly, the men spotted Peg and they all stopped looking at the computer and straightened up. Lester walked around the desk with the Captain close behind.

"How are you, Ms. McGregor?" asked the Captain, a tall, husky man with kind blue eyes.

The Captain and Lester could be brothers. In contrast, Pierre looked very small and insignificant next to the two large men. As if sensing this, Pierre's expression was sullen and guarded; a polar opposite to the other two men.

"We thank you for coming down today. I'll let Hopper fill you in on what's happening here. He'll explain what we hope you will do for the NOPD," said the Captain, as he reached out and shook her hand.

"Sounds intriguing," Peg answered. She liked the Captain. He got right to the point. She decided she would help them if she could.

The Captain smiled at Peg, and turned his eyes back to the computer and a scowling Pierre.

Lester escorted Peg into his office, situated on the second floor, in the back of the station. Peg could see another panoramic view of the river from the large window that faced the Toulouse Street Wharf. She wondered how anyone at the station, who had a river view, got any work done. It was hypnotic and somehow soothing to watch the river barges, freighters and cargo ships maneuver gracefully down the swift currents of the winding river and the busy activities of tourists loading up for rides on the Natchez Steamboat. She could hear the faint sounds of the calliope playing renditions of Red, Red, Robin.

Peg peered down at a ferryboat crossing the river, towing passengers from Canal Street to the Algiers Point. It wasn't so long ago that the ferryboats were the only river passages for city-dwellers to get downtown from the Westbank, where she lived. Now the twin bridges connect the city. But there are still those who prefer the calming ferry ride over the bumper-to-bumper traffic jam on the Mississippi River bridges.

"I'm fascinated by the boats, too. Sometimes, it seems like those ferry boat captains purposely try to get as close as they can to those tugboat barges to scare the passengers," Lester said from close behind her.

"Yes, it does seem that way," she agreed, as she turned to face Lester. His proximity making her nervous.

"Anyway, I guess I'm not here to discuss the perils of ferry boats, am I?" Peg teased as she walked away from the window.

"As a matter of fact, no," he said, as he moved around to sit in the chair behind his desk.

Lester seemed to be in pain, as his fingers massaged his forehead. He saw her gaze and reached for a pencil on the desk. Peg saw a small scar and indent that he had been rubbing. She found herself wanting to ask him about the scar. His voice broke through her thoughts.

"Peg," he said, his voice taking on a more serious tone.

"I know you were a police officer at one time in your life and a member of the SWAT team in Baton Rouge before you resigned. I also know you worked at the 5th ward precinct station for a short time, when you moved here. The reason I am telling you this is because I would like you to help us out."

"Are you kidding?"

She wasn't sure what was more shocking – that Lester knew she had been a cop and a member of SWAT, or that he wanted to know if she would work for them undercover.

"I think I better sit down. Why would you want me to do such a thing? Is New Orleans finest running low on talent?"

"Very funny," Lester said, as he studied her face.

She had suddenly become very flustered and upset. He guessed right when he read her background report. His instincts had told him she eventually left the police force because of the memories of her father's death.

"I don't want you to join the force, Peg. No, we want you to help us with Morelli. I know you have been seeing him and I think he has information about Angela, Caitlin and maybe the vigilante killings. It's the only thing that makes sense to me."

"You've been following me?" Peg angrily jumped to her feet and began pacing.

"No, of course not, it's Morelli we've been following. But we know that you have had dinner with him a few times. Remember, I warned you about getting involved with Morelli. It seems you decided not to take my advice," Lester said firmly.

She could see the disappointment that flickered momentarily in his eyes. Her anger quickly deflated, she sat back down.

"As good as our equipment is, we can't get close to him and most importantly the family," Lester tried to explain. "We need someone on the inside. With your background and relationship with Morelli, you're in a perfect position to get close enough to help us out."

"Oh, so you want me to spy on the Mafia? Sure, why not! Just put the cement on my legs right now and toss me out that window to the river?" But she realized she wasn't really angry and her words had no bite. She was actually intrigued and felt herself rising to the challenge. The danger almost seemed like a bonus.

"You have it all wrong, Peg. We don't need you to wear a wire. We need you to find out if Morelli is really the vigilante, or if he is the one behind the murders. We have to put an end to this vigilantism. And I know you want closure. These Crusader killings are just making it harder for us and stealing time away, not to mention the resources we need to find the abductor of Angela and Caitlin. We have to stop him, before another child becomes a victim. And who knows, they may somehow be connected."

"Do you really think he would tell me anything? I can see it now. Good morning Peg, just calling to ask you for dinner, and by the way, I'm the Crusader," said Peg, but without rancor.

"Peg, look, I know you are trying to lighten the mood here. I admire your spirit. But I am perfectly serious about this. Vincent is not going to tell you, but surely there are some clues, some indication that something is not right. You haven't lost your instincts. What made you a good cop has also made you a good reporter. We also know he is involved with a radical victims support group, but so far efforts to nail down members or a location have been stopped at every turn. Let's face it, he certainly has the motive."

"What do you mean, motive? If he had motive, then so do I, or any other parent in this city, who has lost a child to a monster. Besides, I left that life behind a long time ago. I don't know if I have the stomach for it any more."

Lester ignored her protests and went on explaining his request.

"The way I see it, the Morelli family may have already identified the killer. With all their connections, it would make sense that they might know by now. However, an angry, distraught father might decide to eliminate all known predators. In the process of elimination he kills a bunch of losers. Police are baffled and looking for an off-the-chart vigilante, and not the Morellis."

Chapter Thirty-one

Peg sat down heavily on the couch and looked at Lester with piercing sadness.

"Have you thought for one minute that maybe one of these vigilante victims might have been Caitlin's and Angela's abductor? Maybe the vigilante is doing the city of New Orleans a noble service."

She had been robbed of her anger by Lester's own apparent frustration over having to focus on the Crusader killings. Lester also sat down. His eyes locked with Peg's.

"As one cop to another, you know that is not true. Vigilantism leads to chaos and innocent people are harmed. We have to be allowed to do our job. Peg, help us do our job."

For just a moment she gazed into his eyes and remembered what it felt like to be a cop. She felt the old feelings of honor and pride surge through her. She remembered her father. Maybe she needed to be reminded of where she came from.

Peg found herself already designing scenarios for maneuvering Vincent. She also was mentally reviewing the members of the Survivor's group that she had met recently.

"We don't have proof, and until we do, more people will die. I know these guys, who are getting knocked off, are losers, but what happens when someone innocent is hurt? And if it turns out I'm wrong about Morelli, then it means we still have a child killer out there and a mentally unstable vigilante who may crack and lose the rest of his marbles and decide to start snapping off bullets at anyone who gets in his way. And if that's the case, then we're all in trouble."

"Alright, I'll do it."

She had already made up her mind to help, but liked being around Lester and didn't want to end the conversation. He had a way of making her feel totally comfortable, like putting on an old sweater on a cold day; and the next minute, one piercing look could make her heart jump and thump around in her chest. It was a crazy hot-and-cold feeling.

"Thanks Peg." Lester was smiling again.

She loved his smile — so open and easy.

When she stopped and thought about it, what did she have to lose but her life? Her life without Caitlin was nothing anyway. Her only reason for hanging onto her day-by-day existence was to try to find Caitlin and bring her abductor to justice. In her inner most dreams, she thought of her daughter — alive. But she kept that fantasy from everyone else. They would just shake their head and suggest counseling and acceptance. So, it would really be a benefit for her to work with the police. They might think she was aiding them, but she could use their resources to help with her own agenda. And somehow, Lester's suspicion of Vincent was rubbing off on her. She began questioning her own judgment. She remembered Lester saying that Vincent was knee deep in the mob, and had been a womanizer. She herself had fallen under Vincent's spell and maybe she wasn't thinking clearly. He was the most charming man she had ever met, very smooth. Perhaps Vincent's soft touch was just a way to get close and trick her into thinking that he couldn't possibly be behind the slayings? Maybe Lester's theory was correct. How can you ever know what someone is thinking, what their motives are?

CHAPTER THIRTY-TWO

As Peg drove home, she couldn't help but feel like she was being squeezed at both ends. Lately, Vincent seemed more interested in her than ever, and now Lester wanted her to spy on Vincent.

Now that she was alone, it all seemed ridiculous. She would go along with it anyway. What did she have to lose? What a minute, she thought suddenly. If Lester is right, that means Vincent has known all along who took Caitlin and he has been holding out on her. That suave charm of his may be his way of pointing everyone, including me, in another direction, away from the Morelli's.

"I can play that game Vincent," she said to the empty car.

Tears threatened, but she didn't know if she felt more angry, or hurt. She took a deep breath, trying to control her emotions. She looked at the dial on radio, and decided to turn it on, as a distraction. She tuned into a radio announcer talking about the recent killings, which would be covered in the next edition of "Troy Talk" set to air in 30 minutes. Apparently, they were having a police profiler come on the show to give some insight into the vigilante's mind. The city seemed to be consumed with the recent violence against criminals or parolees.

Peg felt like calling Troy and demand that he should focus on the victims. What was wrong with people? Once again the criminals were all anyone wanted to talk about. Despite what Lester said about vigilantism, who cares if someone killed those losers? People were so afraid of being politically incorrect that they masked their true feelings behind words like justice, forgiveness and mob rule. Peg's main concern was who was killing their children. That's what the people of New Orleans should be talking about! As the mother of an abducted and possibly murdered child, Peg wanted justice any way she could get it. She wanted whoever took her child away from her to be dead. She reached for her cell phone to set them straight, but just as quickly dropped the phone back in her bag. No, it would be a bad idea to expose herself, especially now that she was actually working on the case, instead of writing about it. She didn't realize how much she missed police work until she walked through the headquarters on her way out. She suddenly felt a part of all the activity that was buzzing around her.

Thoughts of her father came out of the blue and she could suddenly see him standing tall and handsome. When he was wearing his uniform; he always seemed invincible. But he was not invincible. He was dead. Now she remembered why she stopped being a cop. God! How was she going to handle all this? She had to; she had to for Caitlin and for her father.

CHAPTER THIRTY-THREE

Troy got hung up in traffic on the expressway and was running late. He needed to get to the station early to meet his special guest, the noted psychiatrist Paul Poulet. Other radio shows were interviewing top police brass, but Troy had the idea to get "a shrink on the case."

Dr. Poulet was often called on as an expert witness for the prosecutor's office. He was highly reputed among law enforcement agencies in several southern states and had written well-known thesis on the criminal mind.

Maybe the doctor could help solve the vigilante killings. Troy, like everyone else in the city, wanted to know the identity of the Crusader. Was he a saint or a sicko? People in the city, in hopes of finding the Crusader's identity, were calling on all sorts of weirdoes — fortunetellers, voodoo priests, palm readers — everyone it seemed had a special vision for these things. But Troy figured a psychiatrist might actually know something scientific.

As it turned out, the doctor was running late too.

"Slow down Troy," said Doobie, his program manager. "our doctor isn't even here yet. We still have 20 minutes till show time."

"Fine, did you get the extra call-in lines, like I asked you to? I guarantee this show will get hot."

"Five extra lines. That should be enough, I'd think."

"Let's hope so," Troy said, as he swiveled around in his chair to observe the short-stocky figure walking into the studio.

"Dr. Poulet, I presume," said Troy.

He had never met the doctor, only spoken to him on the phone. He was a male version of Dr. Ruth, but with a Cajun accent.

"You presume correctly, Mr. Troy Talk," replied the doctor, in a polite, but self-assured voice.

"Just Troy, please." Troy couldn't hide his smile. This was going to be a great show. For once he wished they had video.

"Of course, so how do you want to do this?" Dr. Poulet asked, eager to please.

"We'll start with reading the news about the latest vigilante attacks. I won't go into great detail, because I know everyone has seen those TV reports over and over. But we need to set the scene. After that, I will introduce you as our special guest, who may help shed light on the psychological profile of our Crusader," explained Troy.

"Well at this point, I'm not sure I have a lot of insight on the case. But I can certainly provide some general information and answer questions."

Troy led the doctor to the DJ's booth. Dr. Poulet sat in an orange canvas director's chair next to Troy. He took a sip of water and cleared his throat. Troy gulped his black coffee. He showed the doctor how to work the headphones and mics. Then the show's signature music was signaling the beginning of Troy's show. Troy rushed through his opening dialogue, so there would be plenty of time for questions from callers. He introduced the good doctor and gave his listeners some background information and then they plunged right into the call-in lines.

Doobie had spent the last 15 minutes setting up the callers, after the earlier promo telling listeners the call-in lines were open. Doobie did a great job screening out the really whacked out weirdoes, while leaving just enough borderline loonies to make the show interesting. It was really an art and Doobie was an artist. Troy didn't know what he would do without him. He saw Doobie giving him the thumbs up for the first caller.

"First caller, line one, go ahead."

"My name is John and I want to ask the doctor to give us a psychological profile of the Crusader."

Troy smiled at the doctor and shook his head.

Troy nodded yes, to indicate that the doctor was free to take over.

"Now that's a tall order," Dr. Poulet said in a long slow drawl. "Since I have no information, other than what the rest of us are getting from the media. As you know the police are keeping the case very closed to outsiders."

Seeing Troy's worried expression, the doctor smiled at him and continued.

"However; I can tell you that there have been many cases of vigilantism in our history. Usually, the person starts out with a cause of some sort like the Ku Klux Klan. Someone may join the group thinking that they are going to save the white race and preserve Southern values. But of course, they become killers and the only real driving force is prejudice and their own insanity and insecurity. These people may feel wronged in life and that others are to blame for their miseries. They look for ways to get even.

"These driving forces may be similar in the case of the Crusader. The person may not only be angry, but also filled with a sense of duty. They see their victims as criminals — the very worst sorts. The Crusader is courageously ridding the city of molesters and possible child porn site operators. But the other component: the insecurity. The Crusader may have had a childhood or life experience that left him feeling impotent. And so you have the two themes: a cause to fight and a need to feel strong."

The doctor was warming up to his favorite subject and the words were flowing off his tongue.

Troy was ecstatic. He could hardly sit still in his chair. This was exactly the kind of show he was hoping for.

"Okay let's have the next question."

"Do you think the Crusader will ever be caught?"

"Well, in my opinion: yes. Mass murderers want to be caught. They are crying out for help or seeking attention and they will eventually trip up somehow. That's why a criminal will often return to the crime scene, or purposely leave a handprint somewhere, or in this case, choose a theme. Each time, three have died. I would guess that there are other similarities or another common theme among the six murders that the police are keeping under wraps. Of course, many of them end up taking their own lives in the end — as a final statement. The vigilante wants to be heard and so at some point, something usually happens that gives the police a lead."

"We have a caller on line three," announced Troy, wanting to keep things moving along.

"Hi Troy; love your show."

"Thanks, tell us your name."

"I'm Sam and I live in Westwego. I'm sure you've heard of the place. This town has become famous now — for more than just the swamp tour," he chuckled.

"Thanks. What would you like to ask Dr. Poulet?"

"I would like to know if you think the Crusader is really someone who is insane, or who is maybe someone who could be our next door neighbor...if you know what I mean?"

"Yes, of course. You are asking if a normal person, someone like a neighbor or coworker, could be driven to become a vigilante — or does a person have to have already been programmed to become a mass killer?"

"Yes, exactly," said Sam.

"This brings us to the very nature of animal behavior: genetics versus the environment. Do you know that a larger percentage of criminals have an extra Y chromosome not found in the general population? Or that many of them were abused as children? So there are very strong genetic and environmental explanations for one's behavior – or deviant behavior. On the other hand, many murders are crimes of passion from normal individuals. A jilted lover, for instance. Gang wars, wife battering, random acts of gun violence are crimes of passion, often not premeditated."

The caller interrupted, "But it seems the Crusader killings are premeditated, so that would mean that the person may already have a programmed criminal mind and may have a police record."

"Well, not so fast. It's not so clear. It's very possible that the person is the guy next door – or even the girl next door – and has been waiting for the right trigger so to speak, to act out the rage."

"What kind of trigger might that be?"

"There's no way to know."

Troy interrupted, knowing that Dr. Poulet was starting to get too entwined in philosophical jargon. That was always the problem with doctors; they eventually would ramble their way into their world of Socratic oratory.

"This is talk radio for God's sake," he muttered under his breath.

"Line 4, go ahead."

"You know, I hope the person is the guy next door. You know why, because I got one of them mother-*Bleep*ing child molesters living right down the street."

Troy broke in, "Caller please watch your language we don't want any more FCC fines than we can afford to pay."

"Sorry Troy, but there are two little kids living there, too and nobody knows for sure where they belong. I've talked to the police and they say there is nothing that can be done, since the guy served his time. Now how can someone serve enough time to make up for hurting a child? So Crusader, I hope you *are* my neighbor!"

"So, Dr. Poulet, what do you think about that caller?"

"I would like to tell her, and others, that this kind of thinking that we have to watch our for," his voice growing stern.

"The only thing worse than a town having a vigilante, is a town having a 'mob' vigilante scene when your average citizen crosses the line of civil disobedience. This kind of attitude will really feed the vigilante's ego."

"It looks like that's all the time we have," Troy said, trying to quickly wrap things up.

"Thanks for coming on the show, Dr. Poulet. We'll have to get you back on real soon. Thanks for listening to Troy Talk."

"Great show doc," said Troy, helping remove the headphones from Dr. Poulet's head.

"Well that was very interesting. I think I like radio. You know I always thought I should have a show like that Frasier guy on television. Think of all the people I could help. How did you get started with your show, Troy?"

Oh boy, thought Troy, another one with radio stardust in his eyes. Something about being on the radio, your voice traveling over hundreds of miles really got some people going. Troy should have known he was one of them.

"Doobie our program manager will be glad to give you some background information about how a show is formatted."

Troy smiled at Doobie. As the doctor turned towards Doobie, he mouthed "thanks."

Doobie smiled and led the doctor — and aspiring radio star — back towards the front office. He hoped Doobie could get rid of him easily, or else he was gonna owe him a case of beer. Doobie got his name from his wild hippie-pot-smoking days, but now his only extra-curricular pastime was drinking beer and singing in a band with his other pals at a local bar. Troy thought they had a unique sound and were great songwriters. They could've hit the big-time, but it seemed they never got that one magic break. He had seen it many times being in the radio business. Many talented groups, who had been frustrated that success kept eluding them, would eventually drift apart.

The selfish part of him was glad Doobie worked with him instead of being a famous rock 'n' roll star. Hell, if he thought about it Doobie should be glad too. Being famous would more than likely have propelled him into a darker life of drugs and maybe an early death. Feeling better about how his program director's life had turned out, Troy walked to his office to go over the rest of the week's format.

CHAPTER THIRTY-FOUR

After Peg left the office, Lester headed home. It was already getting dark and he needed time to think. He was hoping his idea to have Peg spy on the Morelli's might yield some new clues, but he knew it probably was a long shot. Peg seemed to go along with the idea, but he could tell she wasn't buying the theory that the Morelli's were behind the Crusader killings. He too was beginning to have his own doubts. The six murders had some connection; if it wasn't tied to the Morelli, then who? Lester was determined to find some answers.

Captain Jackson and other city officials were leaning harder than ever on the department. The whole place seemed to be coming apart at the seams. The frustration was getting to Lester. More and more he was thinking of how easy it would be to just quit now and subcontract for the FBI. Let Pierre and the rest of them handle the vigilante. Lester went back and forth, finally convincing himself that he needed to stick it out.

All six names must have come from some list with the exception of Hart's wife. All these men had been paroled in the last year, but so had hundreds of other men. Why these six? And who's next? These questions went round and round in Lester's mind.

The next morning, Lester planned to call Agent Glen Kyle. He knew the last murders involved interstate crimes and, as such, were being investigated by the FBI. Not to mention, the vigilante had interrupted a major sting operation by blowing up the Harts. I guess you could say that made it "personal" for the FBI. Could there be a leak in the department? Although the FBI files are kept confidential, and not even the New Orleans PD could access them, he thought he might be able to convince his FBI contact to do a search on the Harts. He knew the only way to catch the vigilante was to get one step ahead. Find out the pattern, find out who the next victim is, and set a trap. The next day, Lester placed a call to Agent Kyle.

"Lester, I can't believe you just called. I was planning on calling you. I have found something interesting in the Hart file. You know this was turned over to us because child porn crimes are a federal offense and my bosses are really pissed about your Crusader messing things up, especially since this case was tied to the same ring that we are investigating in Matamoras."

"Oh really, interesting coincidence: Does that mean I can come down and look at your files? I've spent hours of my own time trying to bust this couple, and then boom, they get murdered and all the sudden; I'm out; so you owe me."

"Well, you know Lester, my boss would have my badge if he knew we were giving anything to the NOPD; you know the turf wars that go on around here. But seeing as you are almost one of us. This time, I'll let you in."

"Gee, thanks Glen, that makes me feel so good to think I am almost one of you. What a compliment!"

"Ah shut up Lester, or I'll change my mind. I may have a lead on your Crusader killings. About three months ago, someone pulled information that included Mr. Don Hart as part of an internal search. The weird thing is the search is untraceable. Someone really high up would have had to pull it together, and not leave any trace."

"You're just full of encouragement today. I'll see you at 3 o'clock."

Lester was thinking that maybe this was a break he needed — a new lead, even if it seemed like a dead-end. Lester had the knack for turning a dead-end into a conviction. Could the five other Crusader victims be linked to the Hart FBI computer search? With a copy of the entire search, Kyle mentioned he could, at least, find out who might be the next target of the Crusader. It also brought up the disturbing thought that the Crusader may be one of their own or an FBI agent.

When he arrived at the office, Glen was already conducting another computer search on the Harts. The FBI had confiscated their email list, but there were hundreds of names and addresses to check out. The ring was international. It was going to be a huge job tracking down customers and business associates. It would cross International lines.

"Glen, I've got an idea. Can you tell me if the other five Crusader victims were also a part of the search that included Don Hart's name?" Lester simply continued their telephone conversation, as if he had just walked in from the next office and not driven fifteen minutes across town.

"That was quick, and hello to you too, Lester," said Glen with a smirk. "I already thought of that. Yes, they are."

He swiveled his chair back around to face the computer on his desk. Nervously, he began tapping his pencil on the edge.

"Were there any other names that were linked to the search?" Lester asked his voice barely above a whisper.

"Five more names," Glen said looking closely at Lester.

"So we may have found our next victim or victims and a possible lead to the Crusader."

"Lester, let's say the Crusader is not someone seeking some kind of payback. But someone who is like you, maybe a cop, who is sick of seeing these guys get off; someone who also has connections high up in the FBI. So they find a list of known 'bad guys' and start whacking them off, one by one. You said yourself; the guy's definitely a well-trained shooter.

"But," he continued, as he swiveled back around to face Lester, "These guys aren't exactly random. Three are killed in one night, and in another night, two others including the Hart woman. So someone is narrowing the list to, well, the same area or zip codes. Apparently, this is a more efficient way of killing — three at a time, or maybe he wants to attract attention, or could be just that he wants to show off. And then there is the strange calling card: a child's toy."

Glen looked at Lester, as if measuring him, and must not have seen anything he didn't like, because he slowly pulled a folded piece of paper from under his computer keyboard.

"Yeah, who wants to spend all night going all over town, when they can be gunned down efficiently, in just a few hours? Here's the list. See for yourself."

"What is more disturbing," continued Glen, his voice lowered to a whisper, "is the fact that anyone familiar with the way the FBI database searches, knows that whatever criteria was plugged in to get this particular search, would result in a list that would narrow down suspects with the first name being the most likely per the search criteria. Another very interesting fact is the killer has been following the list in the exact order it was printed."

"So," whispered Lester as he reached for the list, "the Crusader may be FBI."

"It's possible, which is also why I was going to contact you. This is way too hot and high up the ladder for me to check into. I never gave you this list. And, if you should stake out any of the remaining names you were purely working on a hunch. I want nothing to do with this," said Glen, as he slowly held out the list for Lester to take.

"No problem."

Lester had already turned and was headed out the door, when Agent Kyle's next words made him turn around again.

"Oh, by the way, your boy Pierre, keep a good eye on him. I'm working on some of your concerns and it doesn't look too good."

Mentally, Lester changed gears and frowned as he focused on Pierre. Shit, that idiot was gonna land his stupid butt in jail. Lester was sure Pierre would burn all his designer duds if he really thought about spending any time in jail. Cops were very popular in jail, and in ways no one ever wanted to be popular.

"Don't worry, I have him under control. Just let me know when you have enough that will stick. I want to know before anything goes down."

He was already thinking about the aspirin bottle he threw in the glove compartment that morning. The dull thumping that had lurked all morning had begun to turn into a regular pounding.

"No problem," Glen yelled to Lester, who was already through his office door and headed for the elevators.

"I think he needs a vacation worse than I do," Glen muttered to himself, as he sighed and turned back to the keyboard.

CHAPTER THIRTY-FIVE

Peg decided to take a few days off work. She was exhausted and becoming bored at work ever since Bill took her off the vigilante case.

"Sorry Peg, this one's just too big a fish for you; we need our experienced crime reporters on this one."

"Gee thanks, after I was able to provide him with the only decent lead, so far," she mumbled to herself.

After a few days, Peg shrugged it off. She was too tired to care about her so-called career anymore. She was actually anxious to spend all her time on Lester's request.

"Let those big-shot reporters have at it. They want the glory, let them work for it; I'm sure as hell not going to lift a hand to help. Screw them!"

If they only knew that she had just been down to the precinct and could be feeding them classified information, they'd think twice about taking her off the case.

"They're idiots."

Peg called in to work and asked for some time off.

"I'm guess I'm not doing as well as I thought I was. I need some time to rest and get my head straightened out."

"Don't worry Peg; you need to take it easy."

Bill sounded concerned.

"Just take all the time you need. If you like, you can just call us when you are ready to come back to work. Of course, just let us know if there is anything we can do, to help," he added in a patronizing voice.

"Okay, thanks."

At that moment she realized that part of her life was over. She wasn't ever going back to the paper.

She knew what Bill was thinking — she had come to work too soon and was now paying the emotional price. She didn't like it when others perceived her as weak.

She knew time off wouldn't change her mind so she dialed the office back and got a surprised Bill on the phone.

"Peg, hello, what's up?"

"Bill, I've decided to quit. You took me off the one story I was really interested in. I just can't see going back to writing health stories. Please tell Andrea to clean out my desk and box up my belongings. I'll come by next week to pick them up."

"Are you sure you want to do this? Why don't you just think about it, perhaps take that time off we discussed earlier. You can always decide later. We can even talk about some other assignments," pleaded Bill.

"I've thought about it. You can't change my mind. I'm sorry." Peg forcefully hung up the phone. She immediately felt better.

The next morning Peg awoke and actually felt rested; no nightmares had disturbed her sleep. She made the right decision about quitting her job. It was a relief to not have to go through the mundane routine of setting her alarm clock and fighting the bridge traffic. She didn't want to see anyone at the paper. She had her laptop computer and could still follow the

Crusader killings and would have more time to figure out what Morelli was up to.

Peg really didn't need the income from her job. She could live on the bonds and interest from the money that her father had willed to her. Her mother's life insurance money was still almost fully intact. Though she had used some to get her education, Peg was careful to pay it all back a little at a time. She told herself it would be for Caitlin's education, a gift from the grandmother she never knew. Now there may not be a reason to keep it intact.

Thinking about the money sent Peg's mood on a sudden downward course. Her thoughts again moved to her past and her family and all that she had lost. She was only twelve when her mother died; yet, Peg still hung on to some hope of a future with a family of her own.

When Caitlin came along, she was filled with joy. She hadn't been happy since before her father had died. She wished her parents could have seen their granddaughter. She had recovered, because she had Caitlin and the two of them were a family. Now, she was alone again. Peg was overwhelmed by a profound sadness. How quickly her moods changed. For the past months, she was able to go for days without being depressed. Her energy returned. But now she felt the darkness creeping in again.

Suddenly very tired, she decided to go back to bed until the ringing phone jolted her awake.

"Who is it now?" she said as she picked up the phone, still groggy from sleep.

"Peg, it's Vincent, Are you okay?"

"If one more person asks me that question I am going to SCREAM!" yelled Peg.

"Oh, sorry," said Vincent. "I guess you're having a bad day. You do have to tell me why you're not at work."

"I quit my job today. Happy? Now I just want to wallow for awhile and I want everyone to leave me alone."

"Well, no Peg, I cannot leave you alone. You can't give up now, we are getting close. I feel it."

Peg's thoughts darted to her earlier conversation with Lester. The Morelli family has already identified Caitlin's abductor; they're just sending out the Crusader to throw the cops off.

Could it be true? Peg wondered. She realized that she couldn't give up, not until all the facts were there. What was wrong with her? She needed someone to shake her till her teeth rattled. She was suddenly very glad Vincent had called.

"Okay, Vincent, I'll try to get myself out of this wasteland of misery that I seem caught up in."

"Has it gotten that bad?" Vincent asked, the sincerity of his voice calmed her.

"It's just been a hard week. When do you want to meet? I'm pretty flexible now that I'm a lady of leisure," said Peg, with a small laugh, sounding a little more like her old self.

"Let's have an early dinner. I'll pick you up at six."

Peg hung up and headed for a cup of coffee and a shower. She suddenly realized her usual conservative reserve was gone. Since she had tossed her job out the window, any leftover caution was tossed out, too. What did she have to be cautious about? Her future was no longer something she must nurture and protect. The realization was instantly liberating and a little intoxicating. She could be whatever or whoever she wanted. She could hate Vincent one day and be deliciously seduced by him the next. Her life was a blank page. Since she didn't care about the ending anymore, she could be daring and take the chances she would have normally passed up.

Suddenly, she felt a surge of energy. The weighted heavy feeling had left. A light in her mind had been turned on, and made her realize that she had been living too long in the past. From now on, she would take chances, live on the edge and do whatever it took, without thinking about the risks. She felt liberated.

Coffee in hand, she decided after her shower to do a little shopping. Her wardrobe had gotten quite shabby; she hadn't bought anything new in years. The wrinkled tan Dockers, faded white blouse, and worn shoes were a sad statement to the decline of her wardrobe, not to mention the dreary faded red terry cloth bathrobe she was practically living in.

She didn't have to worry anymore about saving for a rainy day. Who would she leave her money to anyway? She was going shopping and would not even look at the price tags. If she liked it, she would buy it.

CHAPTER THIRTY-SIX

Vincent had made reservations at Galatoire's, one of Peg's favorites. She could tell by his continued admiring appraisal that he appreciated her recent shopping spree. She was amazed at how good everything looked on her. She was wearing smooth black slacks with a thin, red low-cut, v-neck sweater and a soft black, leather jacket. The black boots were the finishing touch. She spotted the outfit in the window and tried it on. To the saleswoman's delight, she had purchased the entire ensemble. She remembered not even listening to the total as she held out her American Express card. Next stop was jewelry and makeup. She sat for a make-over and purchased everything the girl suggested. She treated herself to a matching set of designer silver earrings, necklace and bracelet. She had to admit she didn't even recognize herself when she looked in the mirror while she waited for Vincent. She even had her hair trimmed and styled. Soft blond curls framed her face.

The look on Vincent's face when she answered the door was priceless. She was certain that for a brief moment, he had no idea who she was. To be honest she didn't know who she was and that was an intoxicating feeling.

"Peg? Is that you?"

She laughed, grabbed her new clutch and pulled the door shut behind her.

"I like this new lady of leisure," he said, as he recovered and followed her to the car.

She ordered the crabmeat casserole, a rich combination of a tender white crabmeat in a duo of treats, a béarnaise and béchamel cheese sauce. It was the most incredible tasting meal she ever had. It was so rich, she almost didn't finish it.

Vincent ordered the almond-crusted trout with crabmeat stuffing, a specialty of the house, and saved the last bite for Peg. They ended the meal sharing a crème brulee trio.

After dinner, they walked down a few blocks to the Monteleone for the meeting. The latest Crusader killers dominated the conversation.

"I bet the police would love to investigate our group. We sure have plenty of motives to strike back. Though of course, we are a nonviolent group," one woman said.

"Yes, let's get started on something more positive."

Peg was thinking about what an amazing skill Vincent had at putting a positive light on the situation.

"I have an idea that I would like the group to consider, a foundation for victims of crime. I was thinking about distributing funds to help families who are searching for kidnapped children. You know, the police resources go only so far; most families have to use their own money to hire private detectives."

The group spent the hour discussing the idea, and a plan of action was developed. After the meeting ended, Peg and Vincent took the elevator down together.

"I really liked your idea of having a fund set up for families who have missing children. As you say, some families don't have the resources to keep up the search for their children. And some children are eventually returned home," Peg said.

A sad expression flickered across her features. Vincent noticed the change and sought to lighten the mood.

"Peg, I hate to end the evening with you so soon. Would you like to come to my house for a nightcap? There are some things I would like to talk about and I just don't want to go to a noisy bar. How about it?" he said, gazing intensely into her eyes.

Peg felt like Vincent was reading her mind. She too was looking for an opportunity to extend their discussions, and try to find out if Vincent knew something about the Crusader killings. She was also anxious to stretch her wings and see where her new outlook on life would lead her.

"Sure, why not, I'd love to see your house. Isn't it in the Garden District?"

"Yes, but I have to warn you, I haven't been keeping things up like I used to. It's a bit of a disaster right now."

When Peg had first moved to New Orleans, she loved to drive up and down St. Charles Avenue, admiring the luxurious Southern mansions in the Garden District, with their groomed lawns, gazeboes and fish ponds. She wondered what they looked like inside and what it would be like to live in one of them. The charm of St. Charles Avenue was one thing that had never changed about New Orleans. The old-time streetcars clapped their way up and down the avenue.

At Christmastime, garlands of glittering, twinkling lights were strung in scallops across the wrought iron laced balconies of the mansions. Enormous wreaths with large ribbons and bows were hung on the front doors. She and Caitlin would take long drives along the avenues on Christmas Eve and marvel at the extravagant decorations. If Caitlin were here, she would be thrilled to be able to actually go inside one of these beautiful homes that always seemed to be right out of a fairy tale.

Sometimes the memories of Caitlin would make her so sad, she couldn't breathe, but other times she was filled with an unspeakable fury. Having Vincent around, calmed her and gave her a sense of comfort and relief from her frequent mood swings. Despite what Lester thought, she wanted to trust him. She also needed to shake off those thoughts that threatened to drag her back into depression. She was not that person anymore.

"Well, here we are. Like I said, the place is not what it should be."

It was beautiful, breath-taking, really. Black wrought-iron double-door gates opened up into a brick-paved private courtyard. It was hidden by thick vegetation that had woven into the iron fence. The gardeners had cut and trimmed the hedge into a uniform box that encompassed the rails of the tall fence, like skin and muscle covering the bony interior.

Blooming, vibrant color was everywhere. A soft tinkling sound drew her attention to a graceful round fountain. Greek maidens and cherubs danced with urns held high from where the water flowed in a soothing river of sound to refill the wide basin. The flowers and scents assaulted her senses from all sides.

The heavy sweet smell of butterfly ginger floated and mingled with jasmine, camellias, begonias, caladium and impatiens. Rose of Montana blossoms peeked out in bursts of color from the natural green fence that encircled the garden and held it out like a basket bursting with fresh flowers.

Everywhere she looked, color and scent pulled her gaze. She found herself slowly twirling in a circle in her attempt to take it all in.

Vincent laughed softly at her reaction and grabbed her arms, propelling her toward the ornately carved double doors. A mosaic of stained glass adorned the center square of each massive door.

Vincent opened the door to reveal a marbled entryway, and a showcase suspended double oak staircase. A huge chandelier hanging above came to life and soft sparkling light filled the entire area.

"Well, I must agree, Vincent, this place is really a mess. You must fire your housekeeper and the gardener," Peg tried to keep a straight face but laughter bubbled up and twisted her lips into a crooked smile.

Vincent burst out laughing: "I guess I do take a lot of this for granted. It's just that I remember what this place used to look like when I was growing up here. My mother kept it up; now, I really don't have the time."

"Oh, I am sorry Vincent. It was just so funny the way you described the place, as if there would be cobwebs in the corners, a garden overgrown, trees draped in Spanish moss, cracking paint and dusty worn furniture.

"That garden was magnificent and this house is so stunning, so the contrast in my mind was just too funny; I had to bring you down a peg or two. You really should see how the majority of New Orleans lives before you call this place unkept."

Peg sat down on a classical 16th-century designed, red velvet couch.

Vincent walked to a cabinet across the room that concealed a minibar.

She looked incredible sitting on that red sofa. He didn't know what had gotten into him, but he was seeing a whole different Peg. And he liked what he saw.

When he opened the doors, glass canisters filled with liquor and glassware sparkled like diamonds in the refection of the mirrored cabinet. Peg's practical mind was wondering who had the tiresome job of cleaning and polishing everything so that it shown so brilliantly. Vincent would laugh again if he could read her thoughts.

"What would you like to drink? How about a double? It seems my plans for a romantic evening have crumbled on me."

"What are you having?" Peg said as her laughter subsided to a soft smile of amusement.

"How about some Amaretto. I have a special stock that I bought in Venice."

"Amaretto, it is."

They sat silently sipping the sweet, intoxicating drink.

"These are beautiful glasses. Did these come from Italy, too?" asked Peg, holding the glass up to the light.

"Yes, this gold-rimmed style is a Venetian classic. Peg, have you ever been to Italy?"

"The closest I will ever come will probably be that new hotel in Las Vegas modeled after Venice. I hear they have gondolas and a fake river that encircles the inside and if you look up the ceilings are painted like a sky. I think if I ever went to the real Venice, I probably would never want to come back," she said, as they both laughed.

"Yes, that's the worst part, having to leave such a country and come back here. I'll have to take you, give you a personal tour."

While his eyes were still smiling, Peg knew he was being serious. She was stunned by her willingness to run home and pack for the promised trip. Peg was drawn to Vincent's dark, good looks, but flashes of a different more rugged face kept appearing unbidden. The Amaretto felt warm and rich and it helped her relax. She found herself comparing Vincent to Lester. She wasn't sure who she would rather be with.

Vincent was so handsome and sensitive to her needs; Life with him would be one adventure after another; while Lester brought out her temper and a strange longing to run her fingers through his curly brown hair. She kept remembering what it felt like to be held safe and warm in his strong arms.

Aware that she had drifted away to her own thoughts, Peg looked up and caught Vincent staring at her; his own emotions shown clearly in his penetrating gaze. Peg blushed and looked across the room trying to gather her composure.

"Peg, why don't you get away for the weekend? You need some rest. I know the perfect place," Vincent said, pouring on all his charm.

She wanted to talk to Vincent about the case, but he kept directing the conversation to her. Each time he filled her glass with more liqueur, he moved a little closer to her. She tried to break the spell by getting back to her purpose of seeing Vincent. She needed to get information.

"Vincent, you know, just because I quit the paper doesn't mean that I am giving up on the story," she said, trying to direct the conversation back to the Crusader case.

"I know Peg, but right now, let's just relax; you can think about all that later."

Something about the way his cologne mingled with his body scent made her want to close her eyes and pretend she was somewhere else – that she was someone else. Peg felt like she should move away, but she enjoyed the warmth and the closeness – and the way his voice tickled her ear as he whispered, "Perhaps I should get you home now, before we drink this whole bottle."

Peg drank her last sip and turned to Vincent. She did not want to go; she wanted to stay; she needed to stay. It had been so long since she had allowed herself to feel this way. She wanted to follow her emotions – what did she have to hold back for? She remembered how good it felt to be in his arms, to be embraced, and she was free to pursue whatever course she desired. Right now, she desired to be held, kissed and loved.

At that moment, he put his arms around her and pulled her closer for a kiss. His kiss was soft as silk, but demanding and she felt her body respond-ing. She closed her eyes, yielding to his passionate embrace. Her body was surrendering to the effects of the alcohol and his physical attraction, but she didn't care. It had been too long.

"Come to bed with me," he said softly into her ear.

He reached under her sweater, gently caressing her breast, while he pushed his tongue deeply into her mouth. Her answer was to wrap her arms around his neck while losing herself in his kisses.

Next thing she knew, they were naked on smooth silk sheets. The warmth of Vincent's strong body and his urgent lips on her neck and breasts drove every thought from her mind and rushes of pleasure consumed her. Dizzying sensations erupted throughout her body. Long denied release, her body had a mind of its own and took over completely.

Peg was awakened by a soft kiss on the cheek. Vincent sat beside her on the bed, remembering how surprisingly wild and passionate Peg's response had been. He had started out with gentle caresses, but Peg had matched his strength and pushed their lovemaking to an explosive climax. Just the thought of their night together made him want to strip off his clothes and climb back in bed next to her warm yielding body. She rolled over and looked up at him, rubbing her eyes, still half asleep.

"Peg, I'm sorry but I have to get down to the courthouse this morning, but you stay here and sleep. I'll try to make it back by four."

His eyes expressed his desire for her as he smiled, before leaving, he leaned over and kissed her soft lips and walked out of the room, before Peg had a chance to say anything. She pulled up the sheets over her naked body and drifted back to sleep, exhausted from the night's passion.

When Peg finally opened her eyes, the midday sun was filling the room with light. As she sat up in bed, a small note fell down from the covers. She picked it up.

"Peg, please stay. I want to see you again tonight. I'll call you at lunch," signed, 'love' Vincent.

Peg found her clothes neatly hung across the large armchair in the bedroom. She dressed and was about to leave the house, when she heard the phone ring. She was afraid it might be Vincent. She wasn't ready to talk to him. Her feelings about Vincent were all jumbled. She still wasn't comfortable with herself and how easily he had seduced her. Seduced, how could she say that after the way she acted last night! Her cheeks burned remembering her uninhibited passion. God, what must he think of her? Now the entanglements had begun.

She thought of last night as a fling, a surrendering of emotions, but it seemed Vincent had read more into it. She was not ready to become entwined in a new relationship. She didn't think she ever would be. Why was it that life seemed to throw you into relationships at the wrong times; and whenever you look for it, you can never find it?

She let the answering machine take the call. She was expecting to hear Vincent's voice, but it was a woman's.

"Darling, I guess you must be in court. Your father and I would like you to come to the lake house this weekend. We haven't seen you in so long. You need to take your mind off the investigation. It's gone on too long; you know your father is handling it. You have to let go. Anyway, please consider coming down. I love you."

How strange this felt to hear Vincent's mother's voice, thought Peg. It surprised her that he stayed in such close contact with his family. His mother sounded really warm and caring. Maybe she had been to harsh in judging Vincent more by what she had heard from others about him and his family.

"Well, I guess he did manage to take his mind off it for a while anyway," Peg chuckled out loud, as she sat looking at Vincent's bedroom.

But what did she mean about the investigation? Did Vincent still have 'his people' working on the case? It would make sense that the Morellis would probably not give up until they found some answers. But why had Vincent never discussed this with Peg? Suddenly, Peg felt a sense of betrayal. Vincent had mentioned to her that his family had conducted its own investigation, but he made it sound like it was over. Vincent was still hiding something. Maybe he was the type of man that said "love you" the way other people said "good-bye." Now she felt like the stupid one reading so much into a silly note. She had stayed in this house too long. She needed to finish what she came for and get the hell out. What was wrong with her?

Her police instincts took over. She frantically began searching Vincent's room. She opened his closet and rummaged through a few boxes — nothing but old pictures. She found a metal, locked box under the bed, but knew it would be waste of time to try to find a key. She moved on to a wooden file cabinet next to the computer armoire in his bedroom. She pulled open the drawer. The files were organized according to months. She sifted through the files and found bank statements. She opened the envelopes and sorted through the checks. What was she looking for; she wasn't sure, maybe just something out of the ordinary. Just as she had reached the last month, she realized that she may have found some evidence — a check to Mitchell Parks Investigators for $3,000.00. In the same file was a brown envelope with Parks written on the front. The envelope contained monthly reports. She was shocked when she found a photograph of herself in the file. The picture showed her and Lester on the sofa in her house. The photo was fuzzy. Her anger started a slow burn as she realized it must have been taken by someone parked across the street. He had someone spying on her before he ever met her!

The picture of her and Lester made her feel suddenly guilty that she was sitting in Vincent's bedroom after sleeping with him. It was like he could see her as she stared at the picture. The picture totally erased any guilt that she felt for rummaging through Vincent's desk. Too nervous to concentrate on the reports, Peg just put everything back and decided to come later with a camera to make copies. Peg scribbled a note to Vincent: "I can't make it tonight, I'll call you tomorrow."

As Peg was walking out the door, she stopped and began thinking about the files. After learning of Vincent's deception and remembering her vow to take chances, she couldn't just walk away; so she went back and grabbed the envelope.

Peg spent the next 24 hours reading the reports. Most were similar to the reports she had seen from the police records. After Angela's death, there was an intensive search for suspects. The local vendors had been questioned about the missing child. In a city like New Orleans, with tourists swarming the streets, how could anyone really be expected to remember one little girl? But there had been one old woman who said she might have seen her. It was a Haitian woman who worked in the Sweet Shop. The woman said she remembered a little girl who came in looking around at the counter full of candies and different flavored pralines. The woman thought it was strange, because she wasn't with an adult and, she had noticed a strange man lurking around outside the door. Although the child had long dark hair, like Angela's, she couldn't make a definite identification. The police officers working that day were also questioned about the girl. But no one could confirm the woman's story. Vincent had a copy of the precinct's assignment of cops who were working the shifts that day. Peg was surprised to see Lester's name included. Lester had never mentioned to her that he had been working at the station the day Angela was kidnapped — and also was on duty the night of the parade. But then she remembered that Lester was the first to come to see her at the hospital. Yes, that makes sense that he would be the first in line to investigate. The leads later shifted to a possible kidnapping motive: The Morelli's family business and obvious enemies of the family. Most of the information in the files had already been published in the press. Peg kept searching for something new. She began thinking about her own daughter's disappearance. Where would a little girl wonder off to? She remembered Caitlin loved to go to the Sweet Shop on Decatur Street and stand outside the window looking at the assortment of confections being created: Creole pralines, pecan rolls and fudge. She even remembered the old lady who worked in the shop. She was always in the front window, mixing up the sugar, pecans and butter, in a ritual that went back decades. How could a child disappear with no one noticing? And how could it happen twice?

Peg put the files back together and called Vincent. He didn't answer, so she left a message on the machine.

"I changed my mind. I would love to have dinner tonight. Call me."

Peg wasn't ready to spend another night with Vincent, but she had to get the file and envelope back before he noticed they were missing.

The two met for dinner at The Court of Two Sisters. She wore another of her new outfits, a thin cotton shift that hugged her upper body but flowed freely around her legs. She wore strappy sandals without pantyhose and was chilled the minute the sun went down and dusk settled over the courtyard.

Vincent was wearing a pinned-striped shirt that complimented his navy blue silk suit. Seeming to anticipate her every need, he took off his jacket and draped it around her shoulders. She tried not to think about the magical passion of the night before. She longed for the evening to pass quickly.

They ate dinner in a charming corner of the courtyard under one of the spreading branches of the large tree that dominated the restaurant patio. The garden had a gazebo and situated at the near the back wall were the statues the "Sisters" on a fountain pedestal. Strings of tiny white lights decorated the branches and hung across the open areas of the verandas. She was not sure if it was the atmosphere, fine food, or Vincent's efforts to charm and make her feel special, which melted some of the reserve that had threatened to keep the evening on an unromantic keel.

After dinner, and a dessert of bread pudding, they strolled through the French Quarter. Vincent invited Peg back to his place for a drink. She accepted.

While Vincent was in the kitchen, uncorking the bottle of wine, Peg headed to the bathroom. There was a connecting door to the bedroom, so she quickly went to the desk and removed the file and envelope from her large bag and inserted them back in the file cabinet.

Her heart was pounding and her hands were shaking, but she managed to close the drawer slowly, without making a sound. She returned to the library only seconds before Vincent entered with their drinks.

"Vincent, I'm sorry but I'm not feeling well, would you mind taking me home?"

Peg rubbed her forehead in a distracted manner and gave him a pained, but apologetic expression.

"I may have caught a chill during dinner. I keep forgetting summer is gone and fall will soon be winter. I'm very tired; I think I need some rest. I have had some trouble with migraines lately and I think the red wine may have brought another one on. I'm so sorry. It has been such a wonderful evening. I hope you won't be upset with me."

She felt bad to see how disappointed and worried Vincent looked.

"I could never be upset with you," Vincent said, giving her a quick smile.

Vincent drove Peg home and left her at her door with a soft kiss on her lips. He resisted the urge to ask if he could come inside. Peg had awakened a desire in him, one that he thought he would never feel again; He hungered for more.

As she watched Vincent's car drive away, Peg felt strangely alone and regretful. What was wrong with her?

She had a hard time getting to sleep; she kept thinking about Vincent and then the files. She wondered if she had put the brown envelope in the right spot. Oh well, nothing can be done about it now.

CHAPTER THIRTY-SEVEN

The next morning, Peg called Lester. She was anxious to tell him the news about Vincent. She placed a call to Lester's direct line.

"Lester, I have some information that I got from Vincent's house. Can we meet?"

"Sure Peg, I am interested in what you found out. But let's not get into it over the phone. How about you come down to the station?"

As he hung up the phone, Lester felt confused by his reactions. On one hand, he was hoping Peg had discovered something that would help break this case, but on the other, he was jealous that Vincent and Peg had spent time alone. He had asked her to come to the station so he could see her. He needed to see her and reassure himself that she was not getting too involved with Vincent. He didn't trust Vincent when it came to women.

Peg hung up the phone, feeling a rush of excitement in anticipation of seeing Lester. Her feelings confused her. How could she be with Vincent and still have these thoughts about Lester? Her feelings for Vincent weren't purely physical; they also shared many of the same tastes.

Vincent was unreadable, mysterious, dangerous and exciting. Lester was like being home. He was warmth, comfort and stability — a rock to cling to and someone you could always count on to be there. He was also damn sexy, though Peg had done her best not to think about that whenever she was near him. Would she be able to do that now that she had slept with Vincent? How could she look him in the eye without betraying what she had done?

When she arrived at the station, Lester was waiting on the steps to meet her.

"I like that dress, Peg. You look wonderful. How are you?" He was smiling, genuinely happy to see her.

He had also noticed her new wardrobe. He was shaken by the thought that her change in appearance might be due to the fact that she had been with Vincent. He hated the thought that Vincent might have brought out this change in her.

"Well, with those kinds of comments, I'm feeling better all the time," she said blushing.

Lester brought Peg back to the office and offered her a cup of coffee. He didn't seem to be in any hurry to discuss Vincent.

"Peg, have you ever taken one of those plantation tours?" asked Lester, distractedly.

Peg, surprised by the strange off-the-wall question and already feeling anxious about seeing Lester replied, "Why do you ask?"

"Oh, well I was thinking about taking my mother on one."

Peg saw a brochure for the Laura Plantation on his desk. She picked it up and began reading: "Step into a fascinating world of the Creoles, who lived apart from the American life-style more than 200 years ago. It's a real plantation with 150 year-old slave cabins."

"Read on Peg," said Lester, smiling at her reaction to the brochure.

"It says that in these cabins, slaves retold the West-African folktales, most famous of which was 'Compare Lapin,' known to us as Br'er Rabbit. This is also where many of the present day voodoo ceremonies were learned and passed down from generation to generation, even up to the present day."

"No kidding," she said, wondering why Lester was acting strange and wasn't asking her questions about Vincent.

"You know Pierre Martens, my partner, is a Creole. He may even be related to ol' Laura. Those Creoles are a bit spooky if you ask me. But they represent a real underground community here in the city and still practice the voodoo ceremonies; did you know that?" he said, sounding like a schoolteacher.

"Yes Lester, I may be from Baton Rouge, but I still know a little bit about the Crescent City, too," she said smirking back at him and playing along, until she figured out what game he was playing.

"Then, do you know that the Morellis have for the last century been enemies of the Bergeron's, one of the biggest Creole families in New Orleans?" he continued.

"No Lester, but I have a feeling you plan on telling me."

Peg felt blindsided by Lester's sudden change in conversation. She found herself strangely on the defensive again. She was so stupid. Lester was a pro and had used his information gathering skills to make her relax before getting to what he really wanted to talk about. She felt stupid and angry. Why did he feel he needed to use subversive tactics in questioning her? Wasn't she doing all this at his request? She felt betrayed. She tried to hide her emotions, but was sure Lester had already registered each one as it passed across her face. She had revealed everything without saying a word. She crossed her arms across her chest in a defensive pose and gave him her best unimpressed glare.

"The Morellis came to New Orleans during the turn of the century, along with boatloads of immigrants from Europe. As a matter of fact, that's when many Irish and Germans like my family came along. But the Italians were used to running things. When they settled in, they quickly began taking over the shipping industries, cotton, tobacco, and sugar cane plantations. By then, there were no slaves to work the plantations and cotton fields. Those who stayed became live-in servants to the aristocracy.

"The Creoles had become good at business, but they were spoiled and used to a more indulgent social lifestyle of masked balls and parades. Families like the Morellis moved in, bringing low-wage workers from the north. Many Creoles found their own families working as the 'help' for the same businesses that their ancestors had started, while watching their brown-skinned beauties seduced by the wealthy Italian mob sharks.

Peg interrupted: "Somewhere you're going to tell me when the voodoo dolls come in, right? So, the Creoles hate the Italians and think of them all as gangsters. What's new about that! But there's not a lot they can do, except call on the spirits and their mammies' prayers for help – and put pins in dolls – is there?"

"Ha Ha. But Peg, did it ever occur to you that the Morelli kidnapping was a vengeance killing?"

Peg's thoughts shifted back to reality. She was here to discuss the kidnappings.

"That thought had occurred to me, but why would they take Caitlin, too?"

"Exactly, that's why I'm thinking that the two may not be related. I'm sorry but it may not be the same person. I just don't think it fits Peg. I also can't get my mind off thinking that Angela was targeted by one of Morelli's enemies," he said.

"You have to accept that we may be talking about two different cases. We need to rule out the Morelli connection first. So tell me, what have you found out?"

"Well," said Peg, pausing for a moment, because she suddenly didn't want to tell Lester everything that happened. He may suspect, but he wouldn't really know unless she told him. She also felt strangely protective of Vincent and could tell that Lester was totally focused on the Morellis and unable to see any other motives in the case. She didn't like being lectured.

"I can't explain it all to you, but I know for a fact that Vincent still has an investigator on the case, some guy by the name of Mitchell Parks. I found a check made out to him for $3,000. The reports are unremarkable, except for one."

Lester was clearly interested.

"It was an old lady from the Sweet Shop; you know the one down in the French Market."

Lester patted his stomach.

"Yes Peg, I know that shop all too well."

She refused to let him break through her stiff reserve, sticking to the facts.

"The old lady said she saw a little girl that fits Angela's description, wandering around in her store. Shortly afterwards, she saw a man with strange dark eyes, who glared at her and ran off."

"Yes, Peg. The same woman claimed she might have seen Caitlin. We think she is just an old woman wanting to get some attention for her shop. We investigated her, thoroughly. In both cases she told us that she might have seen the child, and a strange man. The woman couldn't give us any other information about the man. She also is very old and practices voodoo, which hurts her credibility as a reliable witness. Pierre was the one who first questioned her, and called her a wacko who clearly held a dislike for the police."

"Why didn't anyone bother to at least show the woman some photos of child molesters on parole? They could have at least brought her down to the station," she said with disappointment.

"Really Lester, this seems like sloppy police work; I would like to go back to that woman and question her. Show her some photos. Let's face it, it's the only lead we have and she claims to have seen Caitlin, too. I have to talk to her myself," she added, softening her voice and giving Lester a genuine smile.

She couldn't stand the way he was looking at her. She knew she was being very defensive. He was treating her so strangely, like he didn't trust her.

"You may be right Peg. Maybe there is something to it," conceded Lester, while thinking maybe if she followed this dead end it would help her accept what had happened.

"Sorry to rush you but I'm late for a meeting. Let me think about this and I'll get back to you."

He couldn't bring himself to ask her about how she got the information about the Mitchell Parks' check. He had pushed her right into Vincent's arms. Then he had ranted and raved like an idiot about Creoles and Italians. What was wrong with him?

Peg felt depression settle heavy on her shoulders as she left the police station. She thought she could throw all her worries out the window by changing her appearance. She couldn't escape who she was by buying new clothes. She wasn't cut out for role playing. She was always the honest type, believing the best of everyone, until they proved her wrong. That's how she wanted to be treated.

Ever since she had met Lester and Vincent, she felt as if she had to hide who she really was. The truth was she didn't know who she was anymore. Without Caitlin, she was lost. Everything was mixed up and crazy. The only thing she really wanted was to find Caitlin and the person who took her away. She decided to focus only on that goal. Vincent and Lester must only be viewed as a means to an end. They both thought Caitlin was dead. That was their reality. She realized as much as she tried deep in her heart she couldn't accept that. She probably never would, until someone showed her Caitlin's body – she hoped that would never happen.

CHAPTER THIRTY-EIGHT

Pierre rose from his chair and stretched his back. Popping noises accompanied his groans of pain. He walked over to the window. Lately, the river didn't have its usual comforting effect on him. He was running a new report on the latest slayings and the stupid computer was taking forever to retrieve and compile the data. It was ridiculous that most criminals had state of the art computer systems, while the police department hacked away at models that were considered obsolete several years ago. If he were running things, it would all be different. If the city didn't allocate funds, there were always other ways to get what you needed. Lester was just slow, stupid and too honest to lead the department like it needed. Pierre could run circles around him and the Captain. Out with the old and in with the new and improved. Anyone who resisted his changes would be put out to pasture.

The thought of running the department made Pierre smile and forget all about his aching back. He heard several beeps that told him the report was finished; He was brought back to reality.

Pierre studied the report. First, that fat creep in the park and the stuffed dog, and then the rich couple into kiddie porn, and lastly, the doll house figurines. There was no doubt now that the city had a vigilante on the loose, with a very peculiar calling card: a child's toy. The toy lead was worth a bundle. Pierre thought maybe he could get away with selling the lead, now that there had been more murders. This kind of evidence was harder to keep silent the longer the investigation went on. He was fairly confident that too many people knew about the "calling card" to keep a lid on it. It could never be pinned on him.

Pierre had the computer run another report to find out if anything linked together the Landers and Hart murders. The latest murders cast doubt on his original theory that the Keaton, Peyton and Winston murders were tied to some drug deal. Three might go down; but six — that spelled vigilantism. Perhaps the so-called Crusader was someone who had been burned by the justice system, someone who wanted retribution — a real life *Death Wish*, Paul Kersey wannabe. Things were definitely heating up and Pierre had a lot of thinking to do.

He had to make a decision soon. This thing was threatening to get way out of hand. He needed to make sure he was not in the crosshairs when all hell broke loose. Pierre marched into the area outside Lester's office, to the division's secretary, Mildred Welker.

"I want a list of all the homicide court cases from the last year. I want names and addresses of all the victim's relatives. I also want any cases that are coming up for appeal. And plan on working overtime for the next week," barked Pierre, walking back into his office.

Pierre saw the Crusader murders in a new light. This was going to be his opportunity for fame. His heart raced with excitement and his mind wandered in the fantasy world of fame and fortune. If he was honored by the city, then perhaps an important talent scout would recognize his natural charisma and good looks and might offer him a role playing a cop on TV or in the movies. He preferred theatre, but he could start anywhere. Pierre was critical of the movies and TV shows about cops. The only respectable shows were the ones written by Joseph Wambaugh, like "The Onion Field." He was somewhat of a hero for Pierre. People thought cops were big lugs with no elegance, class or culture. Wambaugh dispelled that, and brought a new image for policemen. For him, the payoff was big — million dollar book deals and movie rights, to boot. Pierre could hit the media circuit, too. He could go on the radio show with Troy and talk about how he solved the famous New Orleans Crusader murders. The stage had already been set for that with the letter he had delivered to Troy. At the least, he could be given control of the New Orleans Division and make his earlier visions for the department come true.

The next week, Pierre sorted through the stacks of court records. There were 112 homicides in the last year. Only twenty-five were still tied up in the courts. All the defendants were male. One of the twenty-five was on trial for killing his wife and another guy had shot his girlfriend. The cases fit the standard profile of the abuser who finally goes all the way. Most of the other cases involved bar fights, robberies and some hit-and-runs. A couple cases happened in Metairie and the others down in the Quarter. Pierre figured there couldn't have been much cause for retribution for those losers. No relatives or close friends had bothered to show up for the trials.

Pierre focused on the wife slaying. The woman, Amanda Fields, was the mother of two boys and had been married for 18 years. Her parents, Marta and William Harrison, had come to the husband's trial to testify. Amanda's parents were obviously devastated and would expect justice. They had custody of the boys, age 10 and 12. At the trial, photos were shown of the woman, after she had been beaten with a baseball bat in front of the children. The guy confessed, and was given a plea-bargain, so he only had to serve fifteen years. Surely, this must have infuriated the parents.

The other woman, Skipper Danson, was only 21. The boyfriend, apparently, caught in a jealous rage, shot her twice in the head. The girl moved to New Orleans just last year, and was working at "Crazy Joe's" nightclub on Bourbon Street. Her parents from Ohio were contacted. They showed up for the identification, but did not return for the trial.

So that left Amanda Fields. Her parents had a house in Metairie, near the lakefront. Pierre handed the files to Mildred.

"I want a complete background check on the Harrisons. And make sure you check on whether he had ever served in the armed forces. You never know, this guy could be off his rocker."

Mildred looked at the newspaper photo of the parents. Somehow, they didn't look like they could harm a flea. But Pierre could be right, who knew? Her many years working for the police department had taught her that the worst among society were often the most talented at hiding their real person-alities from others. She felt like it would be a dead-end since the guy was still serving his time in prison. Wouldn't the parents wait for his release to kill him? Why kill others in the meantime? Also this was a wife abuse case, not child abuse. The Crusader was killing child predators. Oh well, she mentally chided herself for doubting Pierre. She was sure he had his reasons. She knew Pierre had good instincts. Pierre was almost always right about whether the witnesses were telling the truth. Even though Pierre treated her badly sometimes, she still put up with him, because he could also be so charming.

She liked Lester too, but he wasn't as needy as Pierre. She took pride in helping Pierre and kept his secrets. Sometimes she smelled liquor on Pierre's breath. She knew he kept a bottle of vodka in his desk drawer. She suspected that he had his own supply of drugs, maybe cocaine or speed, which he would confiscate during drug busts. She sometimes noticed him wiping his nose in an odd way. And then there were the girly magazines that she dared not look at.

"Some people just need a little more help than others to get through life," Mildred often found herself thinking. "It's often the creative ones who need an outlet for themselves."

She always thought of Pierre as a larger than life figure…sort of a Dashiell Hammett, the famous detective writer. Pierre, she thought, could be also many things besides a detective, and become famous. He was handsome and brilliant. But not everyone could see that — certainly not Lester. It took someone intuitive, like her, to understand and also have the desire to be his confidant. She had watched him in several plays at Le Petite; and he was wonderful. It was the creative ones who were tortured by inner demons and self-doubt. Didn't many of the great poets and writers end up overdosing in despair at being misunderstood? She was determined that would not happen to Pierre — not if she could help it.

Mildred spent the day running reports and finally, by the day's end, had gathered a cache of documents, news clips and trial reports. She typed a summary for Pierre and took it into his office.

"Here you go, Pierre. It seems your instincts were correct. Our William Buford Harrison served in the Korean War. He was a combat pilot and a decorated soldier. Besides Amanda, he had a son, Jacob, who also had served with the Marines in Vietnam. Seems like this family doesn't duck a fight," said Mildred, beaming proudly. She was so happy to do her small part to help Pierre.

"Let me see this," he said grabbing the folder from Mildred. "You can go now," said Pierre curtly.

Mildred was used to the brisk treatment. She was just happy that Pierre had trusted her to do the research.

"Hmm, a father and a son, both familiar with weaponry, grieving for their Amanda. Every day, seeing the face of Amanda in the lonely eyes of her sons, who were left to be raised by aging grandparents. Definitely worth checking out."

Pierre didn't trust his co-workers with the information. He would call Mitchell Parks, the P.I. he usually worked with on cases that he wanted to take the sole credit for solving. Pierre decided to go to Mitch's office in person. He knew the chances of catching him in the office were slim, but he went anyway. The worst that could happen is that he would have to bullshit with Mitch's gay secretary, Linal. He could never understand why Mitch didn't have a sexy, platinum blond with a prominent cleavage working the front desk, like every other detective. Well, after all, this was New Orleans – anything but the norm.

Mitch shared his office space with his uncle, an optometrist. The building was about 30-years-old, and was located across from an outdated strip shopping center. Pierre walked past the optometry clinic, briefly glancing at the window filled with eyeglasses. Mitch's office was located down a small hallway, behind the Coke machines and restrooms. He opened the door. Linal was at the front desk, talking on the phone. He twisted around in his chair, eyes focused on Pierre.

"Gotta go now; duty calls," said Linal, smiling as he hung up the phone.

He stood up to greet Pierre. "What a surprise! How are you Pierre, I mean, Detective Martens?" said Linal, with a seductive grin, as he held out a limp hand for Pierre to shake.

"Fine, Linal, where's the boss?" said Pierre, who was clearly not in the mood for idiotic banter and ignored the hand hanging in the air between them.

"Well, he's fixing to lock up. You caught him just in time. You're so lucky," said Linal, a little miffed, but still trying to get a grin out of Pierre.

"Yeah, that's me all right," said Pierre, walking by Linal into Mitch's office.

"Just about ready to close up shop; you'll have to come back with your guns and bully club some other time. Sorry, sheriff," said Mitch, sneering.

The two had met during police training, years ago. Mitch had worked on the force for a few years and afterwards he decided to open his own PI business. Mitch always tried to tease Pierre, calling him sheriff. But Pierre usually got his licks in.

"Well, at least I'm not camping out in this filthy dump, sharing an office with the optometrist across from the Piggly Wiggly," Pierre said, grinning at his sharp comeback; he loved to make Mitch squirm.

"My uncle gives me this space for free," said Mitch defensively. "I plan on moving into a remodeled apartment in the uptown area next year. I already have the down payment, thanks to stiffs like you who can't seem to do their own jobs. This place has always been temporary."

His last jab had hit home. He knew Pierre was a pretentious peacock who would do anything for fame and glory.

"All right, enough about housing. I need your help on the vigilante case. I have a lead and I want you to check it out."

"Something you're keeping from Lester again?" Mitch asked, unable to resist another jab. "Don't worry Pierre; your little competition with Lester is what fills my pockets. Besides, I can't stand the smug bastard either," he said, trying to placate Pierre.

He didn't want to get him too pissed off. Pierre was a steady source of income and also a link to police information he found handy on many of his other cases.

"Here's the file. I didn't have time to make a copy. Let Linal make a copy and mail the original back to me. After you've read it, call me tomorrow. One of these two guys may be our vigilante."

"Well, then, I'll get right on it. Let's catch the guy. Although, I think most people wouldn't mind a few more killings, if you know what I mean," Mitch said. He doubted Pierre had anything of value, but the money was the same. He would check it out.

"No, I don't know what you mean."

"Haven't you been listening to the radio? There are people calling in cheering for the Crusader. He's a hero, didn't you know? The victims have been real losers, child abusers, rapists, you know… scum. People don't mind those kinds of murders."

"Just read the file. I'm not paying you for your opinions," said Pierre, walking out the door.

"Aren't you going to say goodbye?" chirped Linal.

Pierre turned around and flipped him off.

"How sweet! Anytime, honey; I'll be waiting right here," said Linal, blowing Pierre a kiss.

Pierre was the biggest homophobe Linal had ever met and was always a source of amusement. Linal would give anything to have a chance to try to show him a good time. He always welcomed a challenge and Pierre had a real cute butt.

CHAPTER THIRTY-NINE

Mitch decided to wait until the next day to open the brown envelope. He was surprised that Pierre had any leads at all on the Crusader killings. His other police contacts said the well had run dry, but the latest theory connected the vigilante killings to the Morelli kidnapping. Mitch had also been working for the Morellis. The family had hired him to help find Angela's killer. They were anxious to solve the case, for many reasons; but primarily because the police were beginning think the family was behind the Crusader attacks. Mitch didn't buy it, but he knew that Vincent was anxious to get information that might squash rumors that threatened to cast a spotlight on the Morelli family and — draw even more attention to the painful memories of Angela's kidnapping.

Old Pops Morelli had even gotten involved, which really set off the alarms. The family had already suffered, and now was forced to live through the media reports, all over again. The family wanted to keep the press out of it and they wanted the case solved. Mitch provided Vincent with monthly reports. The best lead was from an old lady, who said she'd spotted a little girl in the market, with an "evil" man. Already, Pierre had spoken to the woman and reported that she was an "unreliable" source, since she appeared to be "unstable."

The police figured the old woman was just looking for some kind of attention, like many false leads that come in during high profile investigations. She did voodoo on the side and any publicity would boost her business. Whatever Pierre had found, Mitch was sure it would lead to a dead end. Pierre had some good collars to his record, but Mitch knew most of those confessions were gained after a good beating. Pierre was slick, all right. He was just smart and ambitious enough to be dangerous and he had a hidden mean streak. Since there was no one Pierre could beat up to get the answers on this case, Mitch was sure the folder contained busy work from his poor secretary, Mildred. There was another messed up woman, blinded by love and devotion to a guy who could care less if she took another breath.

Pierre was too stupid to realize Mildred was the only reason he was still a cop. Mitch had used Pierre's dirty secrets to get information out of Mildred on several of his cases. Poor Mildred, she was really a decent person. Mitch knew her doctoring of reports and covering up for Pierre would end one day. Last time he saw her, little more than a couple weeks ago, she looked really worn and haggard. Yeah, it was just a matter of time before Pierre crashed and burned. Mitch was anxious to see what the aftermath would leave of Pierre. But Pierre was more slippery than a greased pig at a county fair, and wouldn't go down without a fight. Mitch would pay big money to see him squeal.

The thought made him laugh out loud, as he gathered his things and walked to the door of his small, cramped office. Time would tell who would be left to gloat. Mitch felt pretty sure he would still be alive and kicking long after Pierre bit the dust. Just a few days earlier, Vincent had called and asked Mitch to give him the latest reports and documentation.

As he was leaving for lunch, Mitch left two brown envelopes: one to Vincent and one to Pierre. He put them on the desk with a sticky note on each one with addresses and instructions for mailing. Linal typed the labels, placed them neatly on the envelopes and put them in the mail drop for afternoon pick-up.

CHAPTER FORTY

After leaving Lester at the police station, Peg decided to do some of her own investigating. She used her home computer to access the New Orleans PD official website. Just as she had suspected, there was a section dedicated to the officers with their pictures and the areas they served. Peg printed out the photos of all the officers who worked in the French Quarter and the downtown area. Next, she called the station and spoke to Officer Anne Benoit.

"Anne, I am following up a lead for Lester. Could you tell me who was on duty the day little Angela Morelli disappeared from the French Market area? I also would like to know if anyone, besides Pierre, interviewed the old lady from the praline shop, the one who said she may have seen Angela the day she disappeared."

"I don't have access to the duty rosters, but Mildred, who works with Pierre and Lester, can help you. You know Peg, we have already checked out that lead several times. Mrs. LaRue from the candy shop is a voodoo kook; the only reason she has a job there is because her son owns it."

Peg wasn't buying it. She continued to pump for more information.

"Well I thought she might open up more to a woman. I'm sure I am still capable of prying a few facts from people. I haven't gotten that rusty," said Peg with a laugh, trying to keep a light tone to her voice. Suddenly, she was very anxious to interview Mrs. LaRue, especially since everyone was so sure the lead was useless. It had nagged at her since she had first heard about the possible sightings of both Angela and Caitlin.

"Oh, that's right, you used to work for the paper, I almost forgot. Maybe you will have better luck than the police. I'll put you through to Mildred. Good luck, Peg," Det. Benoit said, with real warmth coming through in her voice.

Peg went through the same spiel with Mildred and eventually got her to agree to e-mail her the list. Mildred promised to have it to her within an hour.

As soon as Mildred hung up the phone, she called Pierre on his cell phone.

Pierre was headed back to the station. Lester had sent him on a wild goose chase back to the site where the Hart's boat had exploded. Lester was sure the crime scene team had missed something. Pierre knew Lester just wanted him out of his hair for a while. There was nothing there, not a fucking thing. They had already recovered remnants of the two bodies. He was damn sure not going to spend his whole day watching divers pull pieces of the boat out of the murky waters of Lake Pontchartrain. He pulled the cell phone from his jacket pocket and answered.

"Pierre, it's Mildred."

She sounded scared and breathless which immediately put him on edge.

"God, Mildred, I'm having a shitty day as it is; what's going on now?" asked Pierre, his irritation and frustration coming through in his voice.

"Pierre, I probably shouldn't bother you with this, but Peg McGregor just called and asked for the duty roster for the day the Morelli girl disappeared. I promised I would send it to her within the hour. She also said she was going to interview Mrs. LaRue from the Candy Shop."

She had rushed through the explanation and then held her breath waiting for his reaction. The silence was nerve-wracking. Pierre could be so unpredictable lately.

Pierre was thankful that he was in his car when he received this bit of information, because he was sure his mouth had fallen open like the village idiot and all the color had left his faced.

"Pierre, can you hear me?" asked Mildred, feeling sure that his cell phone must have dropped out or cut them off.

Pierre had heard every word, and his anger built as the color rushed back into his cheeks.

"What does she want with the duty roster?" Pierre asked, making every effort to keep his voice calm and even.

"Well, she says she is going to interview the LaRue woman again. She plans on showing her pictures of all the officers on duty. She wants her to come down to the precinct to look at some photos of sex offenders who are on parole."

"Who gave her pictures?" The disgust evident in his voice now, "Didn't you tell her we had thoroughly checked that lead out? Why, I talked to that crazy old bitch myself. Even if she identifies someone, no court is going to listen to her crazy voodoo rantings. Besides, I wasn't even on duty either time, was I Mildred?"

"Uh no, Pierre; She said she got the pictures off the web site. You know, the site Lester started last year? Remember, I had to schedule you for the photo shoot in uniform? Is it okay Pierre? She said Lester asked her to check it out. I told her it was a dead end, but she's very stubborn."

The mention of Lester's name made Pierre's anger flare up again. Fuck! He had actually enjoyed the photo shoot. He thought it was one of Lester's less stupid ideas, especially, since it showcased his picture on the Internet. He even used the web address in his bio and on his business cards he sent to producers and casting agents. He should have known anything Lester thought up would turn around and bite him in the ass, sooner or later.

"Well, Lester's the boss, isn't he? Better do what he says for now, but you mark my words, Mildred, things are gonna change around there, and maybe real soon. You'd better decide just whose side you're on, if you know what I mean."

He was afraid his anger had let him to say too much, so he quickly added, "Sorry Mildred, I've had a tough day. I think I'll catch lunch at home. Talk to ya later," he said as he punched the "end" button on the phone.

In a rage Pierre threw the phone, sending it crashing against the front windshield. Plastic bits shattered from the impact and left a pit and small crack in the left side of the windshield.

"Worthless piece of shit!" Pierre screamed, clearly taking his anger out on the phone. Pierre struggled to control his temper by thinking about the new unmarked cruiser he would be driving soon, real soon.

Pierre didn't give Mildred a second thought. She was putty in his hands and worshiped the ground he walked on. She was the one person whose loyalty he could count on. He would bring her some flowers stolen from his neighbor's garden, give her a little sweet talk and she would be glowing for weeks. What a stupid, but useful bitch. Pierre hurried home. He had to think; he had to plan. It was time to put an end to this mess. It was not going to be easy and a chain reaction of events could very well send everything crashing down around him, but he knew the time had come. That McGregor woman was a nuisance, but when he read her file last week and saw her records, SWAT, criminal profiling, he knew she would be more of an opponent than Lester. Lester was a clown in a cop suit. But he would soon be out of the way. In Pierre's eyes there were only two kinds of women. The ones like Mildred on whom his good looks could turn into putty and the ones like Peg, who would have made a better man than a woman.

The Mildred-type, like his own mother, would sacrifice everything, even their own children, for the man in their life. They were nothing more than dogs, ready to lick the hands of their masters at the slightest show of affection. He avoided the other kind, who were unaffected by him. He passed them off as nothing more than dykes or women who wanted to be tough and act like men. From their first meeting, he had placed Peg in the second category. Sure enough, just to prove him right, that McGregor woman had already zeroed in on his one vulnerability. He had already been thinking about a backup plan – now was the time to set it in motion.

He pulled up in front of his house and headed for the front door, once again ignoring the yapping dog next door. It barked furiously from the other side of the fence. Pierre was oblivious to the noise, his thoughts already reeling through scenario after scenario, laying out the scenes in his head, until he came upon the right combination.

CHAPTER FORTY-ONE

Nettie LaRue kept many secrets. After all, it was her profession as a mambo voodoo priestess to be a spiritual healer vowing the same secrecy of confession as a Catholic priest.

LaRue had kept her secret about Elizabeth Morelli. She hadn't even told the police that she knew Elizabeth. She had come to her in confidence, searching for answers. The woman often stopped at the Sweet Shop on her weekly Wednesday trip to the French market. Her little girl Angela, who wore her hair in a long braid of dark hair tied with a bow, liked the chocolate pralines.

Her mother had the same dark, shiny hair, but kept hers wound up in a sophisticated bun. Elizabeth would routinely buy a box pralines and take one out for Angela to snack on while they strolled up the sidewalk to the flea market, looking for bargains.

It was in the early autumn that Ms. LaRue noticed a certain sadness and quickness in Elizabeth's voice. That day, she had chided her daughter about touching the glass counter. Ms. LaRue looked at Angela, and then up at Elizabeth.

"Oh don worry child, it's just a smudge and likely will bring good luck," said Ms. LaRue, smiling at Angela, revealing her large white teeth. In dismay she noticed Elizabeth had tears shimmering in her eyes.

"What is wrong, my dear, such sadness? Tell me what wrong with my good girl, here?"

Elizabeth looked at Ms. LaRue and, at first, was embarrassed. She didn't know how to approach the woman with her problem. A friend told her that Ms. La Rue practiced voodoo, and might be able to help her. But Elizabeth hadn't the courage to speak up and ask the LaRue woman about it. And she wasn't convinced that Ms. LaRue was a real voodoo woman or one of the many charlatans who worked the streets of New Orleans. And truth be told, she was a little frightened of voodoo. New Orleans was full of tarot card readers and other practitioners of magic and witchcraft. They earned large sums of cash from the tourists by casting spells and putting pins in voodoo dolls. They sold tinctures and told fortunes. Most were fakes. The true practitioners didn't advertise; you had to seek them out and they were connected to an underground spiritual world of voodoo that sought to undercover wisdom from their ancestors.

"I know what you want child, you don't have to say. Come back to see Ms. La Rue on Tuesday, when de shop is closed and I will read dhe cards."

Ms. LaRue kept her voodoo world apart from her day job. In the mornings and afternoons she tended the shop, and at night she was a mambo helping those souls who sought healing through the spiritual path of voodoo.

To the outsider, Ms. LaRue's altar, or badji, looked no different than any other. That was her cover. Her son, who owned the store, figured that his mother was just trying to make extra money with the tarot. As long as it didn't interfere with the sweet shop business, he indulged her. He never believed in all that mumbo jumbo from his childhood.

Ms. LaRue had never told her son the truth — that their family's ancestors were voodoo mambos. They were descended from the many families of slaves that arrived from Santo Domingo more than 200 years ago. Ms. LaRue had carried on the tradition and retained her strong voodoo powers. She had healing gifts that surpassed most other voodoo mambos in New Orleans. Ms. LaRue told Elizabeth to come at sunset, a time when the spirits are most friendly and most negotiable.

When Elizabeth arrived, Ms. LaRue had already set out candles, perfumes and fresh cut flowers arranged in a circle around the Madonna on the alter. Two flags hung on hooks above the table, the white drapo of peace and the red drapo of victory. On the back wall, which was painted turquoise, hung a portrait of a snake charmer. The snake charmer was a dark woman with a snake curling around her head. The snake's mouth pointed up toward the woman's chin. Small pouches, the gris-gris, looped at the top, with black strings were placed along the shelves on the adjacent wall. The gris-gris bags contain herbs and rose petals, and sometimes plant roots, and other natural ingredients that bring good luck. Some were adorned with red or purple colored feathers or jewels.

A wooden shelf was on the opposite wall. Small cubicles held a variety of small bags of herbs and jars of flower petals. The ginger and smells of the other herbs were intoxicating. Ms. La Rue was costumed in a red satin dress with a gold scarf tied around her head as a turban, concealing her thick, mostly gray-streaked black hair.

When Elizabeth walked in the shop, she remained silent. She had just come from the 6 p.m. mass at the Cathedral St. Louis and was in a pensive mood. She prayed that Ms. La Rue could help her, knowing, of course, that some good Catholics would consider this blasphemy. But Elizabeth knew that most of the Catholic Creoles in New Orleans had easily combined the two religions; perhaps, an Italian Catholic, like she, could too.

Ms. LaRue led Elizabeth to the back room. She saw the familiar Madonna and candles. The relics of Catholicism made her feel less afraid. It was the picture of the snake charmer that sent chills down her back.

Ms. LaRue, could sense something was wrong.

"Oh, you are afraid of snake charmer? You think it is de devil? But you are wrong. For you, de snake is de serpent, but in voodoo, dis our weapon against evil and de sign of life and victory. It circles the earth and through it we pass — it is the protector. We must learn what de snake knows and where it is leading us. You know, like de fiery serpents in de Bible, God used de snake to punish but also to heal...de snake turns de pole into de healin cross."

Elizabeth, just nodded, and tried to be open.

"Don you worry dear, you das not needed to understand dis, right now. You tell Ms. LaRue what is wrong. I sense dit has to do with love. Somethin not dat right with your husband, perhaps?"

"Yes, that's right. We have been trying to have another child. After months of trying, my husband and I went to the doctors; but they said that nothing is wrong. We had no problems the first time. I had Angela shortly after we were married. My husband says I pressure him too much. When he says that, it makes me feel like he doesn't want another child. I think that maybe he doesn't want me either."

"Tell me mam, why would you think dat?"

"I don't know. It's just something I feel. Things started changing when he entered this campaign for district judge. He's different now. On lots of nights, he' gone and he gets phone calls from women. He says its business; but I worry. He is very good-looking and he is Italian. His father had mistresses and I worry that he might be the same way."

Ms. LaRue was shuffling the tarot cards, as she listened to Elizabeth. This time she turned her gaze away from Elizabeth and began to stare at the tarot cards.

"Well, let's see dear what de cards will say today. Maybe den you don't have to be worry so much."

She gave the cards to Elizabeth and told her to take off her wedding ring and place it next to the deck. Next, she told her to take one of the flowers from the Madonna and place it next to the ring and then spread the cards across the table in a fan-like motion.

"We are going to call Loa of Erzulie. She tells us all about love. Pick five cards from dhe deck, one for each corner and one for de center. Loa is a spirit that will help shine de light on dhe secrets of de past and present."

Mrs. LaRue directed Elizabeth to place the first card in the middle, the second on the right and the third on the left. The fourth card was placed at the top, or north position and the last card was placed at the bottom, or south position. Ms. LaRue asked for the offering. She had told Elizabeth to bring some food. Elizabeth took out an orange, her favorite fruit and a photo of her and Vincent.

Ms. LaRue held Elizabeth's hand and they said a prayer.

Moments later, Ms. LaRue opened her eyes and began studying the cards. She would need to call on the power of Erzulie to help her read the messages. She took out her ason, a ritual rattle, and started to shake it. The ason was wrapped in a string of colorful beads, to symbolize the eternal serpent. She closed her eyes, and began chanting:

"Bring de magic rite of way to me, open de path of mystery; send de way to de souls to me."

She repeated the verse, shaking the rattle. Then she opened her eyes and stared at the cards.

"Who is Erzulie?" Elizabeth inquired.

Mrs. LaRue opened her eyes and stared at the cards, and then looked up at Elizabeth.

"Erzulie is a dancer, full of de force and de fury, but she be alls good. She grinds de corn for her peoples and puts out de fire of anger. She reveals your heart. Now, uncover de middle card," she commanded.

Elizabeth flipped over the card. It was the world egg card, the first card of the deck and a sign of all possibilities – the burst of a new creation. The card showed an oval egg-like shape with snake circling. It represents birth of new creation…the beginning.

Ms. LaRue clapped her hands.

"Dis is good! Erzulie says dat she sees your new baby. She is listening. But de question is, what dis blocking?"

Mrs. LaRue pointed to the west card, which represents past influences. Elizabeth uncovered the card. It was the Gros Bon Ange. The card showed a yellow sun with tentacles of light beaming from it center.

"Dis card brings energy and success. Angela, your star, it means."

She pointed to the eastern card, which represents the future. Elizabeth reached over and flipped the card. She winced when she saw that it depicted a frightening apparition of a woman looking into a mirror. It reminded her of the wicked witch in Snow White, but was even scarier because the mirror was framed with a snake.

"Oh de Magick Mirror. As you can guess, dit speaks of danger. She says what is in our lives now. De mirror says there is de trap, someone hiding behind, maybe? But, no, dis what you are projecting on the mirror, maybe your own fears and demons. It may be teasing you. All de other cards are good. You are a creator, a mother earth egg, surrounded by stars, but dis not enough; somehow, you do not trust your own good luck that says you deserve happiness. You think dat de husband is the deception; but it could be da mirrors talkin to you about your fears. Let's look and see what de fourth card is telling us. It is the one that speaks to the visible world."

Once again, Elizabeth was notably shocked when she recognized the name. Dr. John, the African drummer whose face is tattooed with red and blue lines to symbolize snakes and creation. He is the most famous voodoo priest. He holds the flaming baton, and has a fierce will that brings musical forces and energizes the spirit of the Loa.

When Ms. LaRue saw the card, she nearly fell off her stool.

"Never in my life have dis seen Dr. John so close to de Magick Mirror. Lordy, dem some powerful, manly spirits been brought dere. Letz keep going. We have one more card."

Ms. LaRue picked up an old tattered fan on her alter and began waving it back and forth, as if to cool down the spirits. Meanwhile, Elizabeth uncovered the last card: It was Marie Laveau.

"Oh, I recognize this one too! Ms. LaRue isn't Marie Laveau supposed to be a good voodoo spirit?"

"Oh yes, dear, you are right. Marie is the great Voodoo Queen, with a healing spirit and has come to visit us in de visible world. She will bring together the pieces, because I was a little worried about Magick Mirror, but child, not to worry, Magick mirror says de husband is good, like the Dr. John, holding the baton, drumming and waiting. You are de center, de World Egg and your Angela is de Gros Bone Ange, the sunlight waiting for new stars."

Ms. LaRue smiled and said the reading was all good. The cards were favorable. She rose from her chair and went to the shelves where she kept her potions and gris-gris. She brought two of them, one red and one gold.

"Place de gris-gris beside your bed, one is a filled with petals and jasmine, de other has rosemary and garlic. De first will bring fertility and de other good luck. Place de cloth over a mirror, to hide Magick Mirror. Den she will not scare you too much. You must take the orange back and rub yourself with it for five days. Come back in five days with de orange. We will ask da spirits and see where de egg and snake lead us."

Elizabeth listened carefully and looked up at Ms. LaRue.

"Is that all there is to it?"

"What do you mean? Ha, you were expecting me to go into a trance, roll back my eyes and become possessed, or stick de pins into a doll?"

Ms. LaRue shook her head, rolling her eyes back, laughing.

"Voodoo is not like dat. If you stick pins in a doll, it will come back to haunt you. We mus not practice de dark magic or zombism; we bring de good spirits and good luck. Dolls speak for our dead or ancestral spirits, and are a vessel, but we not stick de pins in dem."

"Oh, I see," Elizabeth said, trying to understand, but still obviously feeling unsure of what it all meant.

"My dear, voodoo is not black magic. We call on de African spirits dat are here to help ya know, and all de ask is that we treat them well and bring offerings of food and flowers and other presents. And you have done a good sacrifice, by giving up your favorite fruit. You will see child. Don be afraid."

Ms. LaRue rose from the chair and led Elizabeth out of the shop. Elizabeth had two twenty-dollar bills that she gave Ms. LaRue, who exchanged that for a sack to put the gris-gris and the orange inside. She unlocked the door and let Elizabeth out to the sidewalk. She squeezed her hand and said goodbye.

Elizabeth wasn't quite sure what to say. She was tongue-tied, but managed to get out a "Thank you, Ms. LaRue; I'll see you on Sunday. Should I come at the same time?"

"Oh, yes, please do come at da sunset, around 7, dat would be good."

But Elizabeth never did come back. That next Wednesday, when Elizabeth was shopping at the market, her daughter disappeared and was later found dead. The mother poured a bottle of sleeping pills down her throat. Doctors pumped her stomach, but it was too late. Ms. LaRue remembered that horrible day. She heard the screams and the police and sirens. The photos of the little girl were plastered along the store fronts, and then the horror of reading in the newspaper about the dead girl. Then two days later the mother was dead of grief and a broken heart.

The police questioned her on the day the girl was lost, but she couldn't tell them about Elizabeth; it would break a trust, so instead, she told them that she had seen the child, and mumbled some words and acted crazy, so they would leave her alone in her own grief and guilt. She did tell them about a strange man who had been watching the girl, but she couldn't see anything but his dark eyes which was not much help to the police.

How could she have missed it and been so wrong about the cards? She thought the Magick Mirror was just blocking the fertility, but it was something much more evil, the sorcerer, the serpent, gathering strength from his own reflection, taking up a different cross. This force was too powerful. Could Dr. John and Marie Laveau in the north and south position been trying to warn her of this mysterious evil?

Then she saw that other little girl, walking with a policeman. When she heard the girl was missing, she tried to report what she saw, but that same policeman came by to interview her. Something about him caused her to play dumb and hide behind her voodoo persona. He eventually wrote her off as a voodoo wacko and left. Something about his eyes chilled her to the soul. These thoughts haunted her, day after day.

Ms. LaRue had not touched her tarot cards, or lit any candles, since that chilly October morning. Instead, she gathered a bouquet of flowers and pleaded for forgiveness and that her powers would be taken away forever, in her daily visit to the St. Louis Cemetery in Congo Square, the final resting place of Marie Laveau and Dr. John. This was a ritual she had been following ever since the day that Angela had disappeared. She prayed that her own spirit will soon join those of Madam Laveau and Dr. John, and she would be at peace among her African ancestors.

CHAPTER FORTY-TWO

Lester spent every night of the last week staking out the seedy part of the French Quarter, where his informant said the man in the photo was last seen. Lester was searching for the sixth man, Fabio Marko, who was listed on the FBI file that Agent Kyle had turned over to him. Fabio was suspected to be hiding out in New Orleans. Lester was making the rounds of the French Quarter, showing Marko's photograph around and looking for anyone who might have a clue. He was hoping to get one step ahead of the Crusader. Lester felt he was onto something big, as he sat in his old car, sipping hot coffee from his large thermos. He noticed an old lady walking slowly down the other side of the street. What could she possibly be doing out at 3:00 a.m.? The buzz of his beeper distracted him, as he unhooked it from his belt to check the number displayed.

On a dark street corner three blocks from where Lester sat, the tip of a burning cigarette slowly grew red hot and then faded away to a dull glow, with each long pull taken by the man standing and smoking in the shadows.

Fabio Marko was deep in thought and his thoughts were not pleasant. He grew more bored of New Orleans with each passing day. At first, he had been taken in by the outrageous atmosphere of the city. The people intrigued him. He thought it was the perfect place for someone like him to hide out. He would blend easily with the darker side of New Orleans. Mardi Gras was a festival of delights, but the last few weeks had been downhill and held nothing but boredom. Lying low was killing him and his nightly excursions among the drunk and homeless had grown unsatisfying. He needed out, but to get out he also needed money. So far, his benefactor had been ignoring his efforts to contact him. He had grown bolder and chanced calling him at work. With each attempt, he grew more and more restless. Fabio was considering a little robbery to finance his journey, but that could also backfire and put him in a jail cell for life, or worse, if he were caught. The kind of money he needed couldn't be found in this area of town. He flicked the cigarette stub into the gutter in disgust, as he turned and headed down Pirates' Alley toward St. Peter Street — looked like he was back to rustling bums for the next few nights.

The first heap of rags he came to barely moved, as he flipped him over and rifled the drunk's pockets...nothing. He moved on to the next, and his mood grew darker, as two more heaps resulted in only one crumpled bill, and even kicking the shit out of the listless heaps did nothing to help his mood. It was not much fun if they didn't even know their face was being smashed or ribs broken.

He was getting restless and it was making him jumpy. All night he had a strange feeling that he was being tailed, but every time he darted a glance behind him the streets and sidewalks were empty...just another sign that it was time to hit the road.

Miz Walker was bone tired as she shuffled home from a very late night at the Le Chateau Hotel, four blocks south of Bourbon Street. A convention was in town and she couldn't resist the extra hours working as a maid, since Lou's medications were draining their meager cash reserves. At eighty-one, she was proud of her ability to make beds and keep up with the girls less than half her age. Lou did not like her coming home so late at night and made her promise to take a taxi. While she made the promise to keep him happy, she knew she wasn't about to put hard earned money into a taxi ride, when she had two perfectly good legs that would carry her the six blocks to their apartment. Besides, who would want an old bag of bones like her? If she was still young enough to turn heads, she might have considered the ride.

As for being mugged, she always carried a small can of pepper spray that was attached to her keys. She also walked with her keys sticking out between her fingers, just as Lou had taught her many years ago.

Many times he had told her: "Maddie, you are a tough old broad."

They'd been married for sixty-four years, as of last Christmas. Six children she had brought into the world, with grandchildren and great grandchildren too numerous to count.

As she reached the halfway point, she was thinking, I am the pepper and he is the salt – together they made a perfect combination.

Wrapped up in her thoughts, Maddie did not even register that she stepped down into the mouth of a dim alley, or the dark form that was waiting there, silently, until she was grabbed from behind and swung into the darkness and shadows. She didn't even have time to think about screaming and only a surprised "hhmmmmff" sound escaped her lips, as air rushed from her lungs before a hand was clamped down over her mouth.

"Filthy mugger scum," she mumbled.

Realizing the hand that held the keys was free, she reached up and brought the sharp edges against the side of her attacker's face. She knew she did damage to her attacker, when she heard the shriek of pain loud in her right ear and she was flung across the narrow alley, landing hard against the brick wall. As she slid to the ground, she scrambled to get the small canister of pepper spray ready. Thoughts of running were dashed by a severe pain in her left ankle. She thought she had heard and felt bones break, as she landed. Besides, she knew her eighty-one-year old legs wouldn't get her very far. Her eyes had adjusted to the darkness and she looked up to face her attacker, ready with the pepper spray.

She looked at the shaggy creature as it whimpered and pawed at its bleeding face, and then it growled at her before breaking into laughter at her frozen expression. Maddie was certain she was facing no ordinary man, but a demon, the kind her friend old Ms. LaRue said stalked the streets at night. The keys hanging from the spray can jangled as she crossed herself and said a prayer.

Fabio had thought the old lady was easy prey. Why, she had ambled toward him, mumbling to herself and he had figured her for an old crazy, who had gotten loose from her keepers. Instead, she had resisted and attacked him. He cringed as he felt the jagged cut that ran from the corner of his eye to his jaw. Blood was warm on his face, but he was pumped and feeling more alive than he had in weeks. He still couldn't believe an old lady had nearly taken his eye out. Now, he could see her fearlessly facing him with a canister of pepper spray held before her. Only the hand holding the spray betrayed her fear, as it shook uncontrollably. He growled at her and then laughed, as she made the sign of the cross on her chest.

"You're a tough old bitch, aren't ya," Fabio said, as he used his shirt to wipe away the blood from his face.

"God can't protect you from me. Didn't you know: God don't come around here? He's afraid," Fabio sneered.

Maddie's answer was to scream as loud as she could.

Lester's head jerked up at the sound of a scream. A quick scan showed the old lady had disappeared. He opened his car door and sprinted towards the last spot where he had seen her.

Immediately, Fabio drew his gun from his waistband and pointed it at the old lady: "Shut up or I'll shoot you," he yelled.

Maddie immediately fell silent when she saw the gun. Acknowledging defeat, she threw her purse across the alley.

"There, that's what you wanted. Now you have it. My hard earned money is yours. Take it demon and get out of here," muttered Maddie, the pain in her ankle was beginning to flare and pulse.

Fabio picked up the purse and rummaged through it, finding the wad of bills folded neatly in a little zippered, beaded bag. Jackpot! There were at least five twenties, a couple tens and some ones. He smiled at the old lady, as he crammed the cash and the beaded bag into the front pocket of his stained and torn jeans.

"You sure are a tough old bitch, aren't ya," he said again, moving closer.

Maddie raised the pepper spray and Fabio easily kicked it from her old hands and then he was on top of her. His breath reeked of stale booze and God knew what else. She instinctively turned her head aside and that's when she saw him, flying towards them, with his cape flared out behind him. It was Doctor John, sent to rescue her from this demon. The demon did not want her money, but was after her soul instead.

Fabio felt someone grab him from behind; He was flying through the air to land hard against the brick wall of the alley. Instinct made him swallow down the pain as he jumped back up and sprinted down the alley. He heard shots ring out and ricochet off the brick wall by his ear. A sliver of brick sliced into his ear and he screamed in pain.

Desperation drove him on as he hefted himself onto the lid of a large industrial metal waste bin. The stench of decaying food assaulted him as jumped to the fence. He climbed to the top and threw himself over, landing heavily on the other side. Ignoring the pain that flared in his knees as he landed on the cement and quickly darted across the lot into the next alley.

When Lester entered the mouth of the darkened alley, his eyes were immediately drawn to a shrouded figure sprinting towards him from the opposite end of the street. The moonlight streamed into the narrow passageway from the other direction and framed the dark figure with a diffused glow. Upon seeing him standing in the mouth of the alley, his gun raised, the dark racing form tried to slide to a stop. It seemed like everything was happening in slow motion, although Lester knew it was only a matter of seconds. Hearing Mattie's cries, Lester forced his attention to the old woman, struggling with her attacker among the floor of the garbage-strewn alleyway. As he picked up and threw Fabio into the wall, he saw a flash of black. The other intruder leaped over Maddie and darted out into the street, disappearing down the alley on the other side of the street. Lester had just enough time to reach with his right hand, but all he got was a black knit hat, and then his attention was immediately drawn back to Fabio, who was back up on his feet and on the move, escaping in the opposite direction.

Lester couldn't leave the old lady lying helpless, to chase Fabio or the other intruder. Instead he fired shots at Fabio, as he ran down the alley and into darkness. Lester felt sure it was only a matter of time before they found the cockroach's hidey-hole, once he got everyone mobilized to scour the area. He frowned as he looked down at the black knit wadded up in his hand. It was not a hat as he immediately thought, but a face-mask. He examined it more closely in the streetlight. Maybe the crime lab could find some hairs or other evidence. He was drawn back to the present by the moaning of the old woman. Unconsciously, he thrust the face-mask into the pocket of his trench coat.

Lester took off his coat and covered to the old women, trying to make her comfortable, as they waited for backup and an ambulance. His thoughts were still distracted, while his mind raced away down strange and startling paths. He had an instinctive feeling that tonight he had met the Crusader. Perhaps the Crusader had been the intruder and Lester had interfered with the Crusaders plans for Fabio.

Miz Walker came to, briefly, while Lester held her and reached up to touch his cheek, "Thank you, Doctor John," was all she said, before losing consciousness again.

The old woman thought he was a character off a tarot card. This was a very strange night. Lester heard sirens pull up in the street by the alley. Suddenly, he wasn't eager to reveal the face-mask or anything about its owner. He needed time to think.

CHAPTER FORTY-THREE

When Fabio finally made it back to his apartment, he grabbed a bottle of whiskey from the counter and began gulping the contents. He flung himself into the nearest chair. He reached in his pocket and pulled out the old lady's beaded bag. He always liked to keep something as a reminder, a way to relive those final moments when their life force left their bodies and entered his. He believed the strength and life force of those he killed became his. He could feel the surge of power that would sometimes last for days. This time the memento felt cursed. The old bag had won; she had gotten away. Now, he was more desperate than ever to get away from New Orleans. Ignoring the late hour, he again called the number that he was given in case of an emergency. His rattled mind poured out the recent events and he threatened to tell everything he knew, if the police grabbed him. He made sure his contact knew that it was in his best interest to help Fabio get out of town fast.

CHAPTER FORTY-FOUR

The next morning as police scoured the Quarter for Fabio Marko, Peg was headed out the door armed with the photos that she had matched to the duty rosters, along with photos of Lester and Pierre. She looked at the photo of Pierre. She passed him off as nothing more than a pretty boy, going through his life trading on his looks.

Peg drove down to the French Quarter and parked her car in the old lot by the river. It was early afternoon and not many tourists were around. Most were probably sleeping off the hangovers from the night before; come back after dark and the Quarter would be teaming with tourists and locals making the rounds of the jazz clubs and bars.

The day was overcast and dreary. Storm clouds had been brewing in the distance all afternoon. She thought she smelled rain in the light breeze. Peg walked down the gravel road, leading from the levee parking lot to the steps and up to the sidewalk on Decatur Street. She glanced across the street toward Chartres at admiring the Cathedral St. Louis. She still viewed it as one of the city's most fascinating relics of the past, and the garden with its landmark Confederate statute of General Andrew Jackson, our own Southern hero, perched upright on a horse standing up gallantly on its hind legs, as if going for last charge on the Yankees!

Blooming azaleas surrounded the square. As the rain began to fall she could smell Magnolia blossoms and coffee and beignets, wafting from the Café Du Monde, right next to the Sweet Shop. The horse-drawn carriages were parked along the road, waiting for the next group of tourists seeking an old-fashioned tour of the city.

The big drops of rain dappled her coat as she approached the store. Her heart was pounding with anxiety. She remembered her earlier conversation with Ms. LaRue. She had finally gotten the old woman to agree to meet with her. She rushed over before the old lady had a chance to change her mind.

"I don't trust de police, but you knows, dear, I will talk to you." Her old voice was deep and rich with the characteristic Creole accent. Peg sensed that she had given the officers a hard time when she had been questioned earlier.

"Dey tink I'm crazy ole voodoo woman, but I know many dhings; I see many dhings; there are bad people all around us. Her modher, she had come for help, but I could not help, it was beyond my power. I saw de devil with the girl, but it was too late. Later de man come for help…I saw de man too; de husband and I tried to help and tell him he was de spirit of Dr. John. He must be the one and used de baton, de good cross, to fight de evil Satan, de evil serpent. I pray for him.

"The cards were a warning for de woman, but I didn't know. Oh God! I must put out the salt to protect me, for I know de devil is coming for me, too. Dr. John cannot protect me, I fear from this devil. I never told the police de whole story, because I do not trust dem, but I will tell you. I saw the face of the devil, his eyes, and he is coming to get me." The old woman hung up before Peg had a chance to reply or ask questions.

Normally, Peg would have stopped listening after the first ranting. But she couldn't help feeling that the women was not just in some kind of spell, but really trying to explain. She grabbed her keys and headed for the door five minutes later. What did it all mean? The cards? The devil? Dr. John and what about the husband? Was she talking about Vincent? Maybe they were right about this woman being off her rocker. Peg was a skeptic and never went for all that voodoo stuff, or tarot cards, but she had to find out for herself. She was intrigued by what the woman had said about Vincent and his wife.

None of the police reports mentioned that the LaRue woman had even met Vincent's wife – how strange. But then, she remembered that the old woman was included in Vincent's report from the private investigator. The woman was holding something back. Peg was determined to find out what it was, so she grabbed the file off the front seat and headed across the street to the shop. She started to pull open the door, but it opened before her hand had even reached the knob. A middle-aged woman with short, dark hair, in a expensive suit, brushed past her in a huff, "Don't bother, no one is working in there. That silly old woman probably took off again and left the place unlocked. Wait till Marie and Charles find out."

The woman threw the words over her shoulder, as she walked briskly down the street, without looking back to see what Peg would do. Peg decided to go on in. She knew the old woman had been expecting her. Maybe she was sick or had a stroke or heart attack? It happened all the time to people much younger. The LaRue woman had sounded spry but ancient. Maybe she had tripped or was lying helpless in the back, and that stupid woman had not even been willing to check it out.

"Ms. LaRue, are you in there? Is everything okay?" she yelled, as she headed around the counter, looking for the way into the back. She found the section where the counter lifted up, and let herself into the area to where the clerk would weigh packages and ring up the candy on the old-style register.

The cop in Peg came alive and she took notice of all details, including the fact that the register appeared to be undisturbed. She couldn't rule out robbery. Maybe some rowdy kids had entered the shop. Peg's sense of foreboding grew, as she headed for the entrance to the short hallway that led to the back room. A beaded curtain separated the space from the main part of the store. Salt was spread out over the floor. A metallic smell filled the air. She immediately recognized the smell of blood from her old days as a police officer. It's a smell you don't easily forget. The hairs on the back of her neck began to tingle. For the first time in years, she wished she had her gun with her.

"Ms. LaRue," she yelled again, her voice softer than before, as she inched her way down the murky hallway and into the dark, back room. She searched for a light switch on the sides of the wall. Finally, she felt what she thought was the switch and flipped it up. Light bathed the small room that was part kitchen, part storeroom. In a small corner on the opposite side was a table, an altar really, with candles and voodoo flags hung on the wall. Vials of colored tinctures were set around the altar. A red skirt was flung across a chair, and several chicken bones were scattered across the tile floor. A stack of tarot cards were also on the table.

As Peg rounded a stack of boxes, she noticed two feet sticking out from behind a stainless steel table. She drew in a deep breath, as she got closer and saw old-fashioned nurse-style shoes attached to frail old legs covered with wrinkly nylons. She was not prepared for the sight that greeted her. She rounded the corner and saw the old woman, or what was left of her. Her throat was savagely cut and the blood that hadn't pooled around her head ran into a nearby drain set into the floor. A dead chicken with its neck twisted horribly was lying beside her and she clutched a homemade voodoo doll in her right hand. Pins were sticking out of the doll's neck. The killer had taken the time to draw a hex sign in the old woman's own blood. Peg felt herself growing dizzy as she remembered to breathe.

"Who did this to you?" Peg whispered.

Her gaze was drawn to something shiny, clutched in the old lady's other hand. Peg bent down and pried the object from the old lady's grip, using an ink pen from her notebook. A leather button with a silver underside bounced onto the floor. Peg bent down and picked it up. She knew what she was doing was wrong, but something made her slip the button into her pocket, before heading to the phone.

She dialed 9-1-1 and then immediately dialed Lester's cell phone.

While she waited for help to arrive, rain began to pound violently against the roof of the building in a torrent of sound. A cold wind whipped open the front door, causing a flood of rain to pour into the store front. Peg closed her jacket to keep from shivering.

CHAPTER FORTY-FIVE

Lester arrived at the Sweet Shop at the same time as the owners.

Marie and Charles LaRue rushed up the walk, huddled together against the rain, just a few steps behind Lester. As he pulled open the door and stepped around the puddles, he encountered a blue uniformed man blocking the entrance.

"Doug, where's Ms. McGregor?" he asked the young policeman who was blocking the door.

"Hi Lester, she's inside with the others," he said, as the couple tried to push their way into the shop with Lester.

"Please, please this is our shop. We have to go in. My mother was working today. Is she okay? They wouldn't tell us anything," the little man's words tumbled out.

"Charles, tell them to let us in. What has your mother done now? Don't let them keep us out of our own shop! Do I have to handle everything?"

The tubby little woman's voice grew to a high pitched whine that caused both the officer and Charles LaRue to cringe. He allowed them out of the rain and into the front part of the store.

"Stay right here. I'll go get someone to speak with you," said the young officer, as he looked at the elderly man with sympathy.

He stuck his head in the door and whispered something to one of the officers dusting the glass countertop. He left his job and went into the back room.

Lester shook the rain off his long trench coat and found Peg huddled on a chair in the far corner of the shop. As soon as she saw him, she jumped up and rushed into his arms. As he held her, he thought how natural it felt to be this way with her. He also thought it odd how circumstances kept throwing them together at the worst times.

"What happened Peg? Tell me everything."

"Oh, Lester, that poor woman. I think the same person who took Angela and maybe Caitlin murdered her." She whispered the last few words carefully so that no one else would hear her.

"Peg, what do you mean? I talked to one of the investigators and he told me that it was a ritual killing. The old woman dabbled in magic and sold potions. He thinks an unhappy customer or victim of her handicraft may have decided to get even."

"Lester, I just know it's related. I talked to her less than an hour ago, right before I headed over here. She said she had things to tell me that she wouldn't tell the cops; and then she turns up dead before I get here. She knew something bad was about to happen. See, she sprinkled salt all over the doorway, a voodoo custom for keeping the bad spirits away. It's too much of a coincidence. Did you know that she had spoken to Vincent's wife and she knew Angela?" Peg, clearly getting more upset, her voice rising. "I think Vincent went to see her, too."

"Look, you've had enough action for one night. Let me take you home," pleaded Lester. "You can tell me all this later."

Just then Lester's beeper went off and his cell phone rang seconds later.

"Lester," he said, and then listened intently to the conversation on the other end. His face took on a grave expression. She instantly knew he was hiding something from her.

"I'm over at the LaRue homicide; I'll be there as soon as I can. Get the Captain to go over there until I can get there," said Lester into the phone.

Concern and worry were etched on his face and he turned to Peg: "Come on, I gotta go. I'll drop you off at home first," he said in a rush.

"Wait, I have my car. I can drive myself home. It sounds like you're needed somewhere else," insisted Peg.

"You've had a bad shock. I would feel better if you let me take you home. It's on the way; I'll have someone bring your car by later."

He led her out the door as two detectives brought the LaRue couple farther into the shop. The old woman was still harping away at the poor elderly man.

Peg and Lester ran for his car as lightning zigzagged across the dark sky and answering thunder rumbled soon after. She wasn't happy about leaving her car, but she could tell he was not going to let her drive, so she gave in and slid in the car as he opened the door. She had recovered from the initial shock but decided not to push Lester. He was really upset and doing his best to hide it from her.

It took no more than fifteen minutes to get to Peg's house. Lester used his lights and sirens whenever they came to any traffic. He was so busy maneuvering the old car that they had no time to speak on the ride over. The rain had made the bridges and streets slick, but Lester effortlessly handled the turns and slides that had Peg clinging to the door handle and cracked dashboard. She knew something was up, but she didn't want to ask any questions that might distract him from the roadway.

As the car slid to an abrupt stop in front of her house, Lester jumped out and came around to her side and opened the door. She had barely gotten out and shut the door, before he was back behind the wheel. He put the car in gear and waited, until he was half a block away before turning the lights and siren back on. Peg watched until he rounded the corner on the next block and disappeared out of sight. It took a few minutes before she realized she was standing in the pouring rain. Her clothes were soaked and clinging to her skin.

Something big was happening; Something Lester didn't want her to know about. She let herself in the house and stripped off her wet clothing and threw the dripping mess into the tub to deal with later. She pulled on her terry cloth robe and walked through to the kitchen. Peg put the teakettle on to boil. She didn't really want tea, but she was on auto pilot, while her mind busily tried to come up with different scenarios that would explain Lester's behavior. Before she knew it, she was sitting in a chair drinking the tea that she didn't really want.

In her hand was the button that she had found clutched in the old lady's hand. She turned the button over and over; the leather was rich-looking, dark brown with distinctive stitching that circled the edge. She knew the garment that it had adorned was expensive, and felt sure she had seen one like it before, but couldn't draw it from her memory. She still couldn't say what had possessed her to take the button — it was pure instinct. As a former cop, she knew what she had done was very wrong. She had taken and concealed vital evidence. But why, she asked herself, again, as she slowly turned the button. Something had told her to keep silent. The reason was on the edge of her memory.

CHAPTER FORTY-SIX

Not far away, around the same time Peg was headed to visit Ms. LaRue, Fabio Marko was coming home from a trip to the liquor store down the street. A familiar depression was settling in again, as he realized that he'd already spent about half of the old lady's money. He also hadn't heard from his contact, even after leaving the threatening message. Now in the light of day, he regretted his threat and decided to cut his losses and get out while he still could.

He was balancing a brown paper bag containing a six-pack of Dixie beer and cigarettes, while reaching into his pocket to find his door key. He struggled to unlock the deadbolt with the one free hand. As he was turning around to kick the door closed, he eyed Pierre sitting in the ratty chair across the room watching him. He dropped the bag in surprise, but quickly recovered as he recognized his visitor. One of the bottles had broken and was sprewing beer and foam. The smell of beer filled the air.

"What are you doing here? I have been trying to reach you for weeks. I'm leaving as soon as you give me what you owe me. Pay me the money you promised and I'll be gone – you'll never see me again. I didn't mean what

I said last night. You know that I would never tell anyone what I know. I would be cutting my own throat."

Fabio's words all tumbled out in a rush of air, leaving him suddenly breathless and fully alert.

"What a wonderful image you make, all surrounded by a lake of foamy beer. From this point forward, I will always think of you when I drink or smell cheap beer. Isn't that just too sweet."

A small smile played around Pierre's lips, while a panicked look crossed Marko's face. He looked like a cornered rat, his beady eyes flicked all around the room, looking for an escape route.

"I fully intend on giving you what I owe you."

Suddenly, Pierre's smile turned into a twisted, deadly grimace.

"I need a drink, you want a drink?" said Fabio, stuttering and stalling for time, as he picked up the dripping bag and put it in the sink in the kitchen. He reached in the bag and pulled out an unbroken beer.

"Put that shit away," said Pierre, who could see Fabio's hands shaking.

Fabio was trying to figure out how he could get to his gun under the mattress in his bedroom. As he turned around he was startled to see Pierre standing right behind him. The guy moved like a cat. Fabio hated cats.

"Looking for this?" said Pierre as he laid Fabio's gun on the counter next to the sink. As Fabio recognized his own gun his heart started pounding wildly in his chest.

"No, hey Pierre, look I don't want no trouble. We had a deal and I'm sticking to it. What's going on? Look, just forget about the money. Float me a couple hundred and I'm outta here tonight," Fabio pleaded.

"It's too late for that and I don't make deals with scum," Pierre said, as he pushed Fabio into the chair that he had recently occupied. He pulled his own revolver from his shoulder holster.

"Bullshit," said Fabio his anger beginning to rise above his fear.

"I may have killed them little girls, but you brought them to me. You knew who I was and what I was and you brought them to me. I bet your fellow officers would like to know that. I did you a favor, Pierre. You said take care of em and I did. You're as guilty as I am and you know it. Why, you're even worse than me. I'm a sick man. I can't help myself, but what will people say about you? You left them with me knowing what I would do to them," finished Fabio, spit flying from his mouth in his efforts to convince Pierre.

Pierre looked at Fabio. His face was stone cold, showing no emotion.

"You were nothing more than a means to an end — my alternate plan. You're gonna make me famous. I'm gonna be a hero and you're gonna be dead for the crimes you have committed." Pierre's voice timbered with the strong southern drawl of a Confederate general. Pierre was now picturing himself as heroic General Andrew Jackson, standing tall against the northern aggressors. He was really getting into the role, his face changing to take on the emotions demanded by the latest part he was playing. He stood up straight, chest out, and filled his voice with righteous anger as he delivered his lines.

"Fabio Marko, child molester, rapist and killer. Meet your judge and executioner. I find you guilty of all these crimes against humanity and I hereby sentence you to death." Pierre's wicked grin broke through, as he watched the dazed expression spread across Fabio's face.

"You're crazy, you're crazy man." Fabio lunged for his gun on the kitchen counter. He grabbed it and spun around all the while waiting for Pierre's bullets to slice through him. He pointed the gun at Pierre and pulled the trigger over and over.

His eyes squeezed shut as he tried to aim at Pierre, while waiting for the bullets from Pierre's gun to tear through him. Sharp clicking sounds filled the air instead of the crashing sound of gunshots. The gun was empty, but Pierre fell back in the chair, his body jerking as he pretended to take each shot in the chest. The unloaded gun fell useless from Fabio's fingers; his jaw was hanging open in surprise.

"Oh you got me, I'm dying here," laughed Pierre.

Slowly, Fabio's face began to lose the tight lines of fear, and he started to slowly laugh with Pierre.

"Pierre, you piece of shit, you really had me going there," laughed Fabio, as he lifted his untouched beer off the counter and downed the contents in one huge gulp. He wiped the foamy residue off his chin, as he laughed foolishly along with Pierre. The pent up stress, suddenly released, made everything funny and he giggled uncontrollably.

"My turn," Pierre said as his wide grin suddenly turned cold again.

Fabio was still giggling when the first bullet hit him in the chest. He groaned and crumpled to the floor.

Quickly, Pierre rushed across the room and grabbed Fabio's gun, loaded it with the bullets in his pocket and put the weapon in Fabio's hand and squeezed off two shots into the far wall. Fabio's hand tightened on the gun as he tried to push it towards Pierre.

"Pierre, you piece of shit," he mumbled as he coughed up blood. Then he again started laughing crazily.

Pierre grabbed his shirt and shook him.

"What are you laughing about you piece of shit. The party's over and you were the entertainment," yelled Pierre.

"Because the laughs on you. I didn't kill the second one," said Fabio as he coughed up more blood. He was wheezing and having more trouble breathing. He was dying and he knew it. He would at least enjoy watching Pierre squirm during his final moments.

Pierre was stunned into silence. "What do you mean?" Pierre clinched his teeth. The vein in his forehead began to pound.

"You're a cheap piece of shit. I needed more money, so I sold her," Fabio wheezed out the last few words.

"You sold her? What do you mean? Who did you sell her to?" Pierre was so angry he was jerking Fabio up and down by his shirt. Fabio's head was banging on the floor. He stopped as he realized he would kill him before he talked.

"Who," he yelled again. Fabio coughed again and then looked at Pierre. His eyes glazed over as the last of his life and breath left his body.

"Christ," he whispered, with his last breath.

Outside the wind and rain crashed against the old building. The walls creaked and thunder rumbled in the background. Pierre rose from the floor and sat back down in the chair.

What the hell! What had he said? Christ? What did that mean? Holy shit, was everything going to hell at the end, right when everything was within his grasp. His heart was racing. He couldn't focus. He had to breathe. He walked over to the window and raised the sash. Rain and wind whipped into the room and lashed at his face. Refreshed he shut the window. What was he doing? Everything was fine. It had been many months. The girl's body hadn't been found and everyone thought she was dead. He would play it cool and everything would be okay. Hell, as far as he knew she could be dead by now.

The people Fabio ran with weren't exactly saints. Who knows where the kid would turn up? Where ever it was, Pierre doubted she would turn up alive. The odds were definitely stacked against it. Everything would be okay he said again, this time out loud. He had already let too much time slip by. He had to get moving. Pierre took off his gloves and stuffed them into his jacket's zippered inside pocket and walked over to the kitchen phone and dialed the station.

"Call Lester and get a team over here. I think we found our child killer. Unfortunately, I had to kill him in self defense."

Pierre sat back down in the same chair again to wait for the action to begin. He needed time to prepare. He would be giving one of his best performances in the next few hours. Damn, he should have shot himself in the arm. The picture of him, lying down in a hospital bed, while being interviewed was great. People loved a hero, but they loved a wounded hero even more. Shit, it was too late for that though. Besides he didn't think he would be able to hurt himself. He found other people's injuries exciting, but the sight of his own blood made him woozy, and he had to appear strong and invincible.

He spent the remaining minutes reviewing all the Dirty Harry movies in his head. He could be Harry, and play the role better than Eastwood. Eastwood was another one of his favorites, except for the roles where he was manipulated by the female lead. He never did see what Clint saw in the thin, sickly, weak and deathly pale blond who had parts in several of his films.

"Do ya feel lucky, punk? Were there six shots or seven?" he spit out at the dead man lying in pools of his own blood.

"Make my day," Pierre said as he fired off an imaginary seventh shot at the dead man. He felt great, charged up and raring to go. Underneath his bravado, a nagging fear still lingered. Fabio's words echoed again in his head. Christ? What the hell did he mean, the crazy bastard?

He soon heard heavy booted footsteps rapidly ascending the rickety wood stairs. Fabio's last words faded from his memory as he did a quick scan of the apartment. Pierre knew a search of the apartment would reveal a child's gold necklace and locket hidden under the bed, Angela's locket. They would also find the princess costume the McGregor girl had been wearing when she was abducted. That is if that stupid idiot hadn't sold it for drugs or beer. He was counting on Marko's penchant for keeping souvenirs. Oh well, if they were missing, they would do a search of local pawnshops and he was sure something would turn up. Pierre's plans for ransoming the Morelli girl may have crumbled because of one stupid old hag, but he had figured out a way to turn this thing around and come out ahead.

The bitch had started talking to police about seeing a man with dark eyes with the girl. When Pierre went to question her, she acted like she didn't recognize him, but he sensed that she was pretending. He didn't want to take chances, so he never made the ransom call, and let all that money slip through his fingers. He delivered the girl to Fabio with instructions that she be dead before the morning. Then, when the Morellis brought all their power crashing down on the police department, pushing to find Angela's killer he freaked out, and decided to grab another kid to throw off the Morellis. The kidnapping angle had to be disputed and another disappearance and murder would take the focus off the Morelli child. It would be seen as a child predator case.

Fabio Marko was also the perfect answer and his ace in the hole that would bring him fame and fortune as the city's hero cop. As for his role in the girl's death, hell he may be able to shoot an animal like Fabio in cold blood, but he couldn't bring himself to kill a kid.

If he couldn't get his money from scum like the Morelli's, he would get it through the reward money and the gullible public who believed whatever they read if it was in *The Times-Picayune* newspaper. Heck, this way would be better anyway. He wouldn't have to hide his newfound wealth and fame. Things couldn't have turned out better, if he had planned them this way from the very beginning. He couldn't be held responsible for what scum like Fabio did for kicks. He probably was a hero for getting rid of him, before he murdered more children. Those two girls were supposed to be sacrificed for the good of many others. Who knew who else had suffered from Marko's evil? He had been turning a blind eye to mounting complaints from the Quarter about someone robbing and beating drunks at night. Then last night, the attack on the old lady and Lester getting to save the day, really spurred him into action. It was a miracle Lester hadn't caught Marko. Marko's call making threats on his cell last night was the icing on the cake. Just one more reason why he needed to make his move, now, before Marko got caught and started running his mouth. Speaking of calls….he quickly riffled Marko's pocket for his cell. Found it and slipped it into his pocket. That would not have been good. Hell, this is why he hated to be rushed…that's when you made crucial mistakes.

The McGregor bitch was also getting too close and stirring up trouble. He couldn't let her talk to the voodoo hack, so took care of that problem.

Pierre felt his plan falling into place and had managed to convince himself of his own goodness as the first officers arrived on the scene. He was on, just as if there were cameras rolling to catch the action. Fabio's final death words were driven from his mind, by thrill of the chance to show his superior acting skills.

CHAPTER FORTY-SEVEN

It was the fourth ring of the phone and Peg struggled to catch it before it was picked up by the answering machine. She had paced the house last night until her car was dropped off around 11:00 p.m. She couldn't stand the anxiety of waiting for Lester to call, so she took two sleeping pills and went to bed. Even with the help of the pills, she felt unrested. She had tossed and turned in her sleep all night. The bed looked like a tornado had hit it.

The new day brought sunshine and the remaining clouds were quickly burned away. Sometime during the night the rain had settled into a steady rhythm after the worst part of the storm had passed.

"Hello," she said sleepily. She needed a cup of coffee bad.

"Peg, it's Lester, and I'm wondering if you could come down to the station."

Peg was momentarily startled. She was still groggy from the sleeping pills she had taken. Lester's voice brought back the memories of the horrible sight at the candy shop.

"Peg, are you there?" he said, concerned.

"Yes."

Peg assumed he wanted her to look at some more headshots. Perhaps there was a new lead to the old woman's killer.

"I need to talk to you."

"Okay. How about after lunch?"

"Okay, but it would be better if I could talk to you sooner. I know you must be wondering what this is all about, but I'd rather wait until you come to the station."

"Fine," she said, looking at her watch. It was already 11:45 a.m. She was still wearing the robe from the night before. Peg released her hand from the phone. She didn't realize until she put the receiver down that she was sweating and her hands were trembling.

Maybe it wasn't about the old woman? If it were, Lester would have said something over the phone. No, it had to be something more serious. Could it be that they found out something about her child? Lester was acting strangely. Why couldn't he tell her what was going on over the phone? Did they find the abductor? Suddenly, Peg dreaded the thought that she might have to face the man in a courtroom. Oddly enough, she hadn't envisioned that aspect of the search – the part where the monster is finally caught. Her thoughts had never gone beyond that point. To consider that he would be treated civilly and be offered all the legal services the state could supply was just too painful. The very fact of his existence would still be an insult to justice. What if he got off, or was given bail while awaiting trial? It happened all the time. Her mind reeled with the possibilities. She knew that if she saw him, she would want to kill him right then and there because she wouldn't be able to stand it – but not before she tortured him and made him tell her where Caitlin was. He would be presumed innocent by the justice system, even when everyone knew he was guilty. The thought made her crazy.

A migraine started to throb on the right side of her head, as she sank in the nearby armchair. She used the heel of her right hand to massage the area, as she willed the pain away. She sighed and relaxed, waiting for the pain to begin to let go, and ease its grip. How could she be so weak? She had police SWAT training, she was physically strong. Why did she feel so tired all the time? What was wrong with her? She had to find a way to bury her emotions; they were beginning to affect her physically. She couldn't allow that to happen. She couldn't let Lester see her this way. It wasn't finished yet. She had to hang on until it was finished. She owed it to Caitlin. She went to the bathroom to shower. She dressed slowly. It seemed to take her forever to get ready. Finally she was grabbing her keys and heading downtown.

CHAPTER FORTY-EIGHT

Earlier that same morning Mildred noticed a brown envelope had been placed on Pierre Martens' desk. Mildred recognized the return address of Mitchell Parks. She was anxious to get the original copies of the Harrison reports back in the file. But when she pulled out the papers, she saw an invoice with attachments made out to Mr. Vincent Morelli. "Uh oh, someone sent the wrong file."

She started scanning the reports. It seemed Morelli had hired Mitch to do some investigation work, too. Everything looked pretty similar to the police reports, except there were two items that didn't make sense. The official police report said that Lester had been on duty the day the Morelli girl was grabbed — and on the night of the Bacchus parade. But Mildred remembered that Pierre had switched duty with Lester on the day of the Morelli kidnapping. Plus, the duty roster she gave Peg had both their names on it, since Lester was scheduled for both days, but Pierre had actually worked Lester's shift. Only the payroll department would have the correct list. The agency's list didn't even have Pierre's name on it. And Pierre reported to the Mitchell Agency that the LaRue woman was delusional. This was the first she had heard of that. She may have been spooky, what with all that voodoo stuff she was into, but she was far from delusional—odd but not a crazy. In fact, Mildred's neighbor swore by the old woman's abilities and said she had cured her lame back. The neighbor had actually learned of her killing before Mildred. The local community was very upset. Mrs. LaRue was a neighborhood icon and respected in the voodoo community.

Mildred knew there were angry rumblings about the reference made by the police that her killing was related to her involvement in voodoo. No one believed that because, as her friend and others had told her the signs left at the murder scene had not been right. LaRue never used pin dolls or live chickens as offerings.

Mildred was getting more confused. She tried to sort it out in her head and remember back to those nights. Yes, Lester was scheduled, but it was tentative. She remembered that she had to call Pierre and ask him to cover. He did. And he was actually pleasant about it, which was unusual. Pierre was never happy about covering for anyone else. That's why it stood out in her mind – Pierre was jovial and laughing about having to cover for Lester, who she knew he despised.

She shook her head remembering how odd she had felt after hanging up, like something weird was going on. Now she was really freaked out as she noticed someone changed Lester from tentative to on duty on the computer roster. Pierre's name was totally missing. Then she looked at the roster for the night Caitlin was kidnapped. Pierre was on duty that night, too. So was Lester. But Pierre was stationed closer to Washington Avenue and St. Charles. No one had her password. Who could have changed the reports? She changed the reports back to their original status and printed out copies and placed a call to Lester. She was forced to leave a message on his cell phone.

Just as she was about to leave her desk, Vincent Morelli walked in.

"Hello," she said quickly.

"Hi, I think this belongs to you. Somehow Mitchell Parks got our mail mixed up. I think you have something of mine," said Vincent. He was not happy about the mix-up.

Vincent looked at Mildred as he took the report from her hands. He could tell something was wrong. Mildred looked horrible. Her face was white and her hands were trembling. She had practically jumped out of her chair as he walked in.

"What's the matter? You look as if you have seen a ghost."

Vincent looked down at the desk. Mildred was trying to conceal the schedule roster. Vincent grabbed it.

He recognized the dates: Oct. 22 and March 5, the days Angela and Caitlin were taken!

Mildred had circled Pierre's name.

"I thought Lester was on duty that night. It was Pierre. Pierre on both nights," said Vincent, suddenly realizing what that meant.

Mildred didn't know what to say. Her mouth opened, but no words emerged. At that moment they had both reached the same conclusions and the shock was evident.

Vincent didn't give her a chance to say anything. He turned around and hurried out of the station, pushing his way through the doors. Mildred sat for another 10 minutes, trying to figure out what to do. Tears welled up in her eyes and she couldn't hold in the despair. She wept softly.

"Oh Pierre, Pierre," she cried out in between the sobs. She wasn't sure what it all meant but she couldn't think of any good reason why Pierre would change the duty roster unless he had something to hide. It may be unrelated to the kidnappings but whatever it was, it wouldn't be good.

She had noticed a change in Pierre over the last year. He was more reckless than ever and had no regard for the rules. She couldn't cover for him anymore. But always the optimist, she dried her eyes and thought that maybe this would be a blessing in disguise.

Pierre needed to hit bottom. Isn't that what they always said should happen in order for someone to recover from addictions? The department would most likely be lenient with him if he admitted his problems and went into counseling or rehab. He may even be able to keep his job. Mildred would make sure she was there to offer any support she could. She was good at picking up pieces and she longed to be the one Pierre could turn to in a time of crisis.

Suddenly, things didn't seem so bleak after all, but then she felt another twinge of doubt as she tried to picture Pierre admitting a weakness to anyone. As much as she tried, she couldn't wrap her mind around that scenario and she began to worry again.

CHAPTER FORTY-NINE

Peg found a parking spot near the station, so she didn't have to walk far. The sun was flooding down and bathing everything in bright, warm light. The sunny day was startling in its contrast to the dreary day before. The fall hurricane season was rearing its ugly head again. She held her hand like a visor over her eyes to shield them from the blinding light and she headed for the station, it was already late afternoon so she quickened her step.

She opened the old wooden door and climbed up the stairs to the second floor and Lester's office, taking a deep breath with each step. Lester was sitting behind his desk. When he saw Peg enter, he looked up and then stood up to greet her. Other than a quick catnap, he hadn't slept all night and his bloodshot eyes served as testimony. It had been a long day. He had been dreading Peg's visit. Peg resisted the urge to hug him as he stood and walked over to shut the door.

"I'm not sure if I am prepared for this. Sorry I'm so late. I just couldn't get moving today."

She sat in the chair across from his desk.

Lester was silent. What could he say? He had rehearsed how he should handle this, but now that it was time he was lost. He tried to be professional and unemotional, as he pulled out a brown paper bag and carefully removed a large plastic evidence bag that contained the princess costume.

"Do you recognize this?" The pain in his voice betrayed him.

Peg carefully reached her hand out to touch it. It was as if she was reaching to hold the sweet face of Caitlin. But there was no Caitlin, only a horrible reminder of the loss. She had known this was coming. Her instincts had tried to warn her about the possible outcome of this trip but it did not make it any easier. Her heart broke as she noticed a few strands of blond hair still clinging to the sparkling pink mesh of the dress.

"How could anyone do this?" She cried out in pain as Lester came around and enfolded her in his arms.

Lester led her to the small sofa by the window. He put his arm around her, while she sat letting the tears stream uncontrollably down her face. Lester went to his cabinet and pulled out a bottle and a glass. He slowly poured her a glass of Jack Daniels.

He kept a supply hidden for times like this. A case that goes bad, another criminal free on the streets, and then for the better times when they successfully solved a case with a good outcome. Unfortunately, it seemed lately the better times were few and far between.

With shaking hands Peg downed the contents and was barely able to set the glass on the edge of the small wooden coffee table.

"I'm going to take you home now. Give me your keys."

Lester put his arm around her shoulder, and she buried her head against his chest. Lester understood that Peg wanted to be invisible, wanted an escape from the world. The costume had brought it all back as if it were yesterday, flashbacks to the day Caitlin was taken. Each memory unleashed new pain.

Pierre watched them leave the station. He shook his head as he mentally crossed Peg off his list of threats. She was weak after all. Lester made him sick the way he catered to her. Lester should have been a woman. He was stupid and weak and Pierre would be running things before long. The Captain had practically shaken his arm off when he realized Pierre had single-handedly solved the Morelli and McGregor cases. He had not felt such a glowing satisfaction since the hunting trip with his father, when he had finally shed the weakness inflicted by his mother and found pride in killing things weaker and stupider than he. He also was a good liar. Pierre told Captain Jackson that he had tracked Marko through an "inside source" who had come to him about a guy who was rolling drunks for money. Pierre said he had been staking out the same area. After hearing about Lester's run in with a perp who beat up and robbed an old lady in the same area, Pierre said he realized Marko matched the suspect's description. Based on the matching description, he decided to pay an official call on Marko. One thing led to another; Marko freaked and went for his gun. Pierre had no choice but to return fire…end of story.

Pierre sensed that Lester didn't believe a word of it, but it didn't matter, he had fooled everyone else. Most people never questioned a hero's story especially when that hero single-handedly solved the NOPD's biggest case in the last decade. Pierre was riding high and loving every minute of it. Lester was just a jealous loser.

Lester was vindicated, apparently, his instincts had been correct. Fabio was on the top ten list – number 7, and part of him secretly wished he had not interfered the other night when that old lady had been attacked. He should have let the Crusader finish the job.

By the time they arrived at the house, Peg was exhausted. Lester had to practically carry her to the door. Once they were inside, he guided her back to the bedroom. He removed her shoes, pulled back the covers and tucked her in.

"You just stay there, and I'll get you some water."

Lester came back with the water, and Peg drank one sip and fell back onto the bed. Lester gently stroked her hair. After thirty minutes the alcohol and depression worked to put her into a restful sleep.

Once he could tell she was sleeping, Lester left the room and pulled the door shut. He went to the kitchen to get himself some coffee. As he walked down the hallway, he noticed that the door to Caitlin's room was slightly opened. After Caitlin's death, Lester had seen the room only once, right after the kidnapping. Whenever Lester had come to the house for other visits, he noticed that the door was always shut. He guessed Peg never went in there. She had probably left the room as it had been since the day Caitlin disappeared. It was strange to see the door ajar. Lester felt drawn into the room. He felt like an intruder, but went inside anyway. Would Caitlin's toys and room still be untouched? He wondered if Peg had begun packing it all up to be stored? What would he have done if he had lost a child? Are the toys and stuffed animals and photo albums a comfort to the grieving, or a horrible reminder of loss? Lester was thinking about the costume and how shocking it was for Peg to have seen it. He wished that he had been able to handle it some other way that wouldn't have been so painful but he had to follow chain of evidence rules.

The room looked exactly the same as Caitlin had left it. Looking around at the bookshelf full of toys and stuffed animals, he could picture Caitlin running in at any minute to play. His heart heavy, he left the room and pulled the door shut behind him.

When Peg woke up early the next morning she found Lester sound asleep on the sofa, covered up with the throw. She reached out and pushed a few stray curls away from his eyes. She brought him a cup of coffee and placed it on the table by the sofa. She shook his arm gently. "Lester," she said softly.

Lester's eyes flew open and he looked startled.

"I brought you coffee...black right?" she said sweetly.

Lester sat up and was surprised to see Peg so calm. He thought that the rest must have helped. It sure helped him. He hadn't realized how exhausted he was.

"I'm frying some bacon and eggs for you," said Peg with a smile.

Lester was always amazed at how quickly Peg seemed to be able to come through the emotional turmoil. Sometimes she seemed so helpless and fragile and then other times, strong and ungiving as steel. She was an enigma.

"That sounds great."

As soon as Lester had washed his face, and was beginning to feel alive again, he joined Peg in the kitchen. As he set at the table, watching Peg finish up breakfast he was hit by how natural it was for him to be here — like he always belonged here sitting in this kitchen.

The morning sun was streaming through the lace curtains making the kitchen glow with warmth. Peg was at the stove bathed in the morning glow. She looked young, fresh and carefree...only he knew that was probably the farthest from what she was most likely feeling today. She turned and smiled at him but he could see the sadness in her eyes. His heart skipped a beat and he smiled back. He wanted to hold her again and drive the sadness away.

She had on a pair of faded worn jeans that clung to her slim curves and a dark blue v-neck pullover that brought out her blue eyes. She walked over and laid a plate loaded with eggs, bacon and buttered toast down in front of him. She sat across from him with a plate that held a much smaller version of his meal.

"You're gonna make me fat, but it sure does look and smell good."

Lester smiled at Peg.

"You look much better today. How are you feeling?"

"Sleep finally found me and I woke up this morning feeling a lot stronger. I thought we both needed a big breakfast since we didn't have dinner yesterday."

"Speak for yourself. I raided your refrigerator last night while you were sleeping."

Lester watched Peg load one piece of toast with the egg and three pieces of bacon and cover it with the remaining slice of bread. She smiled as she looked up and saw Lester watching her.

"My version of the bacon-and-egg McMuffin. I'm usually not a breakfast person"

She took a bite of the assembled sandwich.

As they ate they talked about food and all the personalities at the police station. As they were sitting over their second cup of coffee, Peg broke the spell of the morning.

"Lester, I feel better today because I had a dream about Caitlin. She's still waiting for me to find her. I know she's not dead."

"Peg, I can't even begin to know what you're feeling but maybe you should talk to someone, someone who can help you figure this all out. God Peg, you are a mystery – one minute I can see all the raw pain you carry around and the next you have buried it all and appear as tough as nails. A person can't function that way. It's not healthy and I'm very worried about you."

His was seriously concerned for her emotional well-being.

"I'm fine, really Lester. You must realize what a big shock it was to see Caitlin's costume. I think where ever she is, we have this unbreakable connection. I just feel it. Through all of this I have never really felt she was dead. I just know I would feel it. I know that sounds crazy and delusional but that's how I feel."

She was doing her best to try to convince Lester.

"I've got more to tell you. Come and sit down."

Lester decided he had better go ahead and tell her everything about yesterday's events. She needed to know. Maybe then she could deal with Caitlin's death. Lester was surer than ever that Caitlin was dead. Marko was dead. Caitlin and Angela's things were found in his apartment. He could think of no scenario where Caitlin could still be alive. They moved to the living room and sat down on the sofa. Lester told her the events that led up to that day, his FBI tip, saving the old lady from Fabio Marko, coming to the shop where Ms. LaRue had been killed. He ended with Pierre finding Fabio, while he had everyone patrolling the area, then Pierre finding the evidence and finally Pierre having to kill Fabio in self-defense.

"I need to see him. Do you have a picture?"

"Peg, don't torture yourself. Why do you need to see him?"

"Because something is not right about this, Lester. It all fits together too easily. The other pieces don't add up. What about what Ms. LaRue said? Who wanted her dead? Please Lester I have to see what he looked like."

A bell went off in Lester's head. Peg brought up a question that had been bothering him too. Why would someone kill that old Creole woman, unless she knew or saw something? It was one of those loose ends that he hadn't figured out either. He didn't buy the ritual killing either. He had talked to some local experts and the crime scene had been staged by someone. He had some ideas of his own, that he wasn't ready to mention to Peg. He kept to himself some of the thoughts that were beginning to form in his mind – some of the pieces were coming together, the suicide note from Elizabeth and the LaRue woman's murder. When the police first saw the note, they, like Vincent, figured that his wife must have written it during a psychotic episode. But now, it may make more sense. Elizabeth must have gone to see LaRue and later blamed herself for Angela's death, by "conjuring up the devil with the voodoo."

LaRue was probably afraid to tell the police that she knew Elizabeth, later she became scared, and probably wanted to talk to Peg, maybe even warn her. He wondered if the LaRue woman really did know the killer, and if it was Fabio Marko she saw that night, or some other person. Now that she was dead, there would be no way to know.

"Please Lester. I haven't asked much from you. And I need you to understand that I have to be sure about this. I can't rest until I know in my gut that this whole thing is really over — that justice has been served. Besides, I left my car there," she said with a smile.

"I also noticed there was no blood on Caitlin's costume. Was it ripped at all? She had on a t-shirt and shorts underneath. Were they found in the apartment?"

"No, nothing but the costume. But Peg that doesn't mean she's okay. You have to start accepting that she is gone."

"I can't do that yet." Her voice was strong and firm.

Lester shook his head, knowing that he was defeated.

"Okay, I'll run you down to the station; come on."

"Thanks, Lester."

Peg jumped up off the sofa, grabbing her jacket from the closet.

CHAPTER FIFTY

When Lester and Peg arrived at the station, they headed directly to his office. He deposited her on the couch, while he went to get the report on Fabio Marko. As Peg was looking around the office, Mildred stuck her head in the doorway.

"Have you seen Lester?" she asked Peg.

"I think he went to get a file. He should be right back."

She was surprised at the woman's disheveled appearance.

"Are you okay?"

Mildred forced a smile, "Yes, I'm fine."

Mildred had been thinking all night about the disturbing call from Fabio Marko. He had called the station just last week looking for Pierre. When she told Pierre about the call, he told her to forget it, because it was some screw-up and didn't mean anything.

But Mildred knew he was boiling inside. When he was upset, he always turned red in the neck and ground his teeth, clinching and unclinching his jaw. He'd also left the station ten minutes later and hadn't returned until after lunch. Mildred had tossed and turned all night, after learning about Pierre's escapade at Marko's apartment. She was very afraid; afraid of what she now imagined he was capable of doing.

Still, she just couldn't believe it was true, and was able to ignore all the signs, until she saw the Mitchell Parks report. She ached all over. She should just go home for the day and think about everything. She was tired and scared and might say or do something she'd regret later. She felt caged in and tried to hide her fear but it wasn't working too well. Meanwhile, Pierre was riding high, basking in the glory of being the one to crack two of the most famous New Orleans cases.

As Lester reached the main office area, he saw Pierre looking smug, surrounded by the other detectives.

"Lucky break in the child murder cases, huh?" said Detective Hubert, who was standing with two other police officers. They had just arrived from Marko's apartment.

"Yeah, but when you think about it, it fits together pretty well," Pierre explained. "I mean most kids don't stray too far, and we often find the kidnapper within a few miles' radius. I can't believe we never checked that guy out before; he flew just under the radar since jumping parole in Texas and hiding out here. Too bad we never brought him in before; maybe those little girls would still be alive."

Pierre was really getting into the role of reluctant hero.

"I know what you mean," Hubert said. "The search really sealed it. All that porno crap sickened me. It should be easy to wrap up the Morelli case now. I can't wait to get the political brass off our backs."

"Come on Pierre; we'll buy you a cup of coffee for saving us all from City Hall," said one of the officers. They were all laughing as they walked right by Lester and down the hall towards the break room.

Lester shook his head as he grabbed the file off Pierre's desk. Pierre was enjoying his day in the sun a little too much. He quickly walked down the long hallway to the room at the far end. He had been reluctant to congratulate

Pierre, not out of jealousy, but because he was a part of an internal investigation surrounding Pierre. The net was tightening and if the Marko thing hadn't blown wide-open, Internal Affairs would have already convened. Lester had suspected Pierre of leaking information, but he hadn't had a chance to pursue it until Pierre got so bold as to leak information about major cases. It was not like him to withhold credit from any of his staff. He knew Pierre had picked up on it and instead of being upset and angry, as he would have been in the past, he took pleasure in rubbing the victory in Lester's face. Pierre had gotten too smug, but Lester felt no pleasure in knowing Pierre's day in the sun would soon end. How does the saying go...the bigger they are the harder they fall? Pierre's ego was inflated bigger than ever, and Lester wasn't sure how he would react when they lowered the boom, so soon after this latest bit of glory.

Last week Glen, his friend at the FBI, had called and made the official FBI offer. He'd accepted and was turning in his resignation today. Pierre's removal from the force was to be his last official act. When Lester came back into his office, he pulled the mug and file photos of Marko out and handed them to Peg.

She took the photos and started looking through them. Fabio Marko was rail thin, with greasy unkept hair and a fresh scab that ran from the corner of his left eye down to his mouth, lifting it slightly like a permanent half grimace. Even without the cut he was danger incarnate. She was sure one look at him and Caitlin would have run away or screamed. Maybe he hit her and knocked her out, but still, wouldn't anyone have noticed with all those people around. Yet, despite extensive searches, no one reported seeing anything even slightly suspicious.

She was comforted that Lester had stayed with her, and gave him a small smile of gratitude. They had spent a lot of time together these last few months and she was glad to catch Caitlin's abductor, but was sad to think it might end their friendship. She knew Lester thought this was it...case closed. Caitlin could be laid to rest along with the case. But for Peg, this was just the beginning. She had new leads to explore and would follow them where ever they led. As long as they still hadn't found Caitlin's body, Peg couldn't accept that she was dead.

Peg had no idea that Lester was thinking along the same lines. Except, he was hoping, now Peg could find some peace in her life and their friendship could grow into something more meaningful. Hell, friendship, why didn't he admit it; he wanted it over so he could make it more than that. He was afraid he had fallen in love with her, but he couldn't show it while he was officially linked to her. He also was a man of few words where emotions were concerned.

Instead of pouring out his unspoken love, and completely forgetting Pierre, he returned her smile and dropped down beside her, taking her hand in his.

"Peg, are you okay? Do you recognize him at all?"

"Lester, I have been sitting here thinking and the more I think about it from every angle – something just doesn't add up."

"What?"

He knew they both needed this thing to end. He felt Peg slipping away from reality every day that went by with this case unsolved. It was destroying her and he didn't know what to do about it. His frustration showed on his face.

"Look at him," she said. "No child would go with him willingly. I know Caitlin wouldn't have gone with him. I don't think he forced her or people would have noticed." Peg desperately wanted to convince Lester. She read his frustration as a sign that he was tired of dealing with her, and wanted to put this case behind him so he could move on without her in his life.

Peg didn't know if she was clinging to her feelings of unease, because she truly believed them, or that she still needed a reason to see Lester again.

"But Peg, he had the costume and the necklace. He was a convicted child molester in Texas. He was connected to both girls by evidence found in his apartment."

Lester knew that Peg wasn't convinced, and he hated to admit it, but had his own doubts about how some of the facts were lining up.

"What else have you neglected to tell me, Lester?" Peg's eyes flashed with pain, as Lester turned away, looking out at the river.

"I could see it on your face; you are not convinced either. I thought we were always going to be honest with each other. I guess if I want answers, I'll have to find them on my own."

She jumped up and hurried out of the room leaving Lester to stare after her.

He slammed his fist down with a bang on the oak desk in frustration and jumped up to follow Peg, but Mildred blocked the doorway.

Looking like a hunted animal she slipped into the room, shut and locked the door and handed Lester a file folder.

"Lester, we need to talk; I'm scared, really scared and I need your help."

She was terrified. It stunned him and brought him back to earth.

Lester could tell this was not an act set up by Pierre. In fact he was sure that Pierre did not know Mildred was in his office right now and wondered what he would say if he did. He knew Mildred had been covering for Pierre for some time now.

He quickly opened the file. His eyes widened as he read the contents.

"Mildred, do you realize what you have here? Do you realize what this will mean to you?"

"Yes." Mildred broke down in tears. "I never meant any harm. I thought he needed me. I never thought he was bad, just misunderstood. In the last year things have gotten out of hand. He has changed and it frightens me. That's why I started recording everything, in case something happened to him,"

Tears streamed down her face.

"Mildred, I'll do what I can to help you out. You did come forward and cooperate and that will mean something to Internal Affairs. I can't sit on this thing one second more though, especially if what you recorded in here pans out. It goes way deeper than Pierre making a few bucks selling tips to reporters."

Lester's face was grim and he was doing a mental scramble trying to decide how to handle the information.

"I've got to take this to Internal Affairs and Glen – right away."

Lester looked at a very scared and rattled Mildred, sitting directly across from him.

"You did the right thing. Now I have to make some phone calls. Go home now and don't talk to anyone, especially Pierre."

He waited for Mildred to walk out the door, and then Lester dialed the FBI.

"Glen, it seems we may have to move quicker than expected. Mildred Welker has a file of information going back about a year that I think you should see."

"Yes, that Mildred," he said into the phone. "The case isn't solved yet. I've got Internal Affairs on their way down and thought you'd better show up, too."

CHAPTER FIFTY-ONE

Peg had left in a rush, her anger propelling her towards the door to the station. As she ran down the two flights of stairs from Lester's office, her anger slowly dissipated.

Why was she so angry? The look on his face – poor Lester. He was only trying to shield her from more hurt. He didn't realize how strong she had felt this morning when she woke up.

She had a purpose to fulfill and she intended to continue until she found out exactly what had happened to Caitlin. It was a promise she made that awful day of the prayer service while the rest of the world was mentally laying her daughter to rest. She was more determined than ever to find her. It was her only reason for living. But that wasn't being totally honest.

Her life had taken some strange turns in the last six months. She found herself thinking more and more of the future. Lester and Vincent kept sidetracking her. She pushed the thoughts of them away. She was betraying her vow to Caitlin. Caitlin was her only future. It was time to finish what she had started.

Peg had calmed down considerably as she reached the front desk. The door separating the front lobby opened and a policeman stepped through with a small boy in tow. He looked to be about four-years-old. He was wearing red-stripped shorts and a white shirt sporting a smiling Crocodile on a leash with the words "New Orleans Yard Dog" emblazoned across the front.

A tourist's lost kid from the looks of him. Well there is one frantic mother whose prayers will be answered. The boy will be safe with her tonight.

She watched as the officer picked the boy up and sat him on the desk. He took his patrolman's cap and placed it on the little head. The small boy was clearly thrilled with his adventure and a huge smile lit up his face. At least he was not scared; he knew he was safe.

Peg walked out the door with the vision of the little boy looking up at the officer like he was a superhero. She kept thinking about it all the way home. Something about it bothered her, but she couldn't put her finger on it.

Later that evening, as she roamed around the house, looking for answers to questions unasked, she came to Caitlin's door. The phone had rung several times but she ignored it; she just didn't want to talk to anyone right now. She opened Caitlin's door and went into the room and sat on the bed.

Memories rushed at her and the pain was great but it was also soothing. She smiled even as tears ran down her face. Her Caitlin so beautiful, so funny, so smart. She remembered talking to Caitlin many times about stranger danger. She could see them as they had been, Caitlin lying in bed the day before the field trip to the zoo in the fall, now almost a year ago.

"Now Caitlin you stay with the others and don't wander off by yourself."

"I know Momma, don't worry, I'll be safe. I have Jenny and she's my buddy for the trip and my best friend," Caitlin proudly said.

"And what do you do if you and Jenny get lost?" urged Peg, not ready to let the lesson go.

"We look for a policeman. Always look for a policeman when you're lost. Policemen are good and will help lost children find their mommas."

Peg absently felt the leather button that was still in her pocket. Suddenly a picture flashed before her of a jacket draped over a chair as Lester led her down the hall to his office. She closed her eyes and concentrated on the memory. Whose desk? It was the one by the window. Almost immediately, another picture flashed before her of Pierre bumping into her as she left Lester's office several weeks ago. She remembered the soft feel of the leather jacket as she had placed her palms against him before momentum carried her into him. She rubbed the button between her fingers again.

She jumped up from the bed and rushed to her computer. She remembered that she had saved the police roster from the reports. Lester was working the night Caitlin was taken. No, not Lester, but yet the report said Lester and Pierre were both working, and it all made sense. Pierre could have easily planted the evidence, and Pierre was the one who killed Marko. Lester obviously disliked Pierre. Maybe there were other things about Pierre she didn't know.

Peg picked up the phone and called the station.

This is Peg McGregor. I need to talk to Detective Martens."

It was late; she hoped he would still be at the station, basking in his glory.

"I'll get him for you. He's sitting at his desk. I'll transfer you."

She could barely hear the duty officer who had answered. She could tell he must be holding his hand over the phone as he whispered to Pierre.

"It's Peg McGregor calling, she wants to talk to you."

"Wonder what she wants? Send it through."

"Hello," said Pierre into the phone. His good mood was evident in his voice.

"Detective Martens, you will be surprised at what I have to tell you. I know who took Caitlin and Angela. It wasn't that Marko person you killed. I have the evidence. Meet me and I'll show it to you."

Pierre couldn't believe what he was hearing. He asked her to repeat herself just to be sure. Playing it cool he went along with the conversation. Beads of sweat popped out on his forehead.

"You know the lady in the Sweet Shop saw Angela with someone. I have something she gave me before she died. It belongs to the killer. I talked to her on the phone the day she was killed. There were things she saw that day that she hadn't told the police, but she told me when I called her."

Peg had not made up the part about Mrs. LaRue giving her something that belonged to the killer, but Pierre would have no way of knowing that it was given to her by a dead woman, or even if she was bluffing.

"That is amazing. I would love to know what information she had been concealing. I'm really glad you called me since I was instrumental in solving this case. This is something that needs to be checked out. I can't talk right now. Why don't you meet me at Le Petite Theater tonight around 9:00 p.m? It's down the street from the station. The theatre will be closed, but the court-yard stays open. We can meet there and find a quiet spot to talk. And keep this to yourself. We wouldn't want anything to get out to the media before I have a chance to check it out."

"Don't worry, I will."

Peg hung up the phone. While listening to Pierre, her face had taken on a wooden expression. Next she dialed Lester's cell phone. She got his voice mail.

"Lester this is Peg. I know who took Caitlin and Angela. I have evidence that I am going to confront Pierre with tonight. I'm meeting him at the Le Petite Theatre at 10:00 p.m. Please come as soon as you can."

She knew he only checked his personal cell phone for messages after he got home. Even if he came by the time she stated he would be too late, but she wanted him to be there for the aftermath — she owed it to him.

Peg looked at her watch: 7:45 p.m. She didn't have much time. She didn't question her actions as she walked to the hallway and lowered the hanging stairway. She climbed the wooden ladder and stopped at the top. Peg crawled to the chest she had stored when they had first moved in and flipped the han-dle and threw back the lid. The minute she saw the folded uniform, memories crowded into her brain — flashing across her field of vision like a child's video scope. She saw her mother, her father, Caitlin. All her past – the good and the bad. The memories crowding in all at once.

She embraced her anger and need for vengeance. No longer a woman torn between two men she could never have. None of that mattered anymore.

She would never have any peace unless she finished this – unless she found the truth and whatever answers it brought. She quickly donned her bullet proof vest, old shoulder holster and gun. She finally was thinking clearly. She knew her path. This was her; this was how it had to be.

All these months she had tried to live the life everyone thought she should, but it hadn't worked. She could not ever rest until she found the truth. No matter the price, she would give everything she had to find the truth.

As Peg shut the door and started down the steps, she heard the phone begin to ring. She tuned it out as she continued walking to her car.

After the fourth ring the answering machine picked up. A small scared voice came through the speakers.

"Mommy, are you there? Mommy it's me. Mommy, please come get me. I want to come home," the voice begged as the child on the other end began to softly cry.

There was noise in the background and then a click as the line went dead. The blinking light of the answering machine flashed denoting one call waiting.

CHAPTER FIFTY-TWO

Vincent rushed back to his house from the station. He had received the call from Lester on his cell phone. Lester had told him about Fabio Marko and the evidence found at the scene. He was worried about Peg. Lester had even sounded worried and asked him to look in on her. There was also a message on the machine. It was from Peg.

Her voice sounded urgent but calm at the same time.

"Vincent, they are missing a piece of the puzzle. Fabio Marko didn't do this all on his own. It's Pierre Martens. I can't explain now, but I wanted you to know. I've told Pierre and Lester to meet me tonight at the Le Petite Theatre at 10:00 p.m. I hope you can forgive me for doing this without you. I really feel bad knowing that you suffered at his hands as much as I have. But this is something I need to do on my own. If I should fail I know you will finish what I started. Thank you for everything."

His heart beat loud and fast as he listened to the rest of the message.

"Don't worry about me; I can take care of this myself."

Vincent couldn't believe what he heard. He rewound the tape again and again. He was convinced it was Peg. But this was crazy. He had spoken to

Lester and knew about Marko. Now Peg was calling saying Det. Martens was also involved. It was a shock he had not anticipated. Pierre was the master mind behind the killing of their children. Lester was expecting him at the station. He was supposed to come and identify some jewelry found at the scene. He knew about the princess costume and the hair match. He had been trying to reach Peg for the past two hours. He had to do something fast.

He knew Peg had stolen the FBI list that night at the Survivor meeting. He had been intrigued when he saw her pocket the list. He had her followed and considered making her his partner both personally and professionally. Now she had taken it out of his hands as she sought to end the story for him. He couldn't let that happen. He had come too far and done too much to let her finish what he had begun...he was "the Crusader." It was a role he took on to obtain the vengeance for his inconsolable loss and his final destiny – the Dr. John that the old woman had babbled about.

He had fallen hard for Peg before he ever really got to know her. They belonged together. He didn't want to lose her but he also had to stop her. This was his fight to finish.

Vincent decided he would call Lester. After catching Mildred with that doctored duty report today, he had already been thinking about having Mitch put a trail on Pierre.

A man's voice answered. Vincent got right to the point as he noticed it was already 8:30.

"I have to find Lester. Where is he?"

"Who is this?"

A desk officer he didn't recognize was on the other end. He could hear the indifference in the young man's tone.

"This is Vincent Morelli. You must tell me where he his."

"Lester is in conference and I can't disturb him," the voice on the other end said in a dismissive tone.

"I need to talk to Lester now; it's very important," shouted Vincent before the other party could hang up. "Get him now, damn it or I'll have your job."

If Vincent could reach through the phone the guy would be using his socks for a necktie. He took a deep breath and tried to reign in his anger. He had to remember he wasn't talking to one of his father's cronies or thugs.

"He's in a closed door meeting. I can't interrupt him."

"What about Det. Martens. Where is he?"

"He is already off duty. Look buddy, the Saint Pat's parade is expected to roll down through the Quarter any minute. We're short staffed around here. I gotta go."

"Wait! Tell Lester I've gone to find Det. Martens and that I think Peg McGregor is in danger. He needs to get to Le Petite Theatre pronto. Someone is going to die tonight at that theatre and if Lester finds out you didn't let him know about my call, you will have two of us after you."

Vincent hung up the phone, not even waiting for a reply as he dashed to his study and grabbed his revolver from the locked desk drawer, before shrugging on his jacket and flying out the door. Vincent had to get down to the Quarter. At this point he had no idea what would happen when he got there. But he needed to find Peg.

He rushed to his car and then realized that St. Charles Avenue was blocked all the way to Canal Street because of the St. Patrick's Day parade. Vincent knew the faster way would be on foot. The distance wasn't more than two miles, a thirty-minute jog. But with these crowds, it would take longer. It didn't matter, it was the only way to get there and find Peg.

Lester, Mildred, Glen and several Internal Affairs agents looked up as the young officer on phone duty poked his head into the room.

He looked at Lester and gestured him to the door. Lester pushed him back through the doorway into the hall as he quickly said, "What's up?"

CHAPTER FIFTY-THREE

The crowd in the French Quarter was cheering its approval, as the St. Patrick's Day parade was just getting into full swing. Peg tried to blend into the mass of people who lined the streets in a sea of green t-shirts, hats, beads and cans of beer.

The weight of her shoulder holster bumped against her side under her jacket, as she pushed her way through the drunken crowd. As her eyes looked for spots of blue, or any of Lester's officers among the glittering green hats that seemed to be glued to every head, she nearly tripped on the curb.

She looked down towards her feet, the filthy gutter was a stark contrast to the brightly colored marching band that was crossing directly in front of her.

Suddenly, a band marshal waved his gloved-hand, in sweeping motion to the crowds crushing forward towards the street.

"Move away, move away," he chanted.

It was dark, but the glowing lights and sounds of the parade pulsed around her, swirling her thoughts. She pushed ahead through the dense throng of revelers.

Peg turned to the left and momentarily froze as the twirlers and drummers marched past. The pounding rhythm of the drums were beating as loud as her own heart.

She took a deep breath and steadied herself.

She was oblivious to the stares from the crowd. People were stepping back out of her way. The "POLICE" on her cap was doing what she hoped and helped to part the crowds. The unfamiliar weight of the vest and shoulder hardness helped keep her thoughts focused.

One man who had already consumed more than his share of green beers stumbled back as Peg passed by.

"Hello, and goodbye," he mumbled as he saw the gun poking out from underneath her jacket flap.

Peg turned and glanced at him. She reached for her cell phone and called the station. She had a need to talk to Lester one last time. Mildred answered the phone on the second ring. She sounded upset.

"Mildred, this is Peg. Is Lester there? I need to talk to him," demanded Peg.

Mildred cut in quickly and said, "Peg, Lester is on his way. He told me that if you called to tell you to wait until he gets there. Don't do anything stupid."

"Peg, are you there? Peg, listen hold tight. Pierre is dangerous. Wait for Lester. Peg, Peg," yelled Mildred into the phone before realizing she was listening to a dial tone.

As Peg turned the corner, she saw the front door of the Le Petite Theatre. Peg entered the unlocked theatre door and stood just inside the foyer, her eyes sweeping the empty reception room and ticket booth.

She walked ahead towards the wooden double doors leading to the old French-style courtyard. Strings of lights cast a soft glow and outlined the garden and fountain in the center. The soothing tinkling of the fountain's waters drew her eyes to the center of the garden.

She spotted Pierre sitting quietly on the edge of the fountain, his right hand resting on the side. He was staring at the twin devil statues that spewed water from their horns. The sight of him made her blood boil. He turned and saw her standing in the entryway.

"Ms. McGregor, or may I call you Peg, surely you take your stint with the department too seriously. Did Lester give you the hat?" said Pierre, clearly enjoying the role of hero in waiting.

"What is it you wanted to tell me?" said Pierre, his voice filled with smug self-satisfaction.

He had decided to play his cards up front. He wanted to know right away her purpose in meeting with him.

"What evidence did the crazy old voodoo lady give you? You know this is all unnecessary as I have already solved this case."

"SHUT UP!" Peg yelled, in a very clipped and controlled tone.

Pierre turned in surprise to see Peg take her gun from her jacket and place it on the delicate wrought iron flower stand by the door.

Pierre relaxed as he saw Peg leave the gun on the table, but something was wrong. The scene was not playing out as he expected. Peg looked hard and her eyes were expressionless.

"She gave me this. It was clutched in her dead hand. Did you loose something?"

Peg's voice was like ice as she held up the leather button. The button that belonged to the jacket Pierre was wearing.

Pierre raised his right arm and saw the hanging threads at the cuff of his jacket.

"At least now we know where we stand," he said as he moved menacingly towards her.

They both turned suddenly as Vincent, his face full of sweat and breathing heavily, burst into the courtyard.

Pierre instinctively reached for the gun in his shoulder harness.

"Peg, stay back he's mine."

Vincent pointed his own weapon directly at Pierre.

"Vincent, I have to do this. Don't get in my way," Peg shouted.

Both men were both caught off guard as Peg charged across the short space separating them and sent Pierre crashing into the back wall at full force. Pierre felt all the air leave his lungs as he slid to the ground. He was dazed by the quick attack.

Peg was already up and pummeling Pierre in the face and chest. Hard blows rained down on his crumpled body. He was still gasping for breath as he felt his body being dragged helplessly across the floor. When his head was plunged into the cold water of the fountain, the seriousness of his situation hit him.

Vincent found it strangely satisfying to watch Peg kicking the shit out of Pierre. He thought he wanted to be the one to kill Pierre, but now he knew Peg must be the one to do it. It was only fair since he had taken care of the other scum on his group's list.

Pierre was dying. This was not the part he was supposed to play. His body already deprived of oxygen from the first blow tried desperately to draw in air, but only fountain water flowed into his open mouth. Eyes bulging, close to passing out, his hands scrabbled at his sides before coming to rest on the hilt of his dagger that he always hid in his left boot. Damn, she was crazy strong – how could this be happening. He pulled the dagger out and frantically stabbed at his tormentor, catching Peg in the front of her right thigh.

The immediate and searing pain was enough to get her to let go, as Pierre pushed himself out of the fountain. He ended up on all fours gagging and wheezing before throwing up fountain water. He looked like one of the devil statues, only he was gasping and spewing a fountain of blood. A dark rage poured through him – that bitch. She tried to kill him. What the fuck was wrong with her? She had ruined everything. Now he would have to kill her and that required a new role. He would have to change roles. He could do it though. He was a professional. Now he would play the avenger and Peg was obviously a wolf in sheep's clothing, trying to fool him all that time playing the weak heroine. In his anger and rage, he had forgotten Vincent.

Vincent had rushed over to Peg, while keeping an eye on Pierre, who was retching on the brick floor.

Seeing Vincent rush to Peg brought Pierre back to the present and he scanned the courtyard, finally eyeing his gun, which was lying beside the fountain. He grabbed the gun and staggered to his feet, as he turned to face Peg and Vincent.

The pain of the knife wound had jolted through Peg's body. She realized Pierre was no longer gasping for breath, but standing above her, with his gun pointed at her head.

Vincent lunged forward, in front of Peg, but he raised his own gun a second too late, as Pierre's fired and hit him in the chest. Peg yelled Vincent's name as she turned to see him crumple to the floor. Pierre came up and delivered a crushing blow to the right side of her face, snapping her head around and driving it into the rough brick wall of the courtyard. The pain of the bricks cutting into her skin kept her from loosing consciousness.

Vaguely, she was aware of being lifted and weightlessness enveloped her as she flew through the air. Her body tumbled across the stone floor and then slid into the row of potted plants that lined the entrance. The small table that had held Peg's gun had fallen on top of her. Peg painfully pushed herself up into a sitting position, so she could look Pierre in the face.

Pierre was smiling. As she watched, he left his gun on the fountain's ledge, wordlessly telling her that he had decided to play by her rules and he intended to kill her with his bare hands.

"I think I should return the favor. It's your turn to get wet."

His voice was full of malice as he advanced towards her. Blood ran from his cuts and mixed with the fountain water that still ran in rivulets from his wet hair, making him look like the deranged mad man he was.

"Why?" was the only word Peg could get out as Pierre took two steps towards her.

"Why?" Pierre said back to her, in a high-pitched voice mocking her.

"Why? You want to know why, you stupid bitch? Because you let me. Yeah, you let me. You were a terrible mother and you deserved what you got. What kind of mother lets her child roam around in a crowd full of people?"

Pierre was really getting into the role full of self-righteous anger, taunting her mercilessly.

Peg sat there shaking her head back and forth each word hitting her like a blow.

"I watched you both for an hour. You let her out of your sight. You let her go into the crowd. It was easy. She was lost and I offered to take her to you. She was trusting — too trusting. You killed her, not me. You killed her by not taking care of her. Just like that Morelli bitch. That kid ran wild all over the market. Her mother was to blame for her death too. Just an offer of candy was all it took to lead her away. Her mother busy shopping and talking to that old voodoo lady, oblivious to her daughter's whereabouts. She was a stupid, weak selfish bitch. And she proved it too, by taking her own fucking, worthless life."

"You both deserved what you got. You didn't deserve to be mothers. I know. I had a mother like you both — all sweetness on the outside. But it's just a cover: a cover that hides the weak stupid whores that you are."

Pierre's eyes blazed fire, his body stiffened as he was transported back to his childhood.

"You let him humiliate me over and over; you didn't protect me. You thought only of yourself. You made me what I am, mother. Aren't you proud?"

Blood mingling with saliva flew from his mouth, as he spit the words out at her.

Peg realized Pierre no longer saw her but was looking through her to some other place in time. He had lost all touch with reality. She slowly pushed herself away from him until her back was against the brick wall. Her right hand had stumbled upon and closed over something hard and cold. Her prob-ing fingers had found her gun. She could not take her eyes off Pierre as he advanced closer.

Tears slid down Peg's face as she raised the gun and pointed it at Pierre.

Pierre flung the words at her as he lunged toward her, "You can't kill me Mother. You're weak and useless. You couldn't harm a flea. That's why you couldn't protect me. I had to play all those vile disgusting roles to save myself from him. I had to save myself mother."

He was not just talking to her but through her. Did he even know where he was anymore?

Lester pushed through the crowds. He had never gotten Peg's voice mail, but when the officer pulled him from the meeting with Internal Affairs, he immediately knew something else was wrong. When he heard what Vincent said, he rushed to the nearest exit.

Lester knew he should have had Pierre picked up earlier in the day, but wanted to get everything straight with Internal Affairs before he took any final action. After all, Pierre was now a local hero, and if this thing backfired on him it would be very bad for the department.

Lester had been watching Pierre for some months. He knew he was sell-ing confidential information. It made his blood boil when he thought about all those leads making it to the public and ruining their chances to solve so many cases. It also made him wonder what other things Pierre had done while on the force and that had brought to mind more than a few charges of police brutality against Pierre that somehow always got squashed. Mildred's private notes had answered all his doubts and shocked him to the core at how sick and twisted Pierre really was.

Lester neared the double doors of the theatre. He stopped and gasped for breath. He had been running for the last ten blocks – fear pushing him forward.

A single shot rang out from inside the theatre, followed by two more in quick succession. Lester pushed the doors open, as he lunged through the entrance, his revolver in his hand.

Peg's first shot went wide and glanced off Pierre's shoulder as he lunged at her. She felt his hands tighten around her neck in a viselike grip, cutting off her breath and threatening to crush her windpipe. The pain of the bullet brought him back to the present.

"Now you'll never find out what happened to your daughter," screamed Pierre, as he continued to tighten his grip around her throat.

"Is she dead or alive? Too bad you won't live to find out," Pierre spit out between gritted teeth.

Realizing she still gripped the pistol, she brought it up against Pierre's ribs and fired two more quick shots. Pierre's grip relaxed, as he crumpled on top of her, his body a dead weight. The next thing she knew Lester was dragging Pierre off her and then his hands roamed her body parts taking stock of her wounds.

All she could do was cough and gag trying to get air through her swollen throat that had Pierre's handprints appearing as red marks on her skin.

"Vincent," she croaked and pointed to the left of the fountain.

Lester looked and saw Vincent sprawled across the bricks. His blood had pooled beneath him. He jumped up as he saw Vincent's hand move.

Lester hurried over to Vincent. As he pushed a handkerchief between Vincent's jacket and his wound, Vincent reached up and grabbed Lester's arm.

"Lester, you have to listen. I am the vigilante, the Crusader. I got the list through a FBI contact in my support group. The evidence is in my pocket and at my house, in my daughter's room you will find toys missing...doll house." Vincent started coughing and blood seeped through his lips.

"Vincent, don't talk, we can talk about everything later," urged Lester.

"No there is no time. You have to promise me not to involve Peg. Take care of her or I'll come looking for you, beyond the grave if necessary," said Vincent, conviction lacing each clipped word.

Lester placed his hand on Vincent's shoulder, "Don't worry. She's safe with me. I will always protect her. She did what neither one of us could do — she killed the sick bastard."

Two officers had entered the courtyard and one rushed to help Peg who was trying to crawl over to where Lester and Vincent were, while the other radioed for backup and an ambulance.

"She's pretty beat up but I can't find any bullet holes unless the wound in her leg is from a bullet," he said to his partner.

"Knife," Peg gasped, as the pain of sitting up brought her out of the fog that encircled her tired brain.

She tried to reach Vincent. She wanted to hold him, save him.

"Remember," Vincent said, still clinging to Lester's arm. His strength was fading; he was wheezing and gasping for breath.

"I am the Crusader. My family is waiting for me and I am going to be with them again," he struggled to get the words out, but they were loud enough for the other officer to hear.

He gasped one last time and then fell silent. Lester swept his hands across Vincent's eyes to shut them and made the sign of the cross, a final christening for the now unmasked Crusader.

"That's Pierre dead over there. Peg shot him in self-defense. I witnessed it all," said Lester to the officer who was now standing behind him.

"Pierre? What are you talking about? There is no one else here but you, Peg and him," said the officer, pointing at Vincent.

"Did he just say he was the Crusader?" the other officer asked.

Lester ignored the question and sprang to his feet. He walked over to where Pierre had been laying. He saw the blood stained tiles, but no Pierre.

"Put out an APB on Det. Pierre Martens — armed and dangerous," said Lester sharply.

"Yes sir," was all Lester waited to hear before walking over to Peg.

Peg was still dazed and part deaf from the gunshots fired at close range. She saw Lester's face and knew. Vincent was dead. She began to softly cry.

"Vincent, it can't be," her heart sank; she began to shake uncontrollably.

Lester looked straight at Peg, as he answered the earlier question, "Yes, Vincent has also confessed to being the vigilante."

"Pierre has disappeared," he whispered.

She stopped crying as his words penetrated her pain. It was horrible: a part of her was actually happy he was alive. She would have another chance to find out about Caitlin. Pierre knew where Caitlin was, unless he was just trying to increase her pain during her final minutes of life. She had to know. She had to find him and make him tell her. She would do anything she had to in order to make him talk. She just needed one more chance with the bastard. She would make sure he told her everything.

"He knows where Caitlin is. We have to find him."

"Don't worry we will. I promise."

If it was the last thing he ever did, this was one promise he intended to keep — come hell or high water.

The ambulance weaved through the crowds, which were pouring down the street in the opposite direction.

Peg heard the first sirens, not more than a minute after leaving in the ambulance. Vehicles, sirens and lights blazing forced the ambulance over between two parked cars, as they rushed past them down the narrow, dark streets of the Quarter back towards the Theatre.

Peg had to block out the terrible memory of Vincent, lying there dead in a pool of blood in the darkened courtyard. She wanted to go back, to do it over. Everything had gone so wrong. She couldn't believe he was dead and Pierre was still out there somewhere.

Vincent was the Crusader and he had made the ultimate sacrifice for her. He blocked Pierre's bullet. Tears flowed freely down her cheeks, as she thought about how much she cared about him, how much she owed him, and most of all, how she would miss him. Thoughts suddenly returned to the voodoo woman, what had she called Vincent, the drummer with de baton, "he will take de evil back."

"She knew, she knew," mumbled Peg.

CHAPTER FIFTY-FOUR

Pierre burst into his house. He headed for the bathroom and stripped off his shirt and the Kevlar vest underneath. Two angry black spots stood out against the dusky skin of his ribs and his shoulder was bleeding, where another bullet had grazed him. He wasn't sure if the bone underneath was broken, but it hurt like hell. He absently picked up the vest and pried off the smashed slugs.

It was then that he looked at his face in the mirror. He was a mess. A black eye was appearing and he had various cuts and gashes. His hair and face were smeared with blood. He ran water in the sink and washed most of the blood away. He looked at his reflection again.

"God damn bitch," he yelled into the mirror not liking what he saw.

"I'm gonna make her eat these bullets," he shouted as he smashed his fist into the mirror.

Overcome by rage, he stormed through the house smashing everything in sight. While his house never had been neat and clean – it now looked as if a hurricane had been unleashed inside it.

He found his bottle of bourbon and downed some pain pills with the liquor.

He scooped up his duffel bag, and headed down the walkway to his car. The neighbor's dog was in frenzy, barking and clawing at the fence. Without hesitating Pierre pulled out his service revolver and shot the dog dead. He even stopped and waited for a moment in case the owners were home and came outside. If they did he intended to shoot them also. Anyone who owned such a shitty little dog didn't deserve to live. Actually, there were a few people on Pierre's list who would not live much longer.

Now he was the grim reaper: search and destroy; that was his new mission and role. He would stop at nothing. He would be invincible in finding his targets. He had lost everything, but so would they. He would make sure of it.

It took awhile for him to see how things would have to be. His dreams of fame were gone but he would simply find fame on the dark side. Villains were always more fun to play anyway. Maybe he would take over for the LaRue bitch and be the dark magic voodoo man.

Ha! He figured he could rustle up a few spirits of his own. He would be exceptional. First he had to take care of two people who still stood in his way. He would enjoy this part very much. He looked in the rearview mirror and smiled as he put the car in gear, gunning the engine, racing down the street and around the corner.

Minutes later three squad cars pulled in front of his empty house.

Pierre drove straight to Peg's house. He knew she wouldn't be there but he was in a fit of rage; if he wasn't able to get to her, he could still hurt her by destroying everything she held dear. He would take away all her memories. If he had to lose his home, she would also lose hers. He didn't bother to be quiet or worry about being observed. This would be quick and dirty: in and out.

He ran up the steps and kicked the door in. He immediately began trashing the living room, making sure to dump a bookcase and scatter any papers he found. The kitchen was next; although, he mostly yanked the gas stove from the wall causing the connection to break. Gas fumes quickly filled the kitchen. From there he went to Caitlin's room — again knocking over tables and shelves. The gas smell began to seep from the kitchen and he decided he had better get out.

As he was walking back down the hallway the blinking light of the answering machine caught his eye. Was it worth the extra time? He decided it was because he may hear information that could lead him to either Peg or Lester.

He hit the play button. Two messages were stored. The first one was from Vincent looking for Peg. He deleted it — old news...that bastard would be causing him no more trouble. The next message widened his eyes and dropped his jaw. It was Caitlin. He played it again to be sure. He knew Peg had not heard it as it was displayed as a new message and the date and time stamp backed that up. It had to have come in after she had already left this evening. So the kid was still alive. Too bad she didn't have caller ID. He could have seen where the call was from and get an idea where she might be, or who she was with. That would have been the ultimate revenge...to find Caitlin and finish what Marko didn't. What a shame! But he would make sure she would never get an opportunity to hear it. Although it would be poetic to play it for Peg just before he killed her. He began to feel light headed and realized he had lingered too long. Quickly, he opened the machine and withdrew the micro cassette.

As he went through the front door he stopped on the porch to pull a book of matches from his pocket. After lighting the book, he threw it in the doorway, and pulled the broken door shut. He jumped in the car and took off.

From half a block away, he heard the explosion. Smiling, he headed for a downtown parking garage. He had to get rid of his car.

CHAPTER FIFTY-FIVE

Peg had just finished getting 12 stitches, a tetanus shot and pain medicine when Lester showed up at the hospital with a bag. She didn't recognize the black tote bag on the chair by the bed. When she opened it she found socks, underwear, jeans and a couple t-shirts. The tags were still on the jeans. She wondered how Lester had found the time to buy the clothes for her. How thoughtful of him. She dressed quickly in jeans, T-shirt and tennis shoes minus the socks. The jeans were a little baggy around the waist but overall she was amazed that he got the size correct. Most men weren't very good at that stuff. When she left the room Lester was waiting outside.

"I've called my brother Dale and I am taking you to his wife's family's lake house in Mandeville. You will be safe there until we find Pierre."

"They haven't found Pierre? I'm not going anywhere until he's caught and then I can finish what I started."

Peg's anger had returned.

Lester pulled Peg back into the room.

"Peg, Pierre has gone totally nuts. He has torn his house apart, and yours. Yes, he is looking for you," he said, as he watched her shocked expression.

"That's why I took the detour to get you some clothes. Your neighbor called the police about someone ransacking your home."

"That bastard! I have to go home. I have to see what he did to my house."

Tears sprung to Peg's eyes when she thought about what it would do to her if he had touched Caitlin's room.

Lester pulled her into his arms.

"You are not going anywhere but out to the lake house with me."

He didn't have the heart to tell her right now that she didn't have a home to go to anymore. All that was left was burning rubble. That news could wait until later when this mess was all over with.

As Lester pulled into the long tree lined drive he finally started to relax. He knew she would be safe at the lake house. He had told no one but Agent Kyle where he was taking Peg. He had also taken special care to make sure they weren't followed. He pulled up to the wooden gates, opened them and drove through.

Peg, who had been sleeping for most of the hour and a half trip, woke up when he stopped at the gates. The pain medication had wiped her out. She had started to get some of her strength back. But she still couldn't stop thinking about Vincent. She still couldn't believe it had all happened.

"Lester, take me back. Take me back to the station. I need to see this through. I need to help them find Pierre. Why are you doing this?"

Peg's voice got louder and stronger as anger again filled her heart.

"Stop this car! I want to go back."

She was yelling now.

"I want to tell them all about what that animal, that son of a bitch did to my daughter. He took my daughter, Lester. My beautiful daughter! She may still be alive. That animal is the only one who can tell me what happened."

Peg's voice was gaining a hysterical pitch. She knew she was losing it but was powerless to stop.

Lester could stand it no more as he swung the car off the dirt road and in the darkness sent the right side of the car scraping along the banana trees that lined the mile long road to the cabin. He jumped out the front door and pulled Peg from her seat.

Shocked out of her rage at Lester's behavior, Peg could only stare at him mutely.

"What do you want from me?" Lester yelled back at Peg.

"Yes, he took your daughter. He took Vincent's, too. We will get him. I will not rest until he is dead or in jail. Damn it, what do you want from me — blood? Do you want to make Vincent's death pointless? Are you so shut off, so dried up and dead inside that you no longer care for anyone else?"

Lester had grabbed Peg by both arms and was shaking her, trying to wake up a part of her that was maybe no longer there.

Peg's teeth were clicking together with each shake and her emotions were changing by the second, shock, fear, anger, hurt, and sorrow as Lester's words hit home.

Lester dropped his hands to his side and walked to the middle of the empty road as he turned and faced Peg, his anguish was written clearly on his tired features.

"Don't you realize I love you? I love you more than any woman I have ever known. I can't let you give up. Your anger and pain has been the only thing driving you for the past year. You will have your justice and when it is finished, will you just withdraw and die? Is that what Caitlin would have wanted? What would she think of you now?"

The words flowed into the still evening air and seemed to float gently to where she stood leaning against the side of the car.

All the anger was gone between them and Peg knew the words he spoke were true and could feel his emotions shimmering between them. It was as if time had stopped and they were the only two people left in the world. Peg could see particles of floating road dust, highlighted by the car's headlights, suspended in the stillness of the heavy air. It was so much darker out here away from the city lights.

A storm was coming. She could feel and smell it as a cool breeze suddenly kicked up and swept her hair across her face and cleared the dust from the air. She could breath again. Slowly, her eyes filled with tears and they ran silently down her face. She felt the warmth of Caitlin's presence; could see her smiling face say, "I love you Mommy."

"I'm sorry," she said as she pushed herself off the car and took a staggering step towards Lester.

"He said I would never know what happened to her. Lester, Caitlin may be alive. I have to know. I have to find him."

"Peg, chances are...," he let the words trail off as he saw the pain deepen in her eyes.

"Lester, I know what you and everyone else thinks and wants me to accept. But I can't. I have to know and until I do I can never give up looking. Can't you understand that?"

Lester looked as if he would shake her again but instead kissed her long and hard. Peg wrapped her arms around his neck and kissed him right back, lingering for a closer embrace. Lester finally pulled away, reluctantly.

"We have to get going. We can talk about all this later when I know you are safe. At this rate, Pierre may find us before we find him," said Lester as he put Peg down into the front seat and helped her slide over.

CHAPTER FIFTY-SIX

The trees finally parted and the headlights revealed an open expanse of green lawn. The cabin lay straight ahead. They left the dirt packed road and crunched over gravel that formed a circle drive in front of the cabin. In the middle of the circle was a cluster of rocks and boulders. A pageantry of wild native flowers sprung from every crevice. The landscaping blended perfectly with the surrounding lakeside scenery. A short gravel walkway led to a rustic cedar log porch that totally encircled the house similar to a wrap around porch on an old farmhouse. The big difference was that as the porch went around the south side of the house it extended out over the lake. Outdoor lights illuminated the house and nearby landscape.

The front porch steps were framed on both sides by a low green hedge. The left side that faced the grass and distant tree line had tall bushes that grew level with top porch rail. Peg could not resist mounting the steps and following the decking in the other direction around to the south side that looked out over the lake. Lights from other cabins twinkled in the distance. She drew her breath in sharply, as she realized part of the southeast side and the back end of the cabin actually stretched out over the water.

The cabin was spectacular. It guaranteed a beautiful view from a large picture window, flanked by two windows half as large that could be cranked open to take advantage of cool breezes coming in off the lake. There was also room enough for a table and four chairs and two chaise lounges set up in a grouping on the wide porch deck.

Cedar from the deck logs filled the air with a pleasant scent. Peg realized piers set into the lake must support the back of the house. It was amazing what could be built when you had enough money to make any dream or wish come true. Lester had finished pulling their stuff out of the car and deposited it in the hallway. He walked through the cabin past the den on the right with the large picture window flanked by the kitchen immediately on the left. Another bedroom and bathroom was on the left and then the master bedroom at the rear of the cabin.

The master bedroom also had a beautiful view of the lake. Lester could see Peg standing, her back to him watching the lights on the horizon. The water was dark and smooth as glass.

He walked to the back of the room and opened the sliding glass doors and stepped out onto the back deck. Insects were buzzing their own secret night rhythms. Thunder rumbled in the distance.

He noticed a speedboat tied up in one of two slips built into a floating dock. He walked around to where Peg was standing and put his arm around her. She leaned into him and placed her head against his shoulder.

"It's so beautiful," breathed Peg.

"I knew you would like it here. More importantly, you'll be safe here. Whatever shreds of sanity Pierre had managed to hang onto are totally gone now. He is more dangerous than ever. He has nothing to loose and he is driven by rage."

Peg turned to face Lester.

"I will not rest until he is dead. I will not have peace until he is no longer breathing. But first I have to find out about Caitlin," Peg whispered, conviction and emotion lacing every softly spoken word.

In reply Lester hugged her tighter and led her back into the cabin.

CHAPTER FIFTY-SEVEN

When Peg awoke the next day, she was surprised to see it was almost noon. How long had she slept? She had also slept fully clothed minus shoes and socks. She felt the bandages that still wound around her leg and covered the knife wound and stitches. She could see the bruises on her arms and legs. She ached everywhere. She was afraid to look at her face and neck.

The wind was whipping around the outside window. It seemed the storm she felt coming last night had finally arrived. Within minutes the wind was driving rain hard against the window. She rose stiffly from the bed and hobbled to the adjoining bathroom. She had fallen asleep on the couch in the den. More pain medication, stew and a warm fire had put her out cold. Lester must have carried her into the master bedroom and put her to bed. She could see no sign that he had slept there with her. She washed her face and stared at herself in the mirror. She was worn out and tired and looked it. Her cheek was bruised and she had numerous cuts and scrapes. The smell of brewing coffee brought her out of the room.

Lester silently drew in his breath as he saw Peg enter the room. Other than the limp favoring her right leg and bruises she looked beautiful. She always looked beautiful to him. He flashed on that morning in her kitchen not so long ago. The day he had almost grabbed her and kissed her, but instead had triggered his beeper himself so he could leave before he let his emotions override his brain. He wished he had stayed and he wondered if things would have been different if he had. Regret clouded his face as he smiled at Peg.

After putting Peg in bed Lester had stayed up all night unable to sleep. He had called in several times but there were no leads on locating Pierre. Several cars had been stolen overnight and it was thought that Pierre was in one of them, since they had found his car abandoned in a nearby lot downtown.

Peg saw the strange look on Lester's face and mistakenly took it for disappointment. He was upset with her and wished he had never helped her but he was too good of a person to back off now. He was entangled in the mess that was her life.

She took a seat by the wide panoramic window. The peaceful, serene beauty of the evening before had been replaced by a more savage view. Driving rain and gray cloudy skies whipped the lake into a wild and churning free-for-all. No less beautiful, just different, it was a pure, raw majesty.

Peg took a few minutes to look around. She had been so tired when they arrived; she had fell right asleep barely noticing the cabin's interior. She was impressed. The room was filled with glowing wood walls, baseboard, floor and the ceiling was crossed with rough-hewn beams. A large stone fireplace covered the entire back wall. She realized it was the see through kind that also serviced the master bedroom. The room was filled with comfortable, expensive furniture. Wool rag rugs brought warmth to the room. She fixed her gaze again on the large wide window and was transfixed anew by the beautiful view of the lake even while it was being savaged by the storm. The lake appeared to come right up to the window. Peg looked down and remembered the wooden walkway and deck with lounge chairs and a table was all that separated the house from the lake. The wind was driving large waves over the deck and the chaise lounge chairs were in danger of being swept into the chaotic water.

She felt Lester's presence behind her. She turned around to face him. Lester pulled her to him and gave her a tight squeeze and then released her. They sat down together on the couch.

"You sure you haven't changed your mind since last night. I didn't mean to flip out on you. Really you can leave me here. I am sure I'll be fine. You can go back and search for Pierre," said Peg.

She wanted to give him the opportunity to wipe away his words spoken in haste at the edge of the dirt road. She feared he was now filled with regret.

His response was to pull her close and kiss her.

"In case you didn't hear me yesterday on the road. I said I loved you. I want to know everything about you. But first, maybe you had better start with everything you know about Vincent and his Survivor's group."

Peg decided to tell him everything. He deserved to know it all. Even if it changed the way he felt about her, she owed him that. She kept looking for traces of disappointment on Lester's face, for she knew he was a good cop to a fault and would take a harsh view of anyone taking the law into their own hands. That is why she had resisted the temptation to fall completely in love with him.

She had a fear that in the end he would choose his values and career over his love for her. She was, after all, a renegade at heart. She kept remembering Vincent's warning that Lester would never understand or accept any shades of gray — the law was the law. That is why she had gravitated toward Vincent. She had at first felt safer with Vincent. Vincent could understand her motives and still love her. He had understood putting principal above the law. She had really fallen for Vincent, but in Lester, she sensed a soul mate.

Lester was careful to keep all emotions off his face. He would face a firing squad for her. He would lie to the FBI, Internal Affairs and his own Captain for her and not regret anything. It didn't really matter anymore anyway. That was all past him now. He was officially no longer a part of the department.

"Lester, the only thing I am concerned about is that people know what kind of animal Pierre really was. He is responsible for what happened to Caitlin and Angela just as much as Marko."

Lester reached out and grabbed her hand, "that has all come out Peg. Mildred has turned over phone records and we have eyewitnesses who saw Pierre with Marko months before Pierre killed Marko. Marko was his fall guy. Pierre originally kidnapped Angela to hold for ransom, but that fell through when he feared that the old lady at the candy shop spotted him with Angela. Pierre made sure that no one followed-up on the LaRue lead by saying she was crazy. He didn't want to take the chance that she might realize it was him with the girl, so he killed her. You should have seen the way he lived. All those fancy clothes were just a part of the act. His house was literally falling down around him. His whole life was just a show — which is probably why he wanted the money so he could live his dreams completely. Internal Affairs was already investigating him at my request. He had been selling information to the press for nearly two years.

We also found out there were some questions surrounding his mother's death. She broke her neck after falling down a flight of stairs. She was supposed to be bedridden but just happened to get up for a walk down the stairs one night at 3 a.m. With no proof to the contrary, they couldn't prove it didn't happen the way Pierre said, so the death was ruled accidental. After what you told me about some of Pierre's last ranting words I think we all know what happened," finished Lester, his voice filled with sadness.

"I know what you are thinking Lester, please don't even go there. You are a wonderful man and were willing to risk everything for me. I know what chances you took and I am so grateful. I don't ever want you to feel like you should or could have done any more than you did," Peg's voice trailed off as she cupped Lester's chin in her palm and turned his face so she could look in his eyes.

God, how could he look into those crystal blue eyes without losing himself? He felt himself drawn towards her. Their lips met and he pulled her into his arms. Peg felt like she had come home. But then reality flooded back in and she pulled away.

"One last question, how did you know, or when did you know, it was Pierre?" asked Lester.

He was trying not to push her too much.

"It was the leather button."

"What leather button?" Lester asked with a stern look in his eye.

"Well, I found a button at the LaRue crime scene."

"Just where did you find the button?"

"In the old lady's hand," said Peg guiltily, as she wheeled around so she wouldn't see Lester's expression.

"Peg!"

He turned her around to face him again.

"What am I going to do with you? Withholding evidence, or should I say removing evidence from the scene of a crime is serious."

In answer, Peg held up her wrists, "I know…arrest me….do whatever you have to but I don't regret it."

Lester slowly grabbed her wrist and pulled her closer as he looked into her eyes and said, "By the way. I am no longer a member of New Orleans' finest. I have officially resigned to work as a consultant for the FBI. Freelance, rent-a-cop, whatever you want to call it, but I call the shots and control what cases I work on. So I guess I'll just have to make a citizen's arrest."

He smiled at her stunned expression and then he was kissing her again, deeper, more passionately, as the rain lashed and whipped against the cabin.

CHAPTER FIFTY-EIGHT

Pierre had been sitting in the stolen car a block away from Mildred's house for about an hour. He was unnerved by the patrol car out front. Why would they think he would contact Mildred?

His impatience got the better of him. He needed to talk to her, get her to help him find out where Lester and Peg were and get out of town before the storm hit. He had been hearing about it all night. At 5 a.m., daylight and the storm were both only moments away. Using all his skill he crept up to the house and circled around the back. He peered in the back window and saw Mildred slumped over the kitchen table and a steaming cup of coffee. She looked like she hadn't slept all night.

Pierre quietly tapped on the window.

Mildred glanced up and looked like she had seen a ghost. For a moment, he saw a look of sheer terror in her eyes.

Mildred felt her heart stop as she looked up and saw Pierre at the kitchen window. She was momentarily filled with terror, until she saw how lost he looked, like a small boy. He was hurt too. Before she realized it, she was at the back door and letting him in.

He grabbed her and gave her a big hug. She had never felt so wonderful in her life. She pushed away any nagging thoughts that threatened to ruin this moment for her.

"Mildred, I knew you would be here for me. I knew you wouldn't believe the lies Lester and that McGregor bitch have been telling everyone."

Instantly, Mildred realized her mistake. Pierre did not know she had betrayed him. She grew nervous. Pierre sensed the change in her.

"Mildred, what's wrong? You must tell me!"

Pierre grabbed her by the shoulders and looked at her with those eyes. Those eyes that had incited her to do things for him she would do for no other person. She realized in that moment just how much she loved him.

"Mildred, you know how I feel about you," Pierre went on pleading.

"Pierre, stop! You know I care for you very deeply. I...I love you," she stammered, turning away so she wouldn't see the reaction in his eyes. She couldn't stand it if she saw revulsion.

Pierre was smirking. Good old Mildred; he played her like the pro he was. This is where he reeled her in.

"Mildred, please I must talk to Lester. You have to tell me where he is so I can meet with him privately and get this whole mess straightened out."

Mildred drew her breath in and turned to face Pierre. She had decided to lay her cards on the table. She had to get through to the Pierre she knew was there, buried underneath all the anger he wore like armor.

"Pierre, please stop. I know everything and I still love you. I have money saved and I will get you the best defense trial lawyer in New Orleans. You have to turn yourself in. If you don't, they will kill you and I couldn't stand that. Please, Pierre, please, come with me. If we get married, they can't make me testify against you. Even if you go to jail, I will wait for you. Things can work out for you. You don't have to be angry anymore. We can be so happy together."

Mildred finally stopped talking, as she noticed the look of total disbelief hanging on Pierre's face.

"What in the hell! What in the god-damn-mother-fucking-hell are you talking about?" Pierre yelled.

His face went from surprise to murderous anger in seconds. The red crept up his neck and infused his face at an alarming rate.

Mildred cringed under his anger and started to cry.

"You stupid pathetic bitch. You told them our secrets, didn't you, Mildred? That's why your house is being watched. How stupid could I have been to trust a witch like you? God, and you say you love me. You are just like all the other stupid bitches."

Pierre reached out and grabbed Mildred by the neck.

"Now tell me where they are before I break your scrawny neck," said Pierre, his face twisted in anger.

Tears streamed down her face. Mildred knew she could not fight him. She loved him even though he was choking the life from her.

"Pierre, please," she whimpered, struggling to breathe.

She saw no tenderness in Pierre's eyes, only hatred. Pierre's fingers dug further into her neck.

"Okay," she gasped.

Pierre loosened his grip.

"I can think of only one place he might take her. I have heard him talk about a secluded lake house in Mandeville. He said it belonged to his brother's wife's family and Dale told Lester he could use it whenever he liked. I bet he took her there. The only thing is, I don't know the address," finished Mildred.

She broke down in tears, as she slumped back into the chair at the table to rub her red and sore neck.

"That's okay Mildred, I'm sorry I scared you."

Pierre walked around behind her and soothingly began rubbing her neck.

"You know, I do care about you, Mildred."

Pierre continued to rub her neck and shoulders.

Mildred continued to cry.

"I am so sorry Pierre, please forgive me? Please Pierre forgive me," pleaded Mildred.

"Mildred, it's all right. I forgive you," whispered Pierre, as he quickly snapped her neck.

Pierre was already on his way out of the kitchen as Mildred's lifeless head hit the tabletop.

Finding Mildred's address book by the phone in the hall, Pierre flipped through it looking for Hopper. Finding Hopper, Dale, he called the number. It was picked up on the second ring.

"Hello," said a female voice.

"Hello ma'am. This is detective Charles Moore. I have to get in touch with Lester Hopper. He is staying in a cabin of his brother's. We have had a break in the case and I need to get him to come back to New Orleans right away," Pierre finished, holding his breath.

"Yes, I am Charlotte, Dale's wife. It's my parent's cabin. Have you tried calling him?" she said, a little bit of suspicion in her voice.

"Why, yes ma'am, we did, but we couldn't get through. Maybe the storm could have hit there already," said Pierre, in his most congenial voice, tinged with a southern drawl.

"Oh yes, it could have. That happens quite often. Do you have a pen? I'll give you directions," Charlotte answered.

"Ready when you are," smiled Pierre into the phone.

As Pierre left the house, he gave Mildred one last look.

"What Mildred? No goodbye?" laughed Pierre, his good mood restored.

"I was kinder to you than a traitorous bitch like you deserved."

Quick and painless, thought Pierre, as he went out the back door jangling Mildred's keys, as he headed for her car in the driveway behind the house.

Heading out down the alley, he realized daylight should be breaking. The storm clouds had hidden the sun, as the wind kicked dust and debris across the windshield. Pierre smiled again. He loved a good storm, he thought as the first splatters of rain speckled the windshield.

"I'm going hunting in Mandeville." Pierre laughed and drove on the highway, heading for the country.

CHAPTER FIFTY-NINE

Peg and Lester had passed the rest of the stormy day very quietly talking about everything. The sounds of the storm made the cozy cabin seem like a safe and warm haven, isolating them from the outside world. It was so easy to talk to Lester. She found herself telling him all about her childhood and even about how she became pregnant and how Caitlin had changed her life.

Lester for the first time in a long while was able to open up to someone. He told Peg all about his family, his father and the beating that left him with the scar on his forehead, his life on the force, even his recent feelings of restlessness and lack of purpose now that his family did not seem to need him as much. He even told her about his roommate, Babykitty. Peg laughed out loud picturing Lester with his wily feline companion.

Lester was trying to keep Peg occupied so she wouldn't dwell on the fact that Pierre was out there somewhere. He noticed her pensive expression every time there was a lull in the conversation. He had been making hourly calls to Kyle's cell phone till around 4 p.m., when the phone line went dead. His own cell phone was useless as the storm gained in intensity and crashed against the cabin. Large waves surged across the decking and splashed against the side of the cabin. The new sound changed the previous cozy, insulated feeling of the storm to a more menacing tone. It also didn't help that in his last call to Kyle he found out that Mildred was discovered dead in her kitchen around noon. Her neck was broken and her car missing.

They currently had an APB out on the car and Pierre. The coroner told them that she had been killed early that morning, which meant the stolen car and murderer could be long gone. Kyle told Lester to stay put. Even though they were pretty sure Mildred had been killed by Pierre, so far there was no way he could have found out where Lester was hiding Peg. Lester agreed but long after hanging up he was bothered by a nagging doubt that kept bringing his thoughts back to Pierre and what his next move might be. Kyle's final words, "watch your back Lester" didn't help either. He wracked his brain trying to remember if he had ever spoken about Dale's cabin to Mildred.

Pierre would be desperate but not stupid. Lester had to stay a step ahead. Peg sensed that Lester was worried, even though he tried to hide it from her. As the storm grew in power, Lester used it as an excuse to check the cabin. Suddenly, the power failed in the den. He could see Peg outlined in the glow of the flickering flames, as she had been stoking the fire when the generator failed. Together they went through the cabin lighting hurricane lanterns.

"This must happen a lot out here," said Peg, trying to lighten the mood.

"Yeah," Lester said in a preoccupied voice, as he tried to scan the area that was now a darkened front porch and gravel drive.

He couldn't even see his car through the driving rain and darkness.

"Should I make some dinner? I know I can't cook with the power out, but maybe I could find some peanut butter and jelly."

She was feeling more and more restless and needed to do something to keep her busy. The kitchen's pantry was well stocked with canned food and a commercial refrigerator. A freezer also held an assortment of foods.

Lester's earlier relaxed mood had disappeared, and he was back to his usual "man of few words" persona.

Her question brought Lester back from his thoughts of Pierre.

"No, sorry Peg, let's wait awhile. Besides I'm not hungry yet."

What he really wanted to say is that he didn't want her out of his sight and the kitchen was along the side of the house facing the woods. She would be vulnerable to anyone out there creeping around in the darkness. He grabbed her by the arms and gently turned her away from the front door and back towards the den and the fireplace. As they reached the entrance of the den an explosion outside shook the cabin. Peg heard glass shattering as she was driven to the floor. Lester instinctively threw himself on top of Peg, trying to shield her from the blast.

As the last tinkling sounds of breaking glass grew faint, Lester was up and pulling Peg to her feet. She immediately turned to him.

"What's going on?" she demanded. "What have you been hiding since that last phone call? Don't try to protect me Lester. I'm a big girl. I need to know the risks. I need to know what is going on."

Lester looked into her intent and pensive features. She was right. He had been trying to protect her, but now she needed to know what was going on. Because if it came to a time when he couldn't protect her, and she was on her own, she would need every shred of information he could tell her.

"Okay," he whispered, as he drew her against the bookcase that lined the western wall of the den. He peered around the corner and down the hall. He saw that the long thin windows that flanked each side of the front door had been blown out from the blast, but the door remained intact.

Some rain blown by the high winds was making its way into the foyer of the cabin. A bright flame was shooting into the night; where his old car used to be parked on the gravel drive about 20 feet from the porch. It lit up the deserted area in front of the cabin.

"Listen," he turned and whispered to Peg. "They found Mildred around noon today, murdered. I'm thinking it was Pierre; from the coroner's report he has had since this morning to try to find us. From the sight of my burning car, he has."

Peg began to speak but Lester shushed her by placing a finger against her lips.

"I've got to go out there. Lock the door behind me and go to the master bedroom. There's a shotgun and shells in the closet. I'll knock twice on the door if it' me. You see anything, or anyone else, don't wait to find out who they are – open fire."

"Lester, don't go out there. We are safer trying to stand him off in here."

"Peg, we can't. I didn't want to tell you before, but they also found weapons in Pierre's house. Some hand grenades. If we try to wait him out, he could creep to the front door and roll one through the blown out window, as easily as he rolled one under my car."

Before she could speak, Lester pulled her to him and kissed her fiercely – it might be the last time he would ever kiss her.

"Go to the master bedroom, get the gun and wait. Go out the sliding glass doors and work your way around the side of the cabin and run for the woods. Wait at least ten minutes before you go, so I have time to check out that side of the cabin."

"Don't look so worried. I'll be fine," he said, as he caressed her cheek and then he was headed for the front door.

"Stay in the woods until I come for you. If I'm not there in about 30 minutes, head back to the highway," he whispered as he peered out the side window.

She followed him to the front door and watched; he quickly darted out and hopped over the right porch railing, taking cover in the tall bushes. Peg locked the door and hurried towards the master bedroom and the shotgun.

The wind-driven rain finally quenched the ball of fire that had been his car. It was now a smoking, smoldering mass of twisted metal. He rose slowly from the bushes and checked out the north side of the cabin that faced the woods. He wanted to make sure that side was safe before he canvassed the rest of the house. He didn't want Peg to run into Pierre, while she was trying to make the safety of the woods.

The resulting darkness had hidden Lester's exit from the cabin, but it also concealed Pierre's tracks. Pierre was trembling from the cold of the lake. He had run for the water, after rolling the grenade under Lester's car. He was now lying in wait at the edge of the decking at the south end of the porch. He had heard, but not seen, Lester come out the door. He retreated to the bushes.

He surmised Peg was hiding out in the house. He thought about slipping onto the porch to roll a grenade through the blown out side window. He decided he wanted to get rid of Lester first. That would give him more time with Peg, without interruptions. Blowing her up with the house was too easy. He wanted her to suffer more. He wanted to watch her die.

Pierre watched Lester leave the bushes and head around the side of the cabin. He slowly pulled himself out of his crouched position by the water, over the rail and onto the porch. He crawled across to the other side where Lester had headed.

The wind and driving rain suddenly died down and Pierre wondered if the storm had finally blown itself out, or whether this was just a lull. Thunderous clouds and lightning sparks filled the distant sky.

Without the cover of the noisy rain, each creak of the porch railing traveled far on the night air, as he put his hands on the rail and swung himself over into the bushes.

After quickly checking out the north side of the cabin, Lester had doubled back. He didn't want to go all the way to the sliding glass doors and risk scaring Peg, or risk her shooting him, while she covered the back deck that led to the tiny dock. The speedboat banged loudly as the wind bounced it against the sides of the slip.

As he returned to the front porch and bushes, the rain and wind suddenly died. In its absence, Lester heard the sound of creaking wood and breaking branches, as someone landed in the same bushes where he had recently sheltered. Not wasting a second, Lester reached into the moving bushes, grabbed toward the movement and, with sounds of tearing cloth heaved whatever or whoever was hiding out onto the wet grass with a grunt.

Pierre had no sooner landed in the bush, when someone had grabbed his jacket and pulled him out onto the slippery grass. He landed and rolled to his feet to face Lester, and the barrel of his 9 mm revolver. Pierre's gun lay useless at the edge of the bushes.

"Don't even think about it," Lester threatened. "It won't take much to get me to pull this trigger."

Lester motioned for Pierre to head around to the steps of the front porch. An eerie howl started low and gained in volume as the wind and rain started up again, just as Pierre reached the steps and started up.

"You got this all wrong Lester. It's that McGregor woman. She lied about everything. She's turned everyone against me."

Pierre shouted to be heard over the howl of the storm.

"Shut up, I know about Mildred. You're an animal. Hurry up before I decide to go ahead and shoot you," Lester shouted back angrily.

Pierre just smirked, as he headed from the wet grass up to the front steps of the cabin. The wind was growing stronger each second and buffeted against Pierre as he stood on the middle step. He felt the wind rush in from the lake and try to push him back down the steps.

He felt Lester's gun poke hard into the middle of his back. He pulled himself up the next step. Timing his ascent with the next gust of wind, Pierre let go of the rail and the wind blew him back into Lester. They slipped off the steps and landed hard on the gravel walk. Lester lost his gun, as it flew from his hand in the fall. Both men scrambled for the gun, tumbling and fighting, as they neared the edge of the lake.

Peg was drawn to the front of the cabin by the sound of angry voices shouting on the porch steps; then the storm began battering the cabin again and drowning out everything else. As she reached the broken window by the door, she saw two men fighting at the water's edge beside the porch and decking. She frantically struggled to distinguish which one was Lester, as she opened the front door and raised the shotgun.

The two men suddenly broke apart; one fell back into the churning lake water, while the one left standing fired. In the flash of the pistol flare, she saw Pierre was the man standing firing into the water. In that same instant, she realized Lester had disappeared into the surging lake water and had not reappeared.

"No!" she screamed without thinking as she aimed the shotgun and fired towards Pierre.

Pierre's face was frozen in a grin of triumph, as he continued to fire into the churning lake where Lester had disappeared. With the second wave of fury the storm also unleashed lightning. In a brief glare of light, he noticed the froth of the white water surging towards shore was stained pinkish-red. Well, one down and one to go he thought, as he scanned the churning water.

Thunder crackled, followed by a shotgun blast. Pierre whirled around and fired at Peg, now framed in the front doorway of the cabin. She was too far away for the shotgun to be effective, but the 9 mm drove her back away from the doorway. Peg fell back into the hallway, as wood splintered and showered over her and slugs dug into the beautiful woodwork of the cabin's porch railings, doorway and hallway.

Peg crawled down the hallway, sobbing as she again pictured Lester's body falling back into the surging waves.

Pierre rushed towards the cabin and Peg. He entered the open front door. He kicked it closed behind him in an effort to drown out the storm so he could hear. He advanced silently down the hallway, stopping to peer into the kitchen and the den. The fireplace still sent a soft glow throughout the empty room. Pierre continued slowly down the hallway, searching for Peg. When he entered the master bedroom, wind and rain from the open sliding glass doors blew into the room. The rain was pounding down, a torrent of winds beat against the western side of the cabin. He stepped to the entrance and looked out at the raging storm and the darkness. He stared into the night, trying to decide which way Peg might have gone. The closet door in the far corner of the bedroom silently opened behind him and the barrel of a shotgun leveled on Pierre's back, as he stood outlined in the doorway.

He stepped through the doorway and a shotgun blast crashed through the room, catching Pierre's right side, arm and leg with pellets. Screaming in pain, he whirled around and fired instinctively toward the sound of the blast. Pierre only got off one shot before being driven further into the room by a crashing blow to his head and back.

Lester had made his way slowly around to the back of the cabin by pulling himself through the maze of piers under the decking. By the time he had reached the back dock, where the speedboat was tied, the cold lake water had numbed the pain in his chest. He knew he had lost a lot of blood, but prayed the numbing cold water was slowing down the blood loss. He quietly pulled himself up onto the deck. He used his last burst of energy to close the distance between himself and Pierre. He arrived in time to deliver a crashing blow from behind with a heavy wooden oar, as Pierre turned to fire into the room.

Peg's second blast of the shotgun hit Pierre squarely. At close range, the cluster of metal pellets tore a large hole into his chest. As Pierre crashed to the bedroom floor, Peg's eyes were drawn to a dark form left swaying in the doorway.

"Lester," she yelled, as she scrambled up across the bed and helped prop him up before he fell over. He looked like a ghost. She clutched him tightly, needing to verify that he was real and only letting go as she realized he was in pain. She drew back as she noticed fresh blood soaking his shoulder and running down his chest.

"It's okay, I've lost some blood. I...I just need to rest a moment...just tired," he mumbled as he swayed on his feet.

Peg guided him towards the bed and helped him lay down, while she rushed to the dresser to grab something to press against Lester's wound. She pulled the comforter up and around his cold and wet body.

She jumped again, as she remembered Pierre and looked towards the doorway. She saw Pierre's hand stretched out on the floor at the end of the bed. She watched intently for any signs of movement.

Lester, reading her thoughts through pain-clouded eyes, grabbed her hand.

"He's dead Peg; he's not coming back this time."

Peg looked back at Lester. Lester had lost blood, but she had no way of knowing how much. His lips were blue-tinged and his face was ashen but that could be from the cold lake water. He was shivering all over. Frantic, she rushed back to his side. Pulling the blanket up closer around him, she softly called his name. He wasn't responding to her anymore. God what was she going to do? She couldn't lose him. Please God, not another person she loved yanked cruelly from her life. She realized the life they had set and planned the day before could never be. Pierre was gone but still she felt the pain, resentment and anger. She had not gotten her answers from Pierre. Pierre and Marko's death had changed nothing. Caitlin was still out there somewhere… she knew it. Lester would never accept the way she felt. He wouldn't understand her need to keep searching. He would never understand. Reality hit her like a freight train.

While she sat lost in thought, holding onto Lester's cold hand, silently she made a prayer to God that if he would just let Lester live, she would go away and never see Lester again. She would give him up and go on with her life and search for her daughter. Something she would have to do alone.

As if in response to her prayer, Lester's eyes suddenly opened.

"Hey, don't cry," he said, as he tried to reach up and wipe away a tear that was sliding down her cheek.

"I'm crying because I have to say goodbye. I love you too and I meant everything I said yesterday – all our plans. But I have realized that I can't stay.

It would never work. I couldn't go on not knowing. It would destroy me in the end and I won't do that to you. I refuse to drag you down with me."

Peg looked sadly at Lester's hurt expression.

"Peg, what are you talking about? Pierre's gone now so you don't have anything left to prove. It's time to start living again."

"Lester, it's no good. Pierre's death has made me realize nothing has changed. I still have the same feelings. The anger is still there and more importantly, I still don't have any answers. I can't live that way. It will ruin us. I would only end up bringing you more pain. I can't do that to you. You deserve better. Please try to understand. I'm sorry."

She kissed his lips and started to rise. Lester grabbed her fingers and held tight.

"No Peg, please let's talk. Don't go."

He felt her fingers slide out of his grasp. He watched helplessly as she walked to Pierre's dead body. She had that stubborn look on her face — a face he had come to love. She bent down, and when she came back into view, she was holding a gun. The gun Pierre had shot him with earlier. She walked silently to the open sliding glass bedroom door.

Peg wait, please I need your help. Just stay until help arrives."

He was pulling out all the stops, shamelessly trying to get her to stay. He was suddenly afraid for her and of what she might do.

She turned in the open doorway with a sad smile on her face.

"You'll be fine Lester,"

Peg smiled weakly.

"Listen, help is on the way."

Behind the noise of the storm, which was close to blowing itself out, they could hear the far away sound of sirens. As she turned to leave something caught her eye on the floor at Pierre's feet…a small cassette. She bent down and picked it up and slid it into her pocket.

"Take care of yourself...do it for me," Peg said as she turned and hurried through the doorway.

Lester gritted his teeth, as he slid to the end of the bed. His body protested in agony at each movement. Finally, he could see Peg standing at the edge of the dock, her back to him. He heard a shot ring out and saw her fall in the water.

"No!" he yelled in anguish, as he pushed himself off the edge of the bed in a sudden rush of adrenaline. His feet hit the floor and he stood briefly. As he tried to take a step forward, his legs turned to rubber and folded beneath him and the world went black.

CHAPTER SIXTY

The morning air was fresh from the recent storm. Agent Kyle pensively watched the chopper land on the soaked grass between the cabin and the woods. He ran alongside the paramedics, as Lester was rushed across the grass on a stretcher and loaded into the Care Flight helicopter. A second bag of blood was already flowing into an IV in Lester's arm, but he still had not regained consciousness.

As the helicopter lifted off and tipped to the side, Kyle could hardly recognize the wrecked cabin. The driveway was filled with a charred car, and a cluster of at least half a dozen flashing police cars and an ambulance.

The destruction and chaos contrasted with the sultry orange glow of a magnificent New Orleans sunrise that outlined the house and lake. Lester and Peg had certainly put up a hell of a fight. They still hadn't found Peg. He was hoping Lester would come to and give them some clue about what had happened.

Sensing movement, he turned and saw Lester looking at the same view. His eyes were tired and sad.

"She's in the water," he croaked.

"Where?" Kyle asked, sympathy in his voice.

"At the back of the cabin, at the end of the dock," Lester said through gritted teeth. He coughed, wheezed and spit up a little blood.

"Find her," was all he was able to say before losing consciousness again.

As the EMTs worked on Lester, Kyle was on his cell phone calling for divers to start a search of the lake. It was as he feared – Peg was dead. He hoped Lester would hang on until they got to the hospital. He couldn't have held on this long to die in this damn helicopter. His mouth set in a grim line as he watched the EMTs do their job.

CHAPTER SIXTY-ONE

She sat in the worn, green leather chair that was pulled close to the bed. She hadn't left Lester's side since Dale had brought her to the hospital that afternoon.

It was 8:00 p.m. now and darkness had settled in the square of window high up on the far wall of the ICU unit. He had lost a lot of blood and it was feared he may have some damage to his major organs. He was classified as critical, but in stable condition. The doctors tried to assure them his chances for pulling through looked good. She wanted to believe them, all the while, bracing herself for the worst.

Dale came into the room and handed his mother, Jean, a cup of hot coffee.

"Thank you sweetheart."

Her boys were so precious; she didn't know what she would do if she lost one. A parent was not supposed to outlive their children.

Several of Lester's fellow officers were out in the lobby and his brother George had left California by plane earlier that evening. She silently prayed again and hoped God was listening. She studied the planes of his face as he slept. His tanned face and ruddy cheeks were relaxed in sleep. He had slowly regained his color. When she had first arrived his face was ashen and gray. She longed to see his green eyes open and look at her.

Tears welled in her eyes as she looked at the beloved face of her oldest son now lying so helpless. It brought back memories of that other time she had watched over him in the hospital after his father had beaten him. She slowly caressed the scar on his forehead. The tears blurred her vision as they ran down her face.

"Hey, don't cry," a groggy voice said from the bed. "I'm not dead yet."

It seems he was saying that a lot lately. The memory caused his eyes to shut with pain.

"I'm not crying," she said, as she wiped away the tears and smiled at him.

She grabbed a cup of water sitting on the bedside tray, and held it to his lips for a drink.

"How long have you been here?" he asked, after taking a short sip.

His lips felt cracked and dry, his tongue swollen.

"Long enough," she said as she bent over and placed a light kiss on his cheek.

Dale had heard talking from the hallway and hurried into the room.

"Hey, big brother, you really had us scared there," Dale said, smiling, as he came closer to the bed.

Lester tried to speak again, but his mother raised her finger and placed it against his lips.

"Shhh," she said.

She suddenly knew her prayers had been answered. Her boy was going to be alright.

"Everything is okay, now."

He tried to resist. He needed to talk to Kyle. He needed to know about Peg. But he knew, he knew it was too late. She was dead. He still could feel her fingers sliding through his. Why did he let go? He should have held on. The pain went deep into his soul. His body overruled his mind as he closed his eyes and slept.

EPILOGUE

Jack Thompson sat at his desk working on the final report to a case closed the day before. He leaned back in his chair and heard his back pop several times as he straightened and stretched. It was 10 p.m and he was working late again. It seemed like he never got enough done; he was fanatical about details. When you juggled as many balls as he did, one wrong move could spell disaster.

He jumped when he heard the dim sound of a phone ringing. Instinctively, he looked at the phone on his desk, just to make sure before he turned and pulled open the big drawer of the wooden credenza behind his desk. It was the secure phone. He picked up the black case and fished for keys in his pocket, unlocking and flipping the top to the case in one quick motion, all the while wondering, who could be calling? Only a handful of people had this number and one of them was dead.

He picked up the handset, pushed in a five-digit code, and said, "You got me."

The voice on the other end was soft and low, definitely female.

"I'm a friend of Vincent's. He told me that if anything happened to him I should call this number."

"If Vincent trusted you, then I trust you," replied Jack.

"Vincent said you could help me. Maybe we could help each other."

"Okay, let's meet and talk and then we'll go from there. Go to Muthers restaurant near the Convention Center. A black Suburban with tinted windows will stop there at 11 p.m. The side door will remain open for exactly 3 minutes. If you don't show, lose this number."

"I'll be there."

The line went dead.

"Well, well."

Jack stared at the portrait of a smiling young girl on the far wall, deep in thought.

Vincent said there was someone new in the Survivor group who was special, someone he may have to send to him one day. If his calculations were right, he just had a conversation with that person. The paper last week had been plastered with banners announcing the Crusader's death. It seemed Vincent Morelli had been identified as the vigilante killer, who had been ridding New Orleans of its most vile criminals. The recent phone call just confirmed Jack's suspicions. A good man was dead but the torch had been passed on – the "Crusader" would live again.

Jack picked the secure phone back off the hook and punched in a series of numbers.

"It's me," he stated simply, when the other end picked up.

"Yeah, me too. I've got an urgent pickup."

Four months later

New Orleans Airport

Lester was at the airport with his brother George. When George had arrived at the hospital four months ago, he announced his intentions of moving in and taking care of Lester, until he had recovered. What Lester had thought would be a matter of weeks, had turned into months. Lester feared George was staying for good. But, he finally convinced George he was fine and got him to agree to return to his California life, by promising to make a trip out there next month. Lester was even looking forward to some time in the California sun and lounging on the beach.

When he saw the woman sitting at the next gate something about her drew his attention. Maybe it was the way she sat lost in thought or the turn of her head. She reminded him of someone else. When she stood up and looked at him, she acted like she had seen a ghost. His own expression froze between a smile and a questioning look. Did he know her? She seemed to have known him. But then she turned away and hurried past the ticket counter to her gate. Maybe she had mistaken him for someone else and then felt silly for staring at him. That kind of thing happens all the time

"Lester, come on or I'll miss my flight," said George, who was already walking in the other direction to gate 30.

"Coming," Lester called back as he reluctantly followed his brother down the concourse.

Ten minutes later as he watched his brother board the plane, his thoughts were still drawn back to the strange encounter. What made him think he knew her? Suddenly Peg's face floated in front of his vision. He tried to compare the two but he knew there was no way he wouldn't have recognized Peg. It drove him crazy that Peg's body had never been found in the lake.

At first he was seeing her around every corner. He thought the candle light memorial months ago had helped lay her ghost to rest. Without thinking, he had wandered back down to the other gate and stood staring out the window, as the plane started backing up, waiting its turn to take off. Shaking his head, he walked away, but turned to see the destination: New York.

He worried that maybe George was right in his decision to stay as long as he did. It seemed the minute he was on his own, he started seeing ghosts again and the memories rushed back to haunt his mind. His family had been so good to him. They showered him with their time and affection, Although, at times, it was stifling. He was used to being the caretaker.

Memories of Peg's face filled his mind, "God, I miss you," he whispered as he again shook off the ghosts of the past and headed back to his car.

Sitting in her seat, her earlier tension had evaporated and left her feeling oddly deflated and melancholy. She gazed out the window. There he was standing at the window by the gate to her plane. She momentarily froze again. Had he recognized her? She decided it was unlikely and relaxed visibly. She quietly drank in the sight of him — glad he was healthy and back on his feet. She longed to talk to him...to explain. Even now, with what she had learned she knew he still wouldn't understand. What she had done was too cruel. He would never be able to forgive her. Her melancholy turned to sadness and regret.

Her heart still hurt when she thought of being so close to Lester. She had just heard the announcement for the boarding of her flight, grabbed her things, stood up and looked across the concourse directly into his eyes. She had been frozen momentarily with shock, and then while he was staring at her his eyes full of curiosity, she had come to her senses and darted for the ticket counter. Her composure hanging in tatters, she had boarded the plane. Each step was an eternity and the weight of the distance between them became almost unbearable.

Seeing him like that had definitely caught her off guard and brought back all the old memories that did not have a place in her current life. She had to keep her main goal in focus. She had to find Caitlin. After she had her daughter back she could think about Lester and the possibility of a future. Until then there was only the present and finding Caitlin was her only goal. Everything else was just a means to an end.

She pulled out her iPod and headphones and hit the play button.

"Mommy, are you there? Mommy it's me. Mommy, please come get me. I want to come home."

She played it two more times. Her heart fluttered in her chest and her throat squeezed shut, breath catching painfully. She had listened to the tape a million times over the last four months and her reaction never changed, ever since Jack's people pulled the message off the cassette. She kept it with her at all times. It was her touch stone for when she doubted herself and lost her way.

They had recently learned a religious group was briefly in New Orleans offering to take orphans and find homes for them. When a woman sold her baby for drug money; she later told the cops "Christ" had her baby. Eventually they tracked the information to a group calling themselves "Children for Christ."

By then the group was already out of the country and the case was turned over to the Feds. The telephone records of Caitlin's call had been traced to a payphone in a building that the group had been using as one of their churches. It was their biggest lead and her strongest hope.

She was brought back to the present as the plane lurched and started take off. Looking out the window, she saw Lester turn and walk away. She placed her hand against the thick glass as if she could somehow reach out and touch him. An invisible band tightened around her heart.

"Goodbye Lester, be happy," she said under her breath as the plane turned and headed for the runway. Seeing Lester had served as the catalyst that she had been searching for all these months. It was the closure she had needed. The sealing of an open wound.

"Caitlin, I'm coming for you baby," she whispered against the window.

The plane rolled down the runway, swiftly gathering speed and then lifted into the air. New Orleans grew smaller and smaller, until it resembled a child's board game and then it was obscured by the clouds.

Read an excerpt from the sequel: **Crusader II: Second Adam**

SECOND ADAM

By Karen Parker and Carole Bullock

CHAPTER ONE

Sixth Hour, Wednesday, March 30, AD 36

The Place of The Skull, Calvary

She knelt weeping on the top of the craggy hill just north of the Old City. Far below stretched the well-traveled road leading to Jericho and Damascus. She wished they were on that road and traveling far away from this place of death and suffering. The hill, part of Mount Mariah, is called the "Place of the Skull" because the craggy rock side resembles a human skull. In the sixth hour of that day the skull's face appeared in sharp relief as the sun shined straight down upon the top of the hill. Spring is in the air, a time of rebirth but she only feels endless sorrow. He had counseled her to not be afraid, but instead to rejoice but how could she? She was still a mother who was losing her son.

Her first-born son, hung above her dying a slow and agonizing death. She felt her heart would break and crumble into tiny pieces with pain as she thought of the tortures he had endured since being taken in the garden the night before. He did not deserve it. She wanted to rise up and pull him down and ease his pain but knew the cruel soldiers guarding him would easily prevent her. Why did they hate them so? Why was the world so full of hate and yet he was filled only with pure love for them all? She glanced at the soldiers. The soldier's spear tips gleamed dully in the bright sun. She did not want to risk them further harming him and piercing him with their spears. She did not want to add to his already unbearable anguish.

Mid day had always been her favorite time. But today she could not lift her gaze to the glorious sun. Instead she lowered her head again and prayed for a miracle.

High above the stony hill the light of full day suddenly dimmed as if a giant shadow had passed across the sky. Seconds later a complete darkness fell across the land as sure as if that shadow was a giant's hand that had enclosed the sun within its massive fist. She could hear her sister and Mary Magdalene crying softly in the darkness somewhere beside her but could no longer see them or even make out their shapes in the complete and utter blackness.

"My God, My God, why have you forsaken me?"

As the agonized words drifted down from above she jumped to her feet, "My son, my son. I am here. I am here. I will not leave you," she cried as she stumbled and scrambled over the rocky ground, tearing her clothes and scratching her knees.

She felt for the bark of the olive trees that were bound together and thrust into the unforgiving ground.

All around her, she recognizes the panic-stricken cries of the guards and spectators. Fear is in their voices replacing the earlier laughter and mockery as they cold-heartedly bartered for pieces of her son's clothing. Now they ran and stumbled away in fright of the one they mockingly called, "King." But she feels no pleasure in their terror only anguish for her son's suffering.

The head of the guards calls for a torch amid the din of chaos, and she thought she heard a scream that became distant. She pictured the screamer blindly running off the cliff's edge and plunging to their death. All around utter bedlam reigns amid her son's cries of agony. His cries embrace and uphold all the misery of the world. Her heart was breaking; the shattered pieces scattering to the dark winds that drive relentlessly through the broken and empty void that has become her heart.

Time has lost all meaning as she lives a waking nightmare. Suddenly light creeps forth in the form of several glowing torches. It pushes the complete darkness away in small pools where it gathers and dances around its source. One small pool of light illuminates the head of the guards, a terrible and spiteful man. He approaches the moaning man with angry and purposeful strides. The torch turns his face into a hideous and menacing mask of light and dark caverns.

"You caused this and I will make you pay," he yells as he rams the spear into her son's side. Blood pours forth and glows in the light of the revealing flames.

"No," she screams as she lunges toward her son trying to stop the flow of life from his body. Without thinking, she grabs the empty wine vinegar flask at her feet and tries to catch the glowing stream. She is in shock, temporarily insane, not considering how this might help him. Her only thought is to save his life by saving his blood. Her effort was the futile attempt of someone in denial of the terrible event that has taken place before their very eyes.

"It is done," are the ragged words spoken in a final rush of one last breath as her son dies. She crumpled once again to the hard ground and sobbed. Her sister and Mary Magdalene come to her side and pull her up and lead her away. The giant hand releases its cruel grip and sunlight once again casts its glow across the land. Her heart is not lightened by its glow but stays isolated in darkness as she stumbles away still clutching the flask—the flask that contains the last drops of her precious son's life.

CHAPTER TWO

9:20 P.M., WEDNESDAY, MARCH 11, 2003

TEPIC, MEXICO

The pain was everywhere, but the worst assault came from her tortured and enlarged midsection. How long had she lain there sweating and aching, she couldn't be sure if it was minutes or hours or even days. She had long ago rolled off the pallet of hay she had first laid down on and now felt only hard packed dirt supporting her agonized body.

The constant crescendos of pain caused her feet to jiggle back and forth as she tried to focus. It was dark, darker than earlier when a musty shadow surrounded the small room that had come to feel like a tomb. Focus, she must focus or she would loose what little grip on reality, what minuscule shred of sanity that her ever-looming fear threatened to wrench away from her second by second.

Dank and earthy scents registered with each labored breath. Quiet, she must be quiet, but oh God the pain, the pain was becoming unbearable. She felt her insides ripping apart, and then something broke and trickled through her legs turning a small patch of dirt into mud. This was it. She was going to die here alone in the dark. Not even God would save her now for she had betrayed him. She had become a part of a great evil. An evil made by men in praise of a God that didn't exist. She had no one. Fear riveted her heart as she thought of what she had done. Her life flashed before her in a series of horrific mistakes and reprehensible decisions. She was living the consequences of what she had done. "Reaping what she had sown," as her father was famous for quoting. Her thoughts spiraled down a familiar path of self-loathing and disgust. Plunged into the darkness of depression, fear reared its ugly head and her sanity retreated, replaced by gruesome images, distorted visions, a mixture of the many different science fiction movies she had seen in her lifetime. A soft moan escaped her dried and cracked lips.

Once broken, the silence no longer seemed important, as her moans grew louder and louder, soon drifting beyond the tiny, isolated hut to float eerily on the early night air.

"Listen, hear that? Shine the light over that way."

Keys jingled as many footsteps jogged toward the anguished sounds. The wooden door pushed open and a flashlight beam picked up the huddled shape writhing on the dirt floor.

"We found the package," a soft male voice relayed into the two-way.

"Is it opened?" came the static reply.

"Almost, could happen any minute."

"What are you waiting for? Transport immediately."

A green Humvee backed to the doorway, retrieved the package and left. The hut returned to shadows and darkness. A small muddy spot the only reminder of its previous occupant.

CHAPTER THREE

Amanda Brown stared out the window as the plane rushed down the runway. She laid her head back against the seat and let her body be pressed back as the plane lifts off and heads skyward. Luckily the flight was not crowded and she had no one seated directly beside her. Take-offs and landings drove her crazy because she couldn't put on her headphones and listen to her music which helped quiet her mind and discouraged talkative seatmates. She never went anywhere without her CD player and assorted music collection. She had tunes to ward against any mood that might threaten her equilibrium. Music had become her fortress against the past. The right music could bring her out of a slump or calm her nerves when they threatened to jump out of her skin. When her mind wasn't engrossed in her current assignment she was listening to music. It helped keep the past at bay. She had briefly resorted to alcohol but soon found that was a dead end road. She only wanted to dull the pain not slowly kill herself. She still had things she needed to accomplish. Music turned out to be a healthier addiction.

Although in the nine months since she had become Amanda Brown, she sometimes felt the past receding slowly from her mind. Perhaps it was her new identity trying to take hold. While she was Amanda at times she forgot her true self but it never lasted long. She hoped there might come a day when music didn't have to be her constant companion against the silence her brain tried to fill with flashes of a past too painful to remember.

As the seat belt sign flashed off she reached beneath the seat in front of her and pulled out her briefcase/purse. She removed a manila folder and started scanning the contents. Her eye was drawn to a colorful travel brochure. She briefly scanned the contents.

"Tepic is the capitol of the state Nayarit where you can find peace and quiet at its best. Tepic is located by a beautiful crater lake at the base of an extinct volcano. The City of Tepic is characterized by its urbanism. It serves as the economic focal point for the agriculture related businesses in the area. Cash crops include tobacco and citrus farming. The city's other attractions include several museums and a 10-ft cross made of hay outside a former convent. The cross is said to have displayed miraculous powers of healing since the 17th century. The name "Tepic" comes from an indigenous language and means "hard stone." Tepic has a long history of Roman Catholicism, dating back to the sixteenth century. The latest census tells us that 92 percent of the people of this state, as well as the city, follow the teachings of Rome."

Amanda pulled out several photographs labeled Mary Mueller. Mary was 16-years old and lost somewhere in or near Tepic, Mexico. Her father's last contact with her was when he wired $2,000 to her in Mexico City after receiving a frantic phone call from Tepic. She said she was in trouble and planned to travel to Mexico City, get the money and return home. She was to call him from the airport. That was two weeks ago and the money was never claimed.

The information supplied by her father showed that Mary hadn't exactly been a model child. She began getting into trouble at the early age of 12. Her father, a senator from Ohio did his best to keep her in line but her rebelliousness soon led to drugs. Raised in a Jewish family, at 15 she turned from her own religion and started following an alternate group. She seemed to clean up her act and focused on a belief system that gave her the guidance she was not able to find in Judaism. Too late her father realized her newfound religion was nothing more than a cult. She disappeared with the contents of her private school account. All he had was a note saying she was traveling to Mexico with the church to enlighten and bring others to God. It had almost been two years when he got her frantic phone call. Now at least he had something to go on and also a friend on the hill that ran a think tank called, Justice For All (JFA).

Senator Mueller's friend on Capitol Hill was Jack Thompson, a solid citizen and dedicated man who had lost his only daughter to a murderer/rapist out on unsupervised parole. Everyone on the hill thought JFA was just a think tank organization researching changes needed in the courts and sentencing procedures. To be fair, Jack had started JFA for its original purpose but when a case similar to his daughters occurred, he decided bolder action was needed. His answer was to start the subversive operations of JFA. The members of the special operations group, code named "Jackie" for his murdered daughter, was fully dedicated to JFA. The team was hand selected and untraceable. Jack was like a father and brother to them all. They were a very elite and tight-knit group. They operated right out in the open most of the time. Every few months, they would be alerted to special cases.

Amanda Brown had been the only new member added in the last five years. Being a part of the group had liberated and retrieved her from a dead-end past. It was also a chance for retribution and a salve for her soul. Her life again had a purpose.

This was an unusual assignment for Amanda. She had not ever been sent to investigate a disappearance but usually was sent to punish the perpetrator of a crime. Jack said she was justice's flame, a humorous take on her bright copper hair. She might be justice's flame but it didn't reach her heart, which was cold and hard as stone. It felt appropriate she was journeying to Tepic, the city named after stone.

•

Sighing softly, she pulled out a report on several known cult-type religious groups currently operating in Mexico. The closest to Tepic was "Children for Christ." The group did have earlier roots in the United States but had relocated three years ago to Mexico.

Just looking at the name on the paper, "Children for Christ," made her heart start pounding and her hands shake as adrenaline rushed through her body. Deep breaths, she told herself as she struggled to get control of her emotions. This assignment was more important to her than anything in her life so far. It was so far the only credible lead they had to the group that may also have her daughter.

More than a year had passed since 6-year-old Caitlin had disappeared from the Bacchus parade in New Orleans, it seemed like a lifetime ago and at intense moments like this her heart felt like it had just happened yesterday.

She could try to fool herself and others that she had hardened her heart and moved on but she had not. She would never rest until she found her. She could only hope the time was near. She was tired of waiting.

The pilot's voice came over the PA system and announced the usage of personal electronic devices could begin.

She said a last silent prayer that Caitlin had also not lost hope and was still waiting for her mother's return. Then she put in her ear buds, hit play and lost herself in her music.

###

36949674R00236

Made in the USA
San Bernardino, CA
06 August 2016